KILLING TIME

Also by Elise Title

Hot Property
Romeo
Chain Reaction

KILLING TIME

ELISE TITLE

ST. MARTIN'S MINOTAUR
NEW YORK

www.minotaurbooks.com

Library of Congress Cataloging-in-Publication Data

Title, Elise.
  Killing time : a mystery / Elise Title.—1st ed.
    p. cm.
  ISBN 0-312-28566-3
    1. Women correctional personnel—Fiction. 2. Prison administration—Fiction. 3. Massachusetts—Fiction. 4. Prisoners—Fiction. 5. Prisons—Fiction. I. Title.

PS3570.I77 K55 2002
813'.54—dc21

2001058900

First Edition: July 2002

10   9   8   7   6   5   4   3   2   1

To the dedicated people who struggle to insure the public safety
and rehabilitate those who have paid for their crimes

acknowledgments

There are so many individuals to thank for their support, guidance, and generous assistance in helping me bring this book to fruition. First and foremost, I owe my deepest gratitude to my agent, Helen Rees, who never stopped believing in this project, and more important, never stopped believing in me. Also, a special thanks to Kelley Ragland, my editor at St. Martin's, for her shrewd eye and thoughtful suggestions.

Many people who are currently in the Massachusetts prison system, or who worked with me there in the past, gave unstintingly of their time during the research process. Topping that list are Bill and Marilyn Dawber. Bill headed the Counseling Center at MCI Norfolk and Marilyn was my supervisor for the six years I worked there as a therapist. I would also like to acknowledge John Beaton, at the Massachusetts Executive Office of Public Safety, Department of Correction, for arranging my research tour to a number of prisons and pre-release centers. I much appreciated meeting with Assistant Deputy Commissioner Tim App, Superintendent Steve O'Brian at the Park Drive Pre-Release Center, Kristie Holden at Hodder House, Deputy Superintendent Mark Powers at MCI Cedar Junction, Director of Classification Diane

Silva and Director of Education Carolyn Vicari at MCI Norfolk, and Superintendent Kelly Ryan at MCI Lancaster (the state's only co-ed pre-release program at the time of my research).

I would also like to thank the many male and female inmates who volunteered to talk with me at some of the above institutions. I truly appreciate their willingness to answer my questions and share some of their experiences and feelings.

There were also many staff members—officers, teachers, ministers—who gave of their time and I apologize for not listing everyone's names, but I am grateful to all of them.

As always, love and thanks to my husband, Jeff, my son, David, and my daughter, Rebecca Blake.

KILLING TIME

prologue

CAMBRIDGE POLICE DEPARTMENT: Detective Lois Weaver
VICTIM'S STATEMENT
DICTATED AT CAMBRIDGE HOSPITAL
JUNE 9, 1994

I . . . can't talk . . . about it. Please . . .

I truly understand, Miss Cole. But you don't want to see the man who did this to you get away with it.

I hate . . . him. I hate him so much. How could he . . . ? Oh God. This can't be happening to me.

You're safe now, Alison. It's over. Just tell me what happened.

You know what happened. Everyone knows. He . . . raped me. I want my mother. Please. I need my mother.

She can come in, Alison. But you might not want her here until after I get your statement. Let me try to make it a little easier. You met Dean Thomas Walsh at approximately ten o'clock last night at a party on Commonwealth Avenue, across from Boston University. Was that the first time you met him?

Justine and I knew him from high school. Him and his friend, Rick. But then Dean dropped out and I didn't see him again until . . . last night. Not that he remembered me.

But Dean noticed you at the party.

Both of them were kinda flirting with me, but . . . I guess I . . .

Liked Dean?

He . . . seemed so . . . nice. I never thought . . . Never . . .

Were you all drinking at the party? . . . Is that yes, Alison?

Yes. I . . . don't usually . . . Really. I guess . . . that's why I . . . got sick. I . . . I threw up. I wanted to go home, but I was afraid. My mom woulda killed me. So Dean took me into a bedroom, so I could . . . lie down. Just . . . just until I felt . . . better and could go home.

What did Dean do?

He . . . laid down beside me. Told me he just . . . just wanted to be with me in case I got sick again. I thought . . . shit, I thought he was being so . . . sweet. How could I have been so stupid?

You were drunk, Alison. Drunk and sick. And he took advantage of you. Isn't that what happened?

I didn't know what was happening at first. . . . I was sort of out of it. I think maybe I . . . blacked out. And then . . . then when I did come to . . . it was so dark . . . and I was . . . naked and he was . . . all over me . . . and I tried to make him stop but . . . he wouldn't. And when I tried to scream, he . . . he twisted me over onto my stomach and shoved my face into the pillow. I . . . I couldn't breathe . . . and when I struggled some more he tied my wrists to the headboard with my pantyhose. And then he was ramming me and ramming me . . . and it hurt so bad . . . so bad. . . . I hate him. I . . . I'm going to . . . throw up . . .

Take a few breaths, Alison. That's right. That's better. Here, take a drink of water. Good girl. You're doing just great.

I thought I was going . . . to die.

You thought Dean was going to kill you? Did he threaten you, Alison?

I don't know. I don't remember. I don't . . . I think I must have . . . blacked out again. Next thing I knew, Justine was there, crying, and Rick was untying me. I thought it was . . . just a . . . nightmare, but . . . but Rick kept saying . . . I'll kill the bastard for doing this to you. So I knew . . . I knew it . . . happened. Oh God, it really happened.

And where was Dean?

I don't know. Gone. Dean was gone.

CCI HORIZON HOUSE ORIENTATION HANDBOOK

WELCOME TO CCI HORIZON HOUSE

This experimental pre-release facility, in operation for the past year, is located on Providence Street in Boston in what was once a small hotel for women. The facility currently houses 27 male inmates and 14 female inmates in separate secured quarters—women's rooms on the second and third floor, men on the fourth, fifth and sixth floors with separate staircase access. Two bedrooms are reserved on the main floor for handicapped inmates. Fraternization between the male and female inmates is strictly prohibited, except in administration supervised therapy/skill groups.

Horizon House has three primary goals: security, accountability on the part of staff and residents, and the inmate's successful reintegration into the community. It is the responsibility of the staff to provide the opportunities for each inmate to develop the physical, psychological, and social skills and attitudes necessary for success on the outside. It is the responsibility of each inmate to take full advantage of all the opportunities offered.

While there are no walls or fences, no bars or cells at Horizon House, this **is** a prison facility. All of the inmates housed at HH are either within six to nine months of their parole date or minimum time served. Each inmate here has earned the **privilege** of work-release status. If **any** of the facility's rules are violated, disciplinary action will be taken immediately. In almost all cases, the inmate is returned to a locked facility to finish out his/her term of incarceration. . . .

One

*. . . My husband and my sister worried for my safety
when I chose this work. . . . I admit there's always
the potential for violence. I also admit it isn't for
everyone. . . .*

Natalie Price
(*excerpted from* Boston Monitor)

MAGGIE WAS LATE. Back almost a dozen years when Natalie and
Maggie were college roomies at Boston State, Maggie used to tell
Nat her problem with tardiness was congenital. What else could
you expect, Maggie would say, from someone who was finally
forced from momma's comfy womb close to a month past her
due date? Nat, on the other hand was a stickler for time, and so
she'd spent many a night over the past twelve years getting frustrated, annoyed, finally angry waiting for Maggie to show up—
for dinners, movies, trips. Maggie even showed up late for Nat's
wedding. And since Maggie was the maid of honor, the ceremony

had to be put on hold until she arrived. But Nat knew there was nothing *congenital* about her best friend's tardiness that time. Maggie thought Nat was making a big mistake marrying Ethan Price. And she hadn't minced words about it.

> *"It's a father thing, Nat."*
> *"He's only thirteen years older than me. You make it sound like I'm marrying Methuselah."*
> *"That's not what I mean, and you know it."*
> *"Believe me, Maggie, Ethan is nothing like my father. Thank God."*
> *"Exactly. Ethan's the good father. Or so you think."*
> *"Meaning?"*
> *"Meaning he's totally full of himself. And he absolutely loves your puppy dog adoration—"*
> *"Gee, you make me sound so appealing."*
> *"Come on, Nat. You love me because I tell it like it is. He's the whole reason you decided to major in Criminal Justice. If you hadn't taken his course your sophomore year—"*
> *"I took his course because I was already interested in doing my major in Criminal Justice. I had . . . personal reasons."*
> *"Which you don't want to talk about."*
> *"Which I don't want to talk about."*
> *"You know, it's not fair, Nat. I tell you everything. And you're always playing woman of mystery."*
> *"I tell you more than I've ever told anyone else in my life, Maggie."*
> *"Even Ethan?"*
> *". . . even Ethan."*

Nat picked up her phone, catching a glimpse of herself in the mirror over the mantel. She looked lousy, not so much feeling old as faded. Barely thirty-one and already she could see crows' feet at the corners of her eyes. That morning she'd spotted several threads of gray when she was trying to tame her renegade auburn hair into a French knot. Whenever the humidity rose, her natural curls became coiled springs, refusing to obey. But she was afraid if she cut her hair short, she'd look like Alfalfa. Besides, Ethan always said her hair was her sexiest feature. He used to come up behind her on the bed, slowly, almost ritualistically pulling out her combs and hair pins, letting her wild curls fall down around her shoulders, then he'd bury his face—

Nat scowled and started punching in Maggie's number. Maybe she would get her hair cut. And straightened. *That's right, Nat. Cut off your* hair *to spite your face.* Not that her face was bad. She had an olive complexion that tanned nicely— tending toward sallow, unfortunately, when winter hit; good bone structure that accentuated high cheekbones; an unassuming nose; lips that might have been fuller; hazel eyes that changed color with the light—Ethan used to say they changed color with her moods, glowing almost golden when she was aroused. *Well, they sure as hell hadn't been* golden *for quite some time.*

Her gaze drifted down to her body, clad in blue jeans and a plain white tee shirt. She was slim—a little too slim of late—and while not flat-chested, she could get away without wearing a bra, although she'd only do that around the house. At five foot seven, she was neither too short nor too tall. Average. Attractive in an average way.

Distracted by her clinical self-analysis, she ended up getting a wrong number. She tried again. Three rings and Maggie's answering machine clicked on. Nat figured she was finally on her way. As she was about to hang up—no point leaving a message— Nat was brought up short by an addendum Maggie had tagged on to her recording. "Dean? If that's you, I may be a bit late for lunch tomorrow, so let's plan on 12:30 instead of noon. Same place as usual. . . ."

Dean? As in Dean Thomas Walsh? Same place as usual?

Nat couldn't believe it. Maggie was meeting Walsh outside of class. She was having regular lunch dates with him. Did they squeeze in early dinner dates as well before check-in? What else did they squeeze in?

Maggie, Maggie, Maggie. For all your talk of worldly wisdom, you are so naive.

Nat was already preparing the lecture in her head that she'd deliver to her closest friend. Filled with hard, cold facts. Warnings. Concern. If necessary, threats.

Maggie was going to fight her on this. One trait the two friends shared in common was a thick streak of stubbornness. But no way was Maggie going to win this one. She'd realize the truth and reluctantly go along with Nat's demands. Because she wouldn't have any choice.

But it was bound to cause a rift between them.

Nat felt miserable as she came to this realization. As if she needed more rifts in her life. More estrangement.

She sank down on the couch, pressing her palms into her eyes until tiny silver spots sparkled in the blackness. The *public* Natalie Price—tough, competent, ambitious, fierce in her convictions—blinked out. Despite her many years of concerted effort and determination, the lonely, frightened, insecure little girl remained immutably lodged inside her skin. Still all too painfully alive. With no one there to bear witness to her weakness, Nat let the tears fall.

Crying brought back the memory of just about the only time in her adult life that she'd broken down in front of another person. That person had been Maggie. It had happened just a short time ago. Nat could still recapture the sensation of her friend's comforting arms encircling her. Encouraging her to let go. *It's okay to cry, Nat. It's okay to hurt. That's the only way to heal.* Nat longed for that to be true. But even if it wasn't, she cherished the gift of her friend's tender nurturing. There were so few people in her life who had ever demonstrated such caring. And she'd already lost one of them. She desperately did not want to lose

Maggie's friendship. It would leave a terrible void. And then the thing that Nat had concertedly staved off her entire life, would finally happen. Empty, she would simply cave in.

The echo of Maggie's phone message replayed in Nat's mind.

Maybe, she thought with no real conviction, maybe she'd got it wrong. Maybe it was another *Dean*.

10:40 P.M. Maggie could have *walked* from her South End apartment to Brookline and been there by now. Nat, an alarmist if not by nature then certainly by *nurture*, had learned to curb her anxiety where her friend was concerned. But this was late even for Maggie. Nat was starting to worry that something had happened to her, her mind racing through a minefield of catastrophic possibilities. Of course, the most logical explanation was that Maggie had forgotten altogether. Or thought they were on for the next night. Maybe she had a date tonight. At least it couldn't be Dean. If he were out and about at this late hour she would most definitely have heard about it.

Before giving up and going to sleep, Nat rang Maggie's number one last time, planning to leave a message. To her relief, it was picked up after one ring. Not a *late* date anyway.

"Hey," Nat said before Maggie squeezed in so much as a contrite *hi*, "just wanted to make sure you're still alive and kicking. And no, I'm not pissed you forgot about me. Well, maybe a little. I have still got this wicked craving for that lemon meringue pie you were supposed to bring over tonight. You owe me—"

"Who is this?" A somber voice cut Nat off. A somber male voice she didn't recognize.

"Sorry . . . must have dialed the wrong number."

"Who are you trying to reach?"

Nat hesitated. Maybe this was Maggie's new boyfriend. And Nat had interrupted—*Oh damn.*

"I'm sorry. I'm a friend of Maggie's and—"

"Maggie Austin?"

"Yes. Who . . . ?"

"May I have your name?"

The guy was really putting Nat off. If this was Maggie's new love interest, Nat was not too impressed.

"Are you still there? Is this Nat?"

So Maggie'd told the new guy about her. Nat was irritated that Maggie hadn't told her best friend, who she supposedly told everything, about him.

"What's your name?" Nat countered.

"Leo Coscarelli."

She scowled. Name didn't ring a bell.

"Well, look Leo, I'm just calling to let Maggie know—"

"Detective Leo Coscarelli. Homicide."

Oh God, Nat thought, the air in the room suddenly too thick to breathe. Or else it was her lungs. Something congealing in her lungs. And a lump instantly formed in Nat's chest that felt like a hard knot. "Hom . . . icide?"

"Are you Nat?" he asked again.

"Yes. How did you . . . ? Where's Maggie? What's happened . . . ?" The room started to spin. Nat couldn't focus.

"Can I have your full name please?"

Nat willed herself to be calm. It was a lesson she'd drilled into herself as a child. There was the popular saying—*never let 'em see you sweat*. Nat's was a variation—*never let 'em see you hurting*.

"Price. Natalie Price. I'm Superintendent of Corrections at CCI Horizon House, the pre-release center in Boston." She tacked her credentials on deliberately. To establish authority. To let him know she was one of them. And to remind herself so she wouldn't fold. "Maggie Austin is a close friend of mine. Will you please tell me . . ."

"I'm afraid I have some bad news for you, Superintendent Price."

Bad news. Homicide. Nat knew even as she asked, "Is Maggie . . . dead?"

"Yes. I'm sorry . . ."

"How?" The brusqueness in her voice belied the struggle it had taken to get the word out. She shut her eyes, trying to tell herself this was a nightmare, that it wasn't really happening. An old, sadly familiar litany. Why did she keep at it when it never worked, her nightmares invariably the real thing?

"I'd rather not discuss it over the phone, Superintendent."

"I see." Of course Nat didn't see. She was half blind from the tears flooding her eyes. Sucking in a frayed breath, she held it a few seconds, hoping she wouldn't retch.

"I can drive over to your apartment—"

"I'll come there," Nat said firmly.

"I don't know if that's—"

"I'll be there in twenty minutes."

"I'd prefer to send a car over for you."

"Why?"

"You're very upset. Wait for the car."

"Yes. All right. I . . . I'll do that."

"It's not a pretty sight, Superintendent. You might want to—" The detective hesitated, still with the somber voice but with an added touch of sympathy. He started over. "You might want to prepare yourself."

"How do I do that?" Nat asked starkly. She knew he didn't have an answer. There was no answer.

The receiver slipped out of Nat's sweaty hand and clattered to the floor. She stood there, numb with devastation. A female voice oozed from the phone that hadn't been disconnected—*if you would like to make a call, please hang up and*—

Nat viciously kicked the phone across the living room. Fierce anger warred with her intense sorrow. One name flashed before her eyes. Dean Thomas Walsh. And as soon as she saw it, a sinking feeling, shameful in its self-interest, pushed its way into the fray.

She could not dislodge it. She could not ignore the catastrophic repercussions, not only at the pre-release center but throughout the entire Massachusetts criminal justice system, that could potentially unfold with Maggie's murder. While she had no way of knowing at this point if Dean Thomas Walsh was in any way involved, Nat knew she had to act on that possibility. And act immediately. She crossed the room and retrieved the phone.

"When did Walsh check in?" Amazingly, her voice sounded calm enough when she got Gordon Hutchins on the line, but her hand was shaking so hard she could barely hold on to the receiver.

"5:40. Problem?"

"And he's there now?"

"Of course he's here. Don't you think you'd be the first to know if we had an escapee on our hands?"

Sometimes Nat wondered about being the *first*. She might be the head of CCI Horizon House, but she was still a woman in a macho man's world. Even though she'd risen up the ranks, obstacles had been thrown in her path at every rung.

"You sound funny, Nat." So much for thinking she at least had her voice under control.

"What's wrong?" Hutch pressed. "Walsh in some kind of trouble?"

"I don't know yet." She couldn't bring herself to tell him about Maggie. If she did, she knew she would break down. And she couldn't do that because, for one thing, to have any of her people witness her collapse would only prove she didn't have what it took to be in command. For another, she was terrified she wouldn't be able to pull herself together again. Surely, there was a point of no return. And Nat had never felt so close to that breaking point as she did right then. The only way she knew to fight it off was to shift into *command* overdrive. She started barking out orders. "I want a full battery of drug tests run on Walsh.

Immediately. The works. Dope, coke, uppers, downers, booze."

"He's gonna ask questions."

"You're not going to give him answers. And Hutch, take some backup with you."

"Sounds serious, Nat."

"Serious enough that I want those tests run in lockup. And I want tight security on him. Call in a couple of day officers."

"Word's gonna get out. You're going to have a lot of agitated cons in here."

Hutch wasn't telling Nat anything she didn't already know.

"If a little mouthing off is as bad as it gets we can count ourselves lucky." And then, before she could stop herself, she blurted it out. "Maggie Austin's been murdered, Hutch."

She heard his sharp intake of breath at the same instant her downstairs buzzer rang. She looked out the window. Saw the police car at the curb.

The receiver once again slipped from her hand. She was going to be sick.

two

I agree that by being granted pre-release privileges, I will demonstrate exemplary behavior at all times within the community. If I feel any stress related to coping with sexually deviant behavior I will immediately inform the appropriate Horizon House staff...
(excerpt from Sex Offender Treatment Agreement)

DATE OF REPORT: 7/7/00

CASE #209782

NAME: DEAN THOMAS WALSH

DOB: 6/17/73

PLACE OF BIRTH: NATICK, MA.

DATE OF SENTENCING: December 11, 1994

OFFENSE: Rape (MGL Ch.256, s. 24)

AGE AT ADMISSION: 19yr.3mo.

SENTENCE: 6–8 years

EPRD (EARLIEST POSSIBLE RELEASE DATE): 12/16/00

SECURITY CLASSIFICATION: +2 (medium-low)

PROGRAM RECOMMENDATION: Sex Offender Treatment Program

CCI NORTON EXIT ASSESSMENT:

Dean Thomas Walsh, age 27, a white male, 5'11", 173 lbs., brown hair, blue eyes, has made a good adjustment to incarceration, having had only two (2) infractions, both of which occurred during his first six months at CCI Oakville Reception and Diagnostic Center.

PROGRAM ATTENDANCE:

While serving the bulk of his time at CCI Norton, Dean obtained his GED, attended both art and writing classes, and was a literacy volunteer. He also attended a twelve-week Sex Offender Program while at CCI Oakville. However, his participation in this program was minimal, and he will be required to attend a second Sex Offender program as a condition of his transfer to the pre-release work program at CCI Horizon House. He must also attend AA twice a week.

PRIORS:

The current offense is Dean's first involvement with the law, indicating a low recidivism profile. Chief hindrance to successful reintegration into the community is his continued insistence that he has no recall of the assault and rape. He does acknowledge that alcohol and drug use were a problem at the time of the commission of the crime, and he has had no infractions for either since his incarceration. He also fully understands that he is to have no contact whatsoever with the victim, Alison (Cole) Miller, age 27, while he is on work-release status. Ms. Miller, her husband Richard Miller and two children, a boy age 7 and a girl age 5, presently reside in Newton, MA. She has been notified of Dean's work-release status and has made no negative response.

INFRACTIONS:

Dean's two infractions at CCI Norton both involved physical assault, but it was determined by the chief IPO that in neither case was he the instigator. However, in each instance, the aggressors suffered moderate injury at Dean's hands.

FAMILY:

Parents divorced in 1987. Father, Kyle Walsh, currently unemployed, resides with his girlfriend, Arlene Hayden in Dorchester, MA. Mother, Marion Walsh, a sales clerk at Barton's Jewelry Store in Framingham, remains at the family's two-bedroom ranch home in Natick, MA. with her 22-year-old single daughter, Christine.

VISITATION PATTERN:

Dean had several visits from his mother during his first six months at CCI Norton. Following a heated argument in the visiting room, Dean refused subsequent visits from her. After two attempts, mother stopped coming. Father has never visited. The only consistent visitor Dean has had throughout his incarceration has been his younger sister, Christine who comes to see him at least twice a month.

COMMUNITY SUPPORT:

Other than his sister, the person who has shown the most interest in Dean's rehabilitation is Professor Margaret Austin of Boston, MA. Ms. Austin is a single, 33-year-old English professor at Commonwealth Community College (CCC) in West Roxbury, who has been holding creative writing classes on a volunteer basis at CCI Norton for the past year. Dean has attended all of her classes. Ms. Austin describes Dean as an articulate student with above-average intelligence and excellent writing skills. With her support and assistance, Dean plans to apply to CCC as a part-time student upon release from CCI Horizon House, his plan being to obtain his AA degree and then transfer to a four-year institution for a BA in English.

NOTE:

On 3/14/98, inmate Keith Franklin, another student in Ms. Austin's writing class at CCI Norton turned over to the Charge Officer a copy of a poem written by Dean that he felt was "out of line." Franklin made a point of saying that he was only coming forward with it now because he was up for release. Otherwise, he was scared Walsh would retaliate in some way. CO notes that there has been tension in the past between these two inmates, but neither of them has been written up.

A conference was held with Ms. Austin who viewed the poem as "purely a creative endeavor," although she did admit that it is not uncommon in her experience for students to "feel an emotional attachment" to their teacher. Ms. Austin, it should be pointed out, is an extremely attractive and vivacious young woman.

No disciplinary action taken, but staff psychiatrist Robert Dollard did have a talk with Dean about "transference" issues—(See attached poem) . . .

Nocturne To Maggie

Locked in my cell
I conjure up your shattering scent.
Sanctioned brutality will not prevent me
From breathing in your essence,
From swallowing you whole
Like a communion wafer.

Dean

three

When I'm not fucking up and getting thrown in the slammer I'm really a stand-up guy.

C. T.
Inmate # 64327

FOR SIX YEARS Nat had worked with inmates. Even with an advanced degree in Criminal Justice, it hadn't been easy getting an administrative position within the prison system. Fine if she'd wanted to be a corrections officer, a prison secretary, or some other low-level job. But Nat's qualifications made her eligible, at the very least, for a mid-level position. There were other women at that level, but most of them had been in the system for years, some for decades, and had to work their way up from the lowest ranks. It took Nat nearly seven months to land a job. She started at CCI Oakville, which was primarily a high security men's prison but had a separate section of the institution designated as a Reception-Diagnostic Center. This center was every male inmate's first stop in the system. Nat was hired as an evaluator in the RDC, which meant she put the new inmates through a standard battery of mandated diagnostic tests and interviews before they could be placed in the system. Meaning, prisoners could be assigned a specific section of a specific prison where they were likely to cause the least trouble—hopefully.

Nat would never forget her first day at CCI Oakville. Even though her job was strictly based in the RDC, she was *graciously* taken on a tour of the *big house*. A couple of brawny male officers were her escorts. Nat braced herself for inmate whistles, jeers, curses. They were locked up behind steel bars, and she was a young, attractive woman who was essentially being put on display for them. She started down the first tier—not knowing until later that it was the disciplinary tier—the officers walking behind her. As they put it—"covering her back."

Her number one blunder was deciding to make eye contact with the inmates. Big mistake. The first cell she looked into, she saw a man sitting on the john in one corner of his 8' by 10' cubicle. He grinned at her, making no move to cover himself, and Nat could feel her face redden. Worse, she could hear the snickers of the two officers behind her. But that little incident turned out to be the least of it. Not even halfway down the tier, an inmate slung something at her. Hitting her gray wool skirt. Oozing noxiously down her stockinged leg. Feces. And before she could recover from the shock and disgust of it, an inmate in the cell on the opposite side of the tier hit her on the side of the head with a paper cup filled with a liquid that turned out to be urine.

Revolted and humiliated, she turned to her *tour guides*, ready to call it quits, wanting nothing more than to get out of there. But as soon as she faced them, saw their barely concealed amusement—not to mention that not a drop of shit or piss had landed on either of them—she knew she'd been deliberately set up. Gritting her teeth, she whipped back around, finished walking the tier, which had now gone so silent all that could be heard was the determined click, click, click of her heels on the concrete floor.

The next day she began her job as the diagnostic evaluator. Word spread fast through the institution about her gutsy handling of her hazing and she won a few points. After a while, she developed a reputation among her colleagues for being a "tough cookie." It was a sexist phrase which allowed them to praise her skills while they diminished her at the same time. Nat could have called them on it, but she was not only tough, she was smart. Smart enough to pick her battles where they'd have the most impact.

Eighteen months later she beat out two men for the job of assistant deputy superintendent at CCI Palmer, a men's medium security prison thirty miles north of Boston, *beat* being the operative term. Even though she was the most qualified of the three for the position and had solid recommendations, she had to hire a shrewd lawyer to bully the powers that be to give her her due or slug it out in court. Since being hit with a charge of sexual discrimination was the last thing the department wanted, they reluctantly gave in. Nat made plenty of enemies in her determined fight to get what she deserved, but she made one very important ally. Russell Fisk, one of the state's more forward thinking deputy commissioners in the Department of Corrections.

After more than a year in the new job constantly having to prove herself, she slowly won over many of her detractors. Even Harvey Wilson, the Superintendent at Palmer who'd been most vociferously opposed to her appointment, had to admit she was doing a hell of a job. Their hard won respect was the result of Nat's talent for administration and, even more, her willingness to get her hands dirty.

She sat in on voc-tech programs, AA and Sex Offender meetings. Met with many of the inmates, listening to gripes, legitimate complaints, family difficulties, whatever. She couldn't solve a lot of the problems but she was considered to be fair and earnest in her attempts. And she not only supported but often spearheaded new education and training programs, as well as more in-prison counseling services in an effort to counter the depressingly high recidivism rate. She had dedicated herself to this cause.

Nat knew, up close and personal, how hard it was for an ex-con to make it on the street. When she was fifteen, her sister Rachel eleven, the cops arrested her father, Nathan Graham, who at that time was a law associate in a small estate planning firm in Boston. He was also an alcoholic. The kind of drinker who did his job, worked hard, was respected by his colleagues, provided—at least monetarily—for his family. But he was like a ghost in the Graham house, coming home each night well after the dinner hour, throwing together something to eat and withdrawing to the den where he locked his door and spent the evening getting quietly drunk. Most nights he fell asleep in the den, somehow managing to rouse himself each weekday morning, shower, dress, and make it to work on time. Weekends were, if anything, worse. They gave him more time to withdraw and to drink. Usually he stayed home, spending most of the day in his den, *working*. But if things were turbulent in the Graham household, which they all too frequently were, he'd make a beeline for his car and go find himself a dark, quiet bar. On one of those drunken escapes, he rammed his '85 Buick LaSabre head-on into a '79 Toyota Corolla on I-95.

Nathan Graham was charged with driving to endanger while under the influence of alcohol. He was lucky. He came close to ending up with a charge of vehicular homicide, if the nineteen-year-old boy who'd been at the wheel of the Toyota hadn't pulled through.

Nat took it upon herself to visit her father while he was in prison. She wasn't sure why she went since she certainly had never been close to him. Maybe it was partly because she'd desperately wanted his attention, his affection, his protection. Behind bars, there was no place for him to run from her. And he was sober. How ironic that this would be the place father and daughter would finally make a connection.

At first Nat asked her sister Rachel to accompany her on her visits. She wanted Rach to see their dad in this new light. But Rachel not only refused to go, she refused to even acknowledge that her daddy was behind bars. Even though it had made all the local papers, Rachel insisted on telling everyone that her father was on a business trip.

And then there was Nat's mother. Nat never once so much as considered asking her mother to go with her. Hallie Graham had struggled with a bipolar disorder for most of her adult life. When she was taking her lithium, she managed to hold things together, however tenuously. But she'd invariably go through periods when she stopped taking her meds. This was one of those times. Things got so bad that Hallie's older widowed and childless sister, Joyce, had to move temporarily from northern New Hampshire down to the Graham home in Winthrop, Massachusetts, to look after the family. Not that Aunt Joyce did it out of love. It was strictly obligation born of Christian duty. Nat remembered Joyce treating her and Rachel as if they were contaminated. Nat often feared they were. An alcoholic father, a mother who was nuts. Bad genes any way you looked at it.

For all the closeness to her father Nat felt when she visited him, it was very hard to bear witness to the shame and guilt he wore so visibly. Sometimes, he'd break down and cry, clutching her hand, thanking her through his sobs for sticking by him, making promises he swore he'd keep. Not just to stop drinking but to be more of a father to her and Rachel. Nat had been through enough in her young life to be wary of such assurances, but still a part of her silently prayed it would happen.

She was seventeen when her dad was released. Nat insisted on stringing up Welcome Home signs around the house. She planned a special meal—roast pork and grilled potatoes, her father's favorite. Rachel deliberately arranged a sleepover at a friend's house that night. Her mother, increasingly agitated as the day of her husband's return home approached, had a full-blown manic episode and Joyce ended up having to take her to the hospital where she was immediately admitted. Despite it all, Nat was determined to pull off this celebration, even if it was just going to be her and her dad.

Nathan Graham staggered into the house seven hours after his release. The pork was cold, the potatoes burnt to a crisp. He greeted his daughter drunkenly, weaved his way down the hall to the bathroom where he proceeded to puke up his guts and then pass out. Nat left him there on the cold tiled floor, dumped out the special dinner she'd so painstakingly and lovingly made, and went to bed.

Within three months Nathan Graham was back inside for parole violations—he'd twice shown up drunk for his meetings with his parole officer. Nat never visited her father during his incarceration. She was not so much punishing him for failing as she was protecting herself from any further stinging disappointment.

The second time he was released, much to Nat's surprise, her father functioned like Joe Citizen for almost a month. Although he'd been disbarred, he got a job clerking in a local law firm, showed up for work sober every day, stayed home with his family every evening except for his twice weekly AA meetings. They ate dinner together, watched TV, even played cards on occasion. Rachel stopped sleeping at friends' houses all the time, Joyce returned to New Hampshire, and even her mother was on more of an even keel now that she was taking her lithium faithfully. It was the most *normal* period of her childhood that Nat could remember. As time went by she grew cautiously optimistic that her dad was going to make it.

Then, on a Friday in late November, Nathan Graham picked up his paycheck and cashed it at the bank across from his office.

But on this day—for reasons Nat would never know, never fully grasp—instead of going home, he stopped at a liquor store, walked out with a case of vodka, checked himself into a South Boston motel, and drank himself into a stupor. Five days later, when all the bottles were empty, he sobered up long enough to make a noose out of a curtain cord, tie one end to the ceiling fixture, climb up on the solitary chair in the room, and hang himself. He left an envelope. Inside was an insurance policy for $200,000, naming Natalie as the beneficiary. He didn't leave a note.

When the two police officers arrived at the Graham home, Nat was the one who opened the door. The instant she saw their solemn faces, she knew. They asked that someone come with them to the morgue to identify the body.

It was the last thing in the world Nat wanted to do, but who else could go? Her fourteen-year-old sister? Her mother who'd started messing up on her lithium within a day of her husband's disappearance and was inches away from having to be committed yet again?

There was no one else. So Nat accompanied the two officers in their cruiser to a sterile brick three-story building, let them lead her into a small viewing room that the State had gone to the wasted trouble of making look like a cheerful if deliberately understated lounge with a tweed sofa, two matching arm chairs, a pine Early American coffee table. On one wall was a painting of the Boston Harbor. On the opposite wall was a large glass window with a solemn black curtain pulled across it from the other side. The female officer suggested she sit down for a few minutes, offering her a cup of tea. Nat shook her head. She stood by the glass window, waiting for what seemed an eternity before the curtain parted and there was the cold steel gurney on top of which lay a figure covered by a white sheet. A young man in a white lab coat pulled back the sheet. Nat fixed her gaze on the orderly, but he never once met her eyes. And then, experiencing this inexplicable feeling of being outside herself, quite removed, she finally looked at the haggard yet oddly peaceful face of her father. *Yes, that's Nathan Graham.* The orderly replaced the sheet and, as he began drawing the curtain, Nat fainted.

And now she was viewing the dead body of Margaret Emily Austin. A déjà vu anathema.

This time she didn't pass out, but it was touch and go as she looked down at her closest friend. Maggie lay sprawled naked on her bed, her supple, athletic body twisted like a Raggedy Ann doll, her wrists tied with a pair of her pantyhose to her headboard, her mouth wide open as if her terror-stricken scream was still rushing from her lips. The bedding was in disarray, the quilt puddled at the foot of the bed. The quilt Maggie's Aunt Lou had made for her. *A special gift for a special niece on turning 30*, said the note that came with the birthday present. Nat recalled how she'd envied Maggie that lovely quilt. Even more, the sentiment behind it. No relative had ever made Nat anything. No relative had ever called her special. No blood relative, anyway. Ethan used to say she was special. Once upon a time.

Yes, think about Ethan. Then you can get your anger flowing again. Rage was better than this horror and anguish trapped inside her head.

But Nat couldn't escape the horror. The image of Maggie violated, murdered, was burned in Nat's mind. Nat knew she would never be able to erase it.

She sat stiff-backed in Maggie's living room, on Maggie's gray flannel camelback sofa, fighting her own skin's icy chill despite the almost suffocating warmth in the room, fighting back both tears and nausea.

Oh God, how I want to hear that deep lilting voice of hers, with its hint of a southern twang from a childhood in Georgia, telling me men are such screw-ups.

But some man had really screwed up Maggie this time. Screwed the life right out of her. And Nat was afraid she knew who that man was.

She heard a strangled cry, shocked to realize she was the source of the sound.

Leo Coscarelli, the Boston homicide detective, appeared at the door connecting the bedroom with the living room. He, too, had heard her cry.

"Are you okay?"

"No," she snapped.

"If you want to leave, Superintendent . . ."

"No," she snapped again. She would not leave Maggie alone with a bunch of strangers—cops, medical examiner, the busy-as-bees crime team snooping around the entire apartment. At least they'd all cleared out of the living room. All except Coscarelli.

The detective walked over to the couch. Nat took real notice of him for the first time. His slight build, the ill-fitting blue sports jacket, the just-starting-to-grow-in buzz cut, not even a hint of a five o'clock shadow on his baby-face. All this marked him as a neophyte in her eyes. A kid fresh out of the police academy. How could they put someone so young and inexperienced in charge of a rape and murder investigation?

"We should be through here in a little while, Ms. Price."

"How did you know my name?" she asked warily. "When I phoned here you asked if I was Nat."

"There was a note on the calendar in the kitchen. Friday, September 16. Dinner at Nat's," he said. "I thought it was a guy, but once you started talking about the lemon meringue pie—"

"Yeah." She was sick to her stomach again, but she fought to get the queasiness under control. There was more she wanted to know. "What brought you here? I mean, how did you know something . . . had happened to . . . Maggie?"

"A friend called it in."

"A friend?"

"Karen Powell. Do you know her?"

"She's Maggie's T.A. Teaching assistant." Nat hesitated, not really sure why, before adding, "And her friend as well."

Coscarelli was studying her. As if he'd tuned into the pause and was also wondering about it.

But he let it go. "She came over here around nine P.M. to drop off some test papers. She had a key. Said Ms. Austin had given it to her last year when she first started working for her. Did you know Ms. Powell had a key?"

"No. But, it's something Maggie would do."

"She gave keys out freely?"

Nat didn't like the detective's insinuating tone one bit. "No. I don't mean that. Just to the few people she's close to. I've got a key as well. She has one to my place." She heard herself take in a long, ragged breath as she realized she was talking about her dead friend in the present tense. Her vision clouded. She looked away, took a few moments, then finally put into words the question she found the most difficult to ask.

"How did she . . . die?" Her voice was a hoarse whisper.

He didn't answer right away. And even though she was now staring down at the carpet she sensed his eyes beating down on her. What did he see? A hard-ass woman who was finally cracking?

"It's okay to cry, you know. I won't give you away, Superintendent."

Nat looked up at him defiantly. She did not appreciate this boy detective reading her so easily.

"I don't need your permission or your confidence," she said in that officious *superintendent* tone she'd honed to a razor-sharp edge.

The detective merely nodded at the rebuke. "I can't tell you cause of death definitively until the autopsy. But the ME says it looks to be suffocation." The low, somber timbre of his voice was the only part of Coscarelli that impressed Nat as being grown up.

"When?" *Please let it be after 5:40 tonight.* That would let Walsh off the hook. Which would let her and the pre-release center off the hook as well. Even in her grief, she could not dismiss these self-serving thoughts. She could only feel guilty for having them.

"We don't have an exact time of death. The ME estimates somewhere between twelve noon and three P.M."

The color drained from her face. *It's Walsh. It's got to be Walsh.* Then a reality far worse than a ruined career assailed her. *And it's all my fault. . . .*

Coscarelli was talking. "We found a poem on the floor beside her bed. Signed "Dean." I'm guessing a student."

Her breath jammed in her throat. *All my fault . . . all my fault . . . Oh Maggie, I'm so sorry . . . I'm so horribly sorry. . . .*

"What can you tell me about Dean, Superintendent?" Not even inquiring if she knew him. Assuming she did. Knowing she did?

"His full name is Dean Thomas Walsh. He's been an inmate at Horizon House for the past three weeks. On pre-release. Working in a copy shop in Cambridge. Finishing six to eight for . . . rape."

Nat started replaying in her mind fragments from Walsh's Horizon House classification meeting, trying to figure out how she could have been so wrong about him—

". . . Sure I'm scared of going out there. Almost as scared as I was coming in eight years ago. But I'm going out a different person, Superintendent Price." Walsh paused, smiling sheepishly. "They all tell you that, right?"

"Right now we're interested in what you tell us, Mr. Walsh."

"I've got so much going for me. No way I'm coming back," he said earnestly, his eyes looking squarely into Nat's. Most inmates have trouble making eye contact. And they get visibly uneasy when an authority figure looks too closely at them. Not Walsh.

"The odds are against you," she said.

"Believe me, I know that. I've met plenty of cons here who've been through the revolving door so often they don't know which way is in and which is out. I think a lot of them

deliberately come back for some R&R. Not me, Superinten-
dent. I never should have been here in the first place. And, I
swear to all of you there's no way I'm ever coming back.
Besides, I've got the chance for a real future now, thanks to
Professor Austin. She told me yesterday when she came to visit
I could audit her evening poetry class at the community col-
lege," he told the board with a boyish excitement. *"Do you*
have any idea what it's like to have someone you respect and
admire see something special in you? To have that person tell
you you have real talent? It means the world to me. No way
I'm going to prove her wrong about me."

Nat picked up an undercurrent of irritation from her
deputy. She guessed what he was thinking. That Maggie might
be at least as much swayed by Walsh's good looks as she was
by what she saw as his writing ability. Nat had to admit Walsh,
with his shaggy dark brown hair rakishly tousled, the day-old
growth of tough guy stubble, those electric blue eyes radiating
just the right hint of vulnerability, the lean but solid build, did
look more like a movie star playing an inmate than a real con.

"Forget it, Walsh. You got the handbook. You know the
rules here," Jack cut in. "You got to be back for evening count
at six." His tone was gruff, bordering on surly.

Walsh showed no reaction to Jack's jab. Definitely not a
hothead, anyway.

"There are exceptions to the rules?" Walsh challenged.
"What about the guys and gals that get overnights? Okay,
okay, I know. They're married. But still—"

"Have we moved from education to sex?" Jack asked dryly.

A faint flush rose in Walsh's cheeks. "I'm trying to better
myself. Make something of my life. I've been through hell. Oh
sure, you all think I had it coming. That I deserved it. I know
there's not a single one of you considers even for an instant that
maybe, just maybe, I got a bum rap. But whatever you think,
I've been paying my debt to society, owed or not. You people are

supposed to be supporting my efforts to make it when I get back on the street. So what gives?" Walsh was visibly agitated now.

As were Nat's deputy and her head officer, Gordon Hutchins. Across from Nat her employment counselor Sharon Johnson was clasping her hands tightly on the table, her dark eyes tense, waiting for the explosion.

Nat was about to try to defuse it when Walsh sighed. "You want to know the God's honest truth, the only reason I signed up for that writing class back at Norton was 'cause it got me out of laundry duty early once a week. And, okay, it didn't hurt that Professor Austin was real easy on the eyes. Sure, every guy in the joint who laid eyes on her wanted to . . ."

"Fuck her?" Jack finished off.

Walsh gave him an openly reproachful look. "My mother taught me you don't use vulgar language in the presence of ladies."

"Does it piss you off?" Jack deliberately egged him on.

Nat gave Jack a reproachful look.

Walsh eyeballed the deputy. "What makes me mad is that I'm getting grief because I want an education. Is that a crime?"

"Assault is a crime," Jack said pointedly. "Rape is a crime. An ugly, brutal crime. It's the most insidious violation of one's body and soul."

"You think I don't know about rape?" Walsh said between clenched teeth. Then, completely unexpectedly, he dropped his head to his hands with his broad shoulders jerking spasmodically; Dean Thomas Walsh, a convicted A felon who had served almost eight years hard time, broke down and cried like a baby.

Detective Leo Coscarelli sat down beside Nat on Maggie's sofa, jarring her from her ruminations. Instinctively, she drew away. If he noticed, he didn't show any reaction.

"How close were they? Ms. Austin and Walsh?"

"I don't know." Which, sadly, was the truth.

"Close enough to be having lunch dates."

Nat felt her face burn. Obviously, he'd listened to Maggie's message on the tape. "Pre-release inmates on the street are forbidden from consorting with other cons, ex-cons, and most of all, victims or any member of a victim's family. If they drink or do drugs they're out of the program and sent back inside. Same if they're not on the job when they're supposed to be. We do regular random checks on each inmate work site. The only place they're supposed to be other than their job is a sanctioned activity."

Coscarelli was getting impatient. "Lunch dates with professors are sanctioned activities?"

"No. But they're not unsanctioned, per se. Walsh was auditing a poetry class of Maggie's which was sanctioned." Nat's stomach twisted. Her staff, especially her deputy, Jack Dwyer, had been very much against her decision to okay the classes for Walsh. Jack's protest had been particularly vehement, even going so far as to accuse her of being swayed by Walsh's bedroom eyes. It hadn't been the first time they'd argued, but there'd been an extra punch of animus between them in their clash over Dean Thomas Walsh.

"So these lunch dates—?" The detective deliberately let the sentence hang.

"They weren't *dates*," Nat said acidly. Not the least bit sure she wasn't lying through her teeth. "It might be she met him for lunch to . . ."

"Tutor him?" Coscarelli's smirk didn't go with his wholesome boy-detective looks. Then again, neither did his questions.

"I'm holding Walsh in lockup with an extra security detail, Detective. And I should have a drug report on him in a couple of hours."

"This look like his handiwork?" He gestured toward the bedroom.

Nat nodded wearily. Coscarelli would know soon enough

anyway. But she was quick to add, "Walsh was high on booze and coke when he attacked his original victim." *And tied her to the bed with her pantyhose . . .*

"When was that?"

"Almost nine years ago. He's had no drug use write-ups during his incarceration. And no reports on any substance abuse during pre-release. Before the test I ordered tonight, he's had three others and showed clean." *Listen to me trying to defend the bastard. More to the point, trying to cover my own ass.* Nat's self-loathing warred with her sorrow.

"Any other men Ms. Austin was seeing? Did she have a boyfriend?"

"I'm . . . not sure. I think there might have been someone . . . recently. She's been busy a lot of nights lately." Their planned dinner tonight was the first time Maggie had been free in almost three weeks. A new man on the scene was all that made sense, and Nat was surprised that Maggie kept him so close to her chest. It wasn't like her. Maggie was usually so open about her love life that she could get Nat blushing.

"I assume Walsh was tucked in at pre-release those nights," Coscarelli said, "so we have to look elsewhere for the possible boyfriend."

The medical examiner cleared his throat behind them. He was a rail-thin man in his fifties with stooped shoulders and a sallow complexion. He stood at Maggie's bedroom door. Coscarelli sprang up and met him over there. They conferred for a few moments, then Coscarelli followed the ME back into the bedroom. Before he shut the door, Coscarelli's partner, Mitchell Oates, a burly African-American in his early thirties, approached him and handed him something. A photo, Nat thought. Coscarelli stared down at it, shutting the door behind him.

He came out a minute later, walked slowly back over to the couch and sat down. Placing his hands squarely on his knees, he looked to be examining his neatly trimmed and spotlessly clean fingernails. "Was your friend into rough sex, Ms. Price?"

The question, put so bluntly, sent a shudder of revulsion through her. "No, of course not." Her response was so fierce, he drew back. "Don't think for a second she voluntarily . . ." Nat couldn't even finish the thought much less the sentence. "She was *raped*, Detective. And if you can't see that—"

"There don't appear to be any signs of struggle," he said matter-of-factly. But not without a hint of sympathy.

"Did it ever occur to you that she might have been too terrified to struggle?" Nat countered. "Or that she was drugged? Or . . . or murdered first?" She squeezed her eyes shut, but she was still bombarded with hideous images.

"There are a few messages that were left on Ms. Austin's answering machine," Coscarelli said, again shifting gears. Even as Nat experienced a physical jolt at the switch, she also felt a wave of relief. The last thing in the world she was prepared to contemplate was even the remote possibility that Maggie in any way encouraged the brutality done to her.

"One was a message from Karen Powell," the detective was saying. "Then there were two male callers. Different voices. No names left. I'm wondering if one of them was Walsh. Are you up to listening to the tape, Ms. Price? Seeing if you can possibly identify the two men?"

"I . . . don't know."

"You don't know if you're up to it?"

"I don't know if I can identify them. I mean, I probably don't know them. Maggie and I were close, but we traveled in different social circles. . . ." But all Nat could think about now was how their circles had converged recently. How Dean Thomas Walsh had become the center of this new, shared circle.

"Why don't we give it a try? Do the best you can, Superintendent." Coscarelli was already on his feet, slipping a hand into his jacket pocket, pulling out a small self-sealing plastic bag. Inside was one of those miniature tapes. Nat noticed as he opened the bag that he was wearing skin-colored rubber gloves on his hands. And, she thought, he had touched Maggie with those gloved hands. Her throat burned as she fought down yet another wave of nausea. Though she was far from recovering from the shock, she was slowly comprehending the awful reality. The crushing sorrow was oozing to the surface of her skin. Her dearest friend on earth was dead. Raped. Murdered. And she might have been partly to blame.

"The answering machine's in the bedroom."

He must have seen her blanch, because he quickly added, "I'll go get it and bring it in here. Maybe you want a cup of tea. Or something stronger. I could send a man out . . ."

"No. Let's just get this over with."

Coscarelli returned a minute later with the answering machine. He hit play and sat in the arm chair to the right of the sofa. Nat was grateful for the distance.

"Hi. It's Karen. I just want to say that I still think you should be more cautious about all this. I really wish you'd listen to reason. Would you please think it over some more? And call me. Please. I'm going to a movie at seven so I'll drop the test papers over at your place afterwards. If you're home by then maybe we can talk."

Coscarelli paused the tape. "Know what she's referring to?"

"Didn't she tell you?"

"I'd like your impressions."

"She could have been talking about Walsh." Nat had no doubt Karen was uneasy about Walsh. Only partly because he was a con. Nat was sure the other and likely larger part had to do with Walsh getting so much of Maggie's attention. Karen definitely wouldn't have liked that.

"Would you describe Ms. Austin as a risk-taker?"

Nat shrugged off his question. She hated the idea of telling this boy detective about Maggie's flaws. Let him find her killer, and leave her poor friend's psyche alone. But that was not about to happen. To do the job right, he would have to learn as much as he could about the victim as well as the monster who murdered her.

Nat was relieved when, instead of pressing for more details, he hit play again.

A male voice came on. Low and rasping.

". . . You're never home anymore. I guess I'll have to catch you after class. It's dumb to go around avoiding me like this."

Coscarelli shot Nat an inquiring look.

She shook her head. The low-pitched, scratchy voice was unfamiliar. And disturbing, although the caller's tone had more of a teasing than a menacing quality. Nat supposed it was either a pesty student or a colleague from school that Maggie had been intentionally avoiding. Both possibilities now took on an ominous importance. Nat very much wanted to know the identity of the man who'd left this message.

A couple of hang-ups followed. And then another male voice came on—a voice Nat recognized instantly. It was all she could do not to gasp in astonishment.

". . . thought you'd be home by now. Did you tell her? How'd she take it? Now, do you believe me when I say she doesn't have a thing for me? Like I've been telling you all along, she's still pining over that dead-beat husband of hers. Man, I hate talking to machines. Call me when you get in. If it's not too late, maybe I can come over. Don't worry about my cold. I stayed home today and sweated it out, so I'm feeling a lot better. But I could feel better still, babe."

Nat saw Coscarelli observing her closely. Shrewdly. Maybe he was older and smarter than he looked. Smarter anyway.

He didn't say a word. Waiting for her to abort the silence.

Nat knew the caller. Knew him well. *Then again,* she realized with a jolt, *not well enough to know he was involved with her murdered friend.* There was no question as to her duty. She was obligated to give him up to the cops. But this was one of her people.

She needed to buy a little time. Get some answers before she gave any out. Even as she made this decision, Nat knew there could be serious consequences to withholding information—even temporarily—from the authorities. Were she in Coscarelli's shoes, she'd throw the book at her. But she was in her shoes—

"You look pale, Superintendent."

Nat played the pallor for all it was worth. Easy enough to do considering how she was feeling. "I'm still in shock." *Shock added to shock.* And now there was another puzzle piece that fell into place. And that was grasping why Jack was so overtly hostile toward Walsh during that classification meeting. Jack and Maggie must have been romantically involved already. Given that fact, it was easy to see that Jack had acted more like a jealous lover that day than an unbiased deputy.

Shakily, she got to her feet. Coscarelli popped up. They were just about the same height so he was eye to eye with her.

"Can you give me a few hours, Detective? It's really all hitting me at once."

"I understand," he said.

And now Nat was worrying that maybe he did.

four

HE WAS STANDING AT HIS DOOR, his dark hair rumpled, his face in need
of a shave. His eyes were watery and his nose was red. He'd
taken the day off from work because of a bad cold.

Clad in a short, beat-up faded blue terry robe, his dark chest
hairs and knobby knees were exposed. He was either naked
underneath the robe or wearing only his boxers. Yes, Nat knew
he favored boxer shorts. And it was only one of the many personal things she knew about her deputy, Jack Dwyer.

"I heard," he said, stepping aside to let her in.

His statement, not quite cavalier but certainly far from discon-
solate, infuriated her. She belted him across the face with her

open hand. Hard enough so that her palm stung. Hard enough to leave a clear red imprint.

His hand went up to his cheek, but he was stunned into speechlessness.

"That's all you can say?" Nat was in his face, her words like bullets blasting him.

"What? Glazer didn't tell me anything . . ."

"Glazer?" Nat had expected Hutch to have called him. She was wondering why he hadn't. Must be, he'd had his hands full coping with Walsh and arranging for extra security coverage.

"Yeah, he called around eight to tell me two female inmates, Carmen Rios and Gerry Flynn, got into a rip-roaring cat fight tonight . . ." Jack scowled. "You didn't know?" He stared at her, uncomprehending. "Why'd you lay into me like that, Nat?" He was still rubbing his cheek.

Nat sank against the doorjamb, weak from the realization that they were talking at cross-purposes. "It's . . . Maggie, Jack."

She saw a look of perplexity. And then—a slow dawning as he took in the ravaged look on her face. Thinking the unthinkable, terrified to voice it.

Nat said it for him, easier to manage it now that she was so worked up. "She's dead, Jack."

He staggered back, almost losing his balance. Immediately sorry for her bluntness, Nat reached out to him but he wheeled away.

"I know, Jack. I still . . . can't believe it myself." Her hand remained outstretched. Clutching air.

Jack was clutching his gut, his eyes already haunted with the loss. A wave of resentment coursed through Nat. What right did he have to feel anguish equal to her? Maggie was her dearest friend for more than a decade. Jack couldn't have been involved with her for more than a couple of months since Nat had first introduced Jack to Maggie that past June.

"How?"

She inhaled a lungful of air like she was drawing in smoke from a cigarette, a habit she'd quit over five years ago. And might end up taking up again. "Let's go inside, Jack." They hadn't moved from his open front door. Nat closed it and they started to walk toward the living room.

He grabbed her arm, clenching it tightly. "How, damn it?"

Oddly, she welcomed the pain of his grip. Somehow it made it easier to tell him. She'd barely finished before he spit out without hesitation, "Walsh."

Nat said nothing.

He stared at her, his features darkening with what she knew must be even darker recriminations.

She remembered the argument they'd had right after Walsh's classification meeting.

"Walsh suckered you in, Nat. Admit it. Those baby blue bedroom eyes, the pretty boy tears—"

"You're way off, Jack. Not to mention way out of line."

"Right, boss. Forgot myself for a second there, boss."

"Don't goad me, Jack. It's not going to work. I gave Walsh the okay because that's what this facility's supposed to be about. Giving cons a reason not to end up back here again. Or, worse, end up—" She shook off the rest of the sentence.

"Look, I know you're particularly vulnerable right now, Nat, what with Ethan dumping you for a twenty-three-year-old bimbo. But you can't let your personal problems spill over—"

"That was a low blow, Jack. Furthermore, she's not a bimbo. She's his student. And my decision about Walsh has absolutely nothing to do with anything going on in my personal life."

In hindsight, Nat couldn't help fearing that there was a kernel of truth in Jack's diatribe. Had she been particularly vulnerable?

Had she completely misread Walsh? Had he manipulated her? Had he manipulated Maggie?

Not that hindsight had ever done her much good.

"It's funny. I didn't even like her all that much when we met at that party you threw for her in June. I tagged her as another one of your bleeding heart liberals. The way she went on and on over dinner about igniting the creative spirit in those lowlife cons she was teaching. Oh sure, I thought she was dynamite looking. Incredibly sexy. But once burned . . . Make that twice burned." Jack took a long swallow of bourbon. Nat's glass remained untouched on the breakfast table in his tiny kitchen. She knew if she so much as brought it to her lips, she'd retch again.

The booze was making Jack loquacious although Nat didn't feel he was really talking to her. In fact, she wasn't convinced he knew she was in the room with him. There was a far-off look in his eyes and if he was seeing anyone Nat imagined it was Maggie.

"About a month later, we bumped into each other on line at the Nickelodeon. What was showing?" He frowned, trying to recall. "Hell, I don't remember. I don't really think I remembered while it was on the screen." He took another belt. "I was by myself. Maggie was with some guy—"

"Did she introduce you?" Nat cut in. Any *guy* in Maggie's life now took on a heightened significance. Of course she knew that included Jack as well. Jack was most definitely a guy in Maggie's life.

Jack scowled. Annoyed at being interrupted. "Probably. I can't remember that either. I don't think he could have been someone all that special, though, because she invited me to sit with them."

This didn't surprise Nat. Probably surprised Maggie's date, though. Surprised and irritated him. "Did you?" she asked.

Jack smiled briefly. "Yeah. I sat on one side of her, the dude sat on her other side." He knocked back the rest of his drink, immediately grabbing the bottle for a refill. "I don't know what it was about Maggie that night that made me so . . . aware of her. Maybe it had something to do with being shoulder to shoulder in the dark theater. Maybe it was her flowery perfume. Most likely, it was the crooked little smirk she gave me when she first saw me on line. Like she knew exactly how I'd pegged her, and was putting me on notice that she was a woman who wasn't so easily pigeonholed." His smile grew wistful. Nat had seen Jack Dwyer in all kinds of moods over the past year. Wistful was a first.

"When did you start dating?" Nat asked matter-of-factly, hiding the hurt she felt that he and Maggie had kept their relationship a secret from her. Also masking her embarrassment that Maggie had told Jack she was carrying a torch for him.

There'd been times over the past year Nat had admitted to herself she was drawn to Jack. If she hadn't been married, if they hadn't been working together, if he hadn't come with a lot of excess baggage, if she hadn't come with as much baggage of her own if not more, if he'd have pushed his advantage a little harder—

Nat regretted now that she'd hinted at some of those *if*s with Maggie. She felt betrayed that Maggie had shared them with Jack. Even more so because Maggie had done it behind her back. But all of those feelings paled against the enormity of Maggie's murder. And the stupendous implications it raised.

One of her inmates was probably the perp.

Suddenly an unbidden thought flashed into Nat's head. *Where was Jack between noon and three o'clock this afternoon?*

What was she thinking?

But the thought clung like glue. How well did she really know her deputy? She knew he had an on-again, off-again battle with booze and two failed marriages. From his resume, she knew he grew up in a family of six kids in Dorchester, one of Boston's poorer, mostly Irish communities, joined the marines straight out of high school planning to be a career officer only to decide not to re-up after two stints. Then he went to college, earned a degree in sociology, and went into Corrections. He worked his way up to Deputy Super at CCI Oakridge. He was not only there during the riot of '96, he was credited with negotiating the truce, saving the lives of two officers whom the inmates were holding hostage. A third hostage was killed before negotiations could get under way. Jack left Oakridge soon after, took a three-month hiatus. Before coming on board at Horizon House, he'd spent almost two years in the DOC's head offices downtown, working as an advisor and strategist. Although Jack never spelled it out, Nat believed that after the prison riot, her deputy had experienced a severe case of Post-Traumatic Syndrome. Nat, having suffered enough traumas of her own, knew that they had lasting effects. But they affected different people in different ways.

Jack picked up her glass of bourbon, holding it out to her. "Drink up. You look like you need it."

Nat looked blankly at the glass, shaking her head, trying as well to shake off her disturbing ruminations. Her gaze shifted to her deputy's face.

"The detective in charge of the investigation played the messages that were left today on Maggie's machine for me, Jack. He wanted to know if I could identify two of the callers. One was a guy whose voice I didn't recognize." Nat gave him a rundown of the message. "Do you have any idea who it could be? Did Maggie say anything to you about someone hounding her?"

"No. She wouldn't have. She had this thing about being able to handle troubled creeps on her own. Totally sure of herself. Lot like you, Nat."

Nat sensed he wanted to goad her into a fight. Give him an excuse to strike back at her. At least he needed an excuse. When she was a child and her mother was in the throes of one of her manic episodes, she'd needed no excuse to strike out at her oldest daughter. It wasn't that Nat got singled out by her mother. It was that Nat singled herself out—*It's okay, Rach. Go next door to the Martins. Go. Now.* Wasn't that what being the big sister was all about? The question she'd assiduously avoided asking herself was—*Who is left to protect me?*

"I guess you heard the . . . other message on Maggie's machine. You and the cops." Jack hesitated, watching her.

Nat met his gaze. His expression was unreadable. "I didn't tell the detective it was you. I thought it might be best if you identified yourself to Coscarelli."

Jack nodded slowly, quickly finished off his refill, then shut his eyes. With all that booze in him, Nat thought he'd likely nod off, possibly pass out. Instead, she saw his shoulders shake and a flood of tears spill out from beneath his closed lids. Getting plastered hadn't knocked him out, or made a dent in his emotional anguish.

Then she got it. Painfully. This wasn't just another fling for Jack. He had been truly in love with Maggie.

Maggie was right to keep their affair a secret. Even in this vastly inappropriate circumstance, Nat felt jabbing pangs of jealousy.

Nat made a pot of coffee and poured some into a mug for Jack. She needed him to sober up before they headed over to the House to interrogate Walsh. She watched as he silently sipped the hot, strong brew. They couldn't draw comfort or consolation from each other, she and Jack, even though Nat sensed he yearned for it as much as she did.

She dropped the topic of his relationship with Maggie. He never did answer her earlier question about when they started dating. Nat didn't know at what point Jack fell in love with Maggie. Did Maggie love Jack? That she'd never know. Nat chose to believe that she did. Because she desperately wanted to think of her friend's last days on this earth as happy ones.

But Maggie's very last day was anything but.

Nat let her head fall into the cradle of her arms on the kitchen table.

She heard the scrape of Jack's chair on the floor as he rose. For a moment she thought he was going to come over to her, make the first move. She wanted the solace—the forgiveness—of his touch more than she could admit.

She heard Jack's footsteps retreat from the room.

She was alone. She stopped fighting back her tears.

When a ringing phone jolted her awake, Nat had no recollection of when she'd stopped crying, nor that she'd nodded off. Her head jerked up from Jack's kitchen table, the muscles at the back of her neck and running down her spine achingly tight and cramped, her arms numb from lack of circulation.

She blearily spotted Jack reaching for the wall phone. The clock beside it read 6:45. Nat had been out for a good hour.

Jack, meanwhile, had used the time she'd been sleeping to shower and dress. His still damp dark hair was combed straight back from his freshly shaved face, and he was wearing a crisp blue oxford shirt and khaki slacks. He cleaned up good. For all his boozing during the night, her thirty-eight-year-old deputy looked a hell of a lot better than she did.

She was just starting to rise from her chair when she heard Jack growl into the phone, "Shit!"

She sat back down. She knew she'd need to.

"When? . . . Yeah, yeah . . . Yeah. She's here. I'll let her know."

"What?" Nat asked anxiously as soon as he hung up.

"We got company down at the House."

"Company?"

"Reporters. Camera crews. A small but vocal contingent of

angry, law-abiding, placard-carrying citizens. Woke everyone up at the House. Someone must have leaked Walsh's name to the media. The shit's not just hitting the fan, it's flying out in all directions."

five

*Jack Dwyer may project a tough, even gruff exterior,
but he has always conducted himself in a professional
manner on the job. While he has suffered some personal problems for which psychological treatment has
been recommended, his integrity and dedication to his
work remains unquestioned. . . .*

(excerpt from yearly evaluation report)

THEY SETTLED INTO JACK'S BEAT-UP '94 GRAY SUBARU STATION WAGON, but he
didn't start the engine right off. He looked over at Nat and they
stared at each other like two embattled soldiers teetering on the
edge of a whacked-out world.

Dawn was breaking through a smudge of clouds. It was one of
those Indian summer September mornings and it was an oven in
the car, but neither of them seemed to have the strength to roll
down the windows, which were fast clouding up with their
breath. Jack was clutching the steering wheel with both hands,

the engine still off. He gave little away, but Nat could see that the lines in his face were more pronounced than usual. She guessed his mind was going a mile a minute.

As was hers. Grotesque images of her dead friend competed with images of angry citizens screaming for blood outside the pre-release center.

"Why the hell didn't you listen to me, Nat?"

So much for hoping his rage would subside and they could be allies in grief and mourning. "Jack, this is no time—"

"Walsh had the hots for her," he cut her off brutally, each word squeezed out between clenched teeth, his knuckles turning white as his grip tightened on the wheel. "Anyone with half a brain . . ." His face registered fury and anguish in equal measure.

"You think I'm not wracked with guilt over this? I loved her, too, Jack. I'd give anything . . . anything for this not to have happened to Maggie."

Silence engulfed them again. Nat strained to hold back an eruption of tears. Managing only by focusing on what was facing them back at the House.

"Listen, Jack," she said quietly, "we're in a crisis situation here. Before the morning's out we're going to have the commissioner and maybe even the governor coming down on us. It wouldn't surprise me if they decide to order the whole House shut down. Which I won't fight as long as it's strictly a temporary measure, but there's no way in hell I'm going to meekly step aside and let them close us down for good."

"Maybe it'd be for the best. Keep maniacs like Walsh off the streets for as long as possible," Jack said grimly.

"But they're still going to get out. They're still going to be walking among us. And for every Walsh we've seen dozens of cons benefit enormously from pre-release," Nat reminded him, anxious to help him through this crisis of faith. Because she desperately needed him to help her through hers. "And no matter what we both assume," she added, "we don't *know* Walsh did it."

"Don't give me that crap, Nat. You read his dirty little poems. Walsh was obsessed with her." He slammed both fists into the steering wheel, his rage and anguish coming from somewhere deep inside him. "All you had to do was veto him attending her classes. But no, you didn't want to deprive the perverted little bastard of an education. So what grade do you think he deserves, Nat? Huh? What mark would you give him now?"

"Jack, I'm already suffocating in my own self-recriminations. I don't need any from you," Nat said tightly. Still, a part of her did envy him the ability to lash out rather than self-flagellate.

Jack stared straight ahead, his voice more despairing than hostile. "You knew how Maggie was. She was always a sucker for *creative* types. Especially the ones who had *suffered for their art*, as she'd put it. Well, I don't know how much suffering Walsh has done up to now, but he hasn't experienced the half of it."

"Jack—"

"I don't want to hear it, Nat. I don't want to hear it." He slumped forward as if deflated, dropping his forehead against the steering wheel. "She was the best thing that ever happened to me. I didn't deserve her. And she didn't deserve . . . this." He didn't make a sound, but Nat could see his chest heave.

Her hand reached out toward him, but she hastily pulled it back. Afraid he'd reject her again. She and Jack had been through a lot that past year, and Nat had thought their shared experiences had made them friends if nothing more. But now she felt as if they were little more than familiar strangers.

Pushing aside reporters' microphones and video cameras that were being shoved into their faces, leaving behind them a trail of "No comments," Nat and Jack squeezed through the crowd in front of Horizon House, a narrow, six-story brick Victorian building on the corner of Providence and Berkeley, a few short blocks from Police Headquarters. There was a contingent of Boston cops holding a small but vocal gathering of picketers back behind a makeshift barrier.

Gordon Hutchins, not only Horizon House's Chief Corrections Officer but an embattled thirty-year veteran of the corrections system, held the front door open for them. Normally, the front entrance remained open from 7 A.M. to 7 P.M. but Hutch informed Nat as soon as she and Jack stepped inside the small vestibule that the House was in a 24-hour-a-day lockdown—and all pre-release privileges had been rescinded until further notice. Orders of the Commissioner. The residents had all been confined to their locked quarters.

"We've got people on each floor, keeping an eye on things," Hutch said as he held open the glass door for Nat and Jack that led into the main lobby. "So far there's just been grousing, but—"

"I know," Nat cut him off. She didn't need Hutch to tell her the inmates weren't happy about this situation. And that the longer it lasted, the more vocally unhappy they would get. She just prayed that was as bad as it would get.

As the three of them stepped into the recently painted sunshine yellow lobby, the officer stationed at the entrance behind the check-in/out desk quickly switched off the metal detector, one of the only giveaways that this was a prison setting. He switched it back on when they passed through.

Nat gave the officer a distracted nod, glancing past him into the disquietingly empty visiting room off to the left. In its earliest incarnation as a hotel for young women, the large, high-ceilinged room had served as a dining hall, sunshine streaming into the oak-paneled space from a set of bay windows that faced onto the street. After falling on hard times in the eighties, the hotel became a boarding house, and then stood vacant for several years until it was bought by the state to serve as the pre-release facility.

Nat, who'd been appointed as Superintendent of Horizon House before the building had been revamped and opened, had played a significant role in overseeing much of the renovations. She was the one who'd insisted on designating the sunny ex-dining hall as a den/library for the inmates. Built-in bookcases were put in along one whole wall and the shelves were filled with a wide assortment of books, audiotapes and audio equipment. On Wednesdays and Sundays, from eleven A.M. until two P.M. the area served as the visiting room. This was the only time male and female inmates were allowed to congregate in the same space at the same time beyond a sanctioned house-supervised activity. At all other times, until lights out at ten P.M. the men and women inmates, alternating days, were given open access to use the room to read or listen to music. Small lounges with reading material were also provided on each of the five upper floors. As for sleeping quarters, each floor contained two triples, three doubles and one single—the latter granted as an earned privilege. Each of the inmates was allowed a TV and music equipment in his or her room, the only stipulation being they had to use ear phones so as not to disturb their roommates. Each room had a small bath-room—toilet, sink, shower. Normally, the bedroom doors remained unlocked from six A.M. to ten P.M. Until further notice, they'd be locked round-the-clock, meals having to be brought on carts by the officers to each room.

Nat walked into her office, which was directly across from the visiting room, a mirror image of it down to the warm honey oak paneling and the huge bay windows. Someone, probably Hutch, had had the forethought to close the triple-paned windows to keep out the commotion on the street. The blinds had also been lowered so reporters couldn't peer in. Nat switched on the over-head light/fan fixture. The blades whirled, pushing hot air around the room.

Nat had furnished her office simply but tastefully. An old-fashioned oak desk, two comfortable arm chairs and a wing chair upholstered with a flowered print near the bay window. Framed old photos of Boston Harbor hung on the walls along with a large Georgia O'Keefe poster of a southwest canyon scene. Toward the front of the office, and off to the right, was a large conference table used for classification and staff meetings.

Hutch, the last of the threesome to enter Nat's office, closed the solid oak door behind him, one hand on his gut like he was having a bad case of indigestion. After a sympathetic nod in Nat's direction, the CO's eyes skidded over to Jack and lingered a moment longer. Nat saw it as if it was flashing in neon over Hutch's head. Her CO knew that Maggie and Jack were an item. And he'd kept it to himself. The good ol' boys' club was alive and thriving.

After their row in his car, Jack hadn't uttered another word to Nat during the entire fifteen-minute drive over to the House. Now the first words out of his mouth were, "I want to see Walsh."

"No. I'll talk to him," Nat said firmly. Pulling rank. In the condition her deputy was in, there was no way she'd have trusted him within a mile of Dean Thomas Walsh.

Jack's eyes narrowed and his voice went stony. "Nat . . ."

"Forget it, Jack."

He was just warming up for battle, but before he could say another word, Hutch held up a time-out hand. "Neither one of you's gonna be talking to him for a while."

The "why?" came out of both their mouths at the same time. With the same alert inflection.

Hutch sighed wearily. "A couple of Boston dicks have Walsh holed up in legal. Been in there with him for well over an hour." Legal was what they called the small, secured room at the back of the stairs used for private lawyer/inmate meetings.

Jack cursed under his breath and stormed out of the office. Nat was certain he was heading straight for Walsh's room to conduct a search. Even though she was just as sure the cops had already been through it with a fine-toothed comb.

She watched the door slam, then turned to Hutch. "They can't question Walsh without a lawyer." Nat was ready to head down to legal and break up the interrogation.

"Forget it. Walsh waved his right to representation. Said he had nothing to hide."

Nat hesitated. "How'd he take the news about . . . Maggie?"

"Cried like a baby." Hutch gave her a jaundiced look. "But we know our boy can do that on cue."

So, Nat thought despairingly, *Hutch's blaming me, too.* No big surprise. But still it hurt. It was going to be tough to operate without the support of her top people.

"How come you didn't call Jack last night and tell him about Maggie?"

Hutch lifted one of his bushy salt and pepper eyebrows. "I figured you'd called him before you called me."

"How long have you known? About Maggie and Jack?"

"What do I know?" Hutch wasn't giving her an inch.

Nat let it drop. Not wanting to totally squander her authority.

"Oh, by the way," Hutch said, "one of the dicks, a snot-nose with a baby face called Coscarelli, wants a meeting first with you and then Jack when he's done with Walsh."

Nat was wondering just how much Detective Leo Coscarelli knew about Jack when there was a light rap on her door. Nat stiffened, thinking *speak of the devil* until she heard her clerk Paul Lamotte's muffled voice, asking if she'd like some coffee. As soon as Nat told him "two coffees," he opened the door, two steaming mugs in hand.

Lamotte was one of three Horizon House inmate trustees. Even in a lockdown situation the trustees were given limited privileges as they were integral to the smooth running of the institution. Lamotte was a small, compact African-American man in his mid-fifties, dressed in navy slacks and a whiter than white shirt. He'd already put in twenty-seven years of a life sentence with no possibility of parole. One count of arson and two counts of murder in the first degree. His wife and his little boy. Both burned to death in their beds from a fire set by Lamotte.

The tragic irony was—if he was to be believed—they were supposed to be away for the night that Lamotte burned the house down for the meager ten-thousand-dollar insurance money so he could pay off some of the heavy medical bills from his boy's heart operation.

If he was to be believed.

One thing Nat had learned over her years in corrections—every con had a story. Out of all those stories, statistically, a few of them were true. It was knowing which ones were true for which there was no statistical analysis.

"Coffee's fresh," Lamotte said to Nat with the barest of smiles as he handed one mug to Hutch, then placed the other on her desk.

"What's the word?" Hutch asked Lamotte in that gruff tone he affected for all the inmates.

"The word is lockdown, man."

Nat eyed her clerk. Lamotte was a man the other inmates tended to trust. Some confided in him. Did that include Walsh?

"Anything else?" Nat pressed.

"You got a lot of calls, Super. . . ."

"I'm sure." Nat sighed. "I'll deal with them later, Paul."

Lamotte hesitated. "One's from Deputy Commissioner Carlyle. Actually, he called twice already. He's visiting family in New York for the weekend, but he's driving back to Boston. Said he should be here by nine. Expected you'd be in."

Hutch groaned. Nat wasn't vocal about it, but she was groaning on the inside. Steven R. Carlyle was one of their two Deputy Commissioners of Corrections. He was also one of their less rehabilitation-minded corrections officials. Carlyle was the antithesis of Russell Fisk, their other Deputy who, from the start, had been not only Nat's supporter, but a strong proponent of the pre-release program—especially approving of Horizon House's innovative policies, including their unique co-ed population. Supporting them meant that Fisk had to contend with what continued to be a fervid pro-punishment political climate. And he had to butt heads repeatedly with hard-asses like Steven Carlyle.

Carlyle would no doubt be in all his *I told you so* glory. Not that he and everyone else above Nat wouldn't get tarred with the same dirty brush. The whole slew of them could very well end up pounding the pavement together. Which would definitely temper Carlyle's gloating. But not his rage over an inmate having been blithely handed the opportunity to commit murder.

Nat was trying not to get ahead of herself. A losing battle. Horror, grief, rage, despair sped through her bloodstream in a headlong drug-like rush. If she didn't get a grip, she would OD on all those emotions.

Hutch leaned against the wall, coffee mug cupped in his beefy hands. "So, you think Walsh did it?" he asked Nat without preamble as soon as Lamotte exited the office.

"If you asked me if I thought there was any possibility he *didn't* do it, I'd say . . . I hope to God there is." Not what anyone would have signified as a vote of confidence for the inmate.

Nat sank into her swivel desk chair and took a sip of the hot coffee. Her body slackened and she could feel the catch at the back of her throat as she echoed Jack's earlier words. "She was such a good person."

"Gotta face it, Nat. Bad things are always happening to good people. But after more years in this system than I care to count, I gotta say some of those good people shoulda been a little smarter."

Nat opened her mouth in angry protest, but Hutch barreled right on. "You think she shoulda been smarter, too. Don't go denying it. Your best friend got too involved with these scuzzy characters. Not just Walsh. She was corresponding and visiting with a few of the sleazebags in the joint who took her prison writing course. A CO buddy of mine over at CCI Norton told me he intercepted a real X-rated love letter a lifer from her class wrote her. And word is, some of those little ditties Walsh has been scribbling out are infested with smut. At least that young cop, Coscarelli, seems to think so. I was there when he showed Walsh a poem—his word was *garbage*—that was found in your friend's apartment and asked him if it was his. Walsh not only owned up to having written it, but was real smug-assed about how his professor was planning to enter it in some big-deal poetry contest where the winner walks away with a five-hundred-buck prize." Hutch snickered. "You can bet that piece of shit's gonna win the prize all right."

six

There's more than one side to every situation. Some people don't see that. Some don't want to see that. . . .
                                                    C. L.
                                      Inmate #421765

"WALSH CLAIMS MS. AUSTIN phoned him at the photocopy store yesterday morning around ten o'clock and told him she'd have to cancel their lunch date that day altogether." Coscarelli had made himself at home on the old oxblood leather two-seater in her office. "He says she told him something came up that she had to take care of."

"You don't believe him."

"He says his boss will confirm the call."

"You don't believe him," she repeated. Did she?

"That he got a call? And his boss will back him on it? Sure, I'll believe that."

"But you still think they were together yesterday. At Maggie's apartment."

Nat got a one-shoulder shrug from Coscarelli who, like her, was still wearing the same clothes he had on last night. Obviously, he hadn't had the time to go home and change yet either.

Was it her imagination or was the detective looking not as boyish than he had at their first encounter less than twenty-four hours ago? They'd probably both aged since then, Nat thought wearily.

"Do you want to tell me why you dummied up on me last night about your deputy?"

So much for hoping Jack would get the chance to own up before Coscarelli tagged him. Nat tucked an errant strand of hair behind her ear and noticed the detective carefully observing the gesture. She was sure he interpreted it as a sign of nerves. Or guilt?

"I was in shock," Nat muttered. As if she was out of shock now. Far from it.

Coscarelli shrugged off her evasion. "I bet my partner a fiver you knew who it was."

"A real big gambler. I bet you buy a lotto ticket every week, too," she commented sardonically.

He surprised her by grinning. An irritatingly youthful grin, at that. "Won a hundred bucks once. Of course, I've blown at least twice that on tickets since then," he added, his grin widening, making him look younger still.

Nat felt older. This detective's questions and manner were aging her by the second.

The grin vanished—Nat wondered if he realized it was not his most authoritative expression—and he got back to the grim business at hand. "We played the tape for Karen Powell this morning and she identified Jack Dwyer right off the bat."

"He was planning to tell you himself," Nat said guiltily. After all, she was a Corrections official and she was certainly not supposed to be obstructing the police in their murder investigation. She consoled herself with the thought that she wasn't *obstructing* justice, just briefly delaying it.

"Dwyer was talking about you in that message, right? I understand your husband split on you just around the time your deputy hooked up with your friend."

Nat's spine stiffened. "My personal life is not at issue here, Detective."

Coscarelli slid right by her declaration as if he hadn't heard it. "You didn't fix them up, though—Jack and Maggie—from what I understand."

"You've certainly acquired a lot of understanding in a very short time, Detective. I'm impressed." The snide tone of her voice made it clear that was not all she was. "I assume you collected all these tidbits from Karen Powell?"

"Karen Powell's still very shaken up. I gather she and Ms. Austin were quite close."

Nat made no comment, but she balked inwardly at Coscarelli's conclusion. Karen, who had been one of Maggie's students for a couple of years before becoming her teaching assistant, struck Nat from the start as a very needy and demanding young woman. She had never understood Maggie's choice of Karen for her T.A. Even less, why Maggie went out of her way to befriend her. It probably fed some maternal instinct. Nat could more than identify with that particular instinct, just not with Maggie picking Karen as the one to mother.

Coscarelli lifted a straggly eyebrow. "You don't like her, do you?"

"Who?" Nat hated the obviously evasive tone in her voice. She hated that the detective, for all his presumed inexperience, was so adept at putting her on the defensive. She didn't like it one bit. Maybe because it reminded her too much of herself.

The detective was waiting patiently. Nat felt that damn strand of hair she'd tucked away, fall back down and dangle irritatingly against her cheek. She folded her hands one on top of another on her desk. Again, catching Coscarelli noting the move. Abruptly, she got up from her chair, walked purposely around her desk and over to the leather settee, deliberately looking down at the detective who remained seated.

Yes, that was better. When in doubt, take the high ground.

"I hardly know Karen Powell." Not a total lie even though Maggie had included Karen in a number of their get-togethers, especially over the past year. For some reason which Nat never fathomed, Maggie was invested in Karen and Nat being friends. For Maggie's sake, Nat made a concerted effort, but Karen was always so guarded around her and so proprietary of Maggie, that their get togethers felt more like Arab-Israeli peace talk encounters. The truth was, Nat didn't like Karen. More to the point, she didn't trust her. On both counts, Nat believed the feelings were mutual.

"Ms. Powell tells me that her phone message last night referred to her concerns about Ms. Austin's involvement with Dean Thomas Walsh."

Nat gave him a sharp look. "Involvement?"

Coscarelli seemed perfectly at ease to have her staring down at him. "She thought Walsh was pushing for more than an *education*. Didn't like how he'd always show up real early for class and pull his prof over for private little tête-a-têtes. And then there were his poems which Ms. Powell described as 'smutty.'"

"Karen Powell far from qualifies as a literary critic, Detective."

She caught a smile, both faint and brief, on Coscarelli's face. "Sometimes when a person's in shock they clam up," he said. "You know, pull right into themselves. Then there are others where the shock triggers a real talking jag. Ms. Powell had a hell of a lot to say."

"So I gather."

"Not only about Dean Thomas Walsh."

"Who else?" How nice it would be if Karen came up with another suspect.

"Jack Dwyer, for one."

Wrong suspect. Nat felt her stomach turn over. She'd conveniently pushed that possibility from her mind. Telling herself it was absurd. But Coscarelli certainly didn't look like he was discounting Jack. Absently, Nat tucked that wayward strand behind her ear again.

"Exactly what did Karen have to say about him?" she challenged, wishing she could sit down again since she no longer felt any advantage standing over him. But she didn't want the detective to read the move as a retreat. Which was precisely what it would be. Nat couldn't afford to lose any more ground. Even though she wasn't sure why this had become so important.

Well, that wasn't entirely true. She found it exceedingly uncomfortable, even threatening, having a stranger, and a cop no less, knowing so much about her. And, worse still, not knowing what it was he knew.

As Coscarelli's silence extended, it became obvious he wasn't about to reveal his newly acquired insights—from Karen Powell's perspective, or his—about Jack or anyone else. Nat decided on a different tack. Still attempting to gain ground.

"You interrogated Walsh for over two hours. Without a lawyer."

"His choice," Coscarelli said blithely.

"If you plan to question him again, I'm going to strongly encourage him to get legal representation."

"Good idea."

"Do you plan to question him again?"

Coscarelli's prosecutorial eyes squinted at her. Answer enough.

She turned back to her desk, picked up a report and handed it to the detective. "The drug results on Walsh. He was clean as a whistle yesterday."

Coscarelli gave the sheet a cursory glance, then slipped it in his notepad.

"Are you charging him?" Nat asked, detecting a quiver in her voice. And hoping Coscarelli didn't.

"Walsh can swear to kingdom-come he never saw the victim yesterday, but his alibi is paper thin."

"What is his alibi?" Nat was eager to know.

"He says he ate lunch alone at around noon in a park across from the copy shop. Hung out there for an hour reading a magazine. Didn't talk to anyone, doesn't know if anyone saw him. Got back to the photocopy shop at one. Left again a little past two—alone—to make some deliveries in Somerville and Watertown. Back again at the shop around three-thirty. And his boss'll confirm he was there till closing."

Coscarelli leaned forward on the couch, both of his hands rubbing the muscles at the back of his neck. "Leaves him alone for most of the afternoon. Plenty of time to skip over to his teacher's apartment either between noon and one, or between two and three-thirty if his deliveries don't check out."

The escalating probability of Dean Thomas Walsh's guilt unfolded with a terrible, excruciating inevitability. At the same time Nat felt the intensifying weight of her own guilt for so desperately wanting Maggie's killer to be anyone but Walsh. Anyone without a connection to Horizon House, that was, making Jack an unsatisfactory substitute suspect.

Coscarelli rose slowly to his feet. Once again, they were eye to eye. "Chances are, we'll come up with something more solid by the end of the day. We're canvassing Ms. Austin's building and neighborhood and we'd like to meet with anyone else here who had more than cursory contact with Walsh. While the investigation is on-going, I advise sticking him back in CCI Norton. Security in a setting like this is less than—"

"It's my job to ensure security here, Detective," Nat replied tightly. She wanted to remind him that even an inmate had the right to be assumed innocent until proven guilty. But who was she fooling? She thought Walsh was as guilty as the homicide cop thought he was.

He gave her a mock salute as he started for the door. The detective was getting under Nat's skin like a festering cyst.

"What I'm hearing, Detective, is that as things stand now, you have no hard evidence on Mr. Walsh."

"If I did," he said, hand resting on the doorknob, "we wouldn't be having this discussion."

"No prints? No . . . semen?"

A ghost of a smile crossed Coscarelli's face, but there was no humor in it. He released his hold on the knob, facing her full on. "Just like there were no prints and no semen his last time round when he raped Alison Cole. Tell me, did Walsh see a shrink in prison for his sexual problem? Did he talk about it in his sex offender group? Did he do any better with impotency issues inside the joint, I wonder?"

"Did you ask him?"

"You think he'd tell me if he did better with men than women?" Coscarelli frowned, then shook his head. "Whatever his sexual preferences, you can bet, being young and pretty, he had himself a *daddy* inside."

Nat was not about to bet against the detective. Early on in her career, she learned the ugly truth that one of the only ways inmates had of protecting themselves from constant brutal sexual assaults—especially the young, vulnerable first-timers like Walsh— was to be persuaded to partner up with an older, savvy con—a *Daddy* in prison slang—for protection. The deal was a Daddy protected his punk in exchange for his punk's sexual submission. Most young cons went along with the arrangement—regardless of how excruciating and humiliating they might find it—because the alternative was almost inevitably gang rape and quite possibly death. But only inmates in utter self-denial would view this protection system as truly voluntary. Or as anything but a kinder, gentler rape.

Although Nat was sure Coscarelli was right about Walsh, she wasn't so sure he'd got himself a daddy soon enough. She was remembering the way he broke down in her office during the classification interview. And his words preceding his tears. *You think I don't know about rape?*

She felt a wave of sympathy for him, then lost it totally to a horrible vision of Maggie bound on her bed. No matter how much she detested and felt appalled by what Walsh might have suffered in prison, in Nat's mind it didn't in even the minutest of ways absolve him of his own acts of violence.

Nat made a mental note to do some detailed checking into Dean Thomas Walsh's incarceration history. Coscarelli, no doubt, planned on doing the same thing. She was not about to suggest they team up on this. Something in her gut told her they wouldn't work well together.

Coscarelli broke in on her thoughts. "There's already a lot of press on this. There's bound to be plenty more. We're going to have to walk a thin line here. A lot of folks will be out for blood. Want Walsh strung up by the balls. On the other side we'll have all the liberal do-gooders accusing us of making a rush to judgment and persecuting poor, *innocent* cons."

"It is possible he didn't do it," Nat said without a touch of conviction.

"You have some other names to toss into the ring?"

"What about the man who left that message on Maggie's machine? The one who thought she was trying to avoid him? Did Karen know who he was?"

He shook his head, eyeballing Nat like she might still be holding out on him.

"I have no idea who . . ."

"Like you had no idea about Dwyer? Why were you shielding your deputy, Ms. Price?"

"I wasn't *shielding* him. God, you don't think Jack—"

"If that thought didn't cross your mind, why did you play dumb?"

"I was in shock, Detective," she said angrily. "And that message from Jack . . . took me by surprise. I didn't know . . . he was seeing Maggie."

Coscarelli nodded. Jack's message had made that much quite clear. "Karen Powell seemed to know all about it."

Nat was beginning to think everyone knew about Maggie and Jack. Except her.

"I don't see that Jack's relationship with Maggie has anything to do—"

"Sure you do," he cut her off perfunctorily.

She wanted to throw something at this little twerp. She eyed the flower-embedded Steuben glass paperweight on her desk—a present from Ethan for their last anniversary. *Talk about killing two birds with one stone.*

"Ms. Powell says that Ms. Austin had been complaining to her recently that Mr. Dwyer was getting too serious. Demanding too much of her time and attention."

"Funny, Maggie used to say the same thing to me. About Karen," Nat replied acidly. Okay, she was stretching it a bit. Most of the time she'd be the one telling Maggie that Karen was getting too dependent on her. But it was not as if Maggie disagreed with her. Just that she didn't seem to mind. Or refused to admit it if she did.

He leaned his back against her closed office door. "Do you know where Mr. Dwyer was yesterday between noon and four P.M., Ms. Price?"

"You heard his message. He was home sick with a bad cold. And although it's not exactly an alibi," Nat rushed on, "why would Jack call Maggie late last night asking her how her dinner with me went, if he . . . if he had any knowledge of her . . . death?"

"I don't know," Coscarelli said laconically. "If I didn't have much in the way of an alibi for the time of the murder of my girl-friend, I might think a phone call message after the fact would be worth a try."

"This is crazy. There's not a reason in the world—"

"In my experience, this kind of murder is usually the result of one or more of the three 'R's'—rejection, revenge, retribution."

Nat laughed caustically. "In *your* experience? How much experience is that, Detective?"

Coscarelli merely smiled.

"I'm so glad I can amuse you, Detective," Nat replied. She could really get to hate that man.

seven

What worries me isn't the danger itself; it's being able
to control myself when it hits. . . .

H. M.
Corrections Officer

Innocence is bliss is need is bleeding pleading back and forth
The good that is the ache in this delirium oozes smarts
Sickness unto death damnation redemption

I am your fake foul lover hater
A stony moany heart head soul
Reversible retractable removable

You are my God devil bitch seeker muse
Facing the face that bears the embrace of all the hashy trash
Your being yearning burning shrieking reeking

To feel what is real is real
The illusion and delusion that is me

Dean

NAT SET DOWN THE COPY OF THE POEM she had now read more than a dozen times since Coscarelli had left it for her *perusal*, as he put it. This time she'd read it aloud, voice quivering, as Dean Thomas Walsh sat, cuffed and shackled, on a state-issue wooden chair across from her desk in her office.

"You don't get it either, do you?" His eyes were red-rimmed, the irises more dark gray than brilliant blue now.

"Did Maggie get it?" Nat asked bitterly.

"She said the poem was disturbing. Powerful. Visceral." A half-smile. "I didn't know what that word meant. Maggie had me go look it up." The smile died. "She taught me so much. She believed in my talent. In me." Tears spilled over the rims of his eyes.

Nat had heard it before. This time she was unmoved by his tears. She couldn't imagine what it would take at this point for Dean Thomas Walsh to engage her compassion. She saw him now as arrogant, smarmy. She readily pictured him as a killer. What was unspeakably worse, a killer who chose for a victim the one person who was truly trying to help him.

"I swear to God I didn't do it, Nat—"

"Superintendent Price," she snapped.

He held up his cuffed hands, a pleading gesture. "Sorry, sorry, sorry. It's just Maggie talked about you a lot, always referring to you . . . by your first name. All good stuff," he quickly added. "How smart you are. How dedicated to your job. How you were always such a good friend to her. . . ."

"Where were the two of you when she was saying all these glowing words about me, Walsh?"

He squinted at her. Looking peeved. And then, as if aware of the slip, switched to confusion. "What?"

"I presume she didn't talk about me during her poetry classes."

"No."

"When you got together for lunch?"

"Sometimes."

"And dinner?"

"No."

"She didn't talk about me during dinner?"

"No, we never had dinner together." His tears were giving way to anger. He cast Nat a black look. "It wasn't what you're thinking."

Her own fury was close to boiling over. "Why don't you tell me what I'm thinking, Walsh?"

"You've all got your minds in the gutter. I never so much as touched Maggie. . . ."

"Tell me about it." She snatched up his poem from her desk and shook it at him. She could hear the hysteria seeping into her voice, but she was past caring. "Isn't that what this is about? Your desire, frustration, desperation? You wanted to be her lover and you hated her for rejecting you. Just like you hated Alison Cole nine years ago. Only this time . . . you . . . you—"

He was shaking his head violently. "No. I never hated Maggie. I never hated Alison. I never harmed either one of them." He took in a ragged breath. "You're wrong about all of it. My poems were symbolic. It wasn't . . . it wasn't *me* who wanted *her* that way. It was Maggie—"

Nat's fingers clenched into fists. She wanted to pummel the maggot. Smash in his filthy pretty-boy face.

Ask her before last night, and she'd have told you there wasn't a violent bone in her body.

"If you don't believe me, talk to Karen Powell. She saw what was happening. Even had words with Maggie before class on Thursday. I walked right in on the middle of it. . . ."

"Shut up."

"All I ever did was honor and respect Maggie Austin. Because she had so much faith in me. And because she was a truly good person—"

Nat's blood ran hot. "I don't want to hear it." Hutch was right. Maggie was good, but she should have been smarter when it came to the likes of slick, seductive cons like Walsh. *Nat* should have been smarter, too.

Walsh's cuffed hands went to his eyes, then he slowly lowered them to his chest. "Christ, don't you think I'm hurting, too? But I'm also scared as hell. You're all determined to pin this on me. And what kind of a chance, with my record, will I have to prove I'm innocent? Less by far than last time."

His tears flowed like a faucet now. "I didn't even see her yesterday. She canceled out on me. I wish to God she hadn't. Because if we'd gone and had lunch together, damn it, she'd still be alive." He squeezed his eyes shut, clasped his hands in prayer, pressing them against his lips. "Please, dear God, don't make me go through this whole nightmare again. Please make them see I didn't do this—"

In the middle of Walsh's entreaty to his Maker, Nat's office door burst open. Jack, held at bay until now by Coscarelli's interrogation, exploded into the room.

She watched as though she was viewing a movie. An action flick. She saw Jack making a beeline for a startled Dean Thomas Walsh, literally lifting him out of his chair, propelling him against the wall, then pinning him there with one hand at his collar. Walsh's manacled feet were dangling almost a foot off the floor. Jack's free hand was curled into a tight fist and Nat knew precisely where it was headed.

A part of her wanted to stay removed—pretend this was just a film. And experience the vicarious satisfaction of seeing Walsh's face caved in.

But she was shaken by this base desire of hers and knew if she did nothing to stop the assault, she'd lose her self-respect. Ironically, it was Ethan, lecturing in Philosophy of Corrections, who told them: *You'll spend your days working with men and women you may not ever respect, but you'll never last in the system unless you can respect yourself and be comfortable inside your own skin.*

So she sprang out of her chair, vainly attempting to get between them as she issued a forceful order. "Jack. Don't you lay a hand on him!"

Whether it was her admonition, the arrival of Hutch and Lamotte, or Jack's own impulse control, his fist missed Walsh's face by inches as it slammed into the wall instead.

Released from Jack's grip, Walsh slid down the wall to the floor, gasping, sobbing, cursing all at the same time. Hutch quickly ushered out Nat's clerk and closed her office door.

Jack remained standing over a cowering Walsh. His hand was bleeding, and there was a hole in the superintendent's plaster wall the size of a baseball.

eight

"Do unto others as others do unto you." Most cons get the message right off. Those that want to test it out learn it the hard way. . . .

A. C.
Corrections Officer

"I SUPPOSE YOU'RE waiting for an apology," Jack muttered after Walsh was returned to lockup and Nat was tending to his bloody, swollen knuckles.

She cut a length of white gauze from a roll. "Hey, I can always hang a picture over it."

He watched her as she carefully, neatly wrapped the gauze around his hand. "I'm not talking about the wall."

"I don't blame you for wanting a go at Walsh. I was in line ahead of you—"

Jack withdrew his hand, the gauze unraveling. "I'm talking about me and Maggie."

She gave him a quick glance, then snatched his hand back, resolutely rewinding the bandage, taping it. "You don't owe me an apology. What you do in your private life—"

"Bullshit."

Nat did not want to be having this heart-to-heart. Her heart had taken enough of a beating. Besides, this particular topic was especially dicey. She busied herself putting the kit back in order. "Look, Maggie didn't want you to say anything to me, so you didn't." *That's it. Done. Finished. Ha!*

"I'm not a sheep, Nat. You should know that better than anyone." He formed a thin smile that Nat found herself sharing. "I went along with Maggie because she wanted to tell you in her own time."

Nat snapped the first-aid kit shut. "Was it a test, Jack?" Her tone was suddenly angry, confronting. She could see it took him aback. Nat was a bit taken aback herself. He should have let it be.

"You need to spell that out, Nat." His tone was curt, his gaze challenging. *Itching for a fight, are we? Oh yes we are.*

Even so, Nat could still pull back. If she didn't, she knew she'd regret it later. But she was already so flooded with regrets, what the hell was one more?

"A test of how much Maggie cared for you. If she told me, it would mean she cared for you as much as you—"

"It had nothing to do with me and Maggie. It was about your friendship—"

"Bullshit."

Jack gave her a mock *ya got me* salute.

Nat got up, carried the first-aid kit over to her open closet, moved a few things around on the shelf, and then placed the kit in a cleared-off spot. She made this busy work into a task requiring her full concentration.

"You're right," she heard Jack say behind her, the edge gone from his voice. "Oh yeah, Maggie made it into this thing about you and me, about how you might have . . . feelings for me, but I never really bought it. Not in any kind of serious way."

Nat's back was still to him. "I never said anything to her. . . . I never told her about that time we . . . I never said anything."

"No, I didn't think you had. Neither did I."

She nodded, forcing a weak smile as she slowly turned back to face him. "I was never really sure how much you remembered."

"I was drunk, but not—" He swallowed hard enough for Nat to see his Adam's apple work. "Not that drunk."

"Well, I had no excuse," she muttered acerbically.

"Alcohol isn't an excuse, Nat. You know that better than most. Anyway, you didn't do anything."

"Yeah, but I didn't do it *soon enough.*"

Soon enough would have meant walking out of Jack's apartment on that April night the minute she saw that he was okay. He'd had another drunken row with his now ex-wife, Sally. Like so many times before, it got physical. Nat didn't know who did what to whom as the fight developed. All she knew was this one ended with Sally shattering a beer bottle over Jack's head.

At a little past nine P.M. that night, Nat got a hysterical call from Sally. She told Nat she'd left Jack. *For good, this time.* After ranting and raving about what a bastard he was, etc. etc. she threw in, almost as an afterthought, that maybe she'd killed him.

"Killed him? What did you do, Sally?"

"Nothing. I didn't . . . Look, all I know is there's blood and he wasn't moving when I walked out." Her words were slurred and she began sobbing mightily at this point. *"Maybe you should go see if . . . if he's alive, Nat. I swear, that man is impossible to live with."*

And Nat was thinking, this was not the way for Sally to solve that problem.

Nat would have made Ethan go with her, but Ethan was teaching a night class and wasn't due home until eleven. A few weeks later, she found out that class actually met on Monday and Thursday nights. This was a Tuesday. *Maybe if she'd known the truth that night, things would have gone differently.*

Nat called first, hoping Jack would pick up and she could avoid getting herself in the middle of his mess. But he didn't pick up. And she got scared.

"I was a complete asshole that night, Nat," Jack cut into her thoughts. "You come running to my rescue and what do I do? Try to jump your bones."

"You're such a romantic, Dwyer." Nat laughed dryly. A cover for the jumble of feelings she recalled having when he'd come on to her that night. Not the least of which, she hated to admit then and now, was desire. There were a lot of things that turned Nat off about Jack, his drinking topping the list. But there was no denying her deputy's dark, provocative sexual draw, his bad boy appeal. Nat had always fixated on being so good. A counter-phobic response to the chaos and pain of her childhood. A way to preserve order. While she'd never doubted that she'd married Ethan out of love, the fact that he'd appeared so emotionally grounded, sober, stable, and supportive were all big pluses. And he was attentive, although often his attentiveness did take on a paternalistic cast. Since he'd walked out on her, Nat had begun thinking Maggie had been right. That, unconsciously, she might have been looking for a *good* father. Maybe that was why their sex life, while satisfying—at least she'd thought so—had always lacked heat. She'd lulled herself into believing passion was overrated.

Jack lightly touched her cheek, giving her a start, and sharply bringing her back to the present. "You're a smart woman, Nat. I was definitely no bargain."

"Maggie seemed to think you were." Her voice caught under the strain of her jumbled emotions.

"Yeah, right." He made a big show of inspecting his bandaged hand. "I tried to be romantic with Maggie. Flowers. Candy. I went the whole nine yards. I never really wooed a woman before. One time I even . . . damn, I even tried to write her a poem." His features darkened. "I wanted to show her I had as much talent as those *deep, sensitive* cons she was always gushing about."

"Especially Walsh?"

Jack gave Nat the kind of bleak, resolute look that made her breath catch in her throat. "If he did it, Nat, it'll take . . . I don't know what it'll take . . . to keep me from killing the bastard."

nine

Even after hope's gone, you got to find a reason to get up and face the day . . .

D. L
Female inmate #587091

IN THE MIDDLE of everything else going down at the house, the female inmate who'd gotten into the cat fight with her roommate the night before had begged one of the line officers for a few minutes with Nat. Carmen Rios's face was streaked with blotched tears that had recently dried. Nat was sure she used them full force on the young officer so he would do her bidding. In the staff training sessions Nat did an entire class on teaching her people how not to let themselves be manipulated by the threats or tears or seductive connivances of inmates, especially from pretty, young female cons who could really turn on the jets. Carmen Rios packed a lot of heat within the voluptuous curves of her petite figure. Even the black eye she was currently sporting did not detract from her kittenish sex appeal.

"How long the House gonna be in lockdown, Super?"

"You wanted to see me to talk about the lockdown?"

"It's because of that writing teacher gettin' killed, right? Word is Walsh's ass is grass."

"Whose word is that?"

Carmen frowned. "You asking me to rat?" Nat knew the game. She was supposed to think the inmate was debating whether it was safe to tell her. But Nat knew Carmen was really debating how much mileage she could get out of it.

Carmen paid acute attention to a loose thread on the cuff of her tight black sweater. "You sendin' me back, Super?"

Carmen knew the rules of the House. Nat could return her on the spot. As well as her sparring partner Gerry Flynn. She didn't even need to get any of the details as to why their fight went down. The fight itself was enough to send them both packing. There were some supers who would do it. A smart power move.

If power rang your bell.

Nat would be lying to herself if she said she wasn't into having *and* wielding power. If you didn't want the power, you didn't take the job she'd fought so hard to get. If you couldn't handle the power, you wouldn't last long. And before you quit or got booted out, you'd already have been eaten up and spit out. By the inmates, your staff, your superiors. But Nat was not on a big power trip like some of her colleagues. Power for its own sake. Power as ego. Nat always gave the *troublemaker* a chance to set things right before she took drastic measures. And she'd help in any way she could. Because, the truth was, power meant nothing to Nat if she couldn't use it to somehow make things better. Make what she was doing mean something.

Nat sighed. The woman sitting across from her was one of the inmates Nat had believed really did want to make it on the outside. "You've been doing so well, Carmen. I got a report from

Vickie Lewis at the beauty school and she says you've been a star trainee."

"Look, it was an . . . accident. Gerry and I was just joshin'. I . . . I fell."

Something had to have triggered this encounter between the two inmates. Both of them had had clean slates up to now. And then it came to Nat. She remembered what Gerry Flynn was doing time for. Manslaughter. She'd left her children—a baby girl and two boys ages four and six—alone in her apartment one night while she went out hustling for crack. By the time she'd dragged herself home two days and a lot of drugs later the cops were there, her baby was dead in her crib and the state had taken custody of her two boys.

And Nat remembered that Carmen Rios's child had also become a ward of the state when she was arrested for burglary.

"It was about your little girl, wasn't it?" Nat said.

Carmen stared at her like she had a direct line to the psychic network. The tears started rolling again but this time Nat believed they were legit. "She killed her baby. That's why she won't get her other kids back. But where does she get off telling me, who never so much as hurt a hair on my baby's head, that the state'll never give my baby Maria back to me?" She wiped her eyes with the back of her sleeve. "I just pushed Gerry, that's all. Just a little push. To get her outta my face. It was like she was gettin' off on it, you know."

"She pushed back?"

"Pushed? Man, she went nutso. Jumped all over me, hissing how no one no how's ever gonna lay a hand on her ever again. Next thing I know, I'm flyin' across the room and. . . . She shouldn't a said what she said, but I shouldn't a pushed her, I know. Super, I don't wanna go down for this. But I don't want Gerry to either. . . . Hell, she cries herself to sleep every night over that baby of hers. Besides, if she goes down, my life's gonna be hell at the House . . . everyone blaming me . . . so I might as well go back . . . only then I never will get my baby. . . ." She winced in honest anguish. "Are you sending me back?"

"You both got write-ups, Carmen. That means there has to be a disciplinary hearing."

Carmen didn't say anything for a few moments, but Nat could see the inmate's wheels spinning.

"Remember how you asked me before who's talking? You know . . . about how Walsh is the one?" she asked.

"I remember," Nat answered without inflection.

"I was thinking, you know . . . like we could make a deal."

"I don't make deals, Carmen. Or take bribes."

"Hey man . . . I mean Super . . . it ain't a bribe," Carmen said defensively. Anxiously.

"I must have misunderstood." Nat shifted her gaze off the inmate and slowly, resolutely closed her folder. "If there is something on your mind that you feel I ought to know about, Carmen—" She deliberately let the rest of the sentence hang.

Carmen's shoulders sagged. She'd been in the game long enough to know when she'd been defeated. "It's just that ya gotta be especially careful inside not to go ratting on staff, because, man, they can make your life real miserable, know what I mean? And she's in tight with a few of the hard-ass screws on my floor, pardon my French."

It wasn't her use of *hard-ass* that she was apologizing for so much as *screws*. One of the house rules was that the officers were never to be called or referred to by that pejorative piece of slang. Even the term *guard* was now considered disparaging.

"What's said in here stays in here, Carmen." Her voice had taken on an edge of impatience. It was almost nine. Right before her meeting with Carmen, Deputy Commissioner Carlyle had called in from his car phone complaining that he was stuck in a traffic tie-up just outside of Providence. He said he was unlikely to get to the house before ten. Nat wanted a little breathing time before what she knew would be a trying encounter.

"Sharon Johnson."

Nat gave Carmen a befuddled look.

"That's who's been talking, okay? Your ex-con employment counselor."

"You can do better than that, Carmen. Ms. Johnson hasn't been at the House since yesterday afternoon. She couldn't very well have been talking about a murder that wasn't discovered until late last night."

"I ain't saying she talked about the murder specifically. Just that several of us overheard her talking to P.O. Glazer the other day about how there was people who better watch their backs if they know what's good for them, because Walsh was out for blood. And then this morning, just before lockdown some of the cons were going around saying—see Johnson's right. Walsh was out for blood and he got him some."

ten

Not sure which part's worse ... the coming in or the leaving. Coming in has its humiliations, but going out's got its heartbreak. ...

D. V.
Inmate Visitor

"THANK YOU FOR seeing me, Superintendent. I was half out of my mind when I heard on the radio that Dean ... First let me say I'm so sorry about Maggie Austin. I wanted to offer my condolences, Superintendent Price. I never met her personally, but I feel as if I knew her, my brother would talk about her so much. I still remember that time I came to visit my brother at Norton right after he attended that first writing class. You wouldn't have known it was the same person. There was this light in his eyes and he was literally bubbling over with excitement.

"Every time before, he would be so down, so full of bitterness. For the first couple of years, all he'd ever talk about was his case. How he was going to get justice. How he was going to get his sentence overturned. And when he finally came to see that wasn't going to happen, he just got so hard and cocky, like he wasn't going to let anything or anyone faze him. But I knew it was an act.

"What he really felt was depressed, hopeless. Like the whole world was against him. And there were things going down at Norton that I knew had Dean scared and upset. He dropped hints that there were some inmates who had it in for him. But after he started taking Maggie Austin's writing class, his whole attitude changed. It was like he believed he could cope with his situation because he'd finally found a direction. A purpose. What I'm trying to say, Superintendent Price—"

Christine Walsh finally had to stop to catch her breath.

"I know what you're trying to say, Ms. Walsh. What I don't know is what I can say to you."

Christine's bottom lip trembled. But Nat could see how much effort she was exerting to keep her emotions in check. Still, her eyes—the same vivid blue as her brother's—were bloodshot and puffy.

Neither Jack nor Hutch were happy that Nat had granted Dean's younger sister a brief visit with her brother when she'd shown up that morning. Even though the visit had taken place in a high-security room at the House with Walsh under heavy guard. As soon as her much abbreviated visit ended, Christine had put in an urgent request with Lamotte to see Nat.

Carlyle still hadn't shown up so Nat had time to see her, if not much strength left for the encounter. Besides, she didn't have the heart to turn down Christine Walsh's request. Meeting with family members was something she did all the time, especially since she'd started at the House. She tried to give them emotional support and guidance, or act as a referee during conflicts they were having with inmates. And there were conflicts aplenty.

So many inmates became estranged from their loved ones during their incarceration. Then there were the inmates who deliberately cut off ties with the world. For some, it was shame at having a loved one see them in such a demeaned state, or they found it too hard to do their time with constant reminders of what they were missing on the street. Sometimes family members were too angry, too despondent or too distraught to stay in contact, as was apparently the case with Dean Thomas Walsh's parents. As had been the case with Nat's own sister and mother when her dad was in prison the first time. As had been the case for her as well the second time her father did time.

Even when families and inmates tried to connect, many of the visitors as well as some inmates found the rules and regulations attached to visits too frustrating and degrading.

Nat would never forget during one of her early visits to her father, the wife of one inmate was denied visitation because she wasn't wearing a bra. Never mind that she was as flat as a pancake. Never mind that she'd spent almost two hours on the bus and then walked over a mile just to get to the prison. The poor woman was reduced to tears. Nat felt so bad for her, she offered to lend the woman her bra and skip her visit with her dad that day. But the woman said no, her husband would be able to tell she'd been crying and get all upset. Just like he had a few weeks back when she was subjected to a strip search for possible drugs or other contraband before being allowed into the visiting room. Strip searches were random for both visitors before entering the visiting area and inmates after visits ended. Nat was one of the lucky ones who'd never been subjected to that horror. If she had, she never would have had the courage to go back.

Nat didn't know whether Christine Walsh had ever been refused admittance at CCI Norton because of some dress code infraction. Whether she had ever been subjected to the gross indignity of a strip search. What Nat did know was that Dean's sister had faithfully and consistently visited her brother throughout the nearly eight long years of his incarceration. Now she was facing the possibility of having to visit him behind the wall for the rest of his life.

Whatever Nat might think of Dean Thomas Walsh, she felt nothing but pity, admiration, and sympathy for his sister.

Christine, twenty-five, thin, dark-haired and not nearly as attractive as Dean, was dressed in a pale yellow blouse and a rather matronly floral print skirt. She pulled a tissue out of a smudged white leatherette pocketbook and dabbed at the line of sweat beading the top of her lip. It was another Indian summer day, with the morning temperature already in the seventies. Nat would have turned on the air conditioner but it was on the fritz. Had been for most of the summer.

"If you'd just let me tell you a little about Dean." Still clutching a crumpled tissue, she kneaded her hands together. "There are things you don't know. Things that will help you understand him—"

"Ms. Walsh—"

"Christine. Please. My mother's Ms. Walsh."

"All right. Christine. What I need to make clear is that I'm not a police officer. I'm not the one investigating the murder of Maggie Austin." *Thank God for that. How would I ever be able to maintain even a semblance of objectivity?*

This did not deter Christine from her mission. "My mother was always so hard on Dean. So demanding. He could never measure up. And, believe me, he tried. He tried so hard. But she always found fault."

"Wasn't she hard on you as well?" Nat asked. Wanting to disabuse her of the all too popular *abuse excuse* rationale. Not every child who was treated badly ended up a criminal. She was living proof. So far, at least.

"My mother wasn't the same with me. I was a girl. I didn't really matter." Christine smiled ruefully. "Being ignored is probably what saved me. Dean always used to say I could get away with murder." She gasped, her hand going to her mouth. "I'm so sorry. I didn't mean to sound so . . . so flip."

Nat nodded, wondering if Walsh was jealous of his sister. Angry at having been the one to bear the brunt of his mother's unmet expectations. An anger that had simmered for years. And what about their father? Christine hadn't even mentioned him. In Walsh's case report, the father was described as an alcoholic and physically abusive. The Walsh family picture was ringing some all too familiar and disquieting bells for Nat. There was a kinship of experiences between herself and Walsh she couldn't get around. What she had to do was make sure that kinship didn't cloud her judgment about the inmate.

"Were you and Dean close as children?"

"I adored Dean. He's my big brother. And he always . . . looked out for me." *Another bond, Nat the big sister always looking out for Rachel.*

Christine's eyes skidded off Nat's face.

Nat regarded her closely. "You mean he protected you from your father?"

Christine's pale cheeks colored. Lips tightly compressed, she quietly stared down at her hands. Nat noticed the tiny diamond ring on her left hand. An engagement ring.

Nat's gaze shifted to the thin gold band she still wore on her own wedding ring finger. There never had been an engagement ring there. When Ethan proposed to her, he half-heartedly offered to buy her one, but he believed they had better use for the money. Ethan was so practical. At least, with her. Was it different with his teeny-bopper girlfriend? Did Ethan woo Jill with flowers, candy, jewels, *go the whole nine yards,* like Jack had done with Maggie?

Nat twisted her wedding band around on her finger, telling herself the only reason she was still wearing it was that she didn't want everyone at the House to know what was going on in her personal life. But in her more honest moments, she knew that what she really didn't want was for them to see her as a woman who couldn't hold on to her husband.

"I'm sorry," Nat heard Christine mumble.

She gave her an edgy look. What was Christine apologizing for? Did she catch her staring at her wedding band? Had Maggie told Dean about her break-up with Ethan? Had Dean told his sister?

But Christine was apparently too absorbed in her own troubles to concern herself with Nat's. "It's hard to talk about my father," she said gravely. "We never do."

"You and Dean?"

"Well, him, too. But I meant me and my mother. He's basically a non-person in our house."

"He never visited your brother in prison."

"No, he wouldn't, would he? The last time my Dad saw Dean was at his trial. Right after the jury brought in the . . . guilty verdict." Whatever color had suffused Christine's face earlier evaporated. "My father sat in the back row and . . . applauded when the verdict was read. Of course, he wasn't exactly sober."

Nat stared at Christine, aghast. Nat knew how ugly alcohol could make a person, but she couldn't imagine that level of cold cruelty, drunk or sober.

"As they were taking my brother away, Dad shouted out to Dean that he was the scum of the earth." Christine laughed a hard little laugh, but Nat could see the young woman was close to tears.

"Because he believed your brother was guilty of rape?"

"As if he's one to talk," Christine muttered. And then, realizing she'd spoken those revealing words out-loud, turned ashen-faced.

Instantly, Nat was able to more clearly understand Christine's steadfast devotion to her brother. Dean must have either intervened or prevented their father from sexually abusing his little sister.

Despite Christine's pallor, she regained her poise. "My brother may keep certain things from me, but what he tells me is the God's honest truth. And he tells me that he didn't do this terrible thing to his teacher." Nat wondered if he'd told his sister eight years ago that he didn't assault and rape Alison Cole.

Christine moved to the edge of the chair and leaned forward. "If I'm the only one who believes in Dean, he doesn't stand a chance in hell. Please, Superintendent Price, all I ask is for you to keep an open mind. Dean is so sure you're already convinced he's guilty—"

"He's wrong, Christine." *But not by a lot.*

Her whole face brightened, and Nat realized Dean's sister was reading way too much into her words. Before she could figure out some way to temper what she'd said without demolishing the poor woman's hopes, Christine was on her feet, hands clutched to her chest, that tiny diamond sparkling in the sunlight. "Then you'll help him? You'll—"

Nat's door burst open again. This time it was Hutch. He was so pale and breathing so hard Nat feared he might be having a heart attack.

"Walsh just tried to suicide."

Christine let out a scream and went whiter than Nat's officer.

Nat sprang out of her chair, probably paler than either of them. "How bad?"

Hutch made a line with his index finger across his wrist. "Gashes don't look to be too deep, but he's bleeding pretty heavy. We got him wrapped up best we can. Jack's gonna drive him over to Mercy."

"Oh no he's not," Nat said, worried that Jack might very well decide to take a route to the hospital via China and let Walsh bleed to death on the way. "I'll take him." In the back of her mind, she was ashamed to admit she was thinking this was a lucky break. Now Jack would be left to cope with the Deputy Commissioner. "Can I use your car, Hutch?"

"I'll drive," Hutch said. "You want two or three officers for security coverage? We can shackle his ankles but keep in mind we can't cuff his wrists in his condition."

"Two should do it." Nat was halfway across the room.

"Please," Christine said weakly, grabbing onto Nat's arm as she passed her—almost forgetting she was there, "let me go with you."

Nat was shaken out of her preoccupation with this latest emergency and paused long enough to place a hand sympathetically on the trembling girl's shoulder. "Sorry. I can't do that, Christine. Go home. I'll phone you as soon as I can with a status report. I promise."

eleven

They put me in isolation and took away all my valuables—books, TV, radio. If crap were worth anything they'd have sewn up my asshole!

G.J.
Inmate #593208

IT WAS JUST the prisoner and Nat, curtained off in a narrow cubicle in the emergency room at Mercy. Hutch and a couple of armed correction officers were waiting just on the other side of the curtain. Walsh, looking haggard, both wrists stitched and bandaged, was stretched out on a narrow hospital bed. He was attached to an IV dripping type B blood.

"You think because I wanted to check out I must be guilty. Isn't that what you're thinking?"

Nat was sitting on one of those uncomfortable gray plastic chairs molded to fit some body other than hers. "Why did you want to kill yourself?"

"No way I'm going back inside," he said fiercely. "I'd rather be dead."

He turned his face away from her. She saw his chest heave. "Maybe you worked inside, maybe you've heard stories, even saw some stuff, but believe me, you've got no idea what it's really like. You spend half your time being bored to death, the other half living in terror. I'll tell you something, I never thought I'd live to see my release date. Until I got to Horizon House and felt my first real glimmer of hope that I was actually going to survive. Hell, maybe even have a life." A sharp, raw laugh escaped his throat. "Should've known better. Serves me right for being dumb enough . . . Forget it. You don't give a crap. You've got me pegged a rapist and a killer. You're probably wishing Massachusetts still had the death penalty."

"You're the one who's already got yourself charged, tried and convicted."

He turned back to her, his blue eyes burning into her. "Don't you? Or else why are you having me shipped back to the joint?"

"It's a temporary transfer to the sick bay at Norton."

"Yeah, right," Walsh muttered acerbically.

Nat was not one hundred percent comfortable with her decision to move Walsh back to CCI Norton because, like his accusation, it assumed guilt. But she knew if she didn't do it voluntarily, orders would come down from the Commissioner's office demanding tighter security than they were obviously able to provide at the House, considering Walsh somehow managed to get his hands on a makeshift shank and do a number on his wrists.

A young nurse slipped through the curtain. She was a petite Asian woman with a pixie haircut and lightly glossed lips which were now curved in a strained smile. Nat got up and moved over toward the curtain as she approached the bed. "Doctor's ordered something for your pain, Mr. Walsh. It'll make your travel more comfortable."

Walsh gave a forced laugh. "Yeah, I'll be comfy-cozy."

The nurse nervously asked Walsh to roll over as she readied the hypodermic needle. Walsh cast Nat a wan look. A look that begged for a smidgen of privacy. And dignity.

Nat was not about to leave Walsh unattended, so she parted the curtain and motioned for Hutch to take her place.

Hutch hadn't taken two steps toward her before she heard a high pitched cry. Thinking first it was Dean reacting to the injection, Nat was a little slow to react. Not Hutch. He burst through the curtains in a shot, instantly followed by the two armed officers, their guns cocked.

It looked at first as if the petite nurse had slipped and fallen on top of Walsh. But in the split second that Nat's back was stupidly turned, Walsh had grabbed the nurse and pulled her on top of him, effectively providing himself with the perfect shield. He had an arm clasped so tightly around the nurse's neck that her lovely dark brown eyes were starting to bulge. At least enough air was getting through her windpipe to keep her squirming as she desperately tried to get free. She stopped cold—they all did—when she felt the prick of the hypodermic needle at her temple.

"Don't be stupid," Hutch warned Walsh.

"Tell your boys to take their best shot," Walsh challenged.

But they all knew that the person most likely to get shot in this chilling standoff was the terror-stricken nurse.

Nat heard the mounting commotion out in the hospital corridor—nurses, doctors, ambulatory patients who'd seen the armed guards rush into the curtained area. A young doc pulled the curtain partly open, his jaw dropping when he saw the full extent of the situation.

"Should I call . . . for help?" he asked nervously.

"We got the situation covered," Hutch said. "Go clear the area."

"You're only making things worse for yourself, Dean," Nat said, amazed at the calmness of her voice. A sharp contrast to the rest of her.

"You're wrong, *Nat*. It can't get any worse." Walsh looked past her to the guards. "Drop your guns and kick them over towards the bed." He loosened his grip around the nurse's neck just enough to allow a squawk of desperation to slip past her trembling lips.

"You're a dead man, you little prick," Hutch snarled, rage and loathing and helplessness etched in each word.

"The only question is, do you want a dead nurse as well?" Walsh was addressing them all. But his eyes were fixed on Nat. "I told you I wasn't going back, Nat. Two choices. Get your boys to drop their guns or take us both down." He pressed his lips to the nurse's hair. "No one believes me, but I've been paying all this time for someone else's vicious crime. Eight nightmare years in what should have been somebody else's hell. Well, it's not going to happen again. I'm done paying for what isn't my doing."

"If you're innocent, Dean, then this is the wrong way to go about proving it," Nat said, sounding like a B movie warden. "I'm willing to help you if—"

Walsh laughed sardonically. "You want to help? Then tell your flunkies to drop their guns. Otherwise, this pretty little nurse here is not going to be ministering to the sick anymore."

Nat saw the desperation in his eyes and had to take him at his word. Even if he were innocent of Alison's rape and Maggie's murder, he might well feel driven to commit an act of violence in his panic. Nat felt the breath-robbing impact of holding this young woman's life in her hands.

"Put down the guns." Her voice might be hoarse but it rang with authority. She was not about to risk more senseless killings.

Nat found herself holding her breath until she heard the weapons clank on the floor.

Walsh's arm tightened around the nurse's neck. Then he gave Nat a nod. "Pick them up, Nat. By their barrels. Nice and slow. That's a girl. You boys, on your fat bellies. Hands behind your heads. And just so you know, I see a single cop come through that curtain, and I'm going to have to do this sweet, little nurse, like it or not. Now, hit the deck." Hutch and the guards had little choice but to obey.

The young nurse was no longer squirming. She was frozen with terror. A rivulet of urine streamed down her white stockinged leg, but her face showed no shame or humiliation. Fear absorbed her totally.

"Okay, Nat. Bring the guns over here to me."

"I can't do that, Dean."

"You willing to watch this lovely young woman die before your eyes. I know how to finish her off with this hypo. You want me to prove it to you?"

"How can you protest your innocence and threaten to kill an innocent bystander at the same time?"

"Desperation, Nat. Don't test me. Just bring over the guns. And make it snappy," he added as they all picked up the faint sound of sirens. The doctor had not only cleared the area, but called the police. Within minutes they'd have the hospital surrounded.

Nat picked up the guns, trying to imagine some way to get the drop on Walsh before he could act out his threat. But the point of the needle was right up against the nurse's temple. Drawing closer, Nat saw her name tag for the first time. Carrie Li. She wanted to tell Carrie it would be all right. But the nurse looked too intelligent to be fooled.

"Put the guns right here on the bed," he ordered, his arm continuing to tightly circle the nurse's neck. His eyes were glued to Nat. "I can break her neck as easy as stab her." Carrie's dark eyes silently begged Nat to do what he asked.

Nat dropped the two weapons on the bed. Walsh quickly exchanged the hypodermic needle for one of the weapons, resting the other one close to his side. The gun increased the nurse's terror tenfold.

"Dean . . ."

"Get my clothes," he cut her off.

His clothing was in a plastic bag on the table by the bed. Nat started to toss the bag over to him, flashing on the possibility of throwing it in his face and then making a mad dive for him. Or she could toss it past him, out of his reach, forcing him to shift his gaze, get distracted . . .

"Open the bag and get the stuff out. You're gonna help me get dressed."

He shifted Carrie off his chest. With the gun at her head and the men on the ground, he didn't need her body to shield him. He used his feet to kick off the covers.

He was naked under the hospital gown which had ridden up over his hips. Nat was startled and appalled to see that he'd gotten an erection. She almost lost it right there on the spot.

"Don't tell me you've never seen a hard-on before, Nat. Or maybe it's been a while. What with your husband splitting on you for some hot little coed." *Thanks, Maggie.*

Gritting her teeth, she shoved the jeans on him. He smiled slyly when she reached for the zipper.

"Uh-uh. I can read your nasty little mind, Nat." He nudged Carrie with the barrel of the gun which he now pressed against her breast bone. "You zip me up, Nurse. Very, very carefully. You don't want my hand to accidentally jerk."

She was nodding vigorously, no doubt grateful for even a momentary reprieve from the viselike grip around her red, raw neck.

"Wait," he barked. "First pull out this IV."

She hesitated.

"Now."

She did as ordered.

"Thanks," Walsh said almost kindly. "Now, zipper me up."

She did so with extreme care.

"My shirt, Nat." But Nat was only half listening. Her eyes were riveted on the hypodermic needle that fell off the bed when Walsh flung back the cover.

"Do it," he barked.

While his order really did startle her, she played it for all it was worth, using it as an opportunity to *accidentally* let the shirt slip from her hands to the floor. She quickly bent down, scooping up the hypo with the shirt. Then, using the shirt to conceal her find, she quickly slipped the hypo into the pocket of her black linen jacket.

As she helped Walsh on with his shirt, Nat said, "Take me instead, Dean."

"No . . ." Hutch shouted from the floor.

"Shut up, Hutchins," Walsh snapped. "That's the first smart thing you've said, Nat. Okay, get the car keys from Hutch's pocket and we're out of here. Move it."

She nodded, her heart hammering, like it was suddenly too big for her chest cavity.

"Don't be a hero, Nat," Hutch whispered anxiously as she knelt down to retrieve the keys from his pants pocket. She gave his arm a reassuring squeeze. Like anything could be reassuring in this situation.

The truth was, Nat was not being brave in offering herself as hostage in exchange for Carrie Li. Or selfless. Nor was she foolish enough to think she was somehow going to be able to talk Dean Thomas Walsh down.

Then what? She supposed it all boiled down to having so long played the role of protector—always feeling the pressure and responsibility of keeping those she loved from toppling over into ever-materializing emotional precipices. Not that she was so strong. Merely that everyone else around her was so much weaker.

The same held true now. Besides, Dean Thomas Walsh was Nat's responsibility. No one ever said working with dangerous felons was easy. Or safe.

twelve

. . . so then they order me to strip down and there I am butt-naked facing four screws and damn if one of 'em ain't a woman and they're making me turn around, bend over and "spread your cheeks, asshole." That really gets them chuckling. . . . And that's just the beginning. . . .

K. R.
Inmate #877659

"I KNOW YOU'RE thinking I'm never going to make it. Maybe you're right. But one thing I'm right about and it's that I'm not going back to the joint. They want me, they're gonna have to kill me. If they miss, I'll do it myself." Walsh momentarily shifted the gun off of her and tapped the barrel to his temple.

"Turn left at the corner," he ordered, Hutch's gun once more aimed at her. The other gun was tucked into his waistband. And luck had been on Walsh's side when they'd exited the building, the cruisers still a good block away, hospital staff carefully keeping their distance as Walsh, a gun trained on Nat's head, forcibly led her to the car. He had her drive out a rear exit, making her zigzag up and down narrow side streets, keeping a constant lookout for any sign of cruisers. So far, he hadn't spotted any. There had to be an all-points bulletin out on Walsh, every cop in the city on the lookout for him. They knew the car, the license plate. But if the cops picked up their trail, what next? A wild chase? A showdown? If it came to that, Nat believed Walsh would do as he promised—kill her and then himself. She found herself praying they'd make a clean getaway.

But then what?

Walsh flicked on the air conditioning, angling his vent toward his face. He was sweating profusely. So was she. It must have climbed to eighty degrees by now, but Nat was sweating more out of fear than heat. She guessed the same was true for Walsh.

"If you are innocent, Dean, how do you know the police won't find the real killer?" She slowed the speed down to thirty-five, trying to work up the courage to jump from the car. But she was afraid that Walsh would be able to get a shot off before she even managed to get the door open. She remembered the hypodermic needle in her pocket—a weapon of sorts—and told herself to be patient. That an opportunity to escape would present itself.

"Because they're sure they've already got him. That's why. Just like they were so damn sure the last time."

"Do you have any idea who—?"

"Skip the small talk, Nat. Next you'll be telling me you believe me. Funny what people will believe with a gun pointed at them."

"Dean, Maggie Austin was my best friend. I loved her. I want the person who killed her to pay. If it's you, I hope you burn in hell. If it's not you, I'm going to make you a promise that I won't rest until the true killer's found. I'll hunt him down myself—"

"You think I'm an idiot, Nat? Is that what you think?"

"No. Just the opposite, Dean. Otherwise I wouldn't waste my breath—"

"Turn right here. And shut up. Just . . . shut up."

Walsh made her drive Hutch's almost new red Ford Taurus sedan into a deserted alley a few blocks from the hospital. He ordered her to park it between an old van and a newer pick-up truck. Nat was not great at parallel parking under the best of circumstances. Circumstances at the moment couldn't have been much worse. Her maneuvers were so jerky, she accidentally rammed the Taurus's back fender into the van's bumper. She felt a flash of regret knowing how much pride Hutch took in his car.

"Now what?" She was careful to keep the panic out of her voice. Panic was contagious. And Walsh's gun was kissing her rib cage. She slipped her right hand surreptitiously into her jacket pocket, taking some small comfort as her fingers circled the hypodermic needle. A part of her wanted to whisk it out, stab him and make a run for it. But she'd be lucky to get one good chance. She couldn't afford to be rash. She had to time her attack carefully.

Walsh reached over to the key in the ignition and killed the engine. After a careful survey of the alley, he barked, "Get out."

As terrified as she felt inside the car with Walsh, Nat was even more afraid to step out into this desolate alleyway. Would he shoot her down in cold blood, leave her dead or dying on the filthy pavement, then speed away? She searched his face, saw only desperation there. Making two of them. But he was the one with the gun.

He pulled the key out of the ignition. "Let's go." He leaned across her, throwing open the passenger door and shoved her out, following after her.

"What are you going to do?" Nat couldn't even attempt the pretense of sounding calm, afraid that she already knew what he had planned. The sound of a gun going off might be too risky.

Someone could be in the vicinity, even though no one was in sight. There were quieter ways to do away with her.

Walsh's blue eyes were over-bright. "It wasn't supposed to turn out this way. I've always had such rotten luck. How could I have been dumb enough to think it could ever turn around?" His words held a ringing despair. Was it remorse? Or simply grief?

With his hand gripping the gun, he nudged her toward the back of the car and opened the trunk. "Climb in."

Nat stepped back in alarm. "No."

"Don't worry. You won't be in there too long."

Did he think suffocation didn't require much time? Even with the trunk being like an oven in that heat, it would take several hours. Excruciating, horrifying hours. Of all ways to die, Nat couldn't imagine a worse one. At least a gun, a knife, even strangulation would be quick. She'd be out of her misery—

"I'll send someone to let you out. I just need a little time. Get a little distance—"

Nat didn't buy that for an instant. She tried to reason with him. "How far will you get? If you turn yourself in now—"

"Shut up, Nat. Or I really will let you die in there. Now, go ahead." His hand jerked out and grabbed her left wrist.

Nat's right hand tightened around the hypo. Time to strike was fast slipping away. "Please," she pleaded, her voice catching, her eyes starting to well up. But some part of her didn't want to give him the satisfaction of seeing her reduced to tears. "I really have this thing about tight spaces." Definitely not a lie.

"That's something we have in common, Nat."

She was struck by the tinge of sympathy in Walsh's smile. For a second or two she even thought maybe he'd relent.

"Don't make me hurt you, Nat. Believe me, I will if I have to. Climb in." Walsh's hand intensified its grip on her wrist, his hold so tight it was cutting off the circulation to her fingers.

The tears fell freely now. All pride was gone. Only abject terror remained. She was reduced to praying her tears would move him. "I . . . can't."

"That's not true," he said ruefully. "It's amazing what we can do if we have to."

Oddly, it was that very sentiment that gave her the courage to act.

Even though Walsh viciously yanked her arm, she was so absorbed in planning her attack she didn't feel the pain.

She thought of Maggie as her right hand flew out of her pocket and she aimed the thin steel needle right for Dean Thomas Walsh's neck. And in that instant of contact, she was stunned and horrified by the ferocity of her assault. Walsh was right. You could do anything if you had to.

He cried out, blinking wildly. Jumping back before she could push the plunger and release the sedative. At least he let go of her, both of his hands springing to her makeshift weapon and quickly yanking it out.

In her mind she was flying like the wind. But, in reality, even with the surge of adrenaline shooting through her veins, she was so shaken and sick to her stomach that her legs felt like lead as she struggled to make them run down the alley.

With each step she waited for Walsh to fire. Waited for the explosion. For the searing pain as a bullet pierced her skin, shattering bone. . . .

She barely made it past the van when he was on her. Slamming her to the ground. She knew the impact should have hurt, but she was numb with fear. And despair.

Dragging her to her feet, Walsh twisted her arm behind her back and, pressing her hard against him, literally lifted her off the ground. The sensation of pain finally penetrated her brain, but it wasn't the pain that made her cry out. It was the sight of a man crossing the street at the end of the alley. Her one chance for salvation.

Nat's cry was brutally cut off by Walsh's mouth clamping down on hers in what bore not the slightest resemblance to a kiss. She was despairingly sure, if the man's attention was drawn their way, he'd no doubt write them off as a pair of hot lovers.

Walsh was perversely gallant as he lifted her into the trunk. "I promise, Nat. Someone will let you out soon."

She didn't believe him for an instant. He was going to let her suffocate and die a slow death in this makeshift tomb. She tried to anesthetize herself against her escalating terror. Until the lid of the trunk closed down on her, snapping resolutely shut and she was engulfed in darkness and airlessness, breathing in the sharp smell of gasoline fumes. All hope vanished and she was consumed with gut-wrenching panic. She was going to die. Long buried memories began surging—

Her mommy was shaking her awake. It was so dark she couldn't make her out at first. She stuck her thumb in her mouth and tried to roll over onto her belly so she could go back to sleep. Her mommy's strong hand impatiently gripped her shoulder.

"None of that. We've got work to do, young lady."

Nat wanted to tell her she was not a young lady, she was just a little girl. But she knew mommy was in one of her moods and there was going to be no talking to her.

"What kind of work?" she asked groggily.

She pulled Nat to her feet. The wooden bedroom floor was cold. Her thin frame was one big shiver.

"They're all over the place. We've got to act fast."

Nat tried to remember which they she was talking about. A few weeks back it had been bats. She was sure they were com- ing into the house through the electrical outlets. Nat had to help her cement every one of them over while her daddy was at work and her baby sister was napping. Nat felt safe for a few days. But she was sad because she couldn't watch Sesame Street. No TV since the outlet was plugged up.

Daddy waited nearly a week until he decided Mommy's fears had passed and then called in the electrician.

Spiders. Yes, that's what it was now. For the last few days she'd been cleaning and cleaning and cleaning, making sure there were no webs.

Nat was afraid of spiders, too. But she was more afraid of her mommy when she was like this.

She dragged Nat downstairs to the hall closet.

"Everything must come out of there, Natalie. I know that's where they're breeding." She spoke not with sharpness but with urgency.

At first her mommy helped her, but as the closet emptied Mommy began to whimper. "I can hear them. I can hear all the babies growing."

She ran off to the kitchen and came back with a scrub brush and a bucket of some awful smelling yellow liquid.

"You've got to go in there and scrub every inch. Don't miss a single spot, Natalie."

She was scared to go in the closet all alone. So scared she wet her panties. "Please . . . please, Mommy . . ." But Mommy wouldn't listen. She just shoved her in there.

"I'm just going to shut the door while you're scrubbing so those little demons don't sneak out. . . ."

"No, Mommy. No . . . please . . . no . . ."

". . . No, please . . ."

"Ms. Price? Natalie? It's okay."

The light was blinding. She threw her arm across her eyes. Coiled her huddled, cramped body up in a tighter fetal position.

"Let me help you."

She felt a hand on her arm. She immediately thought of her

mother, afraid what she was going to have her do now. But this hand was gentle. And the voice, a man's voice, was soothing. And familiar.

Nat slowly lowered her arm from her eyes and squinted in the brightness up at his face. "Coscarelli?" She came careening back to the present. Instantly, she felt tears of relief stream down her cheeks. He didn't look like a boy detective now. He looked like a glorious knight in shining armor.

"Are you hurt?" he asked anxiously.

She didn't know. She didn't care. She just wanted out of that suffocating, gasoline-smelling, nightmare-inducing trunk.

Coscarelli was stronger than he looked. Not a hint of strain showed on his face as he lifted all one hundred and twenty sweaty pounds of her out of the trunk. For a couple of crazy seconds she just wanted him to keep on holding her. She wanted to curl up in his surprisingly muscular arms, nuzzle her head into the inviting curve of his shoulder. . . .

Her aching muscles quivered as they stretched out and she stood on wobbly legs.

Coscarelli continued to keep his arm around her for support. They were still the same height but somehow he seemed taller.

"Have you . . . caught him?" she asked.

"We will," he said firmly. And she saw by the rigid set of his jaw that he meant it.

She believed him.

He was giving her a thorough survey, checking to make sure she was still all in one piece.

"Did he . . . ?"

Before Coscarelli could finish, she vigorously shook her head. "He didn't touch me." At least not in the way she knew the detective meant.

"How did you know where to find me?" she asked, slowly regaining her balance and her composure. Enough so that she only felt mildly disappointed when Coscarelli let go of her.

"We got an anonymous call a few minutes ago about where we could find the Taurus."

A quick check of her watch told her she had only been in the trunk for a little over an hour. So Walsh was telling the truth when he said he would send someone to let her out. He hadn't left her there to die. What did that mean?

Nat's brain was still too overheated to sort it out.

"Anonymous? It had to be Walsh. Who else knew—?"

"It was a female voice," he said.

"It could have been Christine."

"Walsh's sister?"

"He must have gotten in touch with her and she pried the information out of him." Made more sense to her than that he truly felt any compunction to voluntarily keep his word.

"I've got my partner and a couple of uniforms sitting tight over at the mother's house in Natick. Mother and sister both claim they haven't heard a word from Walsh."

She was too exhausted and relieved to care how it was she'd been saved. "Well, whoever called, I'm damn glad she did."

Coscarelli appeared visibly agitated. "We weren't sure we'd find you as well as the Taurus. Or, if we did . . ." He let the rest of the sentence fall away.

Nat realized now that when Coscarelli was prying open the trunk it must have crossed his mind that if he did find her in there she'd probably be in much the same condition as he'd found Maggie.

And that if he had, he would have been very upset.

Nat was thinking there might be plusses to this detective being a neophyte. He hadn't become so jaded by too many years on the job as to take violent death in his stride. She was gratified that, like her, Leo Coscarelli was emotionally invested in bringing Maggie's murderer to justice.

She called Horizon House from Coscarelli's car phone. Hutch got on. When he heard her voice he sounded choked up with relief.

She assured him she was okay. He assured her he was holding down the fort.

"Did Carlyle show?" she asked.

"Don't worry about him now. You go home and take it easy, Nat. Oh, and give Jack a buzz on his mobile."

"Where is he?"

"Out looking for you."

And for Walsh, she thought. *God help that con if Jack's the one who catches up with him.*

thirteen

Sometimes, life on the outside's harder than life on the inside. . . .

L. G.

Inmate #224387

WALKING INTO HER empty apartment was the hardest time for Nat. The time she felt most profoundly alone. The time when her rage over Ethan leaving her reverted to despair. With all that had happened, she felt it descending one-hundred-fold as soon as she turned the key in the lock.

But her despair gave way to heart-pounding apprehension the instant she opened the door. Someone was inside. Not that she heard anyone moving about. It was not something she could really explain, but the silence was different. With Ethan gone, she'd become acutely aware of what a truly empty apartment sounded like.

She wished now she'd taken Coscarelli up on his offer to see her to her door. Or given Jack the okay to come over when she spoke to him on the phone, letting him know she truly was okay.

She held her keys in one hand, her other hand was on the door knob, the door itself open only a few inches. A chill rode down her spine while she stood still debating what to do. In her right mind she'd realize it shouldn't be up for debate. She would turn on her heels, get the hell out of there, call Coscarelli—

"Nat? Is that you?" a voice called from inside the living room.

Her sense of relief was rapidly followed by indignation. So much for her ruminations about what she'd do if Ethan ever showed up on her doorstep. She didn't have to agonize over that one now. The prodigal husband had blithely let himself in, uninvited.

Ironically, she was the one at her doorstep trying to decide whether or not she wanted to enter. What was wrong with this picture?

Ethan stepped out of the living room into her long, narrow entryway. "I'm so glad you're safe, Nat." The picture was getting more skewed by the second.

It was totally weird seeing Ethan in her apartment, dressed as usual in traditional weekend hunk garb—a pair of worn hip-riding jeans, a form-fitting black tee-shirt and his favorite snake-skin cowboy boots—Nat had a matching pair. They'd bought them a few years back on a vacation in Santa Fe. Nat could pick up the familiar scent of the lemony Yves Saint Laurent after-shave he'd worn ever since she'd bought him a bottle of the stuff their first Christmas together. His wavy salt and pepper hair showed signs of a recent haircut. He never liked it riding the collar of his shirt.

Nat concluded her inventory. Everything about the outer package was just so. As it always was. Ethan still reminded her of Sean Connery in his prime 007 days. Yet, he looked awful.

A flood of possibilities raced through her mind. Everything from a fatal disease to an improbable attack of conscience, or an even more unlikely change of heart. *Oh Nat, what a jerk I was to leave you. What a terrible mistake I made. . . .*

She stepped fully inside her apartment. Arms folded across her chest, she gave him a searing look. "What are you doing here, Ethan?" She hadn't seen him once since he left six weeks ago. A few days after he walked out, he called and asked if he could come by for some more of his things. Nat told him to come the next day and take *everything* that was his, and she made sure she wasn't home when he got there.

"I came to see you, obviously." He pushed his lower lip out ever so slightly. It wasn't quite a pout, which would be beneath him, but definitely a discernible sign that she'd hurt his feelings.

Screw his feelings.

"I mean, what are you doing inside my apartment?"

"I need to talk to you, Nat. Please—" He stepped closer to her, but she jerked her hand up. A gesture of self-preservation. She was so desperate for consolation and comfort at the moment that she could do something really stupid. Something she'd hate both herself and Ethan for, later.

He stopped a few feet from her. "I couldn't believe it when I heard about Maggie on the news this morning. It was so awful. Unimaginable. I still can't believe it. I must have called here a dozen times. Then I tried you at work, but your clerk said you'd left. So I tried here again, but still no answer. Finally I got so worried I decided to drive over—and then on the radio I heard about you being kidnapped by the inmate who killed her. I was so distraught . . . I didn't know what to do. Other than stay keyed into the news. And then, an hour later, I heard you were found by the cops locked in a trunk—thank God you're all right, Nat."

His voice was thick with concern and sympathy, but Nat was not the least bit receptive.

"I hope you're planning to leave the car when you go," she said bitingly. "That was our agreement. You were supposed to make other transportation arrangements—"

"Don't, Nat." His handsome, craggy face took on a pained look—his *how can you wound me like this* expression.

The sheer gall of the man. "I can't talk to you now, Ethan," she said dismissively. "I reek of gasoline fumes. I need to take a bath and go to sleep. I haven't slept since . . ." She let the sentence hang. She didn't want to say any more. She didn't want to think any more. It was only by sheer force of will that she was not collapsing into a hysterical heap on the floor.

"How about you get undressed while I run your bath and then I'll make you a nice cup of hot tea—"

"I don't want hot tea. I don't want anything from you. Don't you get it? I want you to leave me alone. I want Maggie back. I want this to all be some horrible nightmare." As she was ranting, Ethan bridged the distance between them and wrapped his big, strong arms tightly around her. For an instant, she gave in to her desperate need to be held. To be held by her husband. For the briefest of moments yearning circumvented self-preservation.

But Nat's hurt, outrage and disgust—at herself even more than at Ethan—catapulted her out of that moment. She shoved her husband hard enough for him to stumble back, surprise etched on his features, as she stormed out of the room.

She sank to her shoulders in the pulsating hot bath water. Sliding forward, she let her head drop back until first her hair and then her whole head was submerged. She held her breath, giving herself up to the pounding jets of the Jacuzzi, hoping the roar would drown out her throbbing grief, self-recriminations and desperate worry. Worry she knew wouldn't abate until Walsh was back behind bars. And what if he wasn't caught?

When she surfaced, she let out a gasp of alarm. Ethan was standing at the bathroom door. In his outstretched hand was a fluted crystal wine glass filled with an amber fluid. The goblet was from a set of eight, a wedding present from his sister. When he moved out, he left behind all their wedding gifts. Nat was sure he told himself he was being sensitive and considerate, but she felt it as one more painful slap in the face. Their marriage meant so little to him, he wanted nothing from it. Except her '97 Toyota Camry.

She still had no idea why he was there, what it was he wanted to talk to her about. He'd insisted on waiting until she'd had her bath and calmed down a little.

Ethan's presence in her bathroom wasn't calming her down one bit. She was lying there naked in her tub and he still looked too damn good.

"I've got the tea steeping, but I thought a cognac might be . . ." He hesitated. "I'll just . . . put it down . . . by the tub."

He crossed the room, knelt—his joints making a familiar crackling sound that Nat used to tease him about—and carefully placed the glass on the white and blue checked tile floor within reach of her arm. Putting him within arm's reach as well.

What if Ethan did want to come back? What if he woke up this morning, learned of Maggie's brutal murder, and that news somehow shocked him back to his senses? Assuming he thought the sensible thing was for them to be together. Maybe he hadn't thought that for a long time.

But if he had—

He smiled in a shy, awkward way.

The smile brought Nat up short. Timid smiles were not part of Ethan's repertoire. He was the most polished, self-assured man she'd ever known. Partly it was all this mawkish attentiveness— *let me run your bath, make you tea, bring you cognac.* Not Ethan's style. Not with her, anyway.

Something was up. And Nat was sure now it wasn't about Ethan popping in here unannounced this afternoon to beg her to take him back. It was not only his facial expressions and the solicitousness that were the tip-offs. It was something indefinable, a sense of being with someone who wanted something from her, not someone who wanted to give her something. Ethan was tossing her some crumbs so she'd be more amenable to whatever it was he was after.

The anger generated by those thoughts filled her with relief. Because, for a moment there, she'd been maybe a hair's-breadth away from asking him to wash her back, kissing good-bye whatever pathetic dregs of self-respect she had left.

"I'll be out in a few minutes," she said in a dismissive tone. Thankfully, it was effective enough for Ethan to get up, turn around and leave the bathroom.

"I forgot to tell you, your sister called a few minutes after I got here," Ethan said as she entered the room, dressed in a gray sweatshirt and a pair of jeans. He smiled sheepishly as he added, "She was surprised when I answered."

"You shouldn't have picked up," Nat snapped. Sheepish smiles were not part of Ethan's tried-and-true repertoire either.

She got up abruptly from the couch as soon as he sat beside her. She couldn't bear to have him near her. Not because she was struggling to keep her hands off him—unless it was his neck.

"Look, I'm sorry, Nat." He lifted the steaming mug of tea off the Mexican tile coffee table and extended it toward her. "Come on, drink this."

She ignored his offering. Any second now she'd tell him what he could do with his crumbs. "What are you sorry about, Ethan?"

He scowled. "Answering the phone. I guess it was . . . presumptuous under the circumstances."

"The circumstances being that you don't live here anymore. And you had no right entering this apartment uninvited, using a key you should no longer have—"

"Nat, I don't want us to be enemies. You probably don't believe this, but I've never stopped—"

"Stop now." Her voice was razor-sharp. She wore her harshest face. The man had ripped her life apart and he had the audacity to quote her romance novel clichés? If he finished that sentence she'd slug him.

Ethan was still holding the mug out to her. Nat could see his hand start to tremble. Tea spilled over the edge. He quickly set the mug back down on the table. Then he ran his fingers through his hair, head bowed. "Nat. God, Nat, I know how badly I've hurt you. But couldn't you please . . . cut me some slack. Just this once. I need to talk to you. I need . . . your help. I think I may be . . . in trouble. It's so crazy. I still can't believe it."

"Believe what?" she asked callously. How could he be so selfish and insensitive to show up there asking for help at a time when she was hurting so much she felt like her insides were shredded.

"I can't believe she's dead," he answered hoarsely, his head dropping lower so that his chin was practically on his chest.

It left her staring at the top of his head. And, surely she was well over the edge because even though she knew Ethan was talking about Maggie and that Maggie's death was connected in some way to his being in trouble, the first thought she had was— *ha, Ethan's beginning to lose his hair. He's got a real bald spot starting there. Bet he's already on the* Rogaine *plan.*

"Nat?" Ethan lifted his head and looked up at her plaintively.

She sat down on the club chair across from the couch. "What's this about, Ethan?"

"Did that con do it, Nat? Walsh? The tabloids are already saying—"

"I don't know if he did it."

"You've talked to the cops, right? They believe he's their man, right?"

She regarded Ethan warily. "What's going on, Ethan?"

He leaned heavily against the back of the sofa, closing his eyes. "Let me start at the beginning."

"I'm afraid that's going to take too long," she said acidly.

Ethan opened his eyes and gave her a wilting look. "You can't give an inch, can you?"

"Don't you dare make this about me," she warned.

He got up from the couch. For a minute, Nat thought he was giving up and going to leave. Instead, he crossed over to where she sitting and knelt down in front of her. "I'm only going back a few nights, Nat. To when Jill and I bumped into Maggie at a restaurant in the North End."

Jill and I. Listen to the way the pairing rolls so easily and naturally off his lips. Jill and I.

"What restaurant?"

He blinked at her in confusion. "What—? Pomodoro." It took a couple of moments for the guilty look to surface. Pomodoro just happened to be the restaurant where they had celebrated their last anniversary. At least he remembered.

He got to his feet, clasped his hands together against his chest. "Nat, what do you want me to do? Avoid every restaurant, every movie theater, every shop we were ever in together? It isn't possible. Or reasonable."

"How about avoiding friends, Ethan? *My* friends?"

Ethan sat back down on the couch, sinking heavily into it. "I saw her. I saw Maggie yesterday."

"You saw her?" Nat's throat constricted. She couldn't manage a voice over a whisper.

He gave her an accusatory look. "I spent twenty minutes, maybe a half-hour over at her place. She kind of hurried me out because she said she was expecting someone. And that someone obviously—"

"Why?"

"Why? I don't know why he—"

"Why were *you* there?"

Silence. Ethan stared down at his hands which were still clasped together. "When we met at the restaurant, Jill . . . got sick. Maggie was nice enough to check on her while she was in the bathroom."

"What kind of sick?" She felt like a lawyer. Only ask the questions you already knew the answer to.

Ethan unclasped his hands and held them out to her placatingly. "We didn't plan it. Believe me, Nat, the last thing I want right now is a baby."

Even knowing the answer, it took a few seconds for the shock to wear off. But then she nodded slowly. She did believe him. She believed he didn't want Jill's baby any more than he ever wanted one with her. And finally she was smack up against the truth that she hadn't been able to face for close to two years now. Ethan Daniel Price did not want to be a father, period. All those months when she was trying to get pregnant and Ethan would comfort her while she sobbed each time she got her period, he was secretly breathing a sigh of relief.

"She's Catholic. An abortion's out of the question."

Nat got up, walked over to the coffee table, picked up the cup of tea. She drank it down like it was some kind of a life-strengthening elixir. All it did was give her an instant stomachache.

"Do you want to marry her?"

His eyes searched hers. For understanding? Sympathy? Compassion? *You're barking up the wrong tree, mister.*

"Jill's having my baby, Nat. It's . . . the right thing for me to do."

His response made her already aching stomach churn. "Where does Maggie fit in to all this?"

"Jill told Maggie at Pomodoro that she was pregnant. Maggie called me at school on Wednesday. I begged her not to say anything to you. I wanted to . . . to tell you myself. I knew you'd be . . . upset, hurt. I thought it would help if I talked it through with someone else first. Someone close to you. I asked Maggie if I could stop by either Thursday or Friday. I was hoping she might give me some guidance—"

"And she agreed? Maggie agreed to counsel you about the best way to tell me you knocked up your girlfriend?" Nat didn't know who she felt angrier at, at the moment, Ethan or Maggie.

"She cared about you, Nat. She loved you. That's the only reason she agreed to talk to me. And reluctantly at that. Anyway, she said she had classes all day Thursday." He heaved a heavy sigh. "So it would have to be Friday." Nat watched his muscular chest slowly expand and then contract beneath his tight tee-shirt. "I'm scared, Nat."

She knew his fear wasn't about getting married again or fatherhood. At least those weren't his primary fears.

"What time were you there yesterday, Ethan?"

"I arrived at around 11:45. I couldn't have been there more than twenty minutes. I was back at school by 12:30 for a meeting with one of my students. And it's a good fifteen-minute drive from Maggie's place to school."

"What went on in those twenty minutes, Ethan?"

"Christ, Nat. You sound like a goddamn prosecutor. What do you think happened? We talked. Or, I talked. Maggie was distracted. Kept checking her watch. Her only advice was that I should be straight with you. She gave me the bum's rush. Saying she was expecting someone."

"And this person she was expecting?"

"She didn't say who. I don't even know if it was a man or a woman. But Maggie was . . . I don't know, not exactly nervous, but edgy. And pretty anxious for me not to stick around too long. I thought, maybe she was just uncomfortable talking with me about Jill and everything. . . . She did say that she would have to tell you what was . . . going on if I didn't talk with you by the end of the weekend. I promised her . . ." He leaned forward. "The way I figure it, either she was expecting this escaped ex-con and things got out of hand—"

"Things?"

"I remember that time a few months back when you threw a

party for her, she was going on and on about this brilliant inmate poet. On the news it said he'd been attending one of her night classes. He probably persuaded her to let him drop by to go over one of his poems or something. But she must have had some inkling that poetry wasn't the only thing on that creep's mind." He buried his head in his hands. "And she was right."

"You have it all figured out."

He raised his head. "But, do the cops?"

"You're afraid they'll suspect you?"

Ethan's eyes skidded off her face. "My fingerprints may be there, Nat. I had an iced tea. Maggie may not have gotten the chance to wash the glass. And my prints are on file—"

She'd almost forgotten that when Ethan was fresh out of college, he attended the Boston Police Academy and spent a few months on the force before he decided being a cop wasn't for him. He quit, went on to get his Ph.D. in Criminal Justice and became a college professor.

"Don't turn on me now, Nat. Please. If there was ever a time I needed you—"

"Does Jill know you were at Maggie's yesterday?" She took a little of the edge off her voice. She didn't know what possessed her to feel sorry for him, but she did. In some way, it was freeing. She supposed because pity was the one emotion Ethan would, under just about any other circumstances, hate having anyone— especially her—feel for him.

"No one knows I was there. No one but you, Nat."

"Unless someone saw you going in or out of her apartment. Or her building. A neighbor. A delivery boy. The postman." She stopped because Ethan looked stricken.

"Oh God . . . it's possible."

"Does Jill know you're here today?"

"No. I did tell her I would be seeing you sometime this weekend."

"To ask me for a divorce?"

"Nat—"

"You've got to let the cops know, Ethan. See Detective Leo Coscarelli. He's in charge of the investigation. Better to go to him than the other way around. Explain it all just like you explained it to me—"

"If I'd gone over there any other day—I kept hoping they'd find the killer fast and then I wouldn't have to get involved."

"You *are* involved."

He hunched toward her. "What if they think . . . I did it, Nat?" he asked so plaintively she was tempted to reach out to him—"Can you imagine what that will do to Jill?"

Her sympathetic impulse vanished. So did a lot of other feelings she'd been carting around. Like longing, need, the desperate wish for reconciliation. Suddenly, they were all so much excess baggage.

Nat's phone rang as she was finally about to crawl into bed at a little past eight P.M.

Her best guess was Jack.

She was wrong.

Leo Coscarelli's voice sounded especially grim as he identified himself. Her stomach knotted as she immediately envisioned a bloody showdown between him and Walsh, saw the inmate sprawled bleeding in a gutter. . . .

Nat was caught between horror and shameful relief.

"A missing persons report just came across my desk."

It was not what she was expecting to hear so it took her a few seconds to absorb the detective's words.

"Who?"

"Alison Cole. Walsh's rape victim. Report was filed this morning. Apparently, the mother was the last one to see her. And that was around eight A.M. Thursday when she picked up Alison's children. She baby-sits them while her daughter works as a receptionist in a law firm in Boston. When Alison didn't pick them up at five as usual, Mrs. Cole didn't worry at first. Seems her daughter often had to work late. When she didn't show by seven, Mrs. Cole tried Alison at work but no one picked up. She fed the kids, tried Alison at home and got the answering machine. Alison's husband called his mother-in-law a little while later asking to speak with his wife, I guess figuring she must have hung around at her mother's place. With neither of them having seen or heard from her, they each tried a few more places they thought she might be. Neither of them had any luck. The husband called the police that night around eleven P.M. but they said he couldn't file a missing persons report for at least twenty-four hours. They took the report Saturday morning. Unfortunately, it took all this time for the report to land on my desk because the husband listed her by her married name, Alison Miller."

Nat heard Coscarelli take in a sharp breath. "I haven't been able to reach the husband yet, but I just finished speaking with the mother. She says that her daughter had recently been complaining about getting a lot of hang-up calls all hours of the day. They started about three weeks ago."

Coinciding perfectly, as they both knew, with the start of Walsh's pre-release program.

fourteen

Honey, let me tell you, no matter how bad you think you have it, chances are, the girl in the next cell, she's probably worse off still. . . .

P. W.
Female Inmate #217096

BOTH DEAN THOMAS Walsh and Alison Cole Miller were still missing when Nat phoned Horizon House's employment counselor Sharon Johnson late Sunday morning and told her she wanted to come by her place to talk to her. Sharon's hesitation disturbed Nat but it didn't surprise her.

"What do you want to see me about?" she said finally. Warily.

"Walsh," Nat said succinctly from her cell phone in the 1997 Camry she'd found parked outside her condo that morning. No doubt Ethan viewed this as a gracious conciliatory gesture. *Better late than never.*

"What about if we meet over your way?" Sharon said. "Get a cup of coffee or something?"

"I'm just a few streets down from your place. I'll be there in a couple of minutes."

Nat heard a muffled sigh travel through the line. Sharon should have known her well enough by now to have realized she was not a woman to be easily put off. She had never been to Sharon Johnson's home. Sharon had never invited her over, and there'd never been any reason before for Nat to impose herself on her employee's private life.

Why now? Nat could have met Sharon at a coffee shop as Sharon would have undoubtedly preferred. But she did not want to discuss Dean Thomas Walsh in public. Plus, the truth was Nat was concerned that her employment counselor was holding out on her. Her insistence on seeing Sharon at home was meant to rattle her. It did. She was hoping to capitalize on Sharon's discomfort to prod her into being more forthcoming than Nat was guessing she'd otherwise volunteer to be.

Nat didn't know what she expected, but when she pulled up in front of tree-shaded 17 Perkins Street in Jamaica Plain, she was more than a bit surprised. Sharon Johnson, ex-con, current civil service employee, was living well. Even if all she'd had was a studio apartment in this stately Victorian brownstone across from Jamaica Pond, it was a long way from the mostly black, mostly poor community of Roxbury where she was born, raised, and got into trouble with the law.

Nat was really taken aback when she got to the front door and saw that there was only one mailbox beside the doorbell, indicating a single family dwelling. And the only names on the single brass mailbox were JOHNSON/FORD.

The large oak front door opened before she rang the bell. She was greeted by Sharon herself. She was dressed in an exquisite multicolored West African dashiki, a matching scarf wound around her hair. She looked regal. Exotic. Nat hardly recognized her as the woman from work who'd always worn simple, nondescript business suits.

"Don't look so shocked. You got the right address," she said, a subversively sly smile on her face.

No point in pretending Sharon had misread her, Nat mutely stumbled into the marble-floored foyer, the walls of which were painted a deep burnt umber and decorated with exotic African masks and batik hangings. From where she was standing she could see into the living room through a wide curved archway to her left. And what instantly grabbed her eye were the huge, vividly colored expressionist paintings covering almost every inch of wall space. If she was flummoxed by the outside of the house, Nat was awed by what she was seeing inside.

Working in a prison setting—and that included Horizon House even though it was a definite step up from being behind the wall—there were times when Nat would walk into her pleasant, nicely decorated two-bedroom condo at the end of a day and be pulled up short by the striking contrast between the place she called home and that of the inmates in her charge. What must the contrast have been like for Sharon? Especially given her own experience as an inmate? And why, if she lived like this, had she chosen to return to such harsh surroundings, even if it was only from 9 to 5? Surely, her paltry civil servant salary wasn't going far toward paying for these opulent digs.

"Do you want something to eat? Ray is making omelets and I've put up coffee."

Nat pulled her gaze away from the living room. *Ray?* So there was a man in Sharon's life. Probably explained the upscale digs. In those few short minutes, Nat had learned more about her employment counselor than she'd learned in the seven months they'd worked together.

"An omelet would be . . . nice," Nat muttered, though she didn't even know if she was hungry. She suddenly flashed on the still untouched dinner for two from Wasserman's Deli sitting in her fridge since Friday afternoon and she was overcome anew with grief. She forced down the sorrow with a steadying breath. But not before Sharon noticed.

"I'm sorry about your friend."

Nat nodded.

"Are you okay?"

"No, of course not," she said sharply, instantly regretting her abrasive tone. It was really misdirected anger and frustration. Nat had to be careful not to go dumping on everyone around her.

Sharon's dark brown eyes were smart, observant. "Come on to the kitchen," she said, then turned, leading the way down the narrow foyer.

Nat followed her past the curved staircase to the back of the house and into the small, cozy kitchen with its ceiling-high walnut cabinets set on a pickled wood floor. A tall, compellingly handsome, ebony-skinned woman—also dressed in resplendent African garb—stood at a butcher block center island spreading a thick coating of butter on what looked and smelled like fresh-from-the-oven homemade bread.

"If you're watching your cholesterol, we've got margarine, too," the woman said by way of greeting. Nat caught a flash of a gold-capped front tooth and the hint of a Caribbean accent.

"Natalie, this is Raylene Ford. Ray's the one did those paintings you were staring at in the living room."

"Not just staring at. Admiring. Enormously. You're a fantastic artist, Ray." Nat was babbling. And feeling a bit like Alice after she'd tumbled into Wonderland.

Ray winked playfully at Sharon. "See that, Sharona—somebody appreciates me for more than my fine cooking."

It was not so much Ray's teasingly affectionate tone as it was Sharon's maladroit smile in response that brought it home to Nat that these two women were more than housemates.

*   *   *

It was after ten. They'd finished their high-octane chicory coffee and delicious brie and mushroom omelets (it turned out Nat was starving). Ray'd excused herself; Nat had learned over breakfast that this engaging woman was not only a talented artist but a highly successful one. Nothing had been said about the point of her visit. The truth was Nat had relished this brief respite. She wanted to keep it going a few minutes longer. Even though she could sense that Sharon was waiting for the shoe to drop. Or maybe she was just uneasy about being *outed*.

"Ray's a terrific woman," Nat said, hoping to allay any concerns Sharon might have about the latter.

Sharon set the dishes noisily in the sink. "We met in prison."

She paused, waiting for Nat to make a comment. Nat felt obliged to say something. "You've both come a long way." She shuddered at how inane that sounded.

"Ray didn't seduce me in the joint, if that's what you're thinking. It's what everyone in the joint thought. What we both wanted them to think. Until I teamed up with Ray I used to get hit on all the time. Sometimes it got ugly. Once I was Ray's *woman*—nobody's business what we were or weren't doing— those jail house dykes were all smart enough to keep their distance from me or they knew they'd *hear* about it from Ray. Ray had that kind of reputation in the joint. Still has it. You don't go messing around with Ray." Sharon hesitated, then added "Truth is, not that it's your business either, we were just friends until we were both on the street for quite a while." Up to now, Sharon had maintained a *you don't ask, I won't tell* policy. It was like she'd interpreted Nat's coming up there as her *asking*. So she was telling. Getting it all out in one fell swoop.

Nat walked over to her. "You're right, Sharon, it isn't any of my business. But I would like to share what I am thinking. I'm envious of any two people having such a warm, caring, nurturing relationship. You and Ray, you're very lucky."

Sharon cast Nat a sideways look. Checking to see whether she was for real.

"No, that's not true," Nat said, causing Sharon to frown until she clarified the comment. "It isn't all luck. Having a good relationship must have taken a lot of hard work." Little by little, Nat was coming to face the cold realization that Ethan hadn't been the only one in their relationship who hadn't worked hard enough. She'd been spending so much time focusing on having been betrayed that she'd neatly managed to avoid examining what she'd contributed to the failure of her marriage. Not that she was ready to do much in the way of a thorough examination just yet.

Sharon smiled ruefully. "Hey, don't go putting us up on some kind of pedestal, Nat. In the five years we've been together, we've had plenty of rough times, Ray and me. For one thing, I'm a real private person. Always have been. Now Ray, she's just the opposite. That girl's outspoken about everything. Including being a lesbian. Ray's never once been with a man. I couldn't bend my mind around that for a long time. I used to say to her, how can you really be sure, girl, if you don't try it with a man even once."

Sharon's smile softened. "She turned that same argument against me." She hesitated. "Ray's the first woman I was ever with. The only woman. Truth is, being with Ray's the best thing ever happened to me."

All of a sudden, Sharon looked away and started busying herself washing the dishes.

Nat reached over and shut off the water. Deciding this was the time to put Sharon's truthfulness to the test. "Word's going round you knew Walsh was out for blood. You want to tell me about it?"

Sharon had the good graces not to act as if she didn't know what Nat was talking about. She set the washed plate on the drain board. "I never dreamed he'd go after your friend."

"Then who?"

"It's got nothing to do with what happened." A defensive edge crept into her voice.

"Talk to me, Sharon. Please. If someone else is in danger, you owe . . ."

"I don't owe the bastard crap." Her lovely face was suddenly contorted with hatred. "Wasn't for him I wouldn't have never . . ." She stopped. The fury dissipated. She smiled ruefully. "That's what all us cons say, right? Gotta blame someone for the messes we get into. Someone other than ourselves."

"I thought you were past that," Nat said quietly.

Sharon walked back over to the table. Sat down. "I am. Most of the time. But I got a lot of hard feelings for Owen."

She met Nat's gaze as Nat joined her at the table. "Owen King. My one time . . ." She hesitated. "Boyfriend. He struck a deal with the DA and ratted me out when he got nailed for a B&E over in the South End. Owen got eighteen months in county. I got three to five at Framingham."

Nat was quite familiar with the details involving Sharon's incarceration. The breaking and entering conviction she mentioned was only one of the charges. The other was assault with a deadly weapon. At that time, Sharon was a prostitute running a scam. She'd tag a john with money, get him to take her to his apartment and while she had him busy in bed or wherever, her partner would break in and rob the place. Trouble was, that last john got wind of the robbery and tried to stop it. He got stopped instead. With a cast iron poker. Sharon was charged with the assault although she swore in her deposition that it was her partner who attacked the victim. Nat hadn't recalled her partner in crime's name until now. Owen King.

"Only satisfaction I got," Sharon broke into her rumination, "was Owen got busted for assault and battery not two weeks after he hit the street. That time 'round he got six to ten at Norton." She lifted her eyes skyward. "Thank you, Lord."

Nat's antennae instantly shot up. "King was at Norton same time as Walsh."

Sharon returned her gaze to Nat, her features etched with tension. "King would kill me if I . . ." She didn't finish.

So Nat finished for her. "King was Walsh's *daddy*."

"And his pimp," Sharon added starkly. "Owen traded the boy to his pals for weed, cigarettes, a shank, whatever he wanted. Walsh wasn't Owen's only punk. He had a stable of them."

"How do you know all this?"

Sharon sighed. "Just when you let yourself start to think you've put your miserable past behind you, up it comes and smacks you in the face. When Owen got out of the joint a month back he tracked me down. Saw my setup. Figured I was a sweet touch. I set him straight in no uncertain terms. Didn't hear from him for a time and then about a week ago I get a call. He's all riled up saying as how Walsh had been phoning him up and threatening him. According to Owen, the boy got real graphic. Saying as how he was gonna . . . this is how Owen told it to me . . . cut off Owen's prick and shove it up his ass, then chop off his balls and stuff them down his throat." She shook her head. "Can't say as how I blame Walsh for wanting retribution. There were times I wanted to do all that and more to Owen King."

"I want to talk to him, Sharon."

"Owen? You crazy, girl? He's downright treacherous. Besides, you won't get nothin' from him."

"Walsh may still be looking for him—"

"Yeah, and you can bet Owen's gonna be ready for him if he shows up. If Owen doesn't dig Walsh up first."

"Exactly what I'm thinking. One way or another King might be able to lead us to Walsh."

Sharon's eyes narrowed. "That's not all you're thinking. You're thinking just maybe Owen could have had something to do with what went down with your teacher friend. Like maybe he set Walsh up to take the hit so's they'd lock him back up and throw away the key this time 'round."

"Would you put it past King?"

"Honey, there ain't nothin' I'd put past that mean, ugly bastard. Which is all the more reason you want to stay clear of him."

"But that's not what I want."

fifteen

*Even if you feel uneasy, never let them see it. Let your
confidence and genuine interest in the inmate's welfare
override your fears. . . .*
(excerpt from Correctional Officers Tip Sheet)

"MMM, MMM, MMM. Never saw no *Super* pretty as you when I was
in the joint." Owen King roughly elbowed the young, waif-like
bleached blond slumped beside him in the booth. She flinched,
grabbing her rib cage, but rose without a peep. King patted the
vacated space, wanting Nat to take the teen's place. Make that
pre-teen.

Nat opted for the empty bench across from him and watched
the young girl as she staggered her way to the ladies room in one
of the few remaining topless bars in Boston's ever-shrinking
scummy red light district. Across from them, on a small stage, a
wasted-looking topless dancer with pronounced stretch marks on
her silicone-inflated breasts was mindlessly swaying to the drone

of what sounded like elevator music, her vacant eyes staring into the void. There were five other customers in the dark, dank place on that sunny Sunday afternoon. All men, all on stools hunched over their drinks at the bar, all well over their alcohol limit.

"Is that kid one of yours?" Nat asked, returning her gaze to King whose hooded eyes hadn't left her face. Nor had the smirk left his lips. Even seated, there was no missing that this forty-two-year-old olive-skinned man was large and powerfully built. Nat was sure he'd spent much of his time in prison lifting weights. As if reading her mind, he flexed a tattooed bicep as he reached for his beer.

His eyes continued to survey her with dark amusement as he brought the glass to his lips. He took a long, slow swallow, then cupped the bottle in both hands. "That there's my niece."

That child was as much his niece as Nat was his aunt.

"What'll ya have, *Supergirl?*" King slurred the words, sounding like a man who was high on plenty more than beer. From the torporous look of him, especially the glazed eyes, her best guess was crack cocaine.

"Some answers," Nat said, hoping he wasn't so far over the edge that this meeting would prove to be a waste of her time.

He slid the beer bottle over to the side of the chipped, faded red Formica table and leaned so far forward Nat could smell his sour breath. "Here's an answer for you. I am *all* man, beautiful. Just say the word and I'll prove it to you. So you just forget about what that bitch dyke's been spouting off about me." He was too doped up to sound all that emphatic, but she knew where this macho talk was coming from.

"All Sharon Johnson told me was that Walsh had some kind of beef with you and that you told her he was calling you up and threatening you."

He drilled her a long, penetrating look, trying to discern just how much she knew about that beef. Even though men like Owen King in no way saw their sexual activities in prison as any indication of homosexuality, they knew people on the outside would have trouble comprehending that forcing weaker inmates to assume the role of *women*, gratifying needs that would in the outside world be provided by real women, was considered, in the joint, a sign of being macho. Basically a stronger inmate saying to a more vulnerable one, "I'm more man than you and I'm gonna turn you out to prove it." Rape and subjugation—in prison or out—is always more about violence, control, and politics than it is about sex or gender.

"Sharon didn't tell me what the beef was about, Mr. King. And, frankly, I don't care," Nat said with as much earnestness as she could fabricate. "All I want to know is if you've heard from Dean Thomas Walsh since his escape on Friday. And if you have any idea where he might be."

King ran a hand over his knobby shaven head in a caressing stroke. "And just how much you gonna pay for that kind of information, *Supergirl*?"

"It seems to me you stand to benefit as much as anyone by his capture."

"You think I'm afraid of that little pussy?"

"I think, Mr. King, you can't afford trouble. You're on parole," she reminded him. "I doubt you want to be sent back."

"You ain't got no cause to be threatening me."

"I'm asking for your cooperation."

He grinned slyly. "I be glad to co-op-er-ate with you, *Super-girl*."

"Tell me, Mr. King. Did you take Maggie Austin's writing class at Norton, too?"

He let out a whooping laugh that was loud enough to attract the attention of one of the customers at the bar. But he turned away abruptly when Nat caught him looking their way. No doubt he didn't want a bruiser like Owen King accusing him of being nosy.

But King seemed oblivious of having drawn any notice.

"*Supergirl,*" he drawled, "I got me better things to do in the joint than learn my ABCs."

"Better things than spending a couple of hours a week with a beautiful young woman?" Nat pressed, her throat going raw as she pictured a roomful of leering inmates ogling her beautiful, earnest friend. How many of those men really had the slightest interest in creative writing?

"Beautiful, huh? No wonder that pathetic little pussy had himself a round-the-clock hard-on." He started to chuckle.

"What do you know about Maggie Austin's murder?"

King's laughter stopped abruptly. He eyed Nat with a barely concealed menace that was fierce enough to override his drug-induced lassitude. "Don't you even think 'bout going there, girl," he said in a flat, hard voice.

"Why so touchy?" she countered.

Nat could see all of the veins in King's neck bulge. She was worried that she might be pushing too hard. Her anxiety heightened when she saw the ex-con's large, beefy hands clench into fists, the knuckles on both hands boldly tattooed in blood red—the left with the letters S-A-T-A-N, the right with D-E-A-T-H.

As she was trying hard to think of a way to defuse the tension, amazingly King settled down on his own. Unclenching his fists, he wagged a finger at her. "You playing with my head, *Supergirl.* Now that's not nice."

"Maggie Austin was my friend, Mr. King. My good friend. If you have any information that can help me, I'd very much appreciate hearing it." Nat decided since she wasn't getting anywhere playing tough, maybe she needed to sweeten up her approach a little.

"I like an appreciative woman. Yes I do, *Supergirl.*" King licked his lips like he was already tasting her.

So much for the soft sell. Nat pulled one of her cards out of her purse, placed it on the table in front of King, and started to slide out of the booth. "When you have something to tell me about Walsh or about Maggie Austin's murder, call." She pushed the card over to him, ready to make her exit.

King tapped the card. "I did hear from that little faggot escapee. Just last night. Interrupted me and my lady friend just when we were really gettin' it on." He smiled lasciviously when she remained seated.

"Where was he calling from?" Nat stayed put, but she was far from convinced King wasn't playing with her head now.

"You ain't gonna believe this, but that little punk actually called this time sobbing apologies for disrespecting me and begging for help."

Nat was torn. He could easily be putting her on. Then again, Walsh had to be feeling desperate. And Owen King, for whatever else he might have done to Walsh, had served the role of his protector at Norton. Was it possible Walsh was so desperate he'd turn to his daddy for protection out on the street?

King finished off his beer in one long guzzle, then rose from the booth. "I'm gonna get me another. You gotta have somethin' if ya want any more news about *Deanna*." His smirked took on a darker edge as he feminized Dean's name. Was that what Walsh was called in prison by the inmates who bought him? Who violated him? Debased him? It was unimaginable to Nat what that must have been like for Walsh. What it must have done to him, both physically and mentally. She was momentarily overcome by a wave of horror and pity for the young man.

When King came back with two glasses of what looked like hard liquor, he slid in next to her before Nat could protest.

"Drink up, *Supergirl*," he drawled, lifting the glass to her lips. The smell of cheap whiskey assailed her nose. She shoved his hand away. The drink splashed over the table.

"Get up, King. You either go sit where you were or I'm out of here." Her tone was sharp, authoritative.

"We ain't on your turf now, *Supergirl*. You on my turf. Only one gonna give orders round here is me."

"You're messing with the wrong woman, King." She managed to keep the tremor out of her voice, but there was no denying she was more than a little uneasy. Sober, King undoubtedly would have gotten her message loud and clear. But he might be too coked up to get any message straight at the moment.

Nat was convinced of the latter when he deliberately slid a little closer, crowding her to the far edge of the booth. "Other way round, *Supergirl*," he drawled, his lips repulsively close to her ear.

She felt almost as dumb as she felt angry. She was also seriously aware that she had screwed up royally coming here on her own. Even if she screamed her lungs off, she'd be lucky if any of the losers in that dump would so much as raise an eyebrow.

Stay tough, she told herself. Owen King wouldn't really be stupid enough to make a move on a prison superintendent of all people, coked up or not. In some corner of his addled brain, no matter how minuscule, he knew damn well that once Nat was on her turf again all she had to do was snap her fingers and he'd be back inside faster than he could slur *Supergirl* one last time.

But even as she was stoking her flagging self-confidence, she felt King's mitt of a hand slither up her thigh. "You got legs go on forever. Mmmm." His tongue darted out like a viper and he licked the side of her face. Nat felt sick with fury and disgust.

"You must be out of your mind, King," she hissed, snatching his hand away only to find him pinning hers to the seat. His free hand went up to her neck, his large fingers lightly circling it.

"One hard squeeze, *Supergirl,* and you're history. And all I gotta do is slide on outta here and ain't a soul gonna remember they ever saw me in this place."

"You're forgetting Sharon Johnson," she said between clenched teeth. Mostly to keep them from chattering.

"I can take care of that bitch dyke. Don't you worry about that. So now, tell me, *Supergirl*, what you got to offer in this deal?"

"The deal is you get your dirty hands off of me."

"You heard the lady, Owen." A clicking sound went with the no-nonsense voice.

Nat's frightened eyes darted first to the .38 police special pointed at Owen King's temple and then to the man holding the gun. Detective Leo Coscarelli. To the rescue once again. Not that she was complaining, to say the least.

The press of the barrel shook King out of his drugged stupor like nothing else. Both hands darted up into the air and he started whining, "Hey, man . . . no harm done, man. This here ain't . . ."

"Shut up, Owen," Coscarelli warned.

Awed, Nat watched the seemingly scrawny young detective haul this bruiser of an ex-con out of the booth, shove him face down to the filthy floor, yank his muscle-bound tattooed arms behind his back and cuff him. It didn't even look like it took much in the way of physical effort. *I will never again rush to judge a book by its cover.*

sixteen

IDLENESS IS UNACCEPTABLE. . . .

Plaque
Homicide Squad Room

"DID HE SAY anything?" she asked the instant the weary detective stepped inside his cubicle of an office at the 37th Precinct on Harrison Street.

"Yeah," Coscarelli muttered acerbically as he crossed the tight space and dropped into a seat behind his cluttered desk. "He wants his lawyer."

"I think he really may have heard from Walsh."

The detective slid his chair away from the desk, tipping it against the wall. He gave her a sizing up look not all that unlike the one Owen King had given her in the bar. Only Coscarelli was stone cold sober and he wasn't sizing her up as a prospective lay.

"I know what you're thinking," Nat said, feeling just as edgy as she'd felt with King. But for a different reason. Leo Coscarelli had a way of throwing her off kilter. It was not a feeling she liked. "Okay, I admit it was dumb tackling that asshole on my own. I should have gotten in touch with you. I suppose Sharon Johnson called and let you know what I was up to. She wasn't too happy about my plan, to say the least. I guess I thought my *position* would persuade King to loosen his tongue. I still think we could get him to open up if we cut a deal."

Coscarelli's eyes remained glued to her face, but he didn't say a word. Not that Nat could discern it in his inscrutable expression, but she was willing to wager he was fuming inside.

"Believe me," she prattled on, his silence making her increasingly edgy, "I'm not trying to move in on your territory, Detective. But you have to understand that I am professionally and . . . personally . . . involved. There's no way I can sit on the sidelines in this. At first I thought King was putting me on about having heard from Walsh since his escape, but now . . . it makes sense. Who else could Walsh turn to? Oh, his sister, maybe. But he couldn't be sure she wouldn't turn him in, thinking it was truly in his best interest. Here's what I think. We offer to go easy on King if he agrees to contact Walsh, arrange a meeting—"

Coscarelli's pager went off abruptly, startling both of them. He gave the pager a quick check, frowned, then reached for the phone. The frown intensified as he dialed.

Pivoting away from her, she heard him ask "What is it?" in a low, tense voice.

He listened intently to the person on the other end of the line as Nat observed him with the same intensity.

"How bad?" he asked, springing to his feet.

Nat's stomach muscles tightened. Was it about Walsh? Or Alison Cole Miller?

"Boston Memorial? Yeah, yeah, I'll get right over there—" He dropped the receiver into the cradle. Nat was on her feet now, too.

"What happened?" she asked anxiously, following on Coscarelli's heels as he made a beeline for the door.

He flung the door open without answering.

Angered by his silent treatment, Nat stormed down the hall of the precinct after him, grabbing him by his jacket sleeve as he started down the stairs to the main exit. "Damn it, tell me. Is it Walsh? Alison—?"

"It's my kid," Coscarelli said fiercely. *Kid? He doesn't look old enough to shave much less be a father.* But all at once Nat saw on this young detective's face the desperately worried look of a very grown up parent.

"Let me drive you," she said.

She was speeding down Storrow Drive as Coscarelli, on the cell phone in the passenger seat beside her, finally got through to a resident in the ER. All he knew so far—which he'd shared with Nat—was that his son was jumping on the sofa, lost his balance and fell, crashing his skull against the edge of a glass coffee table.

"No. Coscarelli. C-O-S-C—Right. Jacob. Yeah. I want to know—" He was white-knuckling the phone.

"How many?" he asked. The answer made him squint as though in pain. "Jeez. How's he—"

Again the resident must have cut him off.

A slow smile started to spread on the detective's face. "Yeah. Anna Coscarelli, right. She can be a handful." He glanced out the window as Nat pulled off the exit for Boston Memorial. "I'll be there in a few minutes to collect them both. Thanks, doc. Thanks a lot." He clicked off and leaned back in his seat, closing his eyes.

"Your boy's okay?"

He opened his eyes, slowly exhaling a breath that Nat suspected he'd been partly holding in since he'd received that phone call. "Seven stitches in the back of his head. They had to shave a big patch. But he handled it better than—"

"Your wife?" Nat had already noticed that Coscarelli wasn't wearing a wedding band. Ethan stopped wearing his ring about a year after they got married. Claimed he was allergic to gold. Nat had believed him at the time. Now she thought it would have been more accurate for him to have said he was allergic to marriage. Or to her, in any case.

"My mother," Coscarelli corrected her. "She was so hysterical the doc had to give her a tranquilizer." He sighed. "It's not easy for her looking after a rambunctious three-year-old full time. I keep telling her I'll get someone in to relieve her, but she won't hear of it. And to be honest I don't push it. Jacob adores his grandma."

"What about his mother?" Nat felt her face flush. "I mean, does she work?"

"Turn left here," he reminded her as she almost went past the entrance to the hospital.

She swerved so quickly, Coscarelli fell against her.

"Sorry," she mumbled as he straightened up.

She pulled around to the main entrance. Coscarelli's hand was already on the door handle before she applied the brake. "Thanks. My mom's got her car here. She'll give me a lift back."

Nat nodded, aware that the detective had not answered her question about his wife. But then, she was learning that Leo Coscarelli held a lot of things close to his chest.

Her first thought, when she arrived back at her apartment and found the front door slightly ajar, was that her husband had had the gall to let himself in again. Nat cursed herself for forgetting to get the key back from him and made a mental note to get her lock changed pronto.

"Ethan?" she called out sharply as she stepped into her foyer. She was betting, since Coscarelli hadn't said a word about it, that Ethan hadn't yet talked to the detective about his presence in

Maggie's apartment on Friday. Probably wanted her to go with him. Hold his hand.

When hell froze over.

Nat strode purposefully into her living room, about to give Ethan Price a well-deserved piece of her mind.

The room was empty.

She called out again, but there was no response.

A chill ran through her. If Ethan was there, surely he would have answered.

She nervously scanned the room for signs of—what? Some type of disturbance, she supposed.

Nothing in the room appeared disturbed. Maybe Ethan had simply gotten tired of waiting for her.

She headed for the kitchen. Her husband used to leave messages for her tacked on the fridge. Messages invariably saying he would be staying late at the university. He varied the excuses. Meetings. Research. Work on his book. But never the truth. Never—*Don't wait up for me tonight, darling. I'll be screwing my girlfriend.*

There was no note on the door to her refrigerator. In there, as in the living room, there was no sign of an uninvited visitor.

Could she have simply failed to shut the front door firmly? Since it locked automatically, she didn't have to use a key when she left the apartment. Only when she returned.

She was comforted by the likelihood that she'd simply been careless—not at all liking the idea of Ethan continuing to think he had the right to pop in and out of there uninvited. But as soon as she stepped inside her bedroom Nat knew her hoped for assumption was wrong. There, lying on top of the chenille bedspread of her neatly made up bed, was a single sheet of lined paper. She first thought it was a note from Ethan. Another seductive manipulation, switching from leaving messages on the fridge to what used to be *their* bed?

But it wasn't a note. And the second she picked it up she knew it was not from Ethan.

On the solitary sheet of paper was a poem. The fine hairs on Nat's arms prickled as she read it—

Adrift in the teeming chaos
I cannot inhale freedom.
Only dread sears through my nostrils.
Deep inside the fortress of my heart
lies an abyss of anguish.
Shame and despair scrape away all that remains
of my humanity.
I am a monster
Without soul
Without heart
Without you.

seventeen

There's not a one of us hasn't sinned. You can talk about your degrees of sin all you want. Me? I say "a rose by any other name . . ."

I. L.
Inmate #643028

"I THOUGHT YOU'D be home with your boy," she said to Coscarelli as he showed her into his office for the second time that day.

"Yeah, well, I left him happily eating a big bowl of chocolate chip ice cream and watching a Teletubbies video with his grandma. He's happy as a clam. What are you doing back if you didn't think I'd be here?"

She extracted the poem from her pocketbook. "I was going to leave this with one of your people."

He eyed the paper for a couple of moments, then took it from her with a pair of tweezers. After giving it a quick read, he looked questioningly over at her.

"It's Walsh's. I'm getting to recognize his style. Why he left it for me is another question." Nat shrugged.

"Left it for you where?"

"My apartment." She didn't know why she didn't provide more specific details. Maybe because it gave her such a disquieting feeling to have found it on her bed. To know that Walsh had been in her bedroom.

Coscarelli raised an eyebrow. "How do you know he's the one who left it?"

"Because I could see that my lock wasn't disturbed. Which means someone got in with a key. And only two people have keys to my apartment. My husband and . . . Maggie."

"You think Walsh swiped your key from Ms. Austin?"

"Did you find my key at her place?"

Coscarelli flipped open a black three-ringed binder on his desk. Nat knew what the cops called it—the "murder book." All the grisly details of Maggie's murder investigation could be found on the pages inside that binder. The poem Walsh left for her would, no doubt, be added.

Coscarelli flipped through the pages until he found the one he was looking for. Nat watched his index finger slide down a typed list.

"No keys found in her apartment."

"Walsh must have swiped them. I don't see any other possibility. Do you?"

Coscarelli leaned against the edge of the desk, folding his arms across his chest. Again the silent treatment. This detective was seriously getting on her nerves.

"Look," Nat said firmly, "Walsh is crying out for help. First he calls King, then he leaves me a poem drenched in guilt and sorrow—"

"What makes you so sure it was Walsh who left it," he asked.

Nat was baffled by his question. "Who else?" Suddenly she

was the one set on Walsh and Coscarelli was having doubts. Now that was a switch.

He gave her a look that seemed to suggest she knew who as well as he.

"Did anyone ever tell you you're anal retentive, Leo? I bet your wife's told you," she snapped when he continued giving her *the look*.

Instead of an answer, she got another question. One that threw her for a loop. "What was your husband's relationship with Maggie Austin?"

"Friends. Casual friends. If that." Nat wasn't sure where this question was coming from. Had Ethan finally followed her advice and gotten in touch with the detective? Told him about having been with Maggie on Friday? Or had Ethan's fingerprints been found on that glass of iced tea? Or did Coscarelli know something she didn't know?

"Why don't you sit down?" He gestured to a straight-backed wooden chair a few feet away from her.

Nat remained standing, shifting her weight from one leg to the other. She didn't want to sit down and have a chat about her husband. Especially with Coscarelli holding all the cards. "I really came back to turn over that poem and get in to talk to Owen King." Hoping, as she was sure he'd guessed, that he'd still be home looking after his boy and she could get one of the other cops on the investigation to be more cooperative. "I think, now that King's had a few hours to stew behind bars, he may be more willing—"

But Coscarelli was not about to let her sidetrack him. "Were Ethan and Maggie having an affair, Natalie?"

"No," she said emphatically, "absolutely not. Maggie didn't even like Ethan. Especially after she—" Nat stopped herself from finishing. Why should she have to air her dirty laundry in front of a man who wouldn't even tell her where his wife worked?

"After she learned he was cheating on you with one of his students?"

"Why ask me questions you already know the answers to?" she retorted, glaring at him. Inwardly feeling those all too familiar pangs of shame and humiliation. Surely, the detective, like everyone else, had to be wondering what it was about her that had driven her husband into the arms of another, younger woman. Was she such an old hag?

Coscarelli held her gaze, but maintained his unruffled, inscrutable demeanor. "Your husband is currently living with a girl by the name of Jill Bennett—"

"She's not a *girl*. She's twenty-three years old. And she's pregnant," Nat blurted, instantly feeling transparent, as if the detective could see through her skull to all the misery and disgrace she'd worked so hard at concealing.

Coscarelli had the good graces to look away for a few moments to allow her to regroup.

"There's also Karen Powell," he said quietly.

This time Nat laughed. "Ethan and Karen Powell? That's one pairing I guarantee would never happen. Karen was definitely not Ethan's type. And vice versa."

"I meant Karen could have taken the keys from Ms. Austin's apartment."

She frowned. "Why would she put that poem on my bed?" She caught the slip about the location as soon as it was off her lips. Clearly so did Coscarelli. But he didn't call her on it.

"Let's say, just for argument's sake, that Walsh is innocent," he said in that same irritating evenly modulated voice. "After all, I certainly don't want to be accused of rushing to judgment."

"Especially if you end up with egg all over your face if he isn't convicted," she said dryly.

Coscarelli let the insult roll right off him and continued calmly. "The way I see it, we have at least four other potential suspects besides Walsh at this point in time. I'm talking *means* for now.

The means with which to murder Maggie Austin and the means to set Dean Thomas Walsh up. Let's start with Karen Powell."

"You don't honestly think Karen tied Maggie up and raped her."

"Stranger things have happened. Karen was close to Maggie. And was quick to point the finger at Walsh."

Everybody was all too eager to point their fingers at Walsh. Herself now included.

"There was no sign of forced entry," Coscarelli continued. "Either Maggie let her killer in, indicating it was probably someone she trusted, or her killer let him or herself in. Karen Powell had keys to Maggie's apartment. And there was no semen found during the autopsy. Which means the rapist wore a rubber. Or didn't require one."

He paused. "Then we have our second possible suspect. Your husband."

Nat took an involuntary sharp intake of breath. "That's insane."

"Ethan Price's fingerprints were found on a glass in Maggie's apartment. But you already know that."

Caught out once again. Nat felt the heat rise to her cheeks, but she didn't say anything.

"My partner, Oates, had a talk with your husband this afternoon. Ethan told him pretty much what he says he told you."

And here she'd been trying to keep Ethan off the hot seat and he shoved her into it, instead. Perfect.

Coscarelli looked more disappointed than angry. Even though he had plenty of justification to be furious. After all, she had withheld possible evidence in a murder case.

"I told Ethan to talk with you. I guess he was scared."

"I think that's safe to assume," Leo said.

"I don't mean because he had anything to do with Maggie's murder. That's ridiculous. Ethan went to see Maggie to ask her advice about how to break Jill's pregnancy to me."

"That's all he told you."

Nat remembered something else Ethan had said—something that might be important. "Maggie told him she was expecting someone else and Ethan felt he was getting the bum's rush."

Coscarelli seemed unimpressed.

"He thinks it could have been Walsh," Nat added mordantly. "But we don't have any proof—"

"You're right," he said. "The only proof we have of someone having been in her apartment on Friday are an excellent set of your husband's fingerprints."

"Ethan may be a lot of things, but he's not a murderer. Or a . . . rapist." Why was she defending him so ardently? Why not encourage the detective to be suspicious of her soon-to-be ex? Get a little payback?

Did she still love Ethan? The pathetic possibility of it filled her with mortification.

She hurried on. "You said four people. I assume Owen King's number three. Talk about a person with a motive to set Walsh up. Walsh goes down for the murder and gets put away for life. And Owen King doesn't have to continue keeping his crotch covered," she added, filling him in on her conversation with Sharon.

She felt like she was really on to something now. "King could have made up any lame excuse to talk to Maggie. She would have made time for him, I'm sure of it. And then after . . ." She didn't want to talk about—think about—the murder. "Afterwards, he swipes the keys, finds one of Walsh's poems on her desk or in her briefcase and—"

"She could have been waiting for her boyfriend," Coscarelli cut her off again, his voice even quieter. "Which brings me to the fourth potential suspect."

It didn't register immediately. When it did, Nat felt her face heat up. "You can't mean Jack. He was—"

"I know. Home nursing a cold."

Coscarelli made it sound like such a paltry alibi.

"He was in love with Maggie. He was devastated by her murder. Besides, he's not a violent man." Nat spoke with less conviction than she might, remembering the hole in her office wall left there by Jack's fist. A fist that had missed Walsh's jaw by no more than a few inches.

"How well did you know Sally Weston?"

"Who?" But, of course, she knew very well who Sally Weston was. She was just buying some time to regroup.

"Jack Dwyer's ex-wife," Coscarelli said, lifting the murder book again, rifling through the pages until he found the one he wanted. "Did you know she filed three complaints against him over the course of five months? Battery complaints? Oh, she withdrew them so Dwyer was never charged, but I've got a photo here—"

He turned the book around and Nat saw a police photo of Sally showing abrasions on her neck and a bruise on her face.

"She drank," Nat muttered, sick at heart. "Heavily."

Coscarelli didn't ask her about Jack's drinking habits. She was sure he'd already been checking into that.

The tiny, windowless, drab green office started to feel claustrophobic. Nat was queasy, overheated. She wanted out.

Without a word, she turned and started toward the door.

"I thought you wanted to talk to Owen King," Coscarelli said as she reached for the knob.

King appeared more clearheaded and more hostile when Nat took a seat across from him in the 8×8 interrogation room at a little after seven P.M. On the wall to her left was a one-way mirror. She was acutely aware that Coscarelli was observing them from the other side.

"You ain't got no cause holding me in this pigsty," King spit out, either not knowing or not caring that he was being watched.

Nat folded her hands on the pitted wood table, noticing that his pupils were considerably less dilated. "Let's talk." She was a lot calmer in King's presence now than she had been at the bar. Not half the reason being Owen King was shackled at the wrists and ankles.

He glared at her, compressing his full lips.

"Owen, you must really miss the joint."

He gave her the finger.

She started to rise.

"You cut me a deal, I talk."

She relaxed again in her chair. "Depends on what you have to say."

"Screw that. I need insurance."

"What you need—and need badly—is to satisfy me that you've got something meaningful to tell me. Or else you're looking at another long stretch in the slammer."

"I got plenty'll satisfy you," he sneered, tapping his head. "Walsh give me a cell phone number to reach him at. I got it all memorized right up here."

She leaned forward. "You think if you give me the number and I call him up, he'll come skipping on down to the precinct?"

"I also got some other stuff I could tell you. And it ain't only 'bout that pussy Walsh."

"And why should I be interested in anyone else?" Nat said.

King smiled, knowing he'd piqued her curiosity. " 'Cause your boy wasn't the only poor ass sucker in the joint had the hots for that teacher."

"Yeah, man.——Is cool.——No hard feelin's.——We put that behind us, man. Hey, man, you got a raw deal. I know that. You ain't no lady killer, man. What say we meet up later tonight, man? Where you at?——Hey, screw you, man. You know I could get my ass for helpin' you.—Cash? Yeah man, I got a few C notes I can spot you. No sweat.——Where's that at?——Oh yeah,

yeah, I know where it's at. I be there by ten. With cash and a sweet ol' Eldorado to chauffeur you wherever your sweet ass wants to go."

King dramatically dropped the receiver into the cradle, looking from Coscarelli to Nat. "So, do I walk or what?"

"Or what," Coscarelli said.

King started to spring out of his seat, but got held back down by the two uniforms flanking him on either side.

"We had a fucking deal, you bitch," he spat at Nat.

"Settle down, Owen," she said quietly. "If Walsh's there when we show up at ten, you'll be off the hook. This time." Nat knew Coscarelli wasn't at all happy about the deal she'd struck with King.

"Yeah, well, like I said before, you may just be roping yourselves in the wrong pussy."

King spoke laconically, but there was a hint of knowledge behind his words. How much he knew remained to be seen.

Nat glanced down at the other name King provided her with earlier. Keith Franklin. A recently released inmate from CCI Norton. Although she couldn't quite place it, that name rang a bell.

eighteen

Warning to loved ones when your man's back out in the free world. If you have cheated on, forgotten, snitched on or just plain "messed him over," immediately do one of the following:

    1. Clear out of town
    2. Join the Marines
    3. Try offering big bucks as apology
    4. Kiss your ass goodbye

T.S.
Inmate #435694

"YOU NEVER EVEN BOTHERED TO RETURN MY CALL."

Nat wasn't surprised by the note of petulance in her sister's voice, but she was surprised by the undercurrent of anxiety that she picked up.

"I'm sorry, Rachel. Really—"

"And what's with Ethan being back?"

"He's not. Believe me."

There was a pause. "It must have been awful for you."

Nat didn't know if Rachel meant Maggie's murder, her abduction or what. She simply said, "Yes." Since it had all been awful, after all.

"I thought you might want to come over for dinner tomorrow night. Gary's out of town until Tuesday and Hannah's taking the children over to one of her au pair friend's houses for dinner and a video treat, so it would just be the two of us."

It was unlike her sister to extend an impromptu invitation, especially an intimate dinner at her home, just the two of them. Nat wondered if it was coming from a sense of obligation, guilt or pity. She and her younger sister were not close. Their disparate views of their childhood had been and continued to be one of the wedges between them. Unlike Nat, Rachel had never been able to acknowledge that their father was an alcoholic; that their mother had been mentally ill. Early on, Rachel, an avid sit-com watcher, had transformed her real family into an amalgamation of the countless TV families that she so loved. Nat often blamed herself for her sister's denial. As the *big* sister, Nat had felt it was her responsibility to shelter her little sister as much as possible from the dysfunction that enveloped their family. Too late, Nat realized that she had protected Rachel too well and for too long. As an adult, Rachel was still unwilling to acknowledge the truth. Denial of her parents' problems had generalized to a denial of any problems that caused her too much anxiety. Nat's tendency to tackle problems head-on—a psychologist might label the behavior counter-phobic—had produced a relationship between the siblings that rarely strayed from the superficial.

"What do you say, Nat?" Rachel pressed. This was so contrary to her sister's normal manner, that Nat became truly alarmed.

"Is anything wrong, Rachel?" This to a woman who'd made a career out of all things being right.

"Does something have to be wrong for me to want us to get together?"

To herself, Nat said, *something has to be very wrong.* To her sister, she said, "Sounds like a great idea, Rachel, but I don't know when I'll be able to get away from the center. It's pretty tense over there." She didn't bother with the details since her sister'd always been less than interested in her work. She didn't tell Rachel that Horizon House was on an extended lockdown and that she was sure Carlyle was already busy spearheading a campaign to get her ousted. He'd never wanted her at Horizon House in the first place. Now she'd gone and handed him the perfect reason to have her booted out. He'd jump on it. So far she still had the support of Russell Fisk. And Fisk was still the Commissioner's fair-haired boy. So, she was hanging in. If only by her fingertips.

"Why do you do it, Nat?" Rachel said. "Really, I think it's masochistic. Doesn't what happened give you any second thoughts?"

"Second, third and fourth," Nat admitted. "But this isn't the time—"

"Because you hate to fail at anything," Rachel said with an edge of irritation.

"I fail plenty," Nat countered, equally irritable. She checked her watch. Almost 9:30. "I've got to go, Rach. I was on my way out the door when the phone rang."

"Isn't it late to be going out?"

"I'm a grown woman, Rachel."

"Okay. Fine. So then . . . I'll see you . . . sometime."

There was no missing the disappointment or hurt in her sister's tone. Rachel was awash with surprises tonight. And Nat was awash with guilt. "Look, I'll try to make it for dinner tomorrow night. It might not be until after eight though."

"You can read the children a bedtime story then and we'll eat after they're tucked in."

Nat smiled. Her sister knew how much she adored her niece

and nephew even though she didn't get to see them nearly as much as she wished she could. "I'd like that, Rach. I'd like that a lot."

"Good," Rachel said. Her unambivalent pleasure proved yet another surprise. But Nat didn't deny feeling almost ridiculously pleased by her sister's desire to spend time with her. Especially now that she was feeling so bereft.

A heavily armed plainclothes cop was riding shotgun on the floor behind the front seat of Owen King's '83 gold Cadillac Eldorado. Two cars back, Coscarelli and his partner, Mitchell Oates, followed in an unmarked '96 Ford sedan. Nat recognized Oates as the other detective in Maggie's apartment Friday night, the one who handed Coscarelli what she'd presumed was a photo. Although that was only a guess since Coscarelli had never shown it to her.

Nat was in the back seat of the Ford. Much against Coscarelli's better judgment, she'd convinced him to let her come along for the ride, the proviso being that she did not leave the car.

The agreed-upon meeting place between King and Walsh was Monte's Bar on Madison Place, a narrow side street off of Washington right in the heart of the city. Being that it was late on a Sunday night, the neighborhood was almost eerily empty save for a handful of street people. Nat was guessing at least a couple of them were undercover cops.

Coscarelli confirmed her guess moments later when he checked in with one of them on his walkie-talkie. A static-filled voice came back. "No sign of him yet."

The Caddie pulled up right in front of the bar. Oates slid the Ford into a space at the end of the street that was marked as a loading zone. Not likely to be any loading going on that time of night.

It was 9:55. Nat hadn't said a word since she was picked up outside her apartment twenty minutes ago. And neither detective had said anything to her either. She figured they were trying to pretend she wasn't there.

Oates turned to his partner. "You think he'll show?"

In the dim light from a lamppost a few yards down the street Nat could make out the shrug of Coscarelli's shoulders.

"If he does show, he won't make it easy for you," Nat said.

Neither man responded. They really were pretending she wasn't there.

Nat didn't like being ignored. Nor did she like the mounting tension she was feeling. "He swore to me he'd kill himself before he lets you bring him in. I think he means it."

"Now that would make it easy for us," Coscarelli muttered dryly.

Oates chuckled. "You got it right there, Leo."

"I see why they teamed the two of you up," she said acidly.

This got another chuckle out of Oates, but nothing out of Coscarelli.

Ten very long, very quiet minutes went by. Nat was pretty much convinced by that point that Walsh wasn't going to surface when she spotted a figure emerge from the shadows of a darkened building a few doors down from the bar.

"We got something," a voice hissed over the walkie-talkie.

"We make it," Oates said.

Coscarelli's hand was on the door knob. Nat's hand darted out for his shoulder. "Let me try to speak to him, Leo. It might save more than just his life."

Coscarelli gave her one quick glance. "You move from that seat and I'll have you tossed in the clink for obstructing justice. Do I make myself clear?"

"He's heading for the Caddie," Oates said.

Nat saw Owen King emerge from the Caddie and give a wave.

"Showdown time." Excitement rang in Oates's voice. As he opened the driver's side door Nat could hear the cock of his semiautomatic. The two detectives both sprinted from the car at the same time.

Nat knew Walsh was armed and she was terrified he'd try to shoot his way out of this trap before turning the gun on himself.

She watched the figure freeze no more than five feet from the Caddie as a half dozen armed cops moved in from every direction. Owen King ducked back into the safety of the car.

She heard Coscarelli issue the order for Walsh to drop to the pavement, arms behind his back.

Walsh didn't budge. She knew what was coming.

Nat couldn't stand it another second. Jumping out of the car, she started running up the street. "Dean, don't do anything foolish," she shouted frantically. "It'll only make everything worse."

Walsh looked in her direction, then suddenly started to pivot around as if to bolt. A shot rang out, then a high-pitched scream.

Nat watched in horror as Walsh crumpled to the ground. The cops started to converge on the fallen man when Coscarelli shouted for them to stay put. "You, too, Price," he barked without a backwards glance at her.

Gun cocked and aimed, he alone made his way cautiously over to the body slumped on the pavement. Nat's breath caught in her throat. Walsh might still be alive. Might decide not to go down by himself. Might decide to take Leo Coscarelli with him.

The other cops had their guns trained on the still unmoving body as Leo gingerly bent down over him, checked quickly but thoroughly to see if he was armed, then checked for a pulse.

"Call in," he shouted. "We got a live one." He rose slowly, shoulders slumped. He looked back over his shoulder at his men. Avoiding her. "What we haven't got is Walsh."

The man who'd been shot came around a couple of hours later at Boston City Hospital. Fortunately, the bullet wound turned out to be superficial. It was his head hitting the pavement that had knocked him out cold. Cursing the pain in his head and his shoulder, he identified himself as Roy Sawyer, a 32-year-old out-of-work house painter. He swore up and down that he didn't know Dean Thomas Walsh from Adam—pausing only to swear just as vociferously that he was going to sue the Boston Police Department for a million bucks for shooting at an innocent man.

"Tell me again," Coscarelli said calmly, ignoring his threats, "how you hooked up with Walsh."

"Jeez, how many times do you have to hear this?" Sawyer once more recounted how he and Walsh met at a bar on Clark Street— a few blocks from Monte's Place—around nine that night, punctuating how it was the first time he'd ever seen him in his life. They had a few drinks together, shooting the breeze, Walsh picking up the tab. Next thing he knows, Walsh's offering him a hundred bucks if he'd meet a pal of his at ten and deliver a message for him. On account of Walsh forgot he had someplace else he had to be.

"And where was that?" Coscarelli quizzed him.

Sawyer started to shrug, but grimaced in pain and grabbed his bandaged shoulder. "He didn't say. What did I care where he had to be?"

"And you said yes? No questions asked?"

"A hundred bucks is a lot of dough when you got ten dollars and seventeen cents to your name, man. Besides, the message was just a note in an envelope. Meaning no drugs or anything illegal that could get me in hot water." He let out a weak but gruff laugh.

Nat had watched Coscarelli retrieve the envelope from Sawyer's jacket pocket while the man was still out cold on the pavement. She saw him stick it into his own pocket. She assumed he'd read it, but he hadn't shared its contents with her.

She wasn't sure why he was still letting her tag along with him. Maybe simply to keep an eye on her, afraid she might have otherwise joined in on the police canvassing of the Washington Street area for Walsh. Coscarelli definitely thought she was no match for Walsh and if she was the one that ended up drawing him out of hiding, Walsh would as soon shoot her as shoot himself. Nat knew that was a serious possibility.

They remained for a short time longer while Coscarelli again demanded a recounting from Sawyer of what Walsh was wearing when they met at the bar. More exhausted than angry at this point, the painkillers having their desired effect, Sawyer slurred his words slightly as he described Walsh as wearing a blue work shirt, dark pants, scuffed hi-tops. On the stool beside him was a gray and red windbreaker. Sawyer assumed it was Walsh's because Walsh had that envelope folded up in one of the pockets.

"Was it a long-sleeved shirt?" Nat asked. Her first question to Sawyer.

Both men looked over at her. Sawyer nodded. "Yeah, I think so. Yeah."

"Did you see his wrists?"

Sawyer scowled. "You mean the bandages. Yeah, I spotted one when he reached for the envelope in his windbreaker."

"He say anything about it? Like what had happened?" she persisted.

"He didn't volunteer, but I asked him. He got all weepy—I think a lot of it was probably the booze—and he tells me how his girlfriend betrayed him something bad—and he tried to kill himself. Only then he realized she wasn't worth it, so he didn't slice too deep."

"Yeah, sure, now you gonna let me walk," Owen King said sardonically. "With Walsh still out there on the street, seriously gunning for me since he knows I set him up."

"Hey, you want to stay in jail, we can arrange it real easy," Coscarelli told him.

"No thanks." King glared at him. "But I'm tellin' you both, ain't no way I'm gonna be sittin' back waiting for that punk to come after my ass."

"That would be a switch, wouldn't it," Nat couldn't keep herself from saying.

nineteen

Confusion, grief, depression, anger, changes in sleeping habits are some of the symptoms of a stress reaction. . . .

Dr. James Fenwick
Stress Reduction Program

IT WAS ALMOST one in the morning when Coscarelli brought her back to her apartment. This time when he offered to take her to her door, she didn't argue.

"The bullet the doc pulled out of Sawyer. It wasn't police issue," he told her as they rode up in the elevator.

"You think it was Walsh? But why—?"

"Keep the poor dupe from talking, I guess."

He didn't sound convinced. Neither was Nat. Sawyer didn't know all that much. Unless he was lying or not telling the whole story.

She got her keys out as they got to her floor. "The maintenance man's supposed to change my lock tomorrow."

"Good. Keep your chain on meantime."

She opened the door and flicked on the light, aware of a tightness in her muscles until she saw that everything looked normal.

"Why don't you check around and see if there are any more poems lying about?" Coscarelli suggested, stepping inside behind her. "Don't forget to check under your pillows."

She felt a little shiver creep down her spine.

"You want me to look?" he said in a softer voice.

"No, it's okay." She headed for her bedroom, wanting to get the worst over with first. A minute later she returned to tell him she didn't find anything. Coscarelli wasn't there. Nat found him in the kitchen, pouring out a glass of milk.

"Help yourself," she said sardonically.

"It's for you. I didn't see any honey. Warm milk and honey is just the thing to help you sleep."

"What makes you think I'll need help sleeping?"

Ignoring her, he rummaged around in her spice cupboard, finally extracting a small tin. "The secret ingredient. A few pinches of nutmeg."

"Is that what you give your wife when she has trouble sleeping?"

"No," he said succinctly, using that same *don't go there* voice Nat was so adept at using herself.

Different when the shoe was on the other foot. "I don't get you, Leo. You share secret ingredients for sleep potions, but you can't even acknowledge the existence of your wife. What happened? You two split up? She run off with another guy?"

"I don't have a wife."

Sensing he'd say more if she kept her mouth shut, Nat did just that. It worked.

"Jacob's mother's in prison. She's doing three to five for manslaughter. Killed her crack dealer."

One way to get off drugs. Nat kept the thought to herself.

"It's a long, sad story." Coscarelli frowned. "Maybe not so long. She's only twenty-four. But she's packed a lot of life into those twenty-four years."

He went silent but Nat could see his mind was still going a mile a minute. Remembering. Ruminating. Censoring.

"And your son?" she prodded.

From the look he gave her, she was sure he was going to tell her none of this was any of her business. Nat imagined it was a look he wore a lot. Something they had in common.

"Hey, I don't mean to pry," she said, more to fill up the silence than because she meant it.

Coscarelli smiled. Letting her know he saw right through her.

Nat hesitated. "Is he . . . yours? I mean . . . biologically?"

"You mean did I *knock her up*? Yeah. Guilty," he said gruffly. "Only I don't feel guilty. You get a kid like Jacob and all you do is feel grateful. He's the best thing that ever happened to me in my life." And there was now such tenderness and love in his voice that Nat felt herself start to tear up.

She turned away so he wouldn't notice, but she wasn't quick enough. "What about you, Natalie? Did you and Ethan want kids?"

"One of us did," she said bleakly, glancing back at him.

Although she didn't specify which, Coscarelli nodded. A no-brainer.

The shrill ring of the phone woke her from a sound sleep. She blindly reached for it and grunted, "What?" into the receiver.

"Can I come over?"

"Are you serious?" she said groggily.

"Just for a few minutes."

Nat squinted at the illuminated dial on her clock radio. "It's almost three o'clock in the morning."

"Please, Nat. I'm going out of my mind here. I've got to talk to you. Don't make me beg. I felt rotten enough without having to get down and crawl on my hands and knees. Anyhow, there's something important I've got to tell you."

"And it can't wait?"

"No. I might . . . lose my nerve."

"Is it about Maggie?"

"Yeah. About Maggie."

Fully awake now, she swung her legs off the bed onto the floor. The empty cup of milk and honey was sitting on her bedside table. She'd have to tell Coscarelli it did the trick. Until the phone woke her up.

"All right, Jack."

He appeared in worse shape than he had on Friday night. But he looked to be sober. Which was a good thing or else she would have probably slammed the door in his face.

"Where were you all night?" He walked ahead of her into her living room tossing the question over his shoulder.

"You didn't come here at three o'clock in the morning to ask me how I spent my evening, Jack," she said, deliberately skirting the answer. Nat wasn't sure why she didn't want Jack to know about the failed Walsh sting, but she didn't.

He walked over to the couch, but he remained on his feet. Abruptly changing his mind, he headed over to the window. Her curtains were drawn, but he pulled one side back and stared out into the dark.

"I can't sleep," he muttered, his back still to her.

"What's on your mind?"

"Maggie. Maggie's on my mind."

"Care to elaborate?"

"I think I was in love with her."

No big surprise there.

He turned slowly to face her. "That cop, Coscarelli, thinks I might be . . . the one." Nat saw his Adam's apple bob as he swallowed.

"I'm pretty sure Walsh still tops his list."

Jack squinted. "He sure the hell tops mine."

"Were you home all day Friday, Jack?"

He looked physically pained by her question—a betrayal of trust—and Nat immediately wished she could take it back. Which was why she was shaken to the core when his response was, "No."

He walked back to the couch, sitting down this time. Nat remained standing near the living room entry although her knees were more than a little wobbly. Holding herself up seemed preferable at the moment to getting too close to Jack.

"Did you see Maggie on Friday?" she asked raspily, her throat having gone dry.

She didn't get an answer. Jack didn't look like he was listening.

When he spoke, it sounded more like he was talking to himself than to Nat. "Maggie was a very complicated woman. Which I think would surprise a lot of people."

He cast her a glance like he was including her in that group. Nat felt a surge of resentment. Again thinking, where did he come off . . . ?

"She was real fearless about so many things. But she was scared out of her mind of intimacy. Whenever I'd call her on it, you know what she'd do?"

Clearly a rhetorical question, so Nat remained silent.

"She'd seduce me. Like sex would prove I was wrong. Or maybe she was just hoping to distract me. Which it damn well did. She was good. The best. Maggie put her heart and soul into it. She once told me sex was how she expressed herself creatively."

Nat folded her hands across her chest. "The last thing I want to hear about is your and Maggie's sex life."

"I guess the fact that she loved sex so much was why I got it into my head I wasn't the only one she was *creatively expressing herself* with. One night, about a week ago, I accused her of getting it on with Walsh. She reacted like I'd physically slapped her. She asked me to leave. And the way she said it . . . she meant leave and never come back. I fell over myself, apologizing. Trying to take it back. Calling myself a dumb, jealous idiot."

"Jack," Nat said irritably, "where is all this leading?"

Another pause, this one rife with tension. "I did go over to her place Friday."

Nat was clutching herself now. Holding herself together. Like she might otherwise come unglued on the spot. "You . . . saw her?"

He shook his head vigorously. "See, I knew she was meeting Walsh for lunch. I saw she'd written his name in her appointment book."

Jack was stalking Maggie? The thought turned Nat's blood cold. *Who is this man I thought I knew? This man I trusted?*

"I wasn't thinking straight that morning. Doped up on cold remedies. Drinking a little. My head got going. Picturing them up in her apartment. In her bed. Picturing Maggie in the throes of orgasm. Such a sight. You don't know. I went a little nuts. Don't even remember driving over there. But once I got to her building, I . . . snapped out of it. Realized that if I showed up at her door, she'd see the jealousy and suspicion written all over my face and . . . and that would be it. She'd call it quits. No *ifs*, *ands*, or *buts*."

Nat watched as tears began silently streaming down his face. "I turned the car around and drove home. He might have been raping her . . . killing her . . . as . . . as I did that broken U-turn. I might have . . . saved her. And lost her at the same time. That's irony for you, all right."

Tears were rolling down her face, too.

"Nat, you do believe me?" Jack gave her an imploring look.

Did she? She had to believe him. Anything else was too . . . unimaginable.

Without conscious thought, Nat walked over to Jack, sank down beside him on her sofa.

She didn't know who made the first move. All she knew was they were holding each other. Clinging. Sobbing. Their tears, their pain, their loss, mingling.

You crossed a line and it couldn't be uncrossed; a moment passed and there was no taking it back. But the line was invisible so you didn't know precisely when you'd crossed it. And the moment snuck up on you and flew past before you even realized it had come, much less gone.

They were still holding each other, though no longer crying, when that moment approached. His lips were moving toward her neck and as soon as they touched her sensitive flesh, an involuntary moan escaped her lips. Action. Reaction. At once simple and complex. A moment before, they were merely friends comforting each other. In the blink of an eye—a split second—they had become something more.

His lips found their way to hers. His tasted of salt, desire and despair. Nat imagined hers must taste the same to him.

There was no tentativeness in that first kiss. None of this— testing the waters. The water was deep as hell. They both knew that. They could easily drown in those waters, already swept up in the current as they were.

Their kiss was hard and fiercely sexual. And yet, oddly enough, not passionate. It wasn't a distinction Nat could explain. Only one she could feel. Like she felt the heaviness in the air.

His hands were yanking up her sweater when she broke away. Jack looked stunned by her withdrawal. And then a shadow of some other emotion crossed his face. Irritation? Anger? It had been too quick for her to discern.

Now his expression was contrite. "Nat . . ."

She held up a hand. "Don't." She quickly straightened her clothes. Involuntarily swiped her lips with the back of her hand.

Had she completely lost it? Shame and guilt enveloped her.

And what about Jack? How could he have made a play for her so soon after the cold-blooded murder of the woman he professed having loved so deeply? Was he feeling so desperate, so needy, so lost? Or was he so shallow, not to mention promiscuous?

Or was she merely projecting? Was this as much, if not more, to do with her unresolved feelings for Jack than his for her? And her feelings about Maggie?

Jack rose. "I . . . I didn't mean for this to happen, Nat."

She nodded again, unable to meet his gaze.

"I know what you must be thinking. . . ."

Nat looked directly at him then. "How can you know? I'm not even sure myself."

Something flickered across Jack's face, but Nat couldn't put her finger on what it was. She only knew that she found it disturbing. And, yes, a little frightening.

It was nearly four A.M., less than an hour after Jack left, when her phone rang again. She was wide awake this time, too worked up to sleep. She reached for the phone, certain it was Jack. His departure had been so awkward and uncomfortable for both of them. Neither of them had known what to say. Nat still didn't. And she wasn't sure she was ready to hear whatever it was Jack had come up with to say. Mostly because she didn't know if she could believe him.

"It's late, Jack," she said wearily into the phone, hoping to forestall him.

"You set me up, Nat."

She stiffened at the sound of Dean Thomas Walsh's voice. "No. That's not—"

"I could have hurt you, Nat. But I didn't. I even got my sister to let the cops know where they could find you after I stuck you in that trunk. It was an act of good faith. Because I thought you were the one person other than Chrissy who'd believe me."

"The longer you stay out there, Dean, the harder—"

"I'm not listening to you. You betrayed me. You and that Judas, Owen King. I owe you both. Next time—"

"Dean, let's meet someplace and talk—"

He laughed harshly. "Next time we meet, Nat, I won't be talking. And neither will you."

There was absolute silence on the line. Even though she didn't hear the click Nat thought he must have hung up. She was about to do the same, when Walsh's voice came through in an anguished whisper. "Do you see what you've all made of me?"

And then she did hear the click and the phone was dead.

She held onto the receiver for several moments. There was a tremor that ran down her arm into her fingers. She was aware her breathing had quickened. That she was close to hyperventilating.

She had to get ahold of herself. She had to phone Leo. But there would be so many questions and right now she had no answers. She needed a bit of time.

twenty

When you were a child, your days filled with glee
Did you ever imagine a time you wouldn't be free?
Did you ever imagine a life behind bars?
A life without daylight, a life without stars?
A life without your wife to hold you tight?
A life without your children to kiss you good-night?

K.F.
Inmate #694837

SHE WAS AT Horizon House first thing Monday morning, dictating a staff memorandum to her clerk about what she was desperately hoping would be a short-lived lockdown. She'd had no word from above as to when business as normal could be resumed. Although she kept it to herself, Nat was in strong agreement with the inmates that they shouldn't have to suffer indefinitely because of one bad apple. Just how bad was debatable. Sides were being taken among inmates as to whether Walsh was a murderer or merely an escapee. The staff seemed far less ambivalent. They appeared to be in agreement that Walsh was guilty on both counts. Despite his threatening phone call, Nat still found herself going back and forth—was he a killer or merely an innocent man on the run, terrified of being convicted of a crime he didn't do? And then Nat was brought up short remembering the disappearance of Alison Cole and felt sick with dread.

After her clerk left, Nat shut her eyes, letting the tears slip past her closed lids. She tried to search inwardly for a reserve of strength, but she couldn't seem to locate it. She was just too bone-tired. And yet the few hours of sleep she had managed to grab over the last few days had been so fraught with nightmare visions that, if anything, it made her more tired still.

Ironically, when she opened her eyes she was shocked to realize close to an hour had passed. She saw that her hand was resting on top of the Walsh file on her desk. And this was the strangest thing. She felt a physical vibration move across her palm. As though it was literally emanating from that file. Either she was really losing it, still half-asleep, or this was a symptom of post-traumatic stress. Probably a combination of all three.

Something niggled at her after she flipped through the file. Something in it had struck a particular chord. She started going through each of the pages again. And then she saw it. A notation in the CCI Norton Exit Report—

NOTE: On 3/14/98, inmate Keith Franklin, another student in Ms. Austin's writing class at CCI Norton, turned over to the Charge Officer a copy of a poem written by Dean that he felt was "out of line." Franklin made a point of saying that he was only coming forward with it now because he was up for release. Otherwise, he was scared Walsh would retaliate in some way. CO notes that there has been tension in the past between these two inmates, but neither of them has been written up.

Keith Franklin. The same inmate that Owen King had told her last night had the hots for Maggie. That's why Franklin's name had rung a bell. She'd come across it the first time she'd gone through Walsh's file.

"Hutch is worried about you," Jack told her when she stopped by his office in the late afternoon to tell him she had to go out and ask him to hold down the fort.

"Did he say why?"

Instead of answering, Jack said, "I'm worried about you, too." His eyes lingered on her face a few beats too long for comfort.

"You both worry too much," she said, trying for a light tone.

Jack was not buying. "Let's go get some dinner tonight, then catch some mindless comedy flick."

"I don't think that's such a good idea." She found it hard meeting his intent gaze.

"I knew you'd beat yourself up over what happened," Jack said softly. He started toward her, but she stepped back.

"It shouldn't have happened. We both know that," she said sharply.

"It was a kiss." An impish smile. "Okay, more than a kiss. But it meant something, Nat. To me, anyway."

Jack had stayed put, but now Nat strode up to him. "What does it mean, Jack? Does it mean what it meant when you were seducing Maggie? Remember Maggie, Jack? The woman you were so passionately in love with?"

His turn to back away a step. "That's unfair, Nat. And cruel."

"I'll tell you what's unfair and cruel. Maggie being raped and murdered."

They stared each other down for several seconds. Nat looked away first.

He took firm hold of her shoulders, but there was no hint of an intended embrace. "Don't go playing amateur detective, Nat. It could get you seriously hurt."

"You worried for my safety, Jack? Or yours?"

"Another low blow, Nat. Maybe I was wrong confiding in you." He dropped his hands, sounding more hurt than angry.

Her anger, however, was revving into high gear. "Yeah, maybe you were."

Nat experienced two surprises when she showed up at Keith Franklin's place a couple of blocks south of Watertown Square close to dinnertime on Monday. One was, despite the rundown condition of the three-decker, the ex-con's two-bedroom street-level apartment was freshly painted, expensively decorated with contemporary furnishings of the buttery leather, chrome and glass variety, and tidy as a pin. The second and more disquieting surprise was, not only did Nat find Keith and Terri Franklin at home, but Leo Coscarelli and his partner, Mitchell Oates, as well. Coscarelli didn't seem the least bit surprised by her arrival. That wasn't to say he appeared the least bit pleased either. Ditto for Oates, and for Terri Franklin, a petite brunette with thin, worried lips and premature stress lines on her drawn, twenty-five-year-old face.

As for Keith Franklin, whatever his true feelings, he was obsequiously welcoming. Dressed in a well-tailored dark blue serge suit, stiffly starched white shirt, navy rep tie, he reminded Nat of the earnest young funeral director who'd made the arrangements for her mother's burial two years ago. She knew from Franklin's parole record that the thirty-three-year-old former accountant was now a clerk in a small plumbing and heating company in Somerville. Doubtful his low-level job demanded such formal attire. Maybe he felt better dressing the way he used to in his pre-prison days when he'd held a more prominent position as a CPA. Or maybe he simply didn't have the money to buy a new, more appropriate wardrobe. Nat was presuming the suits, like the upscale home furnishings, were the accoutrements of his former, more financially comfortable life. A life that took a sharp dip the day Franklin got caught cooking the books at a prestigious Boston accounting firm. A question of two hundred grand that the accountant had to make *disappear* as he'd borrowed that sum over the course of six months to cover some very bad stock investments bought on margin.

"Terri was just going to put up coffee, Superintendent Price. Or if you'd rather tea—"

"I think I better go feed the twins, Keith," Terri interrupted, nervously popping up from her seat. "In fact, why don't I take them on down to McDonald's?" As soon as that magic word was spoken a door flew open across the room and two tow-haired children, a boy and a girl, who looked to be around seven years old, sprang into the room and crowded around their mother.

"Yeah, McDonald's, goodie."

"I want the Happy Meal. But no cheese."

"I want cheese but no pickle. And a chocolate shake."

"Can we each have our own, Mommy? Danny always hogs—"

"I do not."

"Children," Keith Franklin scolded. "Company manners, please."

Danny and his sister ignored the admonition and continued to argue over who hogged the shake.

"If you don't behave, no McDonald's," Keith said. More sharply now.

The children scowled. "You're not the boss," Danny piped up.

"Yeah, Mommy can take us anywhere she wants," his twin sister chirped in.

Keith flushed. Nat wasn't sure if it was due to embarrassment or anger.

Terri took firm hold of each twin's shoulder. "Don't be fresh. Now apologize to your father or there'll be no Happy Meals for either of you."

Two half-hearted "sorrys" were mumbled before the twins dashed for the door, Terri close at their heels. A woman in a hurry to leave.

"They're at that age," Franklin said awkwardly. "How 'bout that coffee?"

Coscarelli and Oates both shook their heads. After a brief hesitation, so did Nat.

Franklin brushed off imaginary crumbs from the arm of his butter cream leather armchair. "Three years is a long time when you're a kid. They were just turning five when I was . . . incarcerated. Just starting kindergarten. I missed seeing them their first day of school. Terri sent photos, but—"

"Did she bring them to visit you?" Nat asked, aware of the searing glances from both detectives. She knew they were not happy to have her brazenly butting into their investigation. Stepping on their homicide detectives' toes. If Franklin picked up on the officers' irritation, he gave no sign of it.

"Neither of us thought it was a good idea for them to know where I was." He hesitated. "She told them I had to go away on business. For a time, I guess they'd ask when I was coming back, but after a while—kids that age, they . . . forget. It's been almost four months. I'm back and they're still . . . getting used to having a daddy again. I'm having to get used to it again, too. Sometimes I'm a little short with them. Terri gets upset. Tells me I've got to give it time. I'm trying." Franklin produced a wan smile. "I want desperately to do right by my children. And by my wife. She didn't have to stick it out, but she did. And I swear I'll do everything I can not to make her regret it."

There was something about his earnest recitation that seemed a bit off. Not fabricated of whole cloth, but embellished for their benefit.

"Have you had any contact with Maggie Austin since your release, Mr. Franklin?" Oates asked gruffly, hoping to circumvent any further interruption.

Ironically, Franklin chose to address Nat. "As I told the detectives just before you arrived, Superintendent Price, we didn't stay in touch. I also told them," Franklin hurried on, "that I was at work on Friday when she was—" He left off the rest of the sentence, shaking his head sadly.

"Did you eat lunch at work?" Coscarelli asked.

"No. Actually I came home for lunch. I usually do. It's only two stops on the T."

And only a fifteen-minute cab ride over to Maggie's apartment, Nat thought.

"Saves money," Franklin was saying. "And Terri's cooking is a lot better than I'd get in the local coffee shop," he added with a little smile.

"So your wife was here when you came home for lunch?" Oates asked.

Franklin's smile dipped. "Well . . . no. She works part-time. Teacher's aide at the twins' school. Tuesdays, Thursdays, and Fridays. Pay's not great but she's out by three and like she said, at least we're not raising latchkey kids."

"Did anyone see you here during lunch, Keith?" Coscarelli jumped in.

Franklin frowned. "I don't understand why I'm being interrogated like this. Surely you have no doubts about who murdered Ms. Austin. Walsh was obsessed with her. Everyone in that class knew. It was obvious. Every time she paid attention to any of the rest of us, you could literally feel him seething. There was this one time she read aloud a short story I'd written. I didn't think it was particularly good, but she really liked it. Said a lot of nice things to me. I was . . . flattered. Walsh cornered me that night in the showers. Put a knife to my . . ." He burned scarlet and looked down at his crotch. "Told me not to go getting any . . . horny ideas or he'd . . . castrate me." Franklin looked back up at them. "I never handed in another piece of writing. Never spoke in class again. Tried not to even make eye contact with her."

"You were terrified of Walsh and yet you turned one of his poems over to a CO and tried to get Walsh thrown out of class," Nat said. "Didn't you think that might get him mad enough to carry out his threat?"

"I'm sure it did. Which is why I waited until the day I was getting out on parole." A shadow of fear crossed Franklin's thin features. "Now that he's on the loose, I don't mind telling you that I'm terrified he might come looking for me. To even up the score." He seemed to drift for a minute. "You wouldn't know it to look at him."

"What's that?" Nat asked.

"His capacity for brutality." He drifted again. "She . . . didn't understand. She totally misjudged him. And now . . ." His voice was quivering. "Walsh killed her. As sure as we're sitting here, he killed her."

Coscarelli leaned forward aggressively in his seat. "How can you be that sure, Keith?"

"Either Franklin knows more than he's telling," Nat muttered, "or he's clairvoyant."

"Or he's lying," Coscarelli said, his tone clipped.

They were heading down Lowell Street to their respective cars, Oates having already taken off to question some of Franklin's co-workers. They arrived at Coscarelli's unmarked cruiser first.

"I know what you're trying to do," he said.

"So do I," Nat said, not missing a beat. "I'm trying to find the man who murdered my best friend."

"And you're determined to find someone outside the House to pin this on."

"Let's just say I'm keeping an open mind."

"Bullshit," Coscarelli said.

Nat felt a wave of guilt. Must have looked guilty, too, from the way the detective was studying her.

"I heard from Walsh early this morning," she admitted. She repeated pretty accurately their brief phone conversation. Save for the implied threat. Not that Coscarelli wasn't smart enough to read between the lines. What she was coming to see was that the detective was smarter, in general, than she'd initially given him credit for. And he had more of a temper.

He pointed a trigger finger at her. "You're on damn thin ice here, Superintendent. I could bust your ass for not reporting that call the minute Walsh hung up. Not only could I have you cooling your jets behind bars for withholding evidence, you'd be kissing your career good-bye."

"I'll probably be doing that anyway," she snapped. "So go ahead. Bust me. But if you think that's going to stop me, guess again, Detective. I will not be frozen out of this investigation. I'm in this to the bitter end," she added, with grim determination.

"That's what I'm afraid of," Coscarelli said, his tone equally grim.

"So now what?" she asked.

"We put a tap on your phone."

"I mean where do we go from here?" For all her bravado, Nat silently prayed it wasn't to a holding cell.

Coscarelli's back got a bit more rigid and he crossed his arms over his chest. This was accompanied by a slight head tilt and a lift of the left eyebrow. A lot of body language for one measly question. Only they both knew there was a lot implied behind the question.

He placed his hand on the roof of his car, did a little rat-a-tat-tat on the metal. "I'm heading over to Karen Powell's place. Got a few questions to ask her." He gave Nat a sideways glance. "You know the way?"

Well, Nat thought, the detective was full of surprises. Her eyes fixed on him, she nodded.

"Okay, I'll follow you."

twenty-one

The individual will experience physical, psychological and behavioral changes subsequent to the stress-producing event. . . .

Dr. Roger Harris
Expert in Post-Traumatic Stress

COSCARELLI SWUNG INTO the yellow tow-away zone directly in front of an early nineteenth-century brick building on gas-lit Joy Street in Boston's old money Beacon Hill section. The advantage of having made friends with a cop—although Nat could be overstating their newfound camaraderie—was that she got to park there too. Otherwise, the closest non-resident space was several hilly blocks away at a parking garage on Charles Street. Coscarelli even slipped an official BPD card on her dash to ensure she'd find her car at the curb when they returned.

There was no strategy talk as they approached the apartment house. No talk at all. Nat watched as Coscarelli slid his finger down the set of six buzzers to the side of the carved oak and glass front door to the building. Karen Powell's was the second from the bottom. Coscarelli pressed it.

It took a good thirty seconds before Karen answered. And then there was a long pause after Coscarelli identified himself— he didn't mention Nat was with him or her hunch was the pause might have been even longer.

"Could you give me a couple of minutes? I'm . . . not dressed." And in what sounded like an afterthought, Karen added, "I was napping."

"Where's her money come from?" Coscarelli asked as they stood outside under the ornate copper canopy, waiting to be buzzed in.

"Trust fund from what Maggie told me. She said Karen never gave her much in the way of details. Maggie thought Karen was embarrassed about being so well-off. That was supposedly why she never suggested her place for dinner whenever the three of us got together. I guess she wasn't particularly embarrassed about Maggie knowing since Maggie spent a lot of time over here."

"So you've never been in Karen's apartment?"

"Once, last winter. But I wasn't exactly invited over. Maggie and I had plans that evening and she asked me to pick her up in front of Karen's building. I got here early."

"How early?"

"It was early enough and cold enough so that it would have been obviously rude to keep me waiting outside. Even for Karen."

Nat caught a glint of grief in Karen's dark eyes before she saw her at the door, standing just off to Coscarelli's right. As soon as she spotted Nat, Karen looked clearly shaken and had to take a moment to compose herself.

"Nat," she said with a mix of puzzlement and pained polite- ness as they stepped into a high-ceilinged semi-circular marble foyer lit by a sculpturesque glass fixture that shed a warm glow on the gilt-framed signed Chagall etching hanging on the stuccoed pale mauve wall.

She led the way to her living room. The one-bedroom apartment was small, but what it lacked in size it made up for in stark elegance. The marble flooring gave way to red oak in the bay-windowed living room, but the mauve coloring was carried through, accented here with touches of a deep ocher in the moldings and trim. The spare furnishings, all in varying driftwood shades, were Italian modern. Crisp lines. Sleek. Pristine. Steely cool. The place was devoid of decorative flourishes save for the abstract Kandinsky pen-and-ink drawing over the travertine marble mantel.

Nat could have easily used some of these same descriptive words to describe Karen Powell, whose appearance went so well with her decor. Fashionably slender, a boyish no-fuss blond bob, never a trace of makeup. Her style of dress was simple, tailored, unadorned. She was big on natural fibers. If you didn't know better, you'd wonder why anyone would pay such a fortune for clothing so spare and basic. Nat knew better. So did Maggie. Karen's designer wardrobe—gray cotton slacks and a pale lime silk blouse today—screamed class.

There was only one aspect of Karen's otherwise patrician appearance that didn't quite compute. Her large, dark eyes. Maggie used to postulate that there must have been a gypsy somewhere back in Karen's ancestry. It was the eyes that gave Karen character, that showed hunger, need, curiosity, jealousy. If the eyes were a window into the soul, then all Nat could say was Karen's soul was rife with heavy emotions. She doubted that Maggie's teaching assistant knew how much her eyes gave away.

Nat glanced over at Coscarelli to see if he was admiring the posh surroundings or the posh owner, but his gaze was aimed in the direction of Karen's bedroom. Although the door to the bedroom was only partially open, there was enough of a view into the room to see that the large queen-sized bed was fully made up. And it didn't look like a hurried job. Since neither of the wheat leather and chrome love seats in the living room looked like they'd make a comfy spot for napping, it definitely brought into question the reason for Karen's delay tactics. Could she have had a guest? Someone who'd slipped out the back entrance? Or who was hiding out somewhere in the apartment even now, waiting for them to leave?

Who would be up there that Karen wouldn't want seen by the cops?

"I couldn't bring myself to go into her office today even though there's so much that has to be done," Karen offered in conjunction with some serious hand wringing. "Her classes have been canceled for the week. A number of her students have been calling me. They want to attend her funeral." Karen gave Coscarelli a sharp look. "When is the coroner going to release her body?"

"I'm not sure yet."

"I've spoken with Maggie's aunt. She's too distraught to make the arrangements so I offered to take care of things." Karen announced this without so much as a glance in Nat's direction.

"Maggie wanted to be cremated. And she didn't want a church service," Nat said tightly. There was plenty more she wanted to say, but that would have opened the floodgates. Not only Nat's, but she was sure Karen's as well.

"When did she tell you that?" Karen's intonation was icy.

"When we were in grad school," Nat said, matching the T.A.'s frigid tone. "And she never said anything different to me in the last thirteen years," she emphasized, establishing the long duration of their close friendship.

"Well, she told me quite the opposite."

"Really? When was that?" Nat's mouth pulled tighter.

Karen smoothed the wispy blond bangs off her forehead.

"Maggie and I had many heart-to-hearts. About life, and death. We used to ruminate on who would show up at our funerals."

"Kind of morbid, isn't it?" Coscarelli stepped in.

Karen smiled coyly. "Haven't you ever wondered, Detective?"

Leo wasn't buying the flirtation. Apparently he was a man with a one-track mind. Or maybe, like Nat, he saw that Karen's come-hither smile didn't reach her eyes. No hint of flirtation was reflected there. Only wariness.

"Did Maggie ever feel she was in any kind of mortal danger?" he asked in that same cool, deliberate tone that, when used on Nat, she found so irritating. Nat wasn't irritated now. But Karen was.

She picked up a pack of Kools and a silver Zippo lighter from her green tinted glass coffee table, tapped out a cigarette and lit it. Nat had never seen Karen smoke before. But she dragged on that cigarette like a pro. Like someone who'd recently fallen off the nicotine wagon.

"Ever since she started teaching at that damn prison she was in danger. The terrible thing is she didn't know it. Or she refused to see it." She dragged deeply again, letting the smoke out slowly as if she didn't want to part with it. "And then encouraging them to join her class when they got out. I used to tell her it was one thing to go to the zoo, but would you invite a tiger into your home?"

Comments like that—Nat had heard them from plenty of people, her sister included—usually triggered her spiel about how inmates were not animals. But then Nat thought about Walsh.

Leo was thinking about the escaped convict, too. "How often did she have Dean Walsh to her home?" he asked Karen.

"One time too often," she said with conviction, her dark eyes flashing unmasked hatred. Some of which Nat knew was directed straight at her. Add Karen to her list of people who blamed her for Maggie's murder. Not that Nat hadn't put herself on that list as well.

"Who else visited?" Coscarelli continued, staying unwaveringly on track.

"Jack Dwyer."

Heat rose up Nat's neck the instant Karen said his name.

"He was always popping over. Far more often than he was invited," Karen added, after another long, deliberate drag of the mentholated cigarette.

"What's that supposed to mean?" Nat demanded.

"Maggie told me on more than one occasion that she was thinking seriously of dumping Jack. She was troubled by his possessiveness."

What Nat wanted to say was, *And what about your possessiveness, Karen?* But once again she was thinking about Jack confiding to her that he drove over there on Friday afternoon. Nat was also thinking about his jealousy. Thinking about Maggie's implicit threat to end the relationship if he didn't get that jealousy under control.

What if Jack didn't just turn around and drive home that day? What if, when he got to Maggie's, he saw someone leaving her building? Saw Dean Thomas Walsh? Or even Ethan? What if, filled with jealousy, he went upstairs to confront Maggie? And she, in turn, got angry and told him they were through . . . ?

Nat had seen Jack lose his temper. Lose control.

Her heart was starting to slam against her rib cage. *Is that why Jack tried to seduce me? To keep me in his corner? Keep me quiet? Keep me from suspecting him of anything so heinous as the murder of his lover? Of my best friend?*

Nat felt ill. She couldn't deny that she had come closer to succumbing to Jack's seduction than she liked to admit.

Karen was busy stubbing out her cigarette in an otherwise spotlessly clean crystal candy dish. Leo was busy looking at Nat. Like he was reading her mind. How strongly did he suspect Jack? How angry would he be at her when he found out she was once again withholding potential evidence. He'd let her off the hook when she didn't tell him about Ethan seeing Maggie the day she was murdered. Nat doubted he'd go so easy on her if he found out she'd kept quiet about her deputy's ride over to Maggie's building on Friday. The homicide detective would be well within his rights to charge her for withholding evidence, obstructing justice. Lock her up. And yet, Nat couldn't bring herself to reveal what Jack had confided in her. Couldn't believe, for all her disturbing musing, that Jack had killed Maggie.

So maybe, in a sense, his seduction had worked.

Nat was grateful when Leo directed his focus back on Karen. Asking, "Were there any other visitors?"

Karen mulled this over. "I know some of the inmates used to phone her from prison. Walsh was always calling before—and after—he got out. But there were others from her class."

"Who?" Nat asked, beating Leo to the punch.

She shrugged. "Maggie never said. Probably because she knew I disapproved strongly of the whole business," she added, with those expressive eyes that said *unlike you.*

"No other cons who used to phone her after they got out?" Leo stepped back in.

Another shrug. "Possibly, but I doubt she entertained any of the others. The truth is, even though Maggie proclaimed an open door policy, she was only turned on by the ones with talent. And she thought Dean Thomas Walsh was exceptional in that department."

"Was she sleeping with him?" Coscarelli's question came like an unexpected left hook that caught both Karen and Nat unawares.

Nat felt a second jab from the right when Karen said, after lighting up another cigarette, "I told her she was crazy. That he was probably infected with the HIV virus. He'd told her all kinds of gruesome stories about having had to prostitute himself in prison."

Nat didn't know which emotion was more consuming, her

anger or her incredulity. "You're telling us you know for a fact that Maggie was having sex with Walsh?" she asked.

But Karen didn't pick up the gauntlet. She merely said, almost sympathetically, "You never really knew Maggie."

This got Nat's blood boiling. "And you did?"

Karen's nostrils flared. "Maggie confided in me because she knew that, even if I disapproved of some of her actions—which I readily admit I did—I never judged her as a person."

Either Leo wanted to nip a cat fight in the bud or he simply wanted to get on with his own agenda, because he cut Nat off before she could get another word out.

"I'd like to show you some photos, Karen. See if you recognize any of the people in them." He was already pulling out a handful of snapshots from his inside jacket pocket. Nat was still on a tear, but Karen took up the photos with what Nat viewed as a calculated nonchalance. But then Nat saw all of Karen's remarks and actions as calculated.

"You recognize him?" Nat heard Leo ask as Karen paused on the first of the photos. It was Keith Franklin's mug shot.

Nat was just waiting for her to tell them Franklin was another one of Maggie's sexual partners. Imply that Maggie was not only promiscuous but indiscriminate.

And yet there was this other shameful part of her—a part she was trying without success to disown—that wanted a concrete reason to add Franklin to her list of suspects. A spurned or jealous lover would put him right up there. Along with Walsh and Jack Dwyer and who knew who else.

"I can't put my finger on it," Karen was saying, "but he looks vaguely familiar. Was he one of Maggie's students?"

Coscarelli nodded.

Karen shrugged. "I never saw him with her. I would have remembered that," she said emphatically.

Yes, Nat was thinking. *I'm sure you'd remember anyone who threatened to monopolize too much of Maggie's time.* Was that it? Was Karen jealous of Walsh and Jack just as she had always been jealous of her?

"What's his name?" Karen asked.

"Keith Franklin," Coscarelli said.

A faint frown drew thin lines across her brow. "I recall somebody named Keith calling her. A couple of weeks ago. I had just come over when she was at the end of a conversation with him. I heard her say something like—*Keith, I really don't think that makes any sense.* I don't know what he said to that, but it got Maggie annoyed. She pretty much ended the conversation there."

"And she didn't say anything to you afterward?"

"No. She didn't. And I didn't make anything of it at the time."

"You going to talk to Franklin again?" Nat asked Coscarelli as they stepped outside Karen's building.

"Not tonight." He checked his watch. "Going on home to tuck my kid into bed."

Nat also checked her watch. "Damn. It's almost eight. I was supposed to be at my sister's house in Weston by now." Better call her, Nat was thinking. Maybe suggest another night. So much on her mind. She wasn't up to making small talk with Rachel. Although Rachel had sounded as though she had something on her mind. Well, whatever it was, surely it could keep for another day or two.

"How come you didn't look all that surprised when Karen said that Maggie was thinking about breaking up with Jack?" Leo interrupted her musing. "Maggie didn't tell you. She never even told you she was seeing him. So it must have been Jack."

"Who says I wasn't surprised?" she countered defensively.

"You and Jack are close."

Nat gave him a sharp look. Did he have a cop staking out her place? Jack's? "Not that close." A statement that had as much truth in it as lie.

"He talks to you."

"Look, I've got to go—" Again, Nat was trying to buy some time and distance. Wishing Jack hadn't confided in her. Wishing they hadn't stepped over that damn line. Even if she hadn't stepped as far over it as she might have. She didn't want these burdens. She sure as hell didn't need them.

"We got a witness who's willing to testify she saw Jack Dwyer outside Maggie's building on Friday shortly before one P.M. She was coming home from a hair appointment. Rushing to catch her soap that started at one. That's how she was sure of the time."

"He never went up to her apartment." So much for pretending she was in the dark here. She might as well stick out her wrists and let Leo cuff her on the spot.

Instead of an arrest, she got the lecture she'd been expecting earlier. "You're not helping Jack by withholding evidence, Natalie. Just like you didn't help your husband."

"I'm not the only one holding things back, Leo," she charged, more than anxious to turn the tables.

"Meaning?"

"There's one photo you didn't show Karen. Or me. The one that you found in Maggie's apartment."

Coscarelli met her gaze squarely. "That's true."

"What's the big secret? I know you're under no obligation to share evidence—"

"That's not why," he interrupted. "Not that it wouldn't be reason enough."

"Then why?"

"It would . . . disturb you."

"Is it a photo of Maggie?"

He nodded somberly.

"And she's not alone?"

Another nod.

Tears gathered in Nat's eyes. *Great. I haven't even seen the photo and I'm disturbed.* "When you asked me, Friday night, if Maggie was into . . . rough sex—"pressure was building at her temples "—did that question have something to do with this photo you found?"

"Leave it for now, Natalie."

"Who's with her in the photo, Leo?"

"There's no way to know. Most of her partner's cropped out of the picture. The photographer was clearly more interested in Maggie. Basically, all we can see of her partner is his head. Which doesn't help one iota since he's wearing a black leather full-face mask."

"A mask?"

"It's one of those props you'd pick up in a sex shop," he said quietly.

Nat was having trouble absorbing this. It was all so bizarre. So unlike Maggie. *Or was it?* Nat was discovering that there were many facets to her friend that she'd never seen. "And the photographer? Who—?"

"Your guess is as good as mine." A slight pause before he added, "Maybe better."

"Don't tell me you think Jack took it."

"Maybe he took it. Maybe it's him in the picture. You tell me."

"If it was Jack, do you really imagine that's something he would have shared with me?" Nat said sardonically.

"You do seem to draw people into your confidence."

"Well, no one has confided in me that they are either voyeuristic shutterbugs or into particularly kinky sex." Including Maggie. Nat held her hands out in a gesture of surrender. "You've unearthed all the secrets I've got, Leo."

"I doubt that, Natalie." He gave the hood of her car a little rat-a-tat-tat. "You better get going or your sister will start worrying." He turned and started for his car.

"I want to see the photo, Leo."

He kept walking. "I don't have it on me."

"Tomorrow."

No answer.

*   *   *

Her cell phone rang just as she was digging for it in her bag, her plan being to call Rachel and try to beg off.

Grabbing hold of the phone, there was this moment when she automatically thought, *bet it's Maggie. . . .*

The moment passed, leaving a dark hole in its wake.

"Hello."

There was silence on the other end.

Nat stiffened with anxiety, thinking it was Walsh on the line, wanting to issue another threat. "Hello," she repeated.

More silence. Her heart was racing.

"I . . . need to talk to you."

The voice was so low Nat had to focus all her concentration on making out the words. It was a woman's voice. Vaguely familiar.

"I don't . . . know who else to . . . turn to," the caller pleaded.

Nat picked up both the urgency and the agitation in the woman's voice. She had a pretty good idea who it was. "When?"

"I . . . don't—"

"We can meet right now," Nat said quickly.

And just as quickly, "415 Jordan Street. Cambridge. Apartment 8."

twenty-two

The first few months are the toughest for the released inmate. Anticipate heightened paranoia, disorientation, agitation. There may also be signs of sexual dysfunction. . . .

(excerpt from Parole Board letter to relatives of parolees)

A HEAVYSET MAN with a spreading bald spot that he tried to conceal with a comb-over and a spreading gut that he tried to conceal with an oversized sweatshirt answered the door. Nat had never seen him before but he was definitely expecting her. Which wasn't to say he was particularly welcoming. A jerk of the head was her invitation to enter. He shuffled a couple of steps to the side of the door. But his hulking frame still took up enough space so that she had to strategically maneuver her way around him to avoid contact as she entered.

The front door led directly into a cramped but tidy living

room. The floor was covered with an orange shag rug, the furniture was old, the couch covered with a cheap beige and green plaid throw, the mismatched chairs turned to face the only item of value in the room, a 32-inch color TV. The picture was on—a news show—but the sound was on mute.

Her *host* remained at the open door. "I'm going," he shouted.

For a second Nat thought he was announcing this to her—like he thought she was hard of hearing—but then the door to her right opened and a woman stepped out of what Nat took to be the bedroom.

Nat's guess as to the identity of the caller was confirmed.

Terri Franklin approached, full of nervous apology. "Thanks for coming . . . so quickly."

"It sounded important, Terri."

"Keith doesn't know I'm here. I mean he doesn't know . . . we're meeting. This is my sister's place. She works nights. She's a nurse over at Mercy. Keith doesn't know she's switched to nights. Some nights I tell him I'm coming over here to see Jen. Not too often. And I never stay too long. Maybe a couple of hours. Keith watches the twins. They don't like it. They still don't . . . Well, you saw. It's hard. On all of us. Harder than I . . . thought it would be."

Terri Franklin sucked in a breath, let only a little of it out. "Please . . . sit down. I could get you something. Coffee. It's only decaf. Jen's off caffeine. Says it gets her too hyped up. Sometimes I bring over my own. I hate decaf. Why drink coffee if there's no buzz? But . . . but I didn't bring any tonight. I'm sorry. Of course a lot of people don't do caffeine at night. Keeps them up. Not me, though. Never has. Other things . . . keep me up." She stopped dead. Like all the air had gone out of her. She even looked deflated. Which was only a step away from how she looked to Nat late that afternoon.

Before Nat sat down she turned off the TV, not wanting Terri to be distracted by the flashing images of a recent plane wreckage.

Keith Franklin's wife didn't so much sit as perch birdlike on the edge of the other chair. She tried to rest her hands quietly on her lap but they wouldn't cooperate, fingers nervously twitching. Her solution was to clench her hands together. Nat could see the knuckles whiten with her exertion. "That was Mike answered the door. He's a . . . friend."

"Of yours?" Nat asked quietly.

She lifted her bony shoulders in a helpless shrug. "Jen's too." She blushed scarlet. "Oh, I don't mean . . ." She avoided meeting Nat's gaze. "Jen introduced us. Mike's a cook at the hospital."

Nat nodded, knowing that her silence would increase Terri's anxiety and, hopefully, keep her talking.

Terri straightened her back and unclenched her hands, folding them primly on her lap. Like a child in school wanting to show the teacher how good she was. Only her face belied the image she was trying to convey. Her face was full of guilty shadows.

"I guess you're wondering why I wanted to talk to you so bad."

It was precisely what Nat was wondering.

"Jen . . . my sister . . . she thinks I should talk to the cops. Mike's on my case, too. But it's not like I know anything. It's just . . . feelings. You know? And Keith's had such a hard time of it already."

"So have you," Nat said.

Terri sighed. "I guess it's easier talking to a woman. And, you not being exactly a cop, well, I got to get stuff off my mind, or Mike and Jen are right, I'll end up going nuts." She bit back a yawn. "Sorry. I . . . haven't been sleeping good. For a . . . long time. Since Keith . . . got out."

Nat nodded sympathetically at the haggard woman. She sensed it would not be wise to drill Terri with questions. Best to give her a wide berth.

"Not that I had an easy time of it when he was inside. It got so lonely while Keith was locked up. I never said anything to my sister, but I guess she could tell. See, I was so ashamed. After Keith was arrested, all our so-called friends dropped me like a hot potato. Which hurt, but not so bad as when the kids' friends—"

Her shoulders drooped. "Keith was feeling so sorry for himself the whole time he was locked up. He'd never ask me how I was holding up. How the kids were holding up. I'm not saying it wasn't much harder on him. I know it must have been awful. I was truly sorry for him. But he should have—" She broke off, her hands once again clenched.

"I see a lot of family members of inmates, Terri. Many of them—especially the wives and children—have a very rough time. We even run a group for families of inmates at the House. So they can share their feelings and get support."

"Mike gave me support," Terri said, quickly checking Nat out to see if she was showing signs of disapproval. Seeing none in her face—in large part because Nat sympathized with the young woman's sense of loneliness and isolation—Terri added, "He still does."

"We all need someone who can understand our suffering," Nat said.

"I never misled Mike. It's not like it's anything serious. We're not even . . . doing it now . . . now that Keith's back. But Mike is sweet. He's nothing like Keith. Oh, I don't mean Keith is mean or anything. I don't think he's got a mean bone in his body. Really I don't."

The protestations were a little too emphatic. Was she trying to convince Nat or herself?

"I mean . . . they're different, Mike and Keith, in looks, education and . . . stuff," Terri sputtered on. "Mike never went to college or anything. He hasn't got . . . aspirations. Keith used to have . . . all these plans and dreams. We both did. Neither of us came from money. And I never got past a high school education. My folks were tickled pink, let me tell you, that a guy with a college education and a really good job wanted to marry their daughter. Of course, they didn't know that he'd knocked me up. Keith wasn't the first guy I ever . . . did it with. But he was the first one I loved. And I thought he loved me, too."

"And you don't think that, anymore?"

Terri ignored her question. "For a couple of years there, Keith was doing so well and we were living real high off the hog. I won't say it wasn't nice. It was. Getting things for the kids, especially. Toys, outfits from The Gap, fancy strollers, a big swing set in the backyard. You should have seen the pile of stuff under our tree that last Christmas before . . . he went to prison. 'When it comes to my family, the sky's the limit,' he used to say."

She looked down at the floor. "Only the kids don't remember what it used to be like. How generous their daddy was. How gentle . . ."

"And now?"

Terri compressed her lips. "He'd never hurt the kids. Or me. Not . . . physically. He's never laid a hand on any of us. But sometimes he's . . . short-tempered. Which isn't like him. Well, isn't like he used to be. But that's not what really bothers me. It's more that he's . . . like he's playing a part from memory."

Terri glanced over at Nat to see if she understood what she was trying to say. Nat's nod seemed to satisfy her.

"He's distracted a lot. I'll be talking to him or one of the kids will say something and you can tell he's not really listening. And . . . he's gone a lot. Sometimes I'll get up in the middle of the night even and he's not there. Not in bed. Not in the house. The next morning I'll ask him and all he'll say is he couldn't sleep and needed to just take a drive. He's got his brother's old Pontiac. It's a real gas-guzzler and we don't have the money to keep it up. But I don't say anything. I don't want him to think I'm . . . insensitive."

"Do you know where he goes when he takes these drives?"

Terri shook her head. "When I ask him why he goes off like that, he says because of all that time being locked up. He kind of feels the need to prove to himself he can just get up and leave, whenever. But it's always in the middle of the night. Nights are hardest on Keith. He has bad dreams. Sometimes, he'll whimper or even scream in his sleep."

"Does he talk about his bad dreams?"

"Never. Not that I haven't asked. I try to draw him out, but he shoves up a wall right between us the second I so much as—" Another shrug. "Keith's parole officer came to see me right before Keith got out. He wanted me to understand that Keith would probably seem . . . different than before. That, more than likely, he wouldn't want to talk about his time in prison. That he'd want to try to forget it. Not that he would, but that with time, his experiences inside would begin to recede. That's what the parole officer said. When I asked Sean—that's his parole officer—what he meant by experiences, he just said life behind bars was no picnic."

She hesitated and Nat could see her hands tremble. "You read things, though. See stuff on TV and the movies. I . . . I admit I was scared . . . having sex . . . with Keith. Like maybe . . . oh God, I wanted him to have a test for AIDS, but I just couldn't think of a way to . . . to ask him. But then I figured out I could just tell him I had to go off the pill and didn't trust diaphragms and so he'd need to use rubbers."

She gave Nat a forlorn glance. "Not that I needed to worry so much. We hardly ever have sex. Keith just doesn't seem . . . interested." Another hesitation, before she added, "In me, anyway."

Nat couldn't help thinking about those last months with Ethan and his increasingly waning interest in having sex with her. And how bereft and undesirable it made her feel. Having to listen to his vast variety of reasons for all those *I'm just not up to it tonight, hon* rejections.

Did Keith make up excuses? Were they a front for the real reason? The reason being, like Ethan, he was getting sexually satisfied somewhere else? With someone else?

Fragments of conversations came back in sharp recall.

Franklin commenting on a piece of writing Maggie had praised highly. Karen making a point of saying that Maggie was only truly interested in the cons she viewed as having talent. Was Keith sneaking off to see Maggie in the middle of those nights? Was she having sex with him? Was he jealous of her other lovers? Jealous enough to cause her to break it off with him. As she'd threatened to do with Jack?

Was it Franklin's voice on Maggie's answering machine? The voice of the man she'd been unable to identify on Friday night? His voice sounded different this afternoon, but he was in an altogether different state of mind today.

Did Keith Franklin get fed up with Maggie avoiding him? Did he drive over to her apartment in his old Pontiac during his lunch hour on Friday, determined to confront her? Did he rape and murder her when his attempts to reconcile with her failed?

"Are you sure you wouldn't like something to drink?" Terri asked.

Nat shook her head even though she was aware that her throat was parched. "Do you know why Detective Coscarelli and I came to see your husband this afternoon?"

Terri's face flooded with anguish and her eyes watered. "Keith had a picture of her in this poetry book he bought. Poetry books. Before he went away, he used to read thrillers or sci fi. Poetry? Never. It just wasn't . . . Keith. Now he owns whole shelves full."

"A picture of Maggie Austin?" Nat instantly thought about that lewd photo of Maggie and her masked lover.

"It's not there anymore. I looked. It's gone."

"What kind of a photo? Was anyone in the photo with her?"

Terri gave her a blank look. "There was nothing special about it. And she was just by herself. It kind of looked like one of those professional pictures you have taken at Christmas time or something." The corners of her mouth drew downward. "She was beautiful."

"Did Keith tell you anything about Maggie?"

"He never even told me he was taking that poetry class in prison. I visited him two, three times a month the whole time he was away, and he never said one word about this teacher."

"Did you ask about her when you found the picture?"

"No. I . . . I don't know why. I just . . . thought—" She didn't finish.

"What did you think, Terri?"

"At first I thought she was just a picture. You know, not someone he really knew. Like . . . like a fantasy woman. Because she just didn't look like someone who'd be . . . be interested in Keith." The tears started to spill down her cheeks.

Nat reached over and touched her hand. "My husband recently left me for another woman, Terri."

Terri's eyes met Nat's and they shared a moment of mutual empathy that Nat was taken aback to realize meant as much to her as it seemed to mean to Terri.

"A couple of times when he thought I wasn't there, I heard him on the phone with her. One time I heard him say . . . 'I love you, Maggie. And you can't say or do anything to make me stop loving you.'"

Terri swiped ineffectively at her tears with the back of her hand. "It wasn't even what he said so much as how he said it. He . . . he never told me he loved me in that way. With so much . . . passion."

Nat pulled a couple of clean tissues out of her purse, offering one to Terri and finding she needed one for herself. Whatever their differences, the two women were bonded by the special kind of pain that came from rejection and betrayal.

Terri took her tissue, blotted her eyes and blew her nose. Nat did the same. They sat in silence for a few moments, but there was no air of tension. Just a couple of discarded women taking a little time to regroup.

"Tell me about last Friday, Terri."

She stiffened, Nat's request immediately breaking off the connection they'd shared.

"I . . . was at school. I work at Singer Elementary."

"And Keith?"

"He was at work." She sniffed, then repeated more emphatically, "He was at work."

"What did you leave him for lunch that day?"

She didn't look surprised or puzzled by the question. She looked frightened. Although she was trying her best to cover it up.

"Meatloaf. His favorite. He always used to say it was even better than his mother's." Her dried tears had cut grooves in the liquid makeup she was wearing. Along with black streaks from her mascara. Had she put on the cosmetics for her benefit or Mike's? Was it really true they weren't sexually involved anymore, or was Terri ashamed to admit the affair was ongoing even though Keith was now back home? And if she and Mike were still having sex, who could blame them? Hell, Nat envied Terri having someone who could make her feel attractive. Who desired her when her husband turned his back, literally and figuratively, on her.

Maybe that was the real reason Nat had come so close to going to bed with Jack. A need to be desired. Only Nat wasn't sure she was the woman Jack desired. Nat couldn't shake the feeling that she would have been nothing more than a poor substitute for the woman he could no longer possess.

Nat realized with a start that she'd let her mind wander again. "Meatloaf."

Creases furrowed Terri's brow. "When I was cleaning up from supper that night . . . I saw it all in the trash. The meatloaf, the bean salad, the coleslaw. All things he loved. Or used to. I don't know why but it . . . it just made me mad. It was like a slap in the face. Like now he was rejecting me in the kitchen as well as the bedroom. I lost it. I blew up at him. Started screaming, pounding his chest, shrieking." Her face reddened. "About how I was so frustrated and felt so alone and how it was all his fault. How everything was all his fault." Fresh tears sprang up in Terri's eyes.

"And what did Keith do?"

"He broke down and started crying like a baby. Right there at the kitchen table. And all this—my yelling and Keith's crying—it was all going on right in front of the kids. They got scared."

"Were you scared, Terri?"

"Not . . . then."

Nat waited for more, her stomach churning, her pulse pounding in her skull. But there was no follow-up. Terri's eyes were closed and more tears were slipping out.

"When? When you heard that Maggie'd been murdered?" Nat was trying to keep her voice unthreatening, but they both felt the threat hanging there like a lead weight. Because what Nat was really questioning Terri about was the possibility that her husband, the father of her children, had raped and killed Maggie Austin.

Terri Franklin offered no answer. She didn't have to. Her fear was palpable.

twenty-three

. . . when the blues hit you hard, gain strength by thinking of those you love waiting out there for you, knowing one day you'll be out there with them and this will all be a bad nightmare. . . .

T. C.
Inmate #957693

THE RAIN THAT had been threatening all day was coming down in solid sheets as Nat hurried down the dark, empty side street to her car parked one block away from Terri's sister's place. Her black pants suit was quickly becoming plastered to her body and she was landing in as many puddles as she was missing, which left her black leather pumps so sodden they were squeaking with each step.

Awash with thoughts about Keith Franklin as a primary suspect, relieved as hell to focus on Franklin rather than Walsh—or Jack—as the guilty party, and anxious to make it to shelter, Nat gave only a cursory glance up and down the two-lane road to make sure no cars were coming before stepping off the curb. She was halfway across the street when she was suddenly caught in the glare of blinding headlights not twenty yards away.

Where the hell did the car come from? Out of nowhere.

For what was only seconds but felt like an eternity, Nat was frozen in the car's high beams, unsure whether to run back or forward.

It was not so much a conscious decision as it was the pull of forward momentum that made her sprint straight ahead only to take a couple of steps before catching the heel of her shoe on a sewer grate. No chance to right herself, Nat felt herself flying face forward toward the ground.

She landed so hard on the wet pavement all the air was knocked out of her.

They say that before you die you see your whole life flash before your eyes. All Nat saw were those damn headlights. Bearing down on her. As if the driver didn't see her. But he must have seen her trip and fall unless he was asleep at the wheel. Or so drunk that he literally couldn't see straight.

The car was so close—within feet of her—that Nat could smell the powerful, pungent odor of its exhaust fumes spewing into the air. She started crawling on the wet pavement, trying to get out of the way. But the car kept swerving left, right, left again . . . There was no escaping.

Her breath came back in enough time for her to scream into the empty night. The sound was drowned out by the car's roaring engine. She shut her eyes. Waiting to be crushed to death for there was absolutely nowhere to go.

Amazingly, all she felt was the hard slap of rain shooting off the spinning tires as the car whisked by her. It missed her by inches.

Nat staggered to her feet, badly shaken and furious, waiting for the car to manage a stop. But the speeding vehicle hit its brakes only for a moment as it swerved around the corner. A hit-and-run driver.

Only, by the sheerest good fortune, Nat wasn't hit.

Her first thought was that not only had she been lucky, so had the driver. Her second thought was far more ominous. What if the driver of that car had deliberately tried to run her down? What if he was cursing his bad luck at that very moment for having missed her?

Who'd been behind that wheel? Nat could feel her mind start to spin with possibilities. But the first person to pop into her head was Keith Franklin. He could have followed his wife here earlier. Staked out the building. Saw Nat arrive and leave a good hour later. Had he guessed his wife had confided in her? Was he simply not taking any chances?

She pulled back. She could be wrong. It could have been anyone. It could have been an accident.

"What do you mean you were nearly run over by a drunk driver?" The question was laden with disbelief.

"It's self-explanatory, Rachel," Nat said irritably from her car phone, having opted for anger over panic. "Anyway, I fell getting out of its way and I'm pretty scraped up. Not to mention looking like a drowned rat. I need to go home. Besides, it's too late for me to head over to your place now." The clock on her dash read nine-fifteen.

"It's not that late. I've got a first-aid kit here. Let me . . . take care of you for a change, Nat."

There was something so poignant in her sister's tone, Nat couldn't bring herself to argue. "You're going to have to part with one of your Armani outfits. My clothes are wrecked."

Rachel laughed and Nat could hear the relief in it. "You can have your pick."

"Did you call the cops?" Rachel asked anxiously.

Nat shook her head. "I didn't get his license. Or the make of the car. There's not much they could do." Not true. Nat knew they could do something. They—i.e., Leo Coscarelli—could come down hard on her for pursuing this investigation on her own. And nearly getting herself killed in the process.

Nat and Rachel were sitting at the polished granite counter in Rachel's newly renovated state-of-the-art Eurostyle kitchen, eating asparagus quiche and endive salad. Truth was they were both merely picking at their food even though it was quite delicious. Nat knew why she didn't have any appetite. She wasn't sure about Rachel.

Nat took a sip of crisp Chardonnay. "It was too dark and the car was going too fast. All I do know is it was large." And then she recalled something else. Something that hadn't really penetrated her consciousness until that moment. She pictured the car swerving around the corner. "Wait. One of the brake lights was busted. On the driver's side."

"Well, that's something for the police to go on."

"Yeah right. Take a guess how many cars in the Boston area have busted brake lights. Besides, I've had enough of the police for today." Nat finished off the wine in her glass and went to pour some more only to realize the bottle was empty. They'd finished it off between them. No wonder she was so woozy.

"I'll get another one." Rachel was halfway off her stool.

"No. I'm already over the legal limit."

"Which means you can't drive home tonight. So we can both get soused."

"Since when do you like getting drunk?" Nat asked. Despite Rachel's lifelong denial of their father being a bonafide alcoholic, she had always been cautious around booze. Never so much as touched the stuff before she was married.

Not a complete teetotaler herself, Nat did watch her intake. Usually.

Rachel deposited another chilled bottle of Chardonnay on the counter. "Here, you get this one open while I make up the bed in the guest room."

Nat had never slept over at Rachel's house. She had only a vague recollection of ever even seeing her sister's guest room. And yet Rachel made her staying over sound like such a commonplace event that Nat almost believed it was. She was sure this was partly due to her moderately inebriated state. Rachel's invite was, no doubt, a result of her being in a similar state of intoxication. Although Nat seemed to recall she'd downed at least two glasses of wine to every one of her sister's.

"You didn't open the bottle," Rachel chided lightly when she returned.

Nat found herself growing impatient. This was not the Rachel she knew. "What's going on, Rach?"

Rachel slid onto her stool, her effort at gaiety finally giving out. She cast Nat a withering glance, then busied herself uncorking the wine. Struggling with it, she murmured, "You're all the family I have, Nat."

"You have a husband and two children," Nat reminded her a bit snippily. Maybe she was angry that Rachel seemed to first be realizing this now. Or maybe she was just plain jealous that her sister had her own intact family. Nat was the one who had no one now but Rachel.

"Damn," she muttered as the cork broke off. She pushed it aside, not bothering to try to pry it out. "I'll get another bottle."

"I'm sorry," Nat said. "I've had a bad day. A lot of bad days."

"Forget it," Rachel said, plastering on a bright smile that was as phony as a three-dollar bill.

"Something's wrong." Nat said it as a fact so Rachel couldn't squirm out of it as easily.

Rachel's eyes skidded off Nat's face and she stared out the blackened window over the sink to her right. She didn't say anything, but Nat could feel the tension emanating from Rachel's body. She knew it must be bad, because she knew so well how talented her sister was at covering up. Denying. At least with her.

And yet she was the one Rachel had asked—practically begged—
to come over tonight.

"Talk to me, Rach," Nat said softly, taking hold of her hand.
Feeling her squeeze it tightly.

It took a few moments before she gathered the courage to
respond. "I think Gary's having an affair." Rachel's bottom lip
quivered. "So . . . see . . . you're not the only one."

"Rachel, I'm sorry."

Rachel tried to smile but failed miserably in the attempt. "I
always thought we were . . . the perfect . . . family."

As did Nat. "Are you sure?"

"A woman called . . . She told me . . ." Rachel struggled to
fight back the tears that were already slipping down her cheeks.
"She said Gary loved her. That he was only . . . staying with me
because . . . of the children."

"Who is she? Did she give you her name? Do you know her?
How do you know—?"

"Stop," Rachel screamed. "The last thing I need from you is a
third degree."

Nat sighed. "Sorry."

"Maybe it isn't true," Rachel said. "Maybe it was some bitch
trying to hurt me."

Nat wanted to ask her sister *why* someone would do that, but
she knew that question would only convince Rachel of her lack of
support.

"Have you told Gary about the call?" Nat asked instead.

Rachel got up from her stool, walked over to the window.
When she got overwhelmed, the first thing she wanted to do was
seek distance. In this, the two sisters were very much alike.

"No," Rachel said, turning on the sink, absently washing an
already rinsed dish. She set it carefully on the drain board. "It's
some sick joke. I . . . know it is."

Nat was far from convinced. She wouldn't put it past Gary to
be cheating on her sister. She wouldn't put it past any man to

cheat on his wife. A part of her wanted to shake her sister. *Wake up. For once in your life, face the truth.*

But she held her tongue. She could only imagine how much it must have taken out of Rachel even to mention this phone call to her. They'd shared so little for so long. Nat was not about to sever this fragile connection.

"I love you, Rach," Nat said softly, words she couldn't remember having said aloud in a very long time.

Rachel turned to her, nodded, then returned to the sink. The water continued running, but she was gazing out the window.

"Maybe I should go home." Nat had certainly sobered up enough to get behind a wheel. And something told her her sister would prefer it if she left.

But Rachel wasn't listening. Her attention was on the dark street outside her window. "Nat. Come here. Quick."

"What?"

"Hurry."

Nat started toward her.

"Too late. He's gone."

"Who's gone?" She stood beside Rachel at the window staring out at the dark country lane.

"A car." Rachel turned slowly to Nat, her face flush with alarm. "It slowed down as it passed the house. As it went by and started to round the corner I saw the brake lights go on. One brake light, that is. The driver's side brake light was out."

The hairs on Nat's arms bristled. "Turn out the light, Rach. Let's see if he circles back."

"I think we should call the police, Nat."

"I'll call them if he comes by again," Nat promised and went to turn the lights out herself.

They stood there in the dark at the kitchen window. Nat put her arm around her sister's waist.

The car did not reappear.

twenty-four

*Ninety-seven percent of currently incarcerated prison-
ers will be released at some point. This makes all reha-
bilitative efforts within our institutions an
imperative. . . .*

MCI Deputy Commissioner of Programming

"JESUS. WHERE WERE you all last night? And all morning today? I
called a dozen times or more. I've been worried sick."

Jack did appear pale and upset. Nat wondered if he'd been hitting the bottle again. Not that she was one to talk, having finished off more than her share of that second Chardonnay with
Rachel the night before.

Nat pulled him into her office and firmly shut the door. "I
think Walsh may be innocent, Jack."

He looked at her warily. Like she was about to finally, openly
accuse him of Maggie's murder.

"What makes you say that?"

Nat hesitated. "Something happened last night."

Jack maintained his fix on her. "Look, Nat, if you don't trust me—" He let the rest of the sentence drop and started to turn away.

"Wait." She rubbed her face. She hadn't slept. She'd spent the whole night rehashing in her mind the encounter with Terri Franklin and the subsequent even closer encounter with that car. By the time dawn broke, she'd become more and more convinced that the driver of that car was Keith Franklin. It all fit. His fixation on Maggie. His lack of an alibi. His own wife's suspicions—and her obvious fear of her husband.

Nat told Jack about her meeting with Terri Franklin the previous night and the near hit-and-run accident. "Only I don't think it was an accident, Jack. I think Keith Franklin followed Terri to her sister's apartment, saw me arrive, got frightened that Terri had given him away and tried to run me down. After he sped off, he must have pulled over and waited. When he saw me drive by, he followed me to my sister's house. If I hadn't stayed over there last night—" Nat shivered at the thought of another hit-and-run attempt. An attempt that might have succeeded the second time around. And who was to say there wouldn't be more attempts to come?

"Did you get a look at the driver?"

"No. But it all fits, Jack. I'll lay you odds Franklin's car's got a busted driver's side brake light. And I'll bet you anything it was Franklin who sneaked into my apartment the other day and left that poem Walsh wrote. He must have found it in Maggie's—"

"You never told me about finding a poem. How come?"

Before Nat could respond, he nodded contemptuously. "Because you thought I might have been the one—"

"No, Jack. I never thought that." They both knew she was lying and Nat hurried on so as not to get hung up on that issue. "When Coscarelli and I talked to Franklin—"

"What? You and the detective are a team now?" Jack cut her off this time, sounding a little paranoid and a little jealous.

"No, we're not a team. And the point I'm trying to make here is that Franklin went on and on about Walsh being obsessed with Maggie, but he was the one with the obsession."

"More than one man can be obsessed with a woman, Nat."

Before Nat could sort out whether Jack was talking about Walsh or himself, her door opened and Hutch walked in. He looked grim, an expression that was starting to look all too familiar on his face. "Did you tell her?" he asked Jack gruffly.

Nat looked warily from one man to the other. "Tell me what?"

Jack's expression turned even grimmer than Hutch's. Which was saying something.

"What?" she repeated, the tension settling in the pit of her stomach.

"Carlyle wants to see you."

Neither man said another word. They didn't have to.

Nat's eyes narrowed. "Vacation leave? You mean you want me gone."

Deputy Commissioner Steven Carlyle sat behind his oversized, overly neat mahogany desk. He fit his office perfectly, an oversized man in a perfectly tailored navy blue suit, white shirt, red and blue paisley tie. His gray thinning hair was combed back straight off his face. A thread-like weave of veins showed through his pale skin. Carlyle was a man who liked his lager. Never one of Nat's supporters, he'd made no effort to soften the blow. "At this point, it's temporary, Ms. Price. As for the future—" He let the rest of the sentence hang, but Nat caught a supercilious smile on his face.

"I'd like to talk to the Commissioner," Nat demanded.

Carlyle leaned forward in his black leather desk chair. "I'm going to give you a piece of advice. Let it be. Given what's gone down, you can only make things worse for yourself by being pushy."

"Pushy? Trying to defend myself is being pushy?" Nat leaned forward in her chair as well. "I have an excellent record, Steven." She saw him bristle at her use of his first name. Not that they hadn't, on less inflammatory occasions, been Nat and Steven. But since she'd arrived in his office this morning, he'd made a point of addressing her by her last name. And deliberately omitted her title. It was now *Ms.* Not *Superintendent.* Nat, however, was not about to be intimidated.

"And," she continued, even though she sensed by Carlyle's bland expression, that he'd tuned out, "I take my responsibilities very seriously. Obviously, I bear a large brunt of the blame for what happened, but let's both be clear about what we actually know *has* happened. Not what's been *alleged.* Dean Thomas Walsh escaped from Horizon House. Dean Thomas Walsh is also being sought for questioning in regard to the murder of . . ." Nat swallowed hard before she could go on. "Maggie Austin. He has not been charged with her murder. And, as a matter of fact," here she hesitated, not feeling on solid ground, but desperate to fight for her livelihood, which was becoming a fight for her life. "I have strong reason to believe the man responsible for the murder of Maggie Austin is not Dean Thomas Walsh."

Carlyle must have been half listening, because Nat detected a flash of interest in his expression. After all, as much as he might enjoy seeing her downfall, he was not a stupid man. If she went down, she could bring him and the other bigwigs down with her. It was in all their best interests to have someone outside of the system charged with this heinous crime.

"And do the police share your *strong reason?*" Carlyle asked.

She steeled herself as she phoned Coscarelli from her car, knowing he'd be positively bullshit that she'd waited so long to report the hit-and-run attempt. "Keith Franklin owns an old Pontiac. I need to find out—" Leo didn't give her time to finish.

"We found Alison Cole Miller."

Nat took in a sharp breath. She could tell from the tone in his voice that the news wasn't good. So much for hoping against hope that Alison was in hiding.

"Dead?" she asked, already knowing the answer.

"For at least four days. Most likely five. Bringing us back to Thursday, the day she went missing. We know she was at work until four, left saying she wasn't feeling well, and supposedly headed straight home. Which would have got her there sometime close to five."

"Where was she found?"

"Some guy who stopped to take a leak discovered her body in the woods a little over a mile from her house. Oates is over at the mother's place now. I was just about to head out to Newton to talk with the husband." There was a brief pause. "I'll wait around here a few minutes if you want to tag along. You can tell me why you're interested in Franklin's Pontiac on the way."

Unfortunately, Nat's interest in the ex-con's car had suddenly taken a nose-dive. It was one thing to imagine Franklin as Maggie's killer. But what reason on earth would he have had for killing Alison Cole? Nat realized now how desperate she must have been to latch onto Franklin when the evidence, if you could even call it that, was so pathetically meager.

Alison's husband, Richard Miller, was a tall, good-looking man in his late twenties. He had the front door open to the small, split-level ranch, looking at them with anxious anticipation as they headed up the slate path.

"Did you find her? Is she okay?" Nat guessed Miller'd been hoping what they'd all been hoping. But she could see, from the wear and tear on his face, that it wasn't a hope he could fully believe in.

Coscarelli suggested they go inside and Miller almost roboti-cally led them down a narrow hallway into a sunny family room scattered with toys. The room overlooked a small back yard taken up with an aboveground pool and a metal swing set. Nat was glad to see the children weren't in the room and she didn't see them out in the yard. Coscarelli asked if they were in the house.

Miller shook his head. "They're with Jean. Ali's mom." He looked pleadingly at them. "Please. Just . . . tell me. I haven't been able to sleep, go back to work, eat, do anything . . . since Thursday."

Coscarelli gently broke the news to him.

"I knew it," Miller muttered, sinking onto one corner of an L-shaped denim sectional sofa. "I knew the bastard would get even." His otherwise handsome face clogged with a mixture of anguish and fury. "You don't find him and lock him away for good this time, I'll hunt Walsh down myself and blow his fucking head off."

Yet another man out for Walsh's blood.

"Did your wife ever say anything to you about hearing from Walsh? Seeing him?" Leo asked.

"What? You think they up and started dating again?" Miller retorted cynically.

"Again?" Nat echoed.

A chilly smile thinned Miller's lips, making him look decid-edly less attractive. "She thought they were on a date the night he raped her. Some date, huh?"

"Has he called here?" Nat repeated Leo's question.

"Ali said she'd gotten quite a few hang-ups over the past few weeks. It made her jumpy."

"She thought it was Walsh?" Leo asked.

"Who else?"

"Why didn't she report it to the police? Or contact the pre-release center and let Superintendent Price here know—"

"Know what? Ali couldn't prove it was him. It could have

been any crank caller. It's just . . . she had this gut feeling. Woman's intuition, you know."

"Did any of those calls come while you were home?" Nat asked.

Miller wiped his lips with the back of his hand. He took a few seconds before answering. "I haven't been around much these past few weeks."

"Oh?" Coscarelli said.

Nat was mighty interested in this remark as well. They both waited for Alison's husband to elaborate.

Miller shrugged wearily. "My mother-in-law's bound to tell you, if she hasn't already, that Ali and I were having some marital problems."

A lot of that going around, Nat mused.

"But Jean kept up my spirits, telling me Ali'd come around. And she was right. Just a couple of days before . . . before she . . ." He looked away. "We were talking about giving it a second try."

"What kind of marital problems?" Leo asked.

"The kind all couples have from time to time," he said evasively. "Anyway, like I said, we were going to give it another go. And we would have, too, if—" Miller shook his head as if to shake off the rest of the thought. "Just like Jean told me, Ali was coming around."

He dropped his head into his hands. "We were going to make it work. We really were. If only—"

Nat didn't know why but she found herself wondering if what Miller was saying was true about their reconciliation or just wishful thinking on both his part and his mother-in-law's.

Miller's hands dropped from his face and whatever sorrow was there moments earlier had transformed into dark anger. "You people should have never let that bastard out on the street." His eyes met Nat's squarely. There was no missing the accusatory tone in his voice. Or the hostility.

"Odd, don't you think, that your wife didn't come forward

with any objections to Walsh's pre-release plan?" Leo said, drawing Miller's gaze back to him.

Miller snickered. "What good would it have done?"

"Are you saying she did have objections?" Nat pressed.

"I'm saying she was too damn naive for her own good."

"Then *you* had objections," Nat persisted.

Miller's eyes darkened with disgust. "After what that animal did to my wife? You're damn straight I did."

"Is that one of the things you and your wife argued about?" she asked.

"I don't see that's any of your business."

"Your wife's been murdered, Mr. Miller," Leo said bluntly. "So let's try that question again."

Miller flushed. "Yeah, I guess we argued about it a little. If he'd done to your wife what he did to mine, wouldn't you have wanted the pervert locked away for as long as possible?" he challenged.

"Have you seen Walsh since his pre-release?" Leo asked.

"If he'd have showed up here, Ali would have told me. If . . . she'd had the chance." Miller's eyes watered up.

"I mean, did you seek him out? Your wife was provided with a letter indicating the location of Walsh's residence and his place of employ. You could have easily found him. Confronted him. Warned him to stay away from your wife. If I were in your shoes—"

"Ali never showed me that paper. Probably scared of what I might do to that maggot if I knew where to find him."

"Was she right to be scared?" Nat asked.

Miller sprang up abruptly. "I'm finished with this. I got a funeral I gotta arrange, and two kids to tell that their mother's dead. You got any more questions, you know what you can do with them."

Interesting that Miller should reach his boiling point just when she'd asked him if his wife was right in her fear that he'd take some violent action against Walsh. Nat was also very curious about the nature of the marital problems Miller and his wife were having. Did Alison have reason to be afraid of her husband's explosive temper on other accounts?

Nat was sure Leo would accuse her of wanting to pin Alison Cole's murder on her husband. Just as she wanted to pin Maggie's murder on Keith Franklin. Especially now that she'd been all but suspended for putting a killer on the streets.

Nat struggled to come up with a theory that would explain why Miller would murder not only his wife but Maggie Austin, a woman who was a perfect stranger to him. Just as Alison Cole Miller was a perfect stranger to Keith Franklin. There was only one man who was linked to these two women.

Nat felt her whole world spinning out of control. Walsh was guilty, not of one murder but two. And who knew if that was going to be the end of it?

Walsh, and not Keith Franklin, now seemed the most likely candidate for the driver of the near hit-and-run car. Walsh must have broken into her home and left that poem. It was Walsh who'd followed her to her sister's house last night. So now he knew where Rachel lived, too.

"So, they'd split," Nat said as they headed back to Leo's car. "You didn't look all that surprised when Miller dropped that little nugget."

"The mom told me the second time when I saw her in person. I wanted to see how Miller would handle it."

"What did Mrs. Cole have to say?" she prodded, annoyed that he hadn't filled her in.

"I got the impression she and her daughter weren't particularly close. I also got the distinct feeling Mrs. Cole likes the son-in-law a whole lot. She certainly didn't bad-mouth him. Said he was a good husband and father, hard-working, honest. In her eyes, a real catch. Took her a while to get around to telling me the couple were temporarily living apart, but she said pretty much the same thing Miller said. That all couples have their little spats."

"If his wife threw him out, they were having more than little spats," Nat said, and she knew Leo knew she was talking from personal experience.

"I suppose you've heard I've been suspended."

Leo started up his unmarked cruiser. "I heard you were taking some vacation leave."

"Some vacation," she muttered.

Before he pulled out into traffic, Leo touched her cheek lightly and so briefly she might have thought she'd imagined it save for the electrically charged tingle it left on her skin.

Nat felt embarrassed and a little pathetic by her response to what had been nothing more than a friendly gesture of sympathy. She told herself it had been a while. Ethan's departure had left her so emotionally bruised that it had drained her of much of her sexual appetite. An appetite that in happier times had been, she'd thought, quite healthy and hearty. But apparently not sufficient to sate her husband's appetite.

Anger and bitterness at this realization effectively discharged that electric tingle.

For once, she was grateful.

They were driving a few minutes before she realized they weren't heading back in the direction of the precinct which was east of Newton. Leo was driving west on Route 9.

"The Walsh home," she said, putting two and two together as they passed a sign for Natick.

"If anyone knows where Walsh's hiding out, it's the sister."

"You're probably right, but I doubt she'll give him away," she said. "She's convinced he's innocent. That he's being set up again."

"Yeah, well let's see what she believes when we tell her about

Alison Cole Miller. I want to hit her with it before it makes the twelve o'clock news."

She glanced at her watch. It was a little past eleven A.M. "Won't she be at work?"

"She didn't go in today. Called in sick."

"And you're sure she's home?"

"We've still got the house staked out and the phone tapped. Christine and her mother know we're out there so they're basically sitting tight."

"Mrs. Walsh is home, too?"

"She's taken vacation leave for the week. Can't say I blame her for wanting to stay out of the public eye."

"I bet she's having as much fun on her vacation as I'm having on mine," Nat said dryly.

twenty-five

The way I look at it, any sentence is a death sentence.
Because, no matter if you're long or short, you got to
figure out how to stay alive while you're inside. And,
you better fucking believe me, it ain't easy. . . .

H.B.
Inmate #348528

THE WALSH'S HOUSE was a couple of blocks off the old downtown section of Natick where tired, old shops lined the streets, much of their business gone the way of the endless run of strip malls on both sides of Route 9.

712 Lincoln Road was a small, red, center-entrance colonial—one of eight houses set in a semi-circle around a cul-de-sac. They all had one-car attached garages, sat on quarter-acre lots, and varied only by the color of the exterior paint. A nice, quiet, respectable middle-class community. A place where everyone mowed their lawns, trimmed their bushes, and kept their garbage

cans tucked out of sight. Nat wondered what the neighbors made of the unmarked cruiser parked outside 712.

Marion Walsh answered the door on the first ring. She must have seen them pull up or was on her way out. She was a tall, trim woman with auburn hair heavily threaded with gray. It was not only her age that made her less attractive by far than her son and even her daughter—there was a hardness about her that showed especially in her steely blue eyes and in the dour line of her mouth. For someone on vacation, she seemed incongruously dressed in a beige linen suit, black silk shell and a strand of pearls around her neck.

"I was just about to go out." She snapped out the words practically in Leo's face, not so much as glancing in Nat's direction. "To see my lawyer, as a matter of fact, about filing charges of police harassment."

Leo stepped aside without a word, allowing her to pass. Nat was already standing clear of the door.

But Marion had a change of heart, abruptly turning and striding back into the narrow hallway, then turning right into the living room, dimly lit thanks to the drawn shades. Leo followed her into the room. Nat followed Leo.

Marion didn't offer them seats, nor did she take one herself. Arms akimbo, she stood by the brick fireplace whose spotless hearth looked like it had never seen a single flaming log.

"I've had enough of this," she said tightly. "I want those policemen off my street. My son is certainly not going to be sneaking back home, if for no other reason than he knows I'd immediately turn him in. He's brought me nothing but shame and humiliation. I don't know how I'll ever face my neighbors again. Or my colleagues at work. How much longer do you intend to keep us here, virtual prisoners? We're not the criminals, Detective. And you and those officers parked out there drinking coffee and eating donuts all day and night should be out looking for my son. I assure you, if he does show his face here, I'll be the first to let you know."

She sounded so convincing, Nat found herself believing she really would turn her son in. Or else she was a damn good actress.

"Why are you here?" she demanded, giving Nat a modicum of notice now.

"We'd like to speak with Christine."

"My daughter's not feeling well," she said curtly.

"It's okay, Mom." Christine was standing at the archway to the living room. She was wrapped in an old terry robe. Her feet were bare, and her face, devoid of makeup, looked sallow and washed out.

"I've got a head cold," she said, entering the room, nodding a greeting in Nat's direction and offering a pale imitation of a smile.

"You should be in bed, Chris." Nat finally heard a note of warmth in Marion Walsh's voice.

"I'm feeling a little better."

Leo and Nat shared a look before he said to her, "I'm afraid you might not be feeling better for very long. There's been a new development."

Christine's complexion turned ashen. Marion stiffened as if preparing for a physical onslaught.

Nat knew Leo had deliberately paused here for maximum effect, but unable to bear the obvious suffering this pair was going through, she blurted, "Alison Cole's body has been found."

Surprisingly, it wasn't Christine who broke down, but her mother. Collapsing against the mantel, wrenching sobs broke from the distraught woman. She made no attempt to hide the rush of tears from any of them. It was like they weren't even there.

Christine made no move to comfort her mother. Instead she

stared at her, dazed by this outburst. Nat was guessing Christine was not accustomed to seeing her mother in this emotionally debilitated state.

In the end, it was Leo who approached Marion and gently guided her over to the sofa. He even retrieved a freshly laundered handkerchief from his inside jacket pocket and offered it to her.

Marion took the hanky and clutched it in her hand as her sobbing began to ebb. She looked beseechingly at Leo. "What did I ever do to deserve this?"

Leo either took this as a rhetorical question or he simply had no answer.

Nat's gaze shifted to Christine who was now looking down at the floor, as if the pain of seeing her mother's suffering was too hard to bear.

"You're not helping your brother, Christine," Nat said quietly. Christine didn't look up.

Marion rose, having to hold on to the arm of the sofa to steady herself. When she did find her legs, she moved with purpose straight to her daughter. She didn't grab on to Christine's shoulder so much as clutch it in much the same way she'd moments ago clutched Leo's handkerchief.

"Do you know where Dean is?" she asked her daughter in a cracked voice.

Christine's head remained bowed as she shook it from side to side.

"Tell me, Christine." Marion's voice was a bit stronger. More forceful.

"I don't know where he is," she muttered.

"He's killed two young women, Christine."

"No."

"You think I don't wish to heaven it wasn't so?" Marion cried out. "To have a murderer for a son. Do you know what this is doing to me, Chrissy? Do you think I don't love Dean? But loving a child doesn't mean you can turn away from the truth of what he is. He's a *murderer*, Chrissy. He needs to be put away. Before he does even more harm."

"No," Christine shrieked. "It's not true. He never hurt anyone. I don't believe it. I won't believe it." Wrenching herself free of her mother's grasp, she fled the room and raced up the stairs in the hallway.

Looking after her, Marion said in a pained whisper, "They were always very close." She absently fingered the strand of pearls. "Give us a little time. I'll let you people know if I—" She waved off the rest of the sentence as she, too, left the room.

On their way out, Nat spotted Christine's tote bag in the hall. She slipped her card inside. It had her work, home, and cell phone numbers. Just in case.

"You ever worry about how your son will turn out?" she asked Leo as they were heading back to Boston.

"Because of who his mother is?" he shot back, instantly on the defensive.

"No, I—"

"Like he's doomed because she was a doper?"

"That's not—"

"She hadn't been using for close to six months when she got pregnant. She stayed clean the whole way through. It wasn't easy for her. But Suzanne did it. Our boy was born clean. Healthy as a baby ox." His features softened and he smiled at the memory.

"What went wrong? With Suzanne, I mean."

His smile vanished. "It was all too much for her. She took off the day after she got out of the hospital."

"With your son?"

"She left Jacob with my mother. Told her she just needed a little time by herself. Mom tried to talk her into staying, but once Suzanne had her mind made up about something—good or bad—there was no talking her out of it."

They stopped at a red light. Leo was staring straight ahead at

238 | **ELISE TITLE**

the road. "My mother worked with Suzanne in drug rehab. There was always one or two Mom felt like she could save. Suzanne was one of them. She was smart, pretty, and she wanted desperately to turn her life around. Mom offered her guidance, support, encouragement, and when Suzanne got out of rehab, Mom got her enrolled in some basic college courses, and even gave her a place to stay. Then she roped me into tutoring Suz in algebra and English a couple of nights a week."

The light turned green. Leo was slow to pull out and got beeped by the driver behind him. "I ought to give the creep a ticket," he muttered, deliberately driving down the road at a crawl.

"And you fell in love?" Nat asked as he finally picked up speed.

"We fell in bed," Leo said bluntly. "One time. We'd been fighting off a mutual attraction for weeks, Suz as much as I. So many times, I've asked myself what it was about that particular night that made me give up the fight." He shrugged. "Whatever it was about that night, neither of us could muster up the energy it would have taken to maintain our distance."

He paused, then glanced over at Nat. "I don't want you to think we were plain reckless. I used a condom. Just my luck, it was defective."

"I thought that never really happened."

He laughed dryly. "Me, too." His laugh quickly dissipated. "Suzanne said we were being punished for our sins. That's how she saw her pregnancy," he said sadly. "As punishment."

How sad, Nat thought. All those months trying with Ethan, praying she'd get pregnant, believing it would be the greatest gift. And here Leo gets someone pregnant on the first try. With a defective rubber, no less. And to Suzanne, it was a curse. Life was not fair, as Nat well knew. Still, there were times it really got to her. This was one of those times.

"It wasn't just that we were both horny and physically drawn to each other," Leo said, as if he was worried that was what she was thinking. "I cared about her. And I believe she cared about me. For a short time, I even thought we could make a go of it. But Suzanne never thought so. She wanted to get an abortion until I told her I wanted my child and that I'd raise it on my own. Not ask anything of her."

"That's traditionally the mother's line."

"Nothing traditional about Suzanne Holden. Anyway, Suz agreed, took off once she'd carried out her end of the bargain, and ended up on crack again within a month. One night, her dealer started roughing her up when she refused to go out on the street to pay off her debt and Suzanne pushed him through a plate glass window. It happened to be on the third floor of a crack house. If it hadn't been for her drugging, she'd probably have been able to win a plea of self-defense. But the jury wasn't particularly sympathetic, given that she'd been so heavy into crack. Luckily, there were a few men on the jury. Suzanne was quite beautiful, especially when she was clean—which she was by the time she went to trial." Nat was sure that was what swung them over to handing down a second-degree manslaughter conviction rather than the second-degree murder conviction the prosecutor was going after. That, and the fact that no one in the whole courtroom was exactly crying over the death of another pimp/dealer.

Leo was whipping down the Southeast Expressway now, going a good twenty miles over the speed limit. Chased by demons.

"Do you visit her in prison?" Nat asked, wondering what his relationship with Suzanne was now. Wondering how involved they were. Wondering why she was doing so much wondering.

"I did for the first couple of months—along with my mom and Jacob—but she asked me to stop coming. Word got out I was a cop and some people inside started hassling her. And I'm not just talking other cons who didn't like the idea of an inmate being chummy with the law."

Nat nodded. Not a new story. But when she got wind of officers unfairly coming down on inmates in her institution for whatever reason, she didn't look the other way like some Supers.

Then she remembered with a lurching sensation in the pit of her stomach that it wasn't *her* institution at the moment. What was really going to happen when her *vacation* was up?

Leo pulled off the expressway at the Prudential Center exit. "Mom still goes once a week like clockwork. Brings Jacob even though Suzanne refuses to let him know she's his mother. Doesn't want him to grow up ashamed of who he is and who he came from. Worse, doesn't want him feeling sorry for her. Mom's working on her, though. She keeps telling Suz the worst thing is lying to your child. Having him discover the truth despite you."

"Your mother sounds like quite a woman," Nat said with an admitted touch of envy.

"She is," Leo said without a note of ambivalence.

"Does she still work at the drug rehab?"

"No. She was only volunteering her services, but now she's doing full-time duty as grandma. She sold her house, moved into my condo and looks after Jakey while I go hunting after murderers."

Bringing them full circle back to Dean Thomas Walsh.

"Do you think Christine Walsh will tell her mother where her brother's holed up?" she asked.

"I hope so," Leo said solemnly. "Before someone else gets hurt." He gave Nat a meaningful glance—a glance that said that *someone* could be her.

twenty-six

Even when you've left for the day, you can't get real distance from it. The sounds, the smells—they cling to you like sour air. You come home, take a hot shower, and tell yourself you're doing all you can do. But the shower doesn't help much and neither does your pep talk. . . .

Superintendent Morris Rice
MCI Norton
(excerpt from WBZ radio interview)

A CALL CAME through from Oates as they were heading into Boston. Leo switched to speaker phone so Nat could listen to his partner's report on his interview with Jean Cole, Alison Cole Miller's mother.

"The mom's pretty broken up even though she was expecting it. Spent a good twenty minutes crying and ranting as to how we're all responsible for her daughter's murder. You can expect she'll be talking to the media all about how we're letting rapists and murderers like Walsh out on the street to wreak havoc, etc., etc."

Nat groaned loud enough for Oates to hear. "You got company, Leo?"

"Yeah, Natalie Price. The mom have anything else to say?"

There was a brief pause. Nat sensed that Oates wasn't all that thrilled that she was still hanging around his partner. "Not really," he said finally.

"Not really sounds like yes," Leo pressed. Didn't take too much reading between the lines for either Oates or Nat to get the message Leo was not going to shut her out. She was happy, but she was sure Oates wasn't.

"Well, she did get a call from her son-in-law while I was there," Oates said reluctantly. "And I heard Ms. Price's name come up a few times."

"I gather it wasn't in a positive context," Leo said dryly.

"I wouldn't say so. Guess the hubby didn't appreciate her asking him all kinds of personal questions."

"I'm sure he didn't," Leo said.

"And I may have a few more to ask him before this is over," Nat added.

Leo pulled to a rolling stop in front of Nat's parked car in the visitor's lot at the precinct house. Not cutting his engine, he looked over at her like he had something else on his mind. A more direct warning?

"You got lunch plans?"

Nat wasn't expecting the question and mumbled something that was a roundabout way of saying no.

"You like Italian?" He was mumbling a little, too.

"Food?" she asked inanely. And, inexplicably, that damn tingle was back.

"I know a place close by that serves the best lasagna in town. Not that nouveau cuisine vegetarian crap. The real thing. With pork sausage and ground sirloin. Homemade sauce made from real plum tomatoes and slow cooked for half a day. Even the mozzarella's homemade."

Nat's stomach growled.

They both laughed.

Ten minutes later they pulled into a parking space marked for residents only, on a narrow road off Hanover Street in Boston's Italian North End. Instead of heading back over to Hanover Street which was lined with *ristorantes*, they crossed the quiet side street to an old five-story building that still bore the worn letters CARUSO ELEVATORS. Although the exterior of the brick edifice had been carefully maintained, Nat could tell from the large, modern windows facing the street that it'd been quite some time since elevators were made on these premises.

She was a little slow on the uptake and it wasn't until she heard the jingle of Leo's keys that it hit her. He was taking her *home* for lunch. Home to meet his son. And his mother.

He noticed her hang back as he stuck his key in the lock of the downstairs door.

"What? You don't like lasagna after all?"

'No. I mean, I love lasagna. But—"

He had the door open and he was waiting for her to step into the lobby.

"Your mother won't be expecting me. Maybe there won't be enough food," she muttered nervously.

"Not enough food? In an Italian house? Are you kidding?"

Still, she hesitated. "Are you sure you want to do this, Leo?"

"It's only lunch, Natalie."

She was expecting a buxom, gray-haired, Italian momma in a cotton house-dress and an apron. Instead, she was greeted by a small, slender woman—surely she couldn't eat much of her own cooking—wearing a cerise silk shirt with sleeves rolled up to her elbows and slim-cut jeans. Like Leo, she had dark brown hair which she wore casually short and stylish. She had a warm, vital smile, but there was a sadness in her dark eyes—a sadness that looked like it had been there a long time.

Her finger was pressed to her lips as they entered the apartment. "Shhh. He's still napping."

Leo pecked his mother on the cheek. "Natalie, meet my mother, Anna. Ma, meet Natalie. She's wild for lasagna?"

His mother surveyed her with a warm smile. "Only lasagna?"

Mrs. Coscarelli might not have looked like your typical momma, but looks could be deceiving. Nat felt the heat of embarrassment creep up her neck. And for some reason she stuck her left hand into her jacket pocket so her wedding ring wouldn't show, and she wouldn't look like she was a prospective adulteress. Then Nat replayed Leo's line in her head. *It's only lunch, Natalie.*

Maybe that's all Leo thought it was. His mother seemed to be having a different interpretation.

If Leo was embarrassed or annoyed by his mother's suggestive comment, he kept it close to his chest. Maybe he was used to remarks like this from her. Nat wondered how many women before her he'd brought home for some of momma's home cooking. A better question might have been, why did Nat care?

Anna Coscarelli was nudging them in the direction of the living room. "Go sit down. I'll make a salad. You like escarole, Natalie?" She'd forgotten her own admonition to speak softly. Good, Nat thought, hoping Jacob would hear his grandma talking and wake up. Then the focus of attention would be on him instead of her.

"Please don't go to any extra trouble on my account."

But she was already heading off to the kitchen.

Leo guided Nat into a spacious living room. The first thing she noticed was a child-sized table flanked by two child-sized matching chairs, covered with puzzles and children's books. Beside the table was a long, low bookshelf lined with wire baskets chock-full of LEGOs, toy trucks, wooden blocks, and a huge collection of Star Wars action figures. Save for this child's corner, the rest of the room was very adult and very beautiful. Magnificent exposed beams clearly original to the one-time elevator factory cut vertically across the high white ceiling. The old oak plank floors had been stripped and whitewashed. The walls were stuccoed a pale terracotta. The Swedish modern style furnishings were spare but far from meager. A pair of tweedy sofas flanked a fireplace above which a white marble slab served as a mantel. There were at least a dozen framed family photographs on the mantel.

This was definitely not your typical cop's abode. For one thing, Nat couldn't imagine how a cop could afford a place like this. Even on a detective's salary. For another, it was far classier than she would have credited a man who looked like he bought his clothes at thrift shops. And didn't much care about the fit.

"You're surprised," Leo said.

"Very," she admitted. "But pleasantly," she quickly added.

"And you're dying to know how I managed to swing for it."

"*Dying* is a bit extreme."

He grinned. "I didn't come by it honestly."

His grin widened as he saw the look of surprise on her face.

"Relax, I'm not on the take. I just mean I didn't work for it. My father left me some money when he died. I bought the condo right after they reconverted the building about seven years ago. Figured it'd be a good investment."

"I love the decor. It's beautiful."

"A friend helped me decorate."

A friend? Leo, true to type, didn't elaborate.

She walked over to the mantel and gazed at the photographs. Most of them were of Leo's son and they ranged from infancy to the present. He was an adorable child with dark curly hair and dark eyes to match. In all of the pictures—even the ones when he was a baby—he was smiling brightly. Several of the photos of Jacob included Leo and/or Leo's mother. None with Jacob's mother, although Nat did spot one gilt-framed photo of a striking young woman—a girl, really—in a flouncy white gown. She was looking straight into the lens of the camera and although she was smiling, there was no sense of cheer in the smile. And her large, wide set eyes were serious, almost soulful. Nat didn't know why, but she felt a sadness as she looked at this photo.

"Suzanne?" she asked, turning to face Leo.

He shook his head from side to side, but didn't offer anything else. Was it his friend with the great taste in furniture?

A squeaky little voice piped up from across the room. "That's my Auntie Marie. She's dead." This was announced matter-of-factly and with a pronounced lisp.

Nat turned to see that same bright, intelligent little face she saw in the multitude of photos on the mantel. Jacob Coscarelli came into the room dragging a well-worn blanket after him. His dark hair was every which way and his right cheek was rosier than the left from sleeping on it. He was dressed in a Boston Red Sox shirt and denim overalls. Still eyeing her cheerily, he said, "Did you come to play with me?"

"Hey, Jakey," Leo interrupted, squatting and stretching out his arms. "When do I get my kiss?"

"When do you want it?" the precocious child asked with a giggle. Then, without waiting for an answer, he flung himself into his daddy's waiting arms and they shared a loud, smacking kiss. Leo rose, lifting child and blanket with him. Jakey wound his little arms around his daddy's neck, father and son maintaining their embrace. Leo's expression, which could give so little away when he chose, revealed a transparent joy. It was a loving and enviable sight.

"Jakey, say *hi* to Natalie."

"Hi, Natalie. Wanna build a castle with me?"

"I can't think of anything I'd like better," she said, finding herself meaning every word.

Jakey wriggled out of Leo's arms. "It's hard with LEGOs. I better show you."

"After lunch, little man," Anna Coscarelli interrupted, stepping into the room. "Soup's on."

Jake giggled again. "It's not really soup. It's lasagna." Soup pronounced *thoop*. Lasagna—*lathanya*.

With no hesitation Jakey walked over to Nat and slipped his soft little hand into hers. His child's touch sparked a tingling sensation of a different kind, one that was achingly maternal. "You *thit* next to me, Natalie."

He stacked the colorful LEGO pieces with far more dexterity than she managed. Her clumsy attempts made him giggle.

Jakey and Nat were sitting together on the floor in the middle of the living room, building their castle. Leo was in the kitchen helping his mom clean up the lunch dishes. Anna adamantly refused to let Nat help. Nat wasn't sure if Anna wanted to get her son alone to get the scoop on his *new friend*, or if she sensed Nat's desire to spend a little time with Leo's engaging child. Probably a little of both. Not that Nat imagined Anna would get much in the way of inside dope from her closed-mouthed son. Or did Leo confide in her? Everyone needed someone to confide in. For Nat, it had been Maggie.

She felt a tiny hand press over hers. "You wearing a *th*ad face."

Nat pressed her lips together, then forced a smile.

"Better," he said, sounding a lot like his father.

"You are an excellent castle builder, Jakey."

"You practice more, you be good, too."

"If I had a little boy at home, I'd practice a lot."

"You don't have a little boy?" He asked the question with

such an ingenuous note in his voice, as if everybody had their own little boy. If only—

"No. But I'd like to have one some day. A little boy as smart as you."

"And a little sister?" he asked innocently. "Nanna *thays* Daddy should make me a little *thithter*. Daddy can make everything."

Three was a little young to explain that while Daddy could probably make lots of things on his own, he would need some help in making a little sister. So, she simply agreed with Jakey that having a little sister would be great fun. Nat was guessing Anna Coscarelli would very much like to see her son get married and raise a family. She was sure Anna had shared that wish with him. Remembering that Anna took Jakey to visit his mom regularly in prison, Nat wondered if Anna had hopes of Leo resuming his relationship with Suzanne when she got out. Nat started calculating in her head and realized that Suzanne would be eligible for parole in a little less than a year's time. Nat further realized, this time with a start, that Suzanne could even end up spending a good chunk of that time at a pre-release center before her parole. The usual stay was four to six months, but some of the female inmates had been granted longer placements. Nat had two female inmates who were doing most of their last year at Horizon House.

"Look at me," Jakey scolded, taking hold of Nat's chin and pointing her face at his.

She ruffled his soft, fine hair. "Sorry."

He snuggled in a little closer to her. As if to remind her more solidly of his presence so her mind wouldn't wander. Nat had a fierce desire to lift him up, put him on her lap, hug him tight and drink in his wonderful child scent. But she figured she should let Jakey set the pace here.

"Last piece," he said sadly, topping the tower with a little red flag.

"What do you say we build ourselves a second castle?"

"Okay," Jakey nodded enthusiastically. "This one for the king. And a new one for the queen."

Out of the mouths of babes.

"See what a nice, hot meal will do for you," Leo said as they drove back to the precinct close to two hours, two helpings of lasagna and two very elaborate LEGO castles later.

"Is that supposed to be a backhanded compliment?"

"Yes," he said simply. For a man with such a talent for evasiveness, Detective Leo Coscarelli could be surprisingly candid when he chose.

"I had a great time. I'm glad it shows. Jakey is totally delightful. So is your mother. And she does make the best lasagna I've ever tasted." Nat looked over at him. "You're lucky, Leo."

"She would have given you the recipe."

"I don't mean—"

"I know what you mean. You're right. I am lucky."

"I'm surprised your mother never remarried. She's a great-looking woman. I can't believe she's fifty-seven." Any more than she would have believed Leo was turning thirty-six. "She could easily pass for forty-five." What Nat wouldn't have given for the Coscarelli genes.

"She may not look it," Leo said soberly, "but she's had it rough the last few years. Finding another husband's been the last thing on her mind."

Remembering Jacob's statement about his Aunt Marie being dead, Nat sensed that Leo didn't only mean his mother's widowhood and the pressures of having to look after his son full-time.

She debated whether or not to ask the next question. Not wanting to mar what had been a much needed and appreciated respite. She was guessing it had been a respite for Leo as well.

But, as usual, curiosity got the best of her. Not prurient curiosity, but a growing desire to learn more about this enigmatic detective. *Desire.* Hmm. What would Freud have said about that?

"That photo of your sister—" she began. Immediately spotting Leo's fingers tightening around the steering wheel. "She was very beautiful."

Now his jaw clenched. Nat was getting all the signs she needed to drop the subject. She ignored them.

"How did she die?"

He didn't answer for several moments and Nat knew she'd once again stepped over some invisible line. But Leo surprised her by responding after all, his expression taking on an incongruously fierce nonchalance.

"She ODed. When she was twenty. That photo on the mantel, that was her high school prom night. Taken ten years ago. She got a scholarship to Boston State. Sophomore year, she talked my folks into letting her share an apartment near campus with a couple of other girls. My mother wasn't keen on the idea. Didn't like these girls. Thought they were wild. But my father was a softie. Marie could always twist him around her little finger. Two months after he co-signed the lease for her, she was dead. Before the year was out, my father died of a stroke. Ask my mother, though, and she'll tell you he died from a broken heart."

"Oh Leo, I'm so sorry."

They hooked eyes for a moment. The nonchalance was gone. So was the fierceness. What Nat saw now was a man filled with heartache and despair. Emotions she could identify with only too well.

Leo's eyes returned to the road. "You wouldn't think smart college kids would mess with something as dumb and as dangerous as heroin. But I guess they thought it was street-chic. Two months. That's all it took to hook her. And to kill her."

Nat understood now why Leo's mother had volunteered at a drug rehab center. And why she'd taken certain girls under her wing and tried to save them. Girls like Suzanne. Had all of them failed her in the end?

twenty-seven

Does the subject understand the reasons for the perpe-
tration of his crime?
Does the subject understand the repercussions of his
offense?
Can the subject explain how he would act differently
given it to do over again?
Is the subject manipulative? Provocative? Flirtatious?
            (excerpted from Criminality Questionnaire
            Commonwealth Community College Thesis)

NAT'S ANSWERING MACHINE was blinking when she got back to her
apartment a little after 3 P.M. There were three messages. The first
was a hang up. The second was from Ethan—*It's me. Call me at*
my office. He made it sound like a command, which only served
to irritate Nat and cement her resolve not to return the call. She
wondered if some of that resolve had to do with the last two

hours she'd spent so pleasantly with the Coscarelli family, particularly Detective Leo Coscarelli.

The last message was from Jack. And it instantly grabbed her full attention. *You may be onto something, Nat. Keith Franklin's car has a broken brake light on the driver's side. Please be careful crossing streets from now on. I'm coming over after work to take you out to dinner.*

"You didn't call back."

Nat found Ethan's accusatory tone more than a little irritating. She was sorely tempted to simply hang up on him.

"What do you want, Ethan?"

"I want to know what that cop thinks about what I told him the other day. I'm going nuts here, Nat, thinking they're going to show back at the house or my office and start grilling me again. Or worse, drag me down to the station and give me the third degree like some common criminal. Luckily, Jill wasn't home when they showed on Sunday, so I've managed to keep this terrible business from her so far."

"Do you really think she'd appreciate being kept in the dark?" Nat asked facetiously.

Ethan missed her sarcasm. "She's having a real rough time with the pregnancy. I always thought morning sickness meant you get sick only in the mornings. She spends more time in the bathroom these days than she does in—" Ethan stopped abruptly. As if Nat couldn't fill in the blank. Had he always been this insensitive? This self-involved? Nat knew one thing. His current behavior was beginning to make this split easier for her.

"I've got to go, Ethan. I'm meeting someone for dinner in exactly fifteen minutes." She really had over an hour, but she was anxious to get off the phone.

"Oh," he said with a note of surprise. "A date?"

"You are really something, Ethan."

"Okay, I know it's none of my business. But is it so hard to understand that I want you to be happy, Nat? And let's face it, you haven't really been happy for a long time. A long time before I . . . left."

"Is that what you tell yourself? Does that make you feel less guilty? Well, I have news for you, Ethan. I was happy. I was damn happy. Before I discovered you were cheating on me. That's when I got unhappy, Ethan. Unhappy, disgusted, angry—"

"I never took you for someone who lied to herself, Nat. You wanted things from me that I couldn't give you. And I know that hurt you."

"If by *things* you mean children, I guess I naively thought you'd . . . come around. And you did. Just not with me."

"Let's not go over this again, Nat. I never intended to get Jill pregnant. It just happened."

"Okay, fine. I don't want to go over it again, either. I've got to go, Ethan."

"Wait. Please. Has Coscarelli said anything to you? Did he believe my statement?"

"Was it the truth?"

"What? Of course it was the truth. For God's sake, Nat, why would I lie?"

Why? Because maybe he had something to hide, that was why. Just like he'd hidden his affair with Jill for all those months. The distressing truth was, the more time Nat'd had to think about the story Ethan gave her and the police for going to see Maggie that Friday, the less she was coming to buy it. If he simply wanted advice from Maggie about how to break the news of Jill's pregnancy to Nat, it could have been accomplished with a brief phone call.

What if Ethan had been sexually involved with Maggie? For all Nat knew, Ethan could be the masked man in that vile photo. What if the real reason he went to see Maggie was to beg her not to tell Jill about their sordid affair? Or to beg her not to break it off simply because he'd knocked up a pretty, young student and was being pressured into marrying her? What if Maggie wanted to come clean? Nat doubted Ethan was worried about her feelings. But Jill was another story. All Nat had been hearing from Ethan since Maggie's death was how desperate he was to protect the future mother of his child, his future wife. To prevent her from knowing anything at all about his involvement with Maggie Austin?

Before Friday, while Nat wouldn't have put it past Ethan to have tried to make a move on Maggie, she'd have said that it was ludicrous to imagine Maggie would ever have engaged in a sexual liaison with her best friend's husband. Now Nat was sadly beginning to think that where sex was concerned, Maggie might have had a serious problem with impulse control.

It was unsettling, to say the least, for Nat to discover that she really didn't know Maggie Austin at all. Her friend's heretofore unknown kinky sexual activities put everything Nat thought she knew about Maggie into question. More to the point, it put their whole friendship into question. How could you be someone's close friend and know so little about her? What kind of a friend kept such secrets from you? Deliberately lied to you? Possibly—very possibly—screwed your own husband?

Not since she was a small child, had Nat felt so alone. So abandoned.

"Nat? Nat, are you still there?"

Ethan's voice jarred her from her thoughts. "Yes."

"Jesus, is that what the cops think? That I'm lying? Why the hell else would I have gone over to see her?"

"You tell me, Ethan."

His voice darkened in a way she didn't think she'd ever heard before. "You aren't filling that detective's head with lies about me, are you Nat? To get back at me? Because if you are—" Again, he left her to fill in the blank.

What he left her was decidedly uneasy.

Jack was working on his third Scotch straight up and he wasn't even bothering to play at eating his steak. It sat on his plate untouched. She wasn't doing much better with her grilled salmon.

"What made you check up on Franklin's car?" she asked. "I thought you were convinced it was pie in the sky."

Jack cupped his glass in both hands. "I was hoping you were right and I was wrong." This was the first time he'd conceded the possibility that Dean Thomas Walsh might not have been Maggie's killer.

Jack's gaze fixed on the Scotch. "I gotta cool it on the booze." He resolutely set the half-finished glass down. Nat was relieved to see he could still exert some control. For how long was something else.

He plucked a radish garnish sculpted to look like a rose off his plate and studied it thoughtfully. Like its mock petals might hold some answers. "I still think it's a reach. But maybe not as big a one as I thought earlier. Especially after I tailed Franklin when he got out of work today. He didn't go straight home."

Nat's dinner, slowly congealing on her plate, was now all but forgotten. "Where did he go?"

"He drove straight to Maggie's building." Jack's eyes fell again on the booze but he didn't reach for it. Just looked like he badly wanted to. "He parked across from her building and stared up at her window for about fifteen minutes, then he dropped his head against the steering wheel. I got close enough to see his chest heaving."

"It's pretty clear Keith Franklin was infatuated with Maggie, which is all the more reason why he'd be the last person to kill her," Nat said, playing devil's advocate. Wanting to be convinced otherwise. Jack obliged.

"Unless he was furious that Maggie was sexually involved with someone else. Another con, no less. A con who'd threatened to castrate him." She noticed the faint wince that was no doubt the result of Jack now taking it as a given that Maggie was sexually involved with Dean Thomas Walsh.

"Why go after Maggie and not Walsh?" she asked.

"I don't know. Maybe Walsh is next. If Franklin can track him down. Or maybe it was that old—*if I can't have her, no one can.* Leaves everyone else who loved her to suffer the agony of her loss." His resolve gone, Jack tossed down the rest of the Scotch in his glass, not coming up for air until he'd drained it.

"You're forgetting about Alison Cole," Nat said. "We may figure out a motive as far as Maggie is concerned, but—"

"I'm not forgetting the Cole woman. What happened to her back in '92 is public record." Jack leaned forward in his chair. "After I followed Franklin home, I stopped by the Boston Public Library. Spent a half hour at the Tribune microfiche files looking up the Cole attack and Walsh's trial. Both were covered quite thoroughly. Much against her lawyer's advice, Cole made several statements to the press. Describing the attack in pretty vivid detail and tearing Walsh to shreds."

"So?" she asked impatiently. And then before Jack could respond, Nat figured the answer out for herself. "You think Franklin read up on it, too. And deliberately sought Cole out and murdered her so that when he murdered Maggie, everyone would believe both murders were Walsh's doing? You're talking a lot of pre-meditation here, Jack." She gave him a dubious shake of the head.

"Granted," he admitted, "that's stretching it."

"Still," she said slowly, speaking as she was thinking it through, "you've got to admit that the Cole murder pretty much eliminated any other potential suspects as far as Maggie's murder's concerned."

Jack was studying her closely. "You look and sound less pained now when you speak about her murder. You feel Maggie betrayed you." There was hurt and disappointment in his voice.

And something else. Something she couldn't quite identify. But it made her uneasy.

"No, that's not true," she argued, but even as she denied it, Nat knew there had been a change. She told herself this was merely a result of the passage of time. Getting used to the reality of Maggie's death. And it was partly that. But Jack was also right. There was a sense of betrayal. And Nat wasn't even sure how far that betrayal extended. If Maggie had only been more open with her, more honest. The problem was Nat couldn't honestly say how she would have reacted if Maggie had been truthful.

"What about you, Jack? You believe she was sexually involved with Walsh. Which means she betrayed you, too." Which also meant, although she didn't say it aloud, that Jack had the same motive for murder that he'd so meticulously constructed for Franklin. Surely, he must have known this, too.

Jack didn't answer. He simply reached for his glass again, frowning when he saw it was empty.

Nat felt tension gathering in her muscles. The dull throbbing of a migraine setting in. Again she found herself questioning— was Jack Dwyer capable of murder?

Her head was pounding now as her mind tried to separate out what was her incipient paranoia from what was logical and real. But nothing was black and white. She felt trapped in a nebulous gray zone where every suspicion seemed dreadfully possible.

The waiter came over. Looked askance at their untouched plates. Before he could inquire whether something was wrong with their meals, Jack told him everything was "just great," and to please take the plates away and bring two coffees.

The waiter eyed Jack's empty Scotch inquiringly. Jack gave a reluctant shake of his head, and Nat was relieved. Despite the three drinks—and who knew how many more before she'd showed up—Jack was looking remarkably sober. Sober topics could do that.

He seemed to be watching the waiter walk away, but Nat could see that his eyes had a faraway look. He was silent for several moments. "Maggie was the most sexual being I've ever encountered."

"Did you suspect she had other lovers besides you and Dean Walsh?"

He turned to her, squinting as if he had just gone from darkness into glaring light. "Do *you* suspect she had other lovers, Nat?"

Nat's throat went dry. "Franklin, possibly."

Jack absently tore little pieces off the damp cocktail napkin the waiter had failed to remove, rolling them between thumb and index finger and flicking them away.

"One night a couple of weeks ago when I was staying over at Maggie's, she got a phone call. It was one, two in the morning. We were half-asleep. When she heard who was on the line, she woke abruptly, got out of bed and took the call in the other room. Clearly not wanting me to overhear her conversation."

"Which immediately sparked your curiosity," Nat said.

A faint smile. "My jealousy, Nat. It sparked my jealousy."

"Who was she talking to?"

"It was a conversation between lovers. Current or past, I'm not sure."

Jack's gaze was riveted on Nat. All seriousness now. "I recognized his voice, Nat."

And suddenly, she understood. The confirmation she'd feared came at her like that speeding car had come at her in the dark of night.

Jack must have seen by her expression that she'd got it.

"I'm sorry, Nat."

"Why didn't you . . . tell me?"

"Ethan had walked out on you for Barbie doll by then. I felt you were already suffering enough." He lifted an eyebrow. "You don't look all that surprised."

"I guess I'm not," she managed to say.

"There's something else." He hesitated. "A few times I saw . . . bruises on Maggie's body."

Jack's words took a few seconds to penetrate. "What are you . . . ?"

"In places you don't get bruises unless—" Jack shut his eyes, the muscles in his neck and jaw growing pronounced.

Nat felt physically ill at the thought that Ethan might have left those bruises. But it made no sense. Ethan had never gotten the slightest bit physically rough with her. Then again, maybe Nat had never brought out that side of him.

Crazy, but that thought made her feel even more sexually inadequate.

Of course, it could have been Walsh who'd left those bruises on Maggie. Or Franklin. Or God only knew who else. Maggie Austin's sexual promiscuity seemingly knew few bounds.

"What about you and Maggie, Jack? Did the two of you ever engage in rough sex?"

"Are you accusing me of something here, Nat?" There was no missing the note of wariness coloring his voice.

Nat was not ready to tell Jack just yet about that sexually explicit S&M photograph Leo had found in Maggie's apartment. Then again, maybe he already knew about it. Maybe, he'd been the one posing with Maggie—

This had to stop. She simply could not tolerate this constant bombardment of suspicions. If this kept on, she'd be a basket case. A very lonely basket case.

Nat resolved to get Leo Coscarelli to show her the photo. If she could detect the identity of the man with Maggie, maybe it would put some of her suspicions to rest.

She didn't want to think that the very opposite might prove true.

twenty-eight

The sexual act is only a small part of the sexual encounter. For most partners there is the need for closeness, tenderness, touch, a sense of connectedness, i.e., escape from isolation. . . .

Dr. Simon Moore
Sexologist

NAT WASN'T SURPRISED to find Leo at the Cambridge precinct house even though it was close to ten P.M. He was surprised to see her.

"I was out to dinner with . . . a friend," she said evasively. "Not far from here." A bit of a stretch, considering her dinner had been at a Cambridge restaurant.

Leo remained seated behind his desk, waiting for her to get to the point of her unexpected late-night visit. Maybe he was thinking it was a social call.

Wanting to quickly disabuse him of that possibility, Nat blurted, "I want to see that photo, Leo."

He motioned to a wooden chair across from his desk. Behind her, a door opened as she went to sit down. It was Leo's partner, Mitchell Oates. He nodded an awkward greeting in her direction, then looked past her to Leo.

"Can I see you outside a minute?"

Leo's chair scraped against the floor as he rose closing a black loose leaf file that was sitting on his desk, and slipping it into a drawer. Nat was sure it was the murder book on Maggie Austin. And inside that book was the photograph she'd come to see—slowly becoming obsessed with the idea that she would be able to identify the masked man with Maggie.

"Sit tight," Leo said, brushing her shoulder with his palm as he passed by.

Nat was relieved that there was no electric charge at his touch now. She had enough on her plate without having to fend off sexual feelings that she had no intention of acting on.

Through the glass windows separating the tight two-desk cubicle of an office from the larger homicide squad room, she could see Oates and Leo conferring. A couple of times Leo glanced in her direction, but Nat couldn't get a reading. They were out there a couple of minutes. Oates took off and Leo returned to the office.

Nat couldn't detect any visible change in his demeanor, yet she could strongly sense it. Something was different now. Worse? Better?

"What?" she asked nervously. Praying for *better.*

"A homeless woman walked into the 7th precinct in Cambridge about an hour ago. Wanted to know if there was a reward for information about a wanted man."

"Walsh?"

Leo nodded.

"She knows where he's hiding out?"

Leo shook his head. "She said they shared a park bench in Cambridge last Friday afternoon. Around lunchtime. Oates is going over to question her. Get a statement as to why she waited this long to come forward."

Her heart rate accelerated. "She could provide an alibi—"

Leo held up his hand. "Let's take it one step at a time. Walsh is still a wanted man, Nat. He's an escapee and he's still being sought for questioning regarding the murders of Maggie Austin *and* Alison Cole Miller."

Leo's way of reminding her that one alibi didn't get Dean Thomas Walsh off the hook. Still, it was something. At least it could be something.

In a rush, Nat told Leo about her meeting with Franklin's wife, the miss-and-run, the discovery of Franklin's broken brake light, and ran Jack's theory by him as to Franklin's motive for killing both women. Not telling him that it was her deputy's theory, not hers. Leo still had to have Jack on his suspect list, and Nat didn't want Leo thinking Jack had spun this theory about Franklin as a way of getting himself off the hook. Or, Leo might think, as she had, that the shoe could fit more than one foot. Namely Jack's. Or, for that matter, Ethan's.

"Why the hell didn't you tell me about this sooner?" Leo barked. It wasn't hard to read his expression now. He was boiling mad. No big surprise there.

Since Nat wasn't sure which part of her saga he was ranting about, she opted for an all-purpose shrug.

"You're nearly run down and you don't say a word to me?" Was that a hint of hurt as well as fury in his voice. "That's why you wanted a check on Franklin's car."

"I thought it was a drunk driver at first. I didn't read anything intentional in it until the same car passed by my sister's house later that night. At least, I think it was the same car. Because of the busted brake light." Nat could see she was only digging herself in deeper with this extra piece of information.

"How'd you find out Franklin's car has a busted brake light?"

"I . . . I went to where he works. I saw him get into his car at the end of the day." She hesitated, then figured what the hell, she was already in for the lie. "I followed him. He drove to Maggie's place." She told him about Franklin staring up at Maggie's window, then breaking down. She simply omitted telling him that she was giving a second-hand account of these events.

"So first you think Franklin tried to run you down and then you brilliantly decide to start following him around. Give him more of a reason to want you out of the way."

"He . . . didn't see me following him." At least that much was the truth.

"Look, Natalie, I don't know if Keith Franklin had anything to do with Maggie Austin's murder. And I'm even more dubious about this motive you've concocted for his killing the Cole woman. But I'll tell you what I do know. And it's sure as hell something you should know, too. And that is that Keith Franklin's an ex-con who's having a lot of trouble putting the pieces of his old life back together. His marriage is falling apart. His kids treat him like a bothersome intruder. He's been demoted, degraded, shunned. God only knows—but you and I can certainly guess—what life was like for him in prison. If he thinks there's even a chance of you trying to pin a murder rap on him, a chance he's going to get thrown behind bars again, it could very well put him over the edge. If it hasn't put him there already."

She crossed her legs and began nervously jiggling her foot as she thought over the implicit warning in Leo's tirade. A tirade that wasn't over yet.

"And Keith Franklin isn't the only lowlife who isn't too fond of you. If I were you, I sure as hell wouldn't want to bump into Owen King on a dark, desolate street. And you aren't exactly culling favor with Walsh after that botched set-up, Natalie."

Leo came and sat down in the wooden chair opposite hers. Some of his anger seemed to have dissipated.

"Am I getting through to you here, Natalie?"

"Loud and clear."

He didn't look convinced. "How about taking a real vacation? Cape Cod is great this time of year. Jakey and I spent a terrific week down in Truro last fall right around this time. Crowds are gone, but the weather's still fantastic and the beaches are empty—"

"You ever quit the force, you should think about being a travel agent."

"Seriously, Natalie—"

"I still want to see that photo, Leo."

He threw up his hands in abject frustration. "You could drive me back to cigarettes, you know that?"

"It's good you quit. You don't want to set a bad example for your son. Not to mention subjecting him to second-hand smoke—"

"I don't need to be worrying about you, too, Natalie."

"Are you worrying as a cop or as a . . . friend?"

"I don't make friends easily."

"Neither do I."

There was an awkward silence, neither of them knowing where to take it from there. Nat believed, more than anything else, that was why Leo went, at last, and retrieved the photo she'd come to see.

The 3×5 photo was in her hands, but she hadn't looked down at it yet. Courage was what was needed here and she was finding it sorely lacking.

She didn't want the man in this photo to be Ethan. Or Jack. Or Dean Thomas Walsh.

But there was more involved than her fear of being able to identify the lover in the black mask. Nat didn't want to see Maggie as she would appear in this photo. She didn't want this lurid image of her best friend to be the one she'd be compelled to carry around with her. She didn't want this to be her lasting memory of Maggie.

She was torn about her feelings for Maggie. Yet, however much Maggie'd betrayed her trust, however much she'd kept from her about her sexual life, Nat couldn't dismiss how much Maggie had meant to her over so many years. Maggie was one of very few people in her life that Nat had allowed herself to love.

"Natalie." Leo said her name softly.

Slowly, she dragged her gaze down to the photo.

She had to blink several times before she could see clearly. And even when her eyes were fully focused, the black and white images crisp, it took her several more seconds to sort the scene out in her brain.

Of this there was no question. The photo was pure pornography, the kind of X-rated trash seen in any S&M smut magazine. Nat could only take it in by pretending that the woman in this photo was a perfect stranger. This stranger was nude, on her knees, wrists bound and pulled taut behind her arched back, her neck encased in a studded black leather dog collar which was attached to a metal chain lead.

The lead was being held by her lover, who was positioned behind her, leaning slightly over her. Because of the angle at which the photo was taken, most of the man was obscured. All Nat could see of him was a gloved hand pulling the lead taut and his head, which was encased in one of those bizarre S&M black leather masks that fit full over the face with little slits provided for eyes and nose.

Maggie's face—yes, when she got to the face Nat lost her ability, fragile at best, to pretend the woman was a stranger—had been yanked at an awkward angle toward the camera—although Nat had no idea if either she or her lover knew there was a camera. There was only one way to describe the look on Maggie's face. Ecstasy.

Finding this image far too disturbing, Nat focused on what there was to see of the black masked figure. The only skin visible in the photo was at the curve of the neck as it began to meet the shoulder. How could she possibly identify the man with so little of him exposed?

She stared at the line of the man's neck for a long time as if somehow, if she was patient, its owner would reveal himself.

And in a way, that was what happened.

She wasn't aware her hands had begun trembling, or that her breath was stuck in her throat, until Leo's voice broke through her reverie.

"What is it, Natalie?"

Her breath escaped in a low gasp. "There's . . . something. I think. Here." Leo leaned closer, looked at the tiny smudge just below where the lover's neck would connect with the shoulder that was out of the frame. She could see from his expression he wasn't seeing it. Didn't understand. How could he?

"What—?"

"We need to blow this up." There was a tremor in her voice. Blood was racing through her veins.

Nat remembered the day quite vividly. It was a little over a month ago. A hot, muggy August Sunday, the air so saturated with moisture it felt like you were breathing in the wetness.

"This is definitely a day for the beach," Maggie announced gaily as they headed up Route 1. Indeed, she was the one who had planned this outing to Rockport, a quaint but touristy artist-cum-beach community on the North Shore. Nat was sitting beside Maggie in the front seat of her black Jetta. Karen Powell was in the back. Piled up beside her were beach towels, blanket, picnic basket, thermos bottles and other sundries.

"I hope someone remembered to bring sunscreen," Karen said, having to shout to be heard over the blast of the Beach Boys on the car's CD player. Karen had already complained about the music. She was not a fan of the Beach Boys or their ilk.

Karen was often snippy, at least when Nat was around. But she was particularly snippy this day. The air conditioning wasn't reaching the back seat; Maggie was driving too fast; the noise of the Beach Boys was going to drive her insane.

The complaints continued all the way to the beach. Maggie had forgotten to stick the beach umbrella in the trunk so there was no shade to be had. And the sunscreen she'd brought was too weak a strength. Karen insisted on leaving her blouse on over her bathing suit to protect her skin.

Nat was fed up with Karen's whining and just about ready to bop her, but Maggie seemed to let her assistant's complaints go in one ear and out the other. Until Karen refused to remove her blouse and come into the ocean.

"Look at her, Nat," Maggie chided. "She's got the best body of the three of us and she's ashamed to show it in public."

Karen glared at Maggie. "Will you leave me alone? You're the one that brought along the wrong sunscreen. Do you mind if I don't like getting burnt to a crisp?"

"Ah come on, Karen," Maggie teased, "what's a little burn? No pain, no gain. You know that."

"Be quiet, Maggie." Karen glared at Maggie.

"It's that dumb birthmark on your shoulder, isn't it?" Maggie said, still teasing, but more gently now. "That's why you never wear anything sleeveless. That's why you never want to go swimming."

Karen opened her mouth to say something, abruptly stopped herself and stalked off.

Maggie went chasing after her.

Nat didn't even think to question at the time, how it was that Maggie knew about this birthmark if Karen always kept it hidden from view.

"You suspected it the other day when we left her place, didn't you?" Nat said, setting aside the blow-up of the lurid photo.

"Not fully. I was pretty sure Karen was into women, but I wasn't sure about Maggie."

"But you thought Maggie might be bisexual? What made you—?"

"Cop's intuition, I suppose."

"I guess I should feel pretty inadequate since Maggie never came on to me," she muttered.

"You've got nothing to feel inadequate about, believe me," Leo said. He smiled faintly. "And there's nothing backhanded about that compliment."

"What happens now?"

Leo's smile broadened.

"About Karen," Nat said, looking reprovingly at the detective. "I didn't take you for being the flirtatious type, Leo."

"Is that right?" he responded obliquely.

There was a rap on his door. Oates popped his head in, gesturing to Leo to come outside again. It was almost midnight, well over an hour since he'd left for Cambridge to get that statement from the homeless woman. This time Leo motioned him to come in. Oates hesitated for a second or two and then entered.

"We may have something interesting here," Leo said.

"That makes two of us," Oates said.

"You go first."

Oates gave Nat a quick look, then shrugged. "The woman's name is Eleanor Cray. Says she's fifty-one, but she looks well over sixty. I gave her a modified mental status exam." He gave a thumbs up, indicating she'd passed it, no problem.

"She lived with her daughter over at the Madison housing project, but about six months ago the daughter took off with her boyfriend. Mom was evicted a few weeks later because she didn't have money to pay the rent. Seems her daughter cleaned her out before taking off."

"No job?" Leo asked.

"She picks up the odd job now and then, but nothing steady.

Doesn't make enough, she says, to afford more than a shelter for a few nights at a time. Says she prefers staying on the street, at least until cold weather sets in. Considers it safer."

"She into booze?"

Oates smiled, showing even, white teeth. "Calls herself a social drinker."

"Was she drunk tonight?"

"No. No dough or she sobered up deliberately before showing at the precinct."

Leo sighed. "Okay, so what's her story for last Friday afternoon?"

Oates pulled out a small pad from his jacket pocket. Unlike Leo, his partner was a smart dresser. His dove-gray suit had the look of cashmere and it was perfectly tailored to his broad physique.

He flipped open the pad, referring to it briefly. "She'd been hanging out in Comden Park since last Tuesday. Found a little out of the way nook where she could sleep undisturbed."

Oates glanced down at the pad again. "Oh, yeah. Says she liked this particular park because a lot of the working people in the area eat lunch there and there's usually good pickings. Plus the magazines."

"Magazines?"

"She told me she likes to keep up. *TIME, Newsweek, People.* Pretty much whatever she can dig out of the trash or snatch off a park bench."

Leo nodded. Nat sat quietly, taking it all in.

"So, anyway, she says she remembers seeing a man fitting Walsh's description walk into the park and sit down on the bench right across from her last Friday. Says it was just past noon because she heard a church bell chime twelve times, which is how she knew it was time to go scouting for lunch."

"And what made Walsh stick out in particular?"

"She says she remembers him for three reasons. One, she says he looked like a movie star. Reminded her of James Dean."

"Yeah, what's the rest?" Leo said impatiently.

"Two, he was eating a huge salami sub with all the fixings and she's nuts for salami. She was hoping, given his size and all, he wasn't a big eater which meant she'd be having herself a nice little lunch when he took off. Turns out, he did leave a good half of the sandwich over, only he set it down on the paper bag beside him and, instead of heading off like she was hoping, he pulled out a magazine and started reading. Which brings us to her third reason for remembering him. The magazine was *Entertainment Weekly* and it had a picture of some actress from a soap opera on the cover. Ms. Cray happens to be a big fan of this particular soap— she told me how, at least one or two afternoons a week, she'd go to this nearby laundromat that has a TV and pretend she was waiting for her clothes to dry so she could catch the show. Only the manager of the Laundromat finally got wise to her and kicked her out."

"Get back to Friday afternoon," Leo said with an even more impatient tone.

Oates continued, unperturbed. "Supposedly, the man she identified as Walsh saw her eyeing the magazine. He asked her if she'd like to have it, seeing as how he was finished with it and had to get back to work. He didn't offer the sandwich. She thinks it was because he didn't want to embarrass her. But he didn't toss it in the trash can. Left it right there on the park bench. She says she sat there all afternoon, savoring every last bite of that sandwich and every single page of the magazine."

"And she's sure all this happened on Friday? Not Thursday, say?"

"Definitely Friday." Oates turned a page in his pad. "Says one of the things Walsh said to her when he handed her the magazine was TGIF. She didn't get it. He explained it stood for Thank God it's Friday."

Leo picked up a pencil off the desk and started tapping it in the palm of his hand. "Does she have any idea what time he left the park?"

"She remembers the church bell chiming once right as she snatched up the leftover sandwich. Says Walsh was just walking out the park gate. She wanted to wait until he was far enough away before grabbing the eats."

Nat looked excitedly at Leo. "That verifies what Walsh claimed. That he was in the park from noon to one o'clock."

"If it was Walsh," Leo said, his excitement negligible to nonexistent.

"Showed her a dozen photos of guys around the same age, build, coloring as Walsh. She picked him out without a second's hesitation. It looks pretty solid, Leo," Oates said.

Leo remained unimpressed. "And what was her reason for waiting all this time to provide us with this info?"

"She didn't want to say at first. Kept going on about waiting for some mention of a reward in the paper. Ask me, I'd say she was on a long weekend bender and wasn't exactly keeping up with the news. Probably sobered up some when the money for booze ran out and then caught a headline or saw something on TV at some bar earlier tonight."

"Run a check on her."

"Already in the works. So, what've you got for me?" Oates asked.

Leo held up the blow-up. "Could be this *he* is a *she*. By the name of Karen Powell."

"Well, well, well," Oates muttered, rubbing his square jaw.

Leo checked his watch. "Give her a call now and let's get her in here for questioning first thing tomorrow."

Oates raised a thick eyebrow. "So you thinking we got ourselves another suspect?"

"Maybe more than one," Leo said, picking up the official

statement Nat had made regarding Keith Franklin, while they were waiting for the photo lab to do the blow-up.

Oates took the statement and gave it a quick scan, eyebrows knitted together.

"We'll want to go another round with him as well," Leo said.

Oates, still scanning, nodded agreement.

Nat looked from Oates to Leo. "Still no leads on Walsh's whereabouts?"

Both men shook their heads.

All three of them knew that, guilty or innocent, a very desperate man was still at large. And that made Dean Thomas Walsh a dangerous man as well.

"We've got to find him," Nat said hoarsely. "Before it's . . . too late."

twenty-nine

Without crime, a lot of people would be put out of work—cops, lawyers, prison employees. You think about it, they ought to be grateful to us. . . .

C. T.
Inmate #854929

IT WAS AFTER midnight, but when Leo offered to take her out for a drink before she headed home, Nat agreed without hesitation. She didn't really want a drink, but she didn't really want to go home yet either. What she wanted to do was expel from her mind the image of Maggie and Karen in that photograph. Maybe a shot or two of whiskey would help. Leo was right. She needed a respite.

Leo was right about other things, too. She was making waves and making enemies. Maybe she should butt out. At the very least, Nat was damn sure going to look both ways before crossing any more streets.

They went to an Irish pub not far from the precinct. It was a cheery place done up to look *authentic* right down to the dart board and the strains of "Danny Boy" lilting through the well-placed speakers. There were only a handful of late-night regulars at the aged copper bar. Leo guided her past the bar, calling out to the robust, ruddy-faced bartender for two whiskeys with beer chasers, and led her to a booth near the back.

"I don't like beer," she muttered.

"You don't have to drink it."

"I don't need your permission," she snapped.

"What do you need, Natalie?"

His question, filled with innuendo, only made her more testy. "I need to not talk."

"Okay," he said with an obliging smile. But he held her with his eyes. There was too much understanding there. Now she was both irritable and uneasy. She didn't want to be understood. Not by Leo. And not by anyone else—her parents, her sister, Maggie, Ethan. A lifetime of telling herself otherwise was really nothing more than a lie. A self-deluding, self-deceiving lie. She was terrified of being understood. Because of what others would unearth in the excavation. The pettiness. The ugliness. The multitude of inadequacies. She had been so adept up to now at concealing them. Even from herself. But Maggie's death and its aftermath had slowly but inexorably led to a stripping away of her multiple layers of defenses.

The drinks came. She swallowed down the shot of whiskey and followed it with the beer, not remembering she didn't like it. But then she didn't really taste it either. All she wanted was to re-insulate herself.

Leo downed his shot, but he was taking his time with his pint of beer. "I'll order you another round if you let me drive you home," he offered.

"No. I'll drive myself."

"Fine, then."

She reached for her bag.

"What's your hurry?" he said.

Nat could have come up with a lot of answers. But that might open Pandora's Box. And she was not about to risk that.

So, she stayed put.

Another Irish melody drifted across the room. Leo leaned against the back of the booth, seemingly comfortable with their silence and the ambiance.

"I thought the Italians and the Irish didn't get along."

He gave her one of those smiles. "I try to get along with everyone."

"Are you successful?"

His smile deepened. "I don't have a bad record," he said in a mock Irish accent that made her laugh.

By the time Leo dropped her off, Nat's mood had greatly improved, thanks to a couple of whiskies and beer chasers. And Leo Coscarelli's company?

While she was riding up the elevator to her floor, preparing once again to enter her silent, solitary apartment, she thought about getting a dog. A nice, big, friendly mutt. It would be so nice to come home and be greeted with open arms—well, open paws—by an unconditionally loving creature.

When she and Ethan were first married, she'd brought up the possibility of getting a dog. Ethan was appalled at the idea. Dogs were dirty and messy. Dogs took a lot of care. Dogs tied you down. It was pretty much the way Nat had come to realize he felt about children as well. Would he still feel that way when Jill gave birth to his child? Did leopards ever change their spots?

Ironically, Nat found herself feeling sorry for Jill. Well, it was a welcome change from feeling sorry for herself.

As the elevator arrived at her floor, Nat felt a new sense of freedom. She was no longer tied to her husband's likes or dislikes. If she wanted a dog, she'd get a dog.

By the time she got to her front door, she was contemplating breed, size, temperament, even having a fleeting thought or two about what she'd call her new puppy—*Ollie if it's a boy, Hannah if it's a girl.*

Opening her door, she imagined Ollie or Hannah loping toward her, barking, jumping up and down with joy, lapping her face with its big, wet tongue—

Nat *was* greeted when she stepped into her apartment. But it was no dog that sprang out at her in the darkness. It was something hard. And it struck her squarely on the left side of her head. Before completely losing consciousness, she felt an arm wrap viselike around her waist. Followed by a harsh, whispered, "bitch" as she was being dragged—

Surely, she must be in Hell. The terrible heat, the acrid smell, the all-consuming smoke. She tries to open her eyes, but the smoke stings so badly.

Momma used to say she'd go to hell. When Momma was in one of her states. That was what Daddy called them. States. Pay no attention. Your momma's in one of her states. When she was little she'd once asked him, which states, Daddy? New York State, where she was born? Florida, where we once went on a vacation? California, where Momma went to college? She wanted to know because whichever state her mother was in, she didn't ever want to visit.

Now she was in hell. What had she done that was so bad?

Oh God, she knows. She knows why she's been condemned to hell.

Maggie, I'm so sorry. Alison, I'm so sorry. It's all my fault.

Hot tears burn down her face. A wrenching pain shoots through her skull.

Do dead people cry? Do they feel pain?

It was the pain that shocked Nat fully into consciousness. Into awareness of where she was.

Not in hell.

But close.

She was on her bed and her bedroom was filled with acrid smoke.

At first she couldn't put it together. Couldn't imagine why there was all this smoke.

And then she saw the flames lapping at the pretty paisley cotton dust ruffle around her bed frame, sparks catching onto her blanket. Quickly, she threw the blanket off her and literally sprang out of the bed. Gasping because of the pain in her head, and then gasping a second time instantly afterwards because of the burning sensation in her chest as she gulped down smoke.

Got to stay low. Got to crawl out of here. Got to hold my breath.

She inched along the floor. Disoriented, eyes stinging from the smoke, she wound up, not at her door, but at her closet.

Despair coursed through her. Precious moments wasted.

The fire was spreading fast. And with it, the thick smoke. She held her breath. *Can't let my lungs fill up with smoke or I really will die. And more than likely go to Hell.*

But she couldn't keep herself from coughing. Which forced her to draw in smoke. Provoking more coughing. More inhaled smoke. A vicious cycle.

Got to move faster. Faster.

Finally, she felt a sliver of fresh air in the thin crack between the floor and her bedroom door. This meant the fire had not yet spread to the living room. Safety out there. Almost home free. She was beside herself with relief.

Keeping low, she stretched her hand up to the knob, turning it.

Nothing happened. The door wouldn't budge.

She pulled harder. No give at all.

Jammed. Pull a little harder. Yank. Use all your strength. Forget about the heat, the smoke, the flames turning your bed into an inferno.

P-u-l-l-h-a-r-d-e-r—
H-e-l-l—

Her eyes flickered open to see a face looming over her. She blinked several times.

"Ethan?" Her voice was a bare croak. The effort of forming that one word provoked a spasm of coughing.

"Take it easy, Nat. You're going to be fine."

She started to look around but her head throbbed too much. "Where am . . . ?"

"At Boston City Hospital. I brought you here in the middle of the night. The doctor says you've suffered some minor smoke inhalation—"

"Fire . . ."

"It's out. Our bedroom's pretty much gutted. But the firemen got there before it spread to the rest of the apartment. Don't worry. We've got fire insurance to cover the damage. A few weeks and you won't even know it happened."

She shut her eyes, trying to put the pieces together, but she was definitely not up to sorting out a jigsaw puzzle.

A hand lightly stroked her brow. The touch was familiar. Comforting. Tears spilled down her cheeks.

"You've also got quite the bump on your skull, Nat. You must have fallen—"

"No. Hit," she rasped. "The . . . fire. Someone set . . ."

"No, Nat. It was an accident. What the fire inspector's put together is that you lit a candle by the bed and then you must have fallen asleep. Knocked the candle over with your blanket and it fell on the floor at the side of your bed and ignited the bedding—"

"No. No."

"Shhhh. Don't get yourself all worked up, Nat. It'll all make sense to you by tomorrow. Your head'll clear by then and you'll remember—"

"I . . . do . . . remember."

Now Ethan's strokes were irritating. She weakly swiped his hand away. "You found me?"

"I got there in the proverbial nick of time."

"How . . . ? Why . . . ?"

Ethan sighed. "To be honest, Nat, our phone conversation yesterday afternoon really upset me. I couldn't sleep. I felt we needed to talk. Clear things up. I knew you were out on a date, so I figured you might be getting home late. I decided to drive over, see if any lights were on. If not, wait until you got back. When I got there, I saw the flicker of what I thought was a light coming through the bedroom window. Then I realized . . ." He shivered visibly. "I raced up to the apartment and found you unconscious just inside the bedroom door."

"The door wouldn't open. I . . . couldn't get out." Panic rushed in again as she remembered the terror. The certainty that she was going to burn up inside that room.

"What? The bedroom door? You probably just didn't have the strength to open it. Anyway, I scooped you up and carried you out into the hall, then ran back inside to dial 911. I was just starting to dial when I heard the fire engines pull up. Someone else must have called it in. I didn't know how bad off you were, so I didn't want to waste any time waiting for an ambulance. I just gathered you in my arms again and raced you straight over here."

She tried to track all of Ethan's words. Making sense of them, however, was too much of an effort.

Leo was standing at the foot of her hospital bed, glancing at her chart. It was seven o'clock Thursday morning. She'd been in the hospital for over twenty-four hours, spending most of Wednesday in a stuporous sleep. She had a vague memory of Jack visiting her at some point in the day, but she couldn't remember a word they'd talked about. If they'd talked at all.

Fully awake this morning, she'd already received and rejected a breakfast of lukewarm porridge and bland tea, had her blood pressure taken, blood drawn, and her chest listened to by a bleary-eyed young resident who looked like he was close to the end of a thirty-six-hour shift.

Leo's eyes moved from the chart to her. "How are you feeling?"

"Like I want to get out of here." Her throat was still sore, her voice still raspy. "I hate hospitals."

"That makes two of us," Leo said, letting the chart swing back on its chain and clank against the metal foot board. He had a small overnight case in his hand. He swung it onto the bed. "Some stuff for you to wear," he mumbled. "Get dressed. You've been sprung."

Nat was so elated by the news, she instantly tossed off the thin white blanket only to realize she was wearing nothing but a skimpy hospital gown that had ridden high up on her thighs. Leo noticed, too.

"I'll . . . wait . . . out there," he mumbled, turning toward the door.

"Wait," Nat called to him. "Don't you want to know what happened?"

"I talked with your ex," Leo muttered, not turning around.

"That's not what happened," Nat said tightly. "Someone attacked me. Someone started that fire—"

"You can tell me all about it after we're out of here. I'll be out in the hall."

Nat quickly dressed in jeans and a soft wool gray turtleneck sweater, trying to ignore the pain in her head where she'd gotten thwacked. Trying also to ignore whose clothes she was putting on. Suzanne's? Leo's sister, Maria's? The underwear was new at least. Still had the labels on the socks, light blue panties and matching one size fits all bra. There was even a pair of new-looking black loafers, size eight. Nat's size. A lucky guess? Or had Leo done some checking?

It was only as she was combing her hair with the complimentary comb provided by the hospital that Nat felt the knobby lump which was still tender to the touch, and remembered Ethan being there the night before last, smoothing her hair from her face.

It all came back to her in a rush. Ethan's story about how she'd lit a candle on the bedside table, then proceeded to fall asleep and knock it over, setting fire to her bed. And how she must have hit her head trying to get out of her bedroom.

It was ludicrous. The last time she'd lit a candle in that bedroom was the first night she and Ethan had moved into the condo. She'd wanted to set a romantic mood for their lovemaking. But Ethan blew the candle out, saying he didn't like making love with any lights on. She'd teased him, telling him it was usually the woman who was self-conscious. Ethan reacted badly to her remark. They'd ended up in the dark, not making love at all that night.

Nat wondered if Ethan thought she'd brought her supposed date home last night and lit the candle as a preliminary to making love.

And then she remembered something else Ethan said. That her bedroom door wasn't jammed.

But it *was*. Or else someone was on the other side of that door. Preventing her from opening it.

"A dog?" Leo glanced over at her from behind the wheel of his car.

"You have something against dogs?"

He smiled. "Man's best friend? Are you kidding? I love dogs. Been thinking about getting one myself. I've just been waiting until Jakey's a little older so my poor mother doesn't have to deal with both a kid and a dog who need to be *potty* trained."

"What kind of dog are you thinking of getting?"

"Golden retriever," he said without hesitation. "How about you?"

"After Tuesday night, I'm thinking pit bull," she said sardonically.

"According to—"

"Ethan?" Nat cut him off sharply.

"According to the preliminary investigation, it appears to have been an accident. A lit candle—"

"I never lit a candle, damn it. And, if Ethan's theory is that I had a lover over there, it's a lie."

"No lover? Or no lover over Tuesday night?"

"You drove me home Tuesday night. And whoever was waiting for me in my apartment, it *wasn't* my lover. And not that it's any of your business, but I don't happen to have a lover at the moment."

She tried to get a read on Leo's reaction to that news, but he maintained his poker face.

"These are the facts about that night, Leo. I'd barely crossed the threshold into my apartment when somebody conked me over the head and knocked me out. He must have dragged me into my bedroom, did that little candle trick, and then left me to . . ." She faltered there. Who, besides Ethan, would know about her desire to make love by candlelight? No one. And was she ready to buy his story that he couldn't sleep and drove over to her place in the middle of the night to talk? What would he tell Jill if she woke up and found him missing? Unless she was the world's heaviest sleeper, would he really take the risk of going off on her like that, unless he was feeling completely desperate?

"Lucky for you, your husband showed up in the nick of time." Leo glanced over at her. "Odd for him to be showing up at that hour. Or is it?"

"Very odd," she said firmly, relating the same excuse for Ethan's presence at her apartment that night that Ethan had given her. Saying them aloud made them seem even more unlikely.

"How bad a fight did the two of you have?"

"Not bad enough for him to want to do me harm."

But did she believe that? What if Ethan *did* want her dead? What if he had murdered Maggie and then became frantic because he saw that she suspected him? And that she might go to the police and convince them of his guilt?

But then, why save her? Did he get cold feet at the last minute? Or did someone report the fire too soon and he was afraid she'd be found alive? The fire investigators might suspect arson. Ethan would be in even worse trouble. So, he rushed inside, carried her to safety and came off looking like her savior instead of her attempted murderer.

Nat told herself this was insane. Ethan might be a liar and a cheat. But a murderer?

She looked out the window, trying to absorb herself in the life of the city only to realize they weren't driving in the direction of her apartment.

"Where are we going?"

"You can't stay at your place. It's going to need some major repair. Your husband's arranging—"

"Stop calling him my husband. I know we're not divorced yet, but it's just a formality."

"So what do you want me to call him?"

"Asshole."

They both smiled. Nat started to feel a little better.

"I thought you could stay at my place. Mom'll bunk with Jakey and you can have her room."

"I can't do that, Leo." There was more than polite refusal in her voice. There was panic. She wasn't sure why his offer of hospitality scared the daylights out of her, but it did.

They were still heading for the North End. "You've got time to decide where you want to go," Leo said when they pulled up to a red light. "For now, my mom's cooking up some minestrone soup especially for you. Jewish mothers believe chicken soup cures all ills. Italian moms feel the same way about minestrone."

He smiled. Until he spotted the tears welling up in her eyes.

"Don't say it's just soup," she rasped. "I can't remember a single day growing up when my mother ever made soup or anything else for any reason having to do with me. Certainly never to cure *my* ills."

Leo reached his hand out and placed it over hers. His touch released the tears she'd been fighting so valiantly to keep at bay.

"It's not what you think," she mumbled, swiping at her face until Leo came up with a fresh, laundered handkerchief for her.

"What do I think, Natalie?"

"You feel sorry for me."

"Blow your nose."

"I almost died the other night, Leo. Don't you want to know what really happened?" She blew her nose.

"Someone attacked you, set a fire in your bedroom, and prevented you from getting out."

"You believe me?" She felt a small measure of relief. And then a flash of panic. "You don't think the man who did this was—"

"You sure it was a he?"

"What—? You think a woman—?" And then, before he could respond, a name popped out of her mouth. "Karen? Is that who you think—?"

"She was furious on the phone Tuesday night when Oates called her and asked her to come in Wednesday morning to discuss a photograph we had of her and Maggie. She insisted she had no idea what he was talking about. So Oates described it to her. The line went dead."

"Why would that provoke her to try to kill me?"

"When we interviewed her yesterday, she insisted she had no idea a photo was ever taken of that *encounter*."

"You showed her the photo?"

Leo nodded.

"And she didn't deny it was her?"

"Not only didn't she deny that she and Maggie were having a

sexual relationship, she went so far as to say she was the only lover that ever truly satisfied Maggie sexually and emotionally."

"Easy to say that without Maggie around to confirm it," Nat said dubiously. And then her mind spun off from that thought. What if it was the exact opposite? What if Karen feared that Maggie's physical and emotional attraction to Dean Thomas Walsh—an attraction possibly stronger than the one Maggie felt toward Jack Dwyer—was pulling Maggie away from her? How far would Karen go to hold onto her bisexual lover?

"Leo, what if Karen's lying about the photo? What if she rigged a camera to take the shot and then, out of jealousy and fear of losing Maggie, she confronted her with the photo. Maybe threatened to show it around. To the dean at the college. To me. To Jack—"

"So far, Karen's sticking to her story that she didn't know about the photo."

"Maggie must have known. You found it in her apartment."

"It could have been left there. Afterwards."

"By her killer. Oh God."

"There's more. For some reason, Karen's got it in her head you were the photographer."

"Me?" She give Leo an astonished look. "That's crazy."

"She says you've got a camera with a telephoto lens. She thinks you were spying on them. Climbed up the fire escape outside Maggie's bedroom window and took pictures—"

"That's crazy and sick. Did you ask Karen if she owned a camera with a telephoto lens as well?" Nat shot back angrily.

"She says she doesn't."

"And you believe her?"

"About the camera?"

"About any of it?"

"I believe one thing."

"What's that?"

"She hates you. One of her last remarks to us yesterday was that if it weren't for you, Maggie would still be alive."

Since that was something Nat had thought herself hundreds of times since her friend's murder, she had nothing to counter with.

"Karen could have been behind the fire, Nat. That phone call Oates made to her on Tuesday night ended just around the time we were sipping our first round of drinks. She had more than enough time to make it over to your apartment before you got back."

Leo hesitated. "There's something else. Karen also knew about Maggie and your husband. She told Oates she'd walked in on them one time."

Maybe it was the pause before he dropped this last bombshell or the way he was avoiding eye contact, but something told Nat this wasn't the first time Karen had shared this piece of information with him. She started to confront him for holding out on her, but then she realized—what did it matter at this point?

"Blaming you—in effect, trying to convince us Walsh murdered Maggie—is a way of throwing suspicion off of her," Leo said.

"Is it working?"

"We haven't crossed her off our list."

Nat thought about that list. Karen, Walsh, Jack, Ethan, Keith Franklin. Any one of them could have killed Maggie. And when they threw Alison into the mix, Alison's husband started looking like an excellent suspect, as well.

"I was at your apartment yesterday with the arson team. There was no sign of forced entry. Did your maintenance man change the lock on your front door?"

Nat shook her head guiltily. "He was out sick for a couple of days and I let it slide. He was supposed to get to it Wednesday." It took a second for her to remember Wednesday was yesterday. Post-fire.

"Well, that means your husband had a set of keys. And then there was the set Maggie had—the ones we think the killer nabbed."

A shudder coursed straight down her spine.

"I'll make sure new locks go in before you move back."

Nat was wondering if she ever wanted to move back into that condo. Would she ever be able to sleep in that bedroom again? Not only would she have to contend with the torturous thoughts of her marital break-up, but now there'd also be nightmarish dreams of shadowy figures striking matches and burning infernos.

thirty

"You can be a king or a street sweeper, but everybody dances with the Grim Reaper."

R.A.H.
Death Row Inmate gassed 1992

LEO'S MOTHER LADLED out another serving of minestrone into Nat's bowl. "He likes you. You know that."

At least Leo wasn't around to hear his mother's comment. He'd dropped her off and headed straight back to the precinct.

"Who likes Natalie, Granny?" Jakey asked after loudly slurping his soup.

Anna ruffled his hair. "You."

"Daddy, too," he announced.

Nat could feel herself blush. "Well, I like all three of you."

"Wanna build a rocket ship?"

"Not now, Jakey," Anna said. "Natalie needs more soup and a little rest."

"She can take a nap in my bed. It used to be a crib but it isn't anymore. I'm way too big for a crib."

"I can certainly see that, Jakey."

He puffed out his chest and climbed off his chair. "I know. I'll build a rocket ship and you can play with it after your nap."

Anna sat down across from Nat as Jakey toddled off for the living room. "You sure you won't spend a night or two here? We've got plenty of room."

"I really appreciate the offer but—"

Anna held up her hand. "Don't explain. I understand."

Nat ate a few spoonfuls of her second serving of minestrone. "Has Leo been involved with anyone since—?"

"Since Suzanne? Depends what you mean by *involved*. Leo isn't a monk. There've been occasions—not too many, but a few—where he's gone out and didn't show up until the next morning. Maybe sometimes it was the same woman, maybe not. He's not one for sharing when it comes to those things. But this I'll tell you, Natalie. You're the first woman Leo's brought home. The first one he's let Jakey meet. That boy means the world to him."

"I know."

"Leo tells me you and your husband are separated. Maybe there's a possibility you'll get back together." She didn't pose it as a question, but Nat was sure she meant it as one.

"Not a chance in the world. I'm filing for divorce." Nat surprised herself with this announcement. Up until now she'd taken a totally passive approach to the dissolution of her marriage. Ethan was the one who'd left. Ethan was the one who'd have to get the divorce. Or was Nat hoping he'd have a change of heart and not go through with it? Had she still been holding out the possibility that somehow they'd work things out? *Things*. The fetus implanted by her husband in Jill's womb wasn't a *thing*. Ethan was going to be a father. That was a given. Whether he wanted the divorce in the end, whether he married Jill—and most important, whether he was a murderer—were all still open for debate. What was no longer open for debate was Nat's decision to start acting in her own best interest. And that meant, for one, not waiting for Ethan to file for divorce, but to file herself. ASAP.

Anna was watching her in much the same way Nat sometimes caught Leo watching her.

"You've had a hard life, Natalie."

She winced at the truth of her words. "So have you. Losing your daughter and your husband—"

"You know the old saying, it's better to have loved and lost than never to have loved at all? There is no pain worse than losing a child, Natalie. Still, that I had my beautiful Marie to love, even for a little while . . ." Tears spiked her eyes. "When you love fully and deeply, you accept how vulnerable it makes you. But it's worth it. For all the pain. It's still worth it."

Nat nodded slowly but it was more out of reflex than confirmation. A big part of her still felt like she'd have been better off if she'd never fallen in love with Ethan Price.

"Thanks for picking me up, Hutch," Nat said as she climbed into his red Ford Taurus. Instantly remembering her last time in this vehicle: her nightmare ride with Walsh, and then being entombed in the trunk.

Hutch looked over at her. "You're shivering. Want some heat?"

"No, I'm fine." The sweater Leo had brought her at the hospital was more than enough to keep out the mild autumn temperature. The chill she was feeling came from bad memories.

Hutch turned up the heat despite her response.

"You sure it's okay to put me up for a couple of days? Rosie doesn't mind?" she asked.

"You can stay for a couple of days, a couple of weeks, whatever. You know that. Rosie welcomes the company."

Nat let a few minutes go by in silence before asking, "How are things at Horizon House?"

"Getting a little slack from the powers that be. Lockdown's over. About a third of the cons are still house-bound—anyone with violent crimes on their record. We've had to send their files downtown for re-evaluation. Expect a few of them to be sent back. The rest have got the okay to resume work release. But no more outside activities or programs. Everything's gotta be in-house. Spot checks at work sites have been upped. Call-ins have been added every two hours. Which is putting a hell of a strain on the staff. But we're holding down the fort."

"And Jack?"

"He's real upset about this fire business, Nat. Don't mind telling you, so am I. Do me a favor. No more candles, okay?"

Nat felt guilty not telling Jack or Hutch that the fire was no accident, but Leo had been insistent that she keep the truth under wraps. For her own protection. Of course, Ethan knew she wasn't buying the fire as an accident, but he wasn't likely to be chatting about it to Hutch or Jack. Besides, he was too busy trying to convince her and the police that it was an accident.

"Jack told me about that scumbag, Franklin. You spot any car with a broken brake light cruising my neighborhood, you dial 911 pronto. And stay put. Rosie's gonna keep an eye on you and see you stay out of trouble."

She balked. "I don't need a watcher. And Rosie doesn't need to be responsible for my welfare. Maybe staying at your place isn't—"

"We all know you're tough. And pigheaded."

"Hey, I'm still officially your boss, Hutch."

He laughed dryly. "What am I telling you that you don't already know?"

"Nothing," she admitted. "Anyway, maybe I won't be your boss for much longer."

"You'll be back, Nat. That is, if you want to come back."

"How's Jack doing?"

"Not winning any prizes. Bitches a lot. Wants you back as

much as the rest of us. Says he doesn't need the headaches. Not only are the cons bitching and complaining, we've got our *friendly* protesters wearing out the sidewalks, and the press crawling up our asses."

Nat nodded. She'd had phone calls and attempted visits from the media as well. Less, though, then when she was still at the helm. Out of sight, out of mind.

Oh well, she thought, that was one benefit of being on vacation leave.

Hutch dropped her off at her car which was still parked in the lot of the precinct house. He beeped his horn and opened his window as she opened the door. "I'll lead you out to my place."

"I know my way to Stoughton, Hutch."

"Okay, then I'll follow you."

Nat shrugged, aware there was no point in arguing with him. He was determined to make sure she got to where she was supposed to be going. And got there safely.

Hutch delivered her to Rosie at the door of their small 1950's green bungalow. The cottage, bought as a fixer-upper back when Hutch and Rosie first had their daughter Elizabeth nineteen years ago, was on a winding dead-end road that led to a small pond. There were only a half-dozen homes on the street. Across from their place was an old one-room schoolhouse that was being converted into a living space. Builders were busy at work putting on a large addition. Rosie, a small, trim woman in her late fifties, apologized for the noise.

"They stop by four P.M. and don't start up again until seven in the morning, so it's really not too bad." She had to raise her voice over the din of hammers and saws.

Taking Nat firmly by the arm—she was surprisingly strong for such a small woman—she deposited her into their cozy front parlor, waving Hutch off at the same time.

"We'll see you for supper, Gordy." If anyone other than his wife had dared to call Gordon Hutchins *Gordy*, no question he'd bite their heads off. Rosie merely got a grunt.

"You'll need some clothes," she informed Nat as she shut the front door. "My Libby was your size before she went off to Smith College. Just rummage through her closet and drawers, pick out what you want. Nothing here she wears anymore. Put on some weight since she's been away at school. Well, more than some. Not that I say anything about it to her when she comes home to visit. And when Gordy opens his mouth, I tell him to shove a sock into it. She's got Gordy's build, so it's not like it's her fault. And really, if anyone should drop some pounds it's Gordy more than Libby. You know how many corrections officers suffer heart attacks? He's lost at least three friends in the past couple of years. And knows a handful more who fortunately pulled through. A couple of them were forced to take early retirement."

"Has Hutch had any heart problems?" Nat asked anxiously.

Rosie rested a cool hand on hers. "No, the man's healthy as an ox. But he's carrying a lot of weight. In more ways than one. He's worried sick about you, Natty." Rosie was the only person who called her Natty. And got away with it.

"You want something to eat?"

"No, I had lunch at . . ." Nat stopped, not wanting to go into her burgeoning relationship with the Coscarelli family. "Actually, a cup of tea would be great." She figured this would give Rosie something to do and give her a few minutes to catch her breath.

All she managed was a few seconds. No sooner did Rosie disappear into her kitchen than Nat's cell phone rang.

"It's Christine Walsh. You said I could call . . ."

"Of course, Christine. In fact, I was going to call you. I've got some terrific news. The police have someone who can provide an alibi for your brother for the time of Maggie Austin's murder."

"Really? I . . . can't believe it. I mean . . . I never doubted he was innocent. I just can't believe there's someone out there who can verify it."

"I need to speak to him, Christine."

"That's actually why I called. My mother's been hounding me ever since you and that detective were here. I wasn't lying when I told you I didn't know where he was. But . . ."

"Yes?" Nat prodded when Walsh's sister hesitated.

"He calls me. Not at home. I have a friend at my office. She's got a cell phone. I don't want her to get into any trouble. She doesn't know it's Dean calling me. She thinks it's my fiancé."

"When will he call again?"

"At four o'clock."

Nat quickly checked her watch. It was ten after three.

"Christine, listen. This is important. Tell him a woman has come forward with a solid alibi for him for the afternoon of Maggie's murder."

"You mean . . . he's been cleared?"

Nat heard the desperate note of hope in Christine's voice. "It's looking good. Very good."

"What about Alison Cole?"

Good question, Nat thought. And one to which she wished she had a good answer. "Let me talk to Dean about Alison."

"He didn't kill her. He swore to me—"

"We need to track down his whereabouts on Thursday. He may also have a solid alibi—"

"*We?* You mean the police? Forget it."

"Let Dean just phone me. I won't involve the police yet. That's a promise."

"I don't think he'll do it. He doesn't trust you anymore. Do you blame him?"

Rosie walked in with a steaming mug of tea, a frown on her face as she saw Nat on the phone. Nat surreptitiously clicked off and then said, "No problem, Rach. I'll come right over."

She clicked off again, this time purely for effect. "My sister.

She's in a pinch. She has a four o'clock doctor's appointment and her baby-sitter just backed out. I told her I'd fill in."

Rosie was still frowning, her shrewd eyes zeroed in on Nat's face. "Well, have your tea first."

"No time. I'm sorry. Just save it for me. I'll nuke it when I get back. I shouldn't be any later than six."

Nat was out the front door before Rosie could argue.

The insurance company where Christine worked was in a strip mall on Route 9 on the Natick-Framingham border. Fighting the traffic and speeding wherever there was the slightest opening, Nat managed to make it to the door of The Lewis Rice Agency at five minutes past four.

There was a young, blond receptionist at the front desk of the long, narrow storefront room which accommodated eight other desks, four on each side. There was an insurance agent at every desk but one, the second on the left. And Christine Walsh was nowhere in sight.

"Can I help you?" the receptionist asked without much enthusiasm.

Nat was busy scanning the room, spotting a door at the rear marked STAFF ONLY. She swung open the gate that divided the receptionist's space from the agents, mumbling and pointing to one of them. The receptionist resumed browsing a fashion magazine.

It was only as she passed the last desks on the left and right that the two agents sitting there realized she wasn't in the back to see either of them.

"You can't go in there," the middle-aged woman on the right called out as Nat opened the Staff Only door.

"I'm a friend of Christine's," she called back as she stepped into a small storage room lined with boxes of insurance forms and the like. There was a small couch at the back of the room. Christine popped up from it and looked nervously at the door as

Nat shut it behind her. Walsh's sister had a cell phone to her ear. Her expression confirmed that she was talking to Dean.

Nat headed straight for her.

"Dean, listen—" was all she managed before Nat snatched the phone.

"Dean, it's Natalie Price. Please don't hang up. We've got to talk. Has your sister told you that someone's come forward who saw you in the park?"

"So you believe me now?" Dean's voice had an edge to it, but he was not nearly as hostile as she'd anticipated.

"Yes." How much, Nat wondered, was the note of confidence in her voice the result of certainty, how much wish fulfillment? Alibis, as she well knew, didn't always stand up on continued scrutiny. But this one had to. For everyone's sake.

"And Alison?"

"Talk to me about her, Dean. Were you calling her and hanging up?"

"No."

"Did you see her at all since you've been at Horizon House?"

"No."

"You've had no communication whatsoever?"

"This is getting old, Nat."

"Okay," she said, not sure where to go from there.

"If your next move is to try to get me to turn myself in, forget it."

"It will go a lot easier on you than if you wait for the police to track you down."

"Another old story. They're not finding me. And if they do, they're not taking me in."

"That's old, too, Dean."

"Old but true," he said fiercely.

"Can we meet? Just the two of us. I swear it won't be a set-up."

"Find Alison's killer, Nat. Then maybe we'll get together for a little chat. I gotta go. Tell Christine we're halfway there. And that I love her." This time Nat heard a distinct click and she knew the phone was dead.

"Will he meet with you?"

Nat nodded slowly to give herself a few seconds to trust her voice to the lie. "If you'll come with me. He says that's the only way. And he says it has to be right now. Otherwise I might call the police."

"But they're watching my building. They follow me every-where."

Well, at least this established Christine did know where her brother was hiding out. Not that Nat had ever doubted it.

"My car's parked out back behind the Stop & Shop at the end of the strip mall." Away from the watchful eye of the cop parked in an unmarked car in front of the insurance company. "We can slip out together through the back door and the cops won't be any the wiser." She was guiding Christine toward the exit as she talked.

"I've got to let my boss know I'm leaving. . . ."

"Call from my cell phone. You can say there was a family emergency."

What could have been more truthful than that?

thirty-one

None of you get it. I am the victim here. They took my
body, my soul. Whatever's left, I'm keeping. . . .

                                                    D.T.W.
                                        Inmate #209782

"WHAT WILL YOU do if he won't turn himself in?" Christine asked
nervously as they pulled out of the lot.

"It's up to the two of us to convince him," Nat said firmly.
"Which way? Right or left?"

"Left."

They headed west on Route 9. Away from Natick. Away from
Boston.

"He can't do another five years. Which is still what he's looking at for the escape even if he's cleared of Alison's murder as
well as Maggie Austin's."

Nat gave Christine a quick glance. "Did you know Alison
Cole?"

She hesitated. "Not . . . really."

"Not really sounds like yes."

"She was . . . at the trial. She testified."

"You spoke with her at the trial?"

Christine shook her head.

"Before?"

"She hardly knew Dean. I wanted her to . . . understand why he never could have . . . done to her what she said he did. See, I knew a few of the girls he dated. One of them was a good friend of mine. And we'd . . . talk."

Nat caught a flush of color staining Christine's cheeks. "Dean'd die of mortification if he knew Kelly and I'd talked about him. Talked about . . . their sex life."

Her blush deepened. "Dean was a very . . . gentle lover. He was—according to Kelly—almost too gentle. He was always asking her if she was . . . liking it. Wanting to be sure he was pleasing her, you know?"

Nat nodded. "Do I stay on this road?"

"Yes. Until Shrewsbury. He's staying at my fiancé's brother's place. Marty, that's Peter's brother, is a computer troubleshooter. And his company sent him to some place in Arizona for a month. Peter had an extra key to Marty's apartment and he . . . sent it to me." Christine nervously twisted a loose thread from her skirt around her index finger. "Peter won't get in trouble, will he? He's in the Air Force. Stationed in South Carolina until December. That's when we were planning—are planning—to get married. I mean . . . Peter only did this for me. And Marty doesn't even know Dean's staying there."

Nat was not about to tell this terrified, wary young woman that both she and her fiancé were accomplices after the fact and that criminal charges could very well be brought against both of them. "If Dean turns himself in, there's no reason for the police to ever know either you or Peter were involved."

"It isn't fair. Even if he had solid alibis for both murders, he's still facing five more years for a crime he never did in the first place. There's got to be something you can do."

Not having any solution at hand, Nat asked Christine to tell her more about her long-ago meeting with Alison Cole.

"Her mother wouldn't even let me in to see her. She threatened to call the cops and charge me with harassment. But I knew where Alison and her friends hung out—a coffee shop near the high school—and I found her there."

Tears spiked Christine's eyes. "I made a complete fool out of myself. Gushing on about Dean and Kelly. About how he would never be rough with a girl, much less do all those terrible things Alison said he did."

"What did Alison say?"

"She said . . . 'you weren't there. I was.' And then she started calling my brother every vile name in the book." Christine put her hands up to her face. "I made it worse for him. The district attorney made Kelly testify and . . . oh God, she'd broken up with Dean over what supposedly happened with Alison, so she wasn't exactly in his corner. She started saying that Dean did get a little rough with her a few times. And that she found some dirty magazines in his room and she just made it seem like he . . ." Christine's hands dropped away, revealing a look of pained betrayal on her face. "It wasn't true."

"Are you saying Kelly lied under oath?"

"It was the way the prosecutor asked the questions. And Dean's court-appointed lawyer was a complete loser. He never even asked Kelly to describe what she meant by rough. It was like he already believed Dean was a goner and wasn't even going to try to get him off. He just wanted to get it over with fast."

Nat spotted the sign for Shrewsbury. "Let me know where to turn off."

"Next light. Right turn," she answered automatically.

"How long did the trial last?" Nat asked.

"Three days. And the jury was out for less than two hours. Dean didn't stand a chance."

"And no luck with appeals?"

"Appeals cost money. My mom certainly wasn't about to remortgage the house, which was about the only asset we had. Dean did try writing letters and we both tried to get a lawyer to take the case on a pro bono basis, but neither of us had any luck."

Nat pulled to a stop at the red light and flicked on her right-hand blinkers. As she started to turn the wheel, Christine's mounting tension filled the confines of the car. "I don't know if this is right," she muttered to herself.

"Why don't you stay put and slide behind the wheel and if you see any sign of police activity you can beep the horn and Dean and I will make a dash for the car." Before she had time to mull this over, Nat was asking for the street address.

"240." She pointed to a gray triple decker on the right, next to the last house on the block. Nat saw a spot on the other side of the street and quickly pulled in. Leaving the car running, she opened the door and started to exit.

"Apartment number?" She had one foot on the curb.

"3A." Nat was shutting the door as she heard Christine add, "He's got a gun."

All the way to his door, Nat was telling herself she was crazy. Walsh could shoot her before she even stepped over the threshold. He might have been at his window and caught her arrival. Maybe he wouldn't even open the door. Just plug her right through it as soon as she rang his doorbell. Maybe she should have had Christine come up with her. But what if a stray bullet hit Walsh's sister? What if he was so furious at Christine for leading Nat to him that he shot her deliberately? Nat didn't need Christine's death on her conscience, too.

Then again, if she were dead, as well, she didn't have to worry about her conscience.

She hesitated a couple of feet from apartment 3A. There was one other apartment, 3B, directly across the hall. Nat's luck, Walsh's apartment faced the front of the triple-decker and the street, increasing the odds that he might already be laying in wait for her.

But if he was innocent as he claimed—and as Nat was coming to believe, thanks to the confirmation of his alibi by that homeless woman—would he shoot her down in cold blood?

For all her fledging confidence, she stood to the side of the door when she rang the bell. Holding her breath. Half expecting a volley of gunfire to pierce the wooden door like it was little more than cardboard.

Silence.

Could be the doorbell was busted. Or Walsh was making a dash for his gun. Or escape.

She knocked, trying to ignore the obvious tremor in her hand. Hand, nothing. Her whole body was one long tremor.

"Dean, it's me. Natalie Price. I know you're in there. I'm alone. Your sister's downstairs. In my car. Making sure I keep good on my promise that this isn't a set-up. That there are no cops on the way. They don't know you're here, Dean. I swear. Please let me in. I want to help you."

Not a sound. Was it possible he wasn't there? Had he made a run for it, guessing somehow she'd figure out some way to get Christine to bring her there?

She was so busy playing over these possibilities in her mind that she didn't realize the door was opening a crack. When she did notice, all she could see was the black barrel of a gun.

At the sight of it, she stood there frozen.

The door opened wider.

"You must have a death wish, Nat." Walsh's voice was more tired than threatening.

But his words struck a chilling chord.

"I'm hoping you have a wish to live, Dean." It was about all she could come back with. Apparently it was enough to get him to open the door fully. But not enough to get him to veer the gun away from her chest, except briefly when he used it to motion her inside.

Nat paid little attention to the small, tidy apartment, her focus directed at the escaped inmate—although it would have been hard to discern from his appearance that he was a convict. Walsh was clean shaven and nicely dressed in tan pleated trousers and a black turtleneck sweater. Did the outfit belong to his brother-in-law-to-be's brother or had his sister provided him with a street wardrobe? Walsh's brown hair was neatly combed. Observing the bags under his eyes, he hadn't, however, been sleeping any better than she had that past week.

Unlike her hands, however, his were rock steady, especially the hand wrapped around the butt end of that gun.

Beyond casting her a look of undisguised dislike, he was not saying anything. Nor was Nat convinced he was waiting for her to speak. More than likely he was merely deciding how best to deal with her unexpected visit.

Nat decided her only hope was to start talking, if for no other reason than to keep him from reaching an unsavory conclusion about what to do with her.

"Here's what I think, Dean—"

"I don't give two cents for what you think," Walsh snapped contemptuously, before she even had the chance to tell him in more detail about the witness who'd come forward to support his alibi. "I'll tell you what I *know*. I didn't kill anyone. Why would I? I loved Maggie. And as far as Alison is concerned, whatever happened that night nearly nine years ago, I don't hold her to blame. I don't think she lied. I just think she was as out of it as I was and it could have been a creature from outer space who raped her for all either one of us knew."

"You believe in space aliens, Dean?"

"Why do I waste my breath? You believe me about as much as you believe in space aliens."

"That's not true."

"I've been reading about you in the papers, Nat. On suspension thanks to me." He leaned against the wall, his gun unwaveringly trained on her chest.

"That's not true, either," she said wearily, knowing it was more the truth than that she was on a *voluntary* vacation.

"You wouldn't know the truth," he said, "if it slammed you in the face. As far as the lot of you are concerned I was guilty eight years ago. I'm guilty now. Déjà vu all over again." He smiled, but there was about as much warmth in that smile as in an iceberg.

"Do you know, I actually thought for a brief moment there that, innocence aside, I'd served my time and I would really be able to put it behind me." A crack of sorrow broke through the hard shell that had formed over his handsome face. "It was Maggie made me believe that. Maggie who gave me hope. Who made me think I had a future." He shut his eyes for a second, but the gun didn't waver. When he opened them back up moments later, he fixed his gaze somewhere over her right shoulder. A glistening of tears spiked the rims of his eyes.

"I told her everything in the end. It took a while for me to open up. Trust isn't exactly a commodity I put much store in after all that's happened to me. Maggie wouldn't let up, though. She could see a lot of the truth in my poems, but she kept telling me I was fighting it and that holding back was affecting my writing in a negative way." His eyes slowly came back to rest on Nat.

"The first time I told her I loved her, she told me that I couldn't love her if I didn't love myself. That's when I broke down. I must have sobbed for a good half hour and Maggie just held me in her arms the whole time, not saying anything. Just keeping her arms wrapped tightly around me while I bawled like a baby." Errant tears escaped over the rims of his eyes, slipping unchecked down his cheeks.

"I told her I hated myself. She asked me why. I screamed at her that I was a coward beyond description. That, from the first day I was thrown in jail until literally the very last day I spent behind the wall, I'd let myself be . . . used." His deep and impotent anger was etched in every word.

"I know about Owen King, Dean," Nat said quietly.

A look of pure hatred shadowed his features. Making him look almost ugly. "I should have killed him. I'd have gotten life for it, but at least no one would have . . . messed with me again." His voice cracked mid-sentence. "What a choice, huh? Daily rape or a life sentence?"

"Did you ever go to the authorities—?"

He cut her off with a snigger. "Like you all don't know damn well what goes on."

Nat looked from the small vestibule where they were standing, into the living room. "Can we go inside and sit down, Dean?"

He mulled this over for a few moments, then jerked the gun in the direction of the living room.

Nat took a seat in one of the arm chairs, but Walsh walked directly over to the window, slightly parting the brown and tan paisley drapery that was drawn across it. The window looked out on the street. Nat was sure he was checking to see if his sister really was parked out there in the car.

Apparently satisfied by what he saw, he let go of the curtain and turned around to face Nat. "How'd you get Christine to—?"

"I lied," she said simply.

"She's all I've got left." There was sorrow and fear in his voice. "Chrissie's only helping me because she believes in me. Whatever happens to me, nothing bad better happen to her." The words might be vague, but the message was as clear as the cold-blooded look in Walsh's eyes. Nat had better not let any harm come to Christine unless she wanted to find a shank in *her* back.

"Despite what you believe, I want to help you," Nat said. "Even if you're fully cleared of Maggie's murder, there's still Alison Cole. You're going to need a solid alibi for the time of that murder as well. So, let's talk about last Thursday night, Dean."

Dean shrugged. "I was nowhere near Alison's place Thursday night or any other night."

"I know you had class that night with Maggie. It ran from 7 to 8 P.M. And that you checked in at the House at 8:45 P.M. Fifteen minutes over your extended curfew."

"Maggie talked with me after class about one of my poems that she was going to enter into that journal. We ran a little over. I told that to Martini when I checked in. He gave me a warning, seeing as how it was the first time, and let it go at that."

"Those extra fifteen minutes wouldn't have given you enough time to leave class, get the T to Newton, kill Alison and be back at the House at 8:45. Of course, that presumes we can verify that you and Maggie did chat for thirty minutes after class."

"Ask that dyke T.A. of hers, Karen. She was there, breathing down our necks the whole time. Like maybe I'd try to cop a feel or something."

"Dyke?" Nat was curious whether this slur was based on guesswork or actual knowledge. Had Maggie told him? Had he discovered it on his own? That photo of Maggie and Karen flashed in Nat's head again. Could Walsh have snapped that picture?

"Karen was so hot for Maggie, you could practically see steam coming out of her ears. She hated me because she knew damn well Maggie and I were . . . close."

"You were about to say lovers."

He was a little shaken. "Karen's the one told you about us, right?"

"Why'd you lie about it before if you knew you'd be found out?"

"I knew none of you would understand. And I wasn't lying when I hinted as how Maggie made the first move. I wasn't putting any moves on her, I swear." He looked away. "I was freaked to do it with a woman again because of all that had happened to me in the joint. I didn't know if I could . . . satisfy her." He smiled cockily. "But I did. She was the best. She was incredible. I never felt more like a man than I did when I was with Maggie."

Nat remembered Jack saying almost the same thing. And Karen had said as much as well. "How did Karen know about you and Maggie?"

He shrugged. "Maggie may have told her. Not that she hadn't already figured it out on her own." He hesitated. "I thought, though, that Karen wouldn't tell anyone about me and Maggie."

"Why is that?" Nat asked, thinking that Walsh may have threatened her.

"I got the feeling Karen was scared of me." And then, no doubt reading Nat's mind, he added, "Not because of anything I ever said or did to her. Just 'cause I was a con. And a man. A lethal combo in her book."

"Okay, let's say Karen can corroborate your after-class chat with Maggie—"

"You kidding? She'd as soon see me gassed as provide me with an alibi. But I got it covered anyway. I bumped into an old pal on my way out of the building."

There was obvious sarcasm in his tone as he said *old pal.* "Who was that?"

"A guy I went to school with." Still that sarcastic tone.

And then Nat put it together. "You mean, someone from your prison writing class." And there was only one person that could be. Only one other person from that class was out on the street. "You saw Keith Franklin outside the building?"

"Yeah. How'd you know—?"

"Were you surprised to see him there?"

Walsh pursed his lips. "Surprised? Not really. I'd caught a glimpse of him on campus before. Last Thursday night, though, was the first time we exchanged words."

"What were the words?"

"I asked him what he was doing hanging out there. And he made up some bullshit story about how he was taking some night class in computers."

"What made you think his story was bullshit?"

"The computer building's clear on the other end of campus."

"So what do you think his real reason was for being there?"

Walsh gave her a knowing look. "You can put two and two together just like I can."

"You add it up for me."

"You want it added up? Sure, Nat. What it adds up to is, Franklin wanted in Maggie's panties so bad it wasn't funny. If that con wasn't scared of his own shadow, I'd put him on top of the list as a suspect. Because the only way he'd have ever gotten Maggie into bed would have been by force. And that pissant wouldn't have had the guts to rape her or—" He looked pained as he let the rest of the sentence drop off.

Nat wasn't so sure Keith Franklin didn't have the guts, considering she believed he had what it took to try to run her down, but she kept that thought to herself. She also made a mental note to find out what Leo had learned about Franklin's whereabouts Thursday night, prior to that accidental meeting with Walsh.

"Putting aside the time after class was over, Dean, there is a gap between when you got out of work at five P.M. and started class at seven. A pretty big gap." Meaning, as they both knew, big enough to have plenty of time to get from Cambridge to Alison's place in Newton, kill her, and get to school in Boston.

Walsh was going through his alleged movements. "I did what I did every other night before class. I took the T straight to school from work, had a quick bite in the cafeteria, went over to the library and did school work until about 6:30 and then I went over to class. Maggie was usually there early and we'd have some time to talk—"

"Let's go back over each step. You rode the T. Did you talk to anyone during the train ride? Sit next to someone or near someone who might recognize you?"

He shrugged. "No to the first. And I doubt it to the second."

"Okay, the cafeteria at the school."

He shook his head. "I found a table off in a quiet corner. Had a book in front of my face most of the time."

"But you got some dinner."

"Salad bar. Help-yourself. And I doubt the cashier would remember me. I don't think she even looked at me. Just at the scale that weighed my salad. You pay by the ounce."

"But there were other people in the cafeteria. Someone might have noticed you," she pressed.

A weary shrug. "Yeah, but why would they? I mean, it's possible, I guess. But it's not likely."

"Still, it's a place to start," she said, trying to sound upbeat.

There was a slight shift of the gun in Walsh's hand. It was aimed closer to her foot than her chest. Nat breathed a silent sigh of relief, believing she was beginning to win his confidence.

That confidence was cut abruptly short by the sudden honking of a horn outside.

They both leaped out of their seats. Walsh rushed over to the window, drew the curtain aside wide enough for Nat, standing behind him, to see a police cruiser pulling up to her car.

Walsh spun around to face her, rage turning his complexion a bright red.

"No," Nat cried out, terror draining her color as she drew back from him. "It isn't what you think, Dean. It's a mistake—"

Gun aimed, he came at her with lightning speed. Frozen, she felt him ram into her and waited for the explosion, the searing pain of a bullet ripping through her—

But instead of firing the gun at her he used it to whack her across the head. Practically in the same damn spot she'd gotten whacked back at her apartment the other night. This time, before she blacked out, all Nat heard was the loud slam of a door.

thirty-two

Screws are always saying how we got it easy in here. That the hard part's being on the street again. That's why so many of us can't wait to come back.

S. V.
Inmate #953503

"YOU LOOK LIKE hell."

Nat felt even worse—not so much because of the added injury to her head but because she'd botched up so badly. After Walsh took off, Christine showed up at the apartment to let them know it was a false alarm. Turned out the cop in the cruiser was merely telling her she couldn't park where she was because it was a Residents Only area. Nat was just coming around. Walsh was gone. Christine was distraught, blaming herself for everything—bringing Nat there in the first place, hitting the horn in a panic when she saw the cruiser, causing Nat to get conked on the head, being responsible for her brother's flight. But none of it was Christine's fault. It was all Nat's.

"Let's go over this again," Leo said soberly as he sat across from her in Hutch's living room. Christine had driven her there twenty minutes ago. Well, Nat drove the last block, having first left Christine off. She didn't want to chance Rosie spotting Christine. Nat waited while Christine used her cell phone to call a cab, then tried to give her money for the fare, but Christine had adamantly refused. When Nat arrived back at Hutch's, she found not only Rosie, but Leo, waiting there for her. Rosie made herself scarce after getting her an ice pack and a couple of aspirin, but Leo was in her face.

"You get a call from Walsh sometime around four P.M. He tells you he wants to meet with you—" He paused for affect, "alone"— another pause, "in a back alley somewhere in Worchester—"

Nat knew he didn't believe a word of her story, but at the moment she was feeling too lousy to put on a convincing act. Her major concern was to keep Christine Walsh out of it. If Leo got wind of Christine's involvement, he could hit her with a laundry list of charges—aiding and abetting an escaped inmate, withholding evidence, obstructing justice, being a material witness, to name a few. Nat's next concern was keeping Leo from slapping her with those same charges. From his grave expression, it looked like he was seriously considering this action.

"Can't we go over this tomorrow, Leo?"

"Will that give you enough time to concoct a clearer story?"

"Okay, you're angry. I don't blame you. But I don't have anything else to say."

Leo dropped his notepad on the floor and stared at her in silence for what was probably only a few seconds but felt like forever. Finally, he heaved a weary sigh, rose and crossed over to the sofa where she was half-reclined with the ice pack on her head. He knelt down in front of her so that they were combative eyeball to obstinate eyeball.

"You're damn straight I'm angry. Not so much because you're lying through your teeth, but because you still think I'm not only inexperienced but dumb to boot."

"No I don't—"

"At approximately 3:10 P.M. you receive a call on your cell phone here at the Hutchins' residence. You hightail it out of here right after the call. At approximately 4:05 P.M. a woman is spotted entering the Lewis Rice Agency in Framingham which just so happens to be where Christine Walsh works. At approximately 4:10 P.M. the aforementioned Christine Walsh took a powder from her office. And here's an interesting aside. She doesn't leave in her car. Nor does she return home, even though at approximately 4:15 she phones her boss, Francis Kelman and explains she's had to rush home because of a *family emergency*." He said all this rote, in a flat, professional monotone.

"You've proved your point, Leo. You're very experienced. Very smart. Would you like me to write that on the blackboard one hundred times?"

"Talk to me, Natalie."

"I don't know where he took off to. Leo. I swear."

"Where did you meet?"

"I told you. In an alley off—"

"Bullshit."

Okay, he saw straight through her, but as long as she didn't say anything more, she wouldn't be implicating Christine, getting the poor girl charged with aiding and abetting a killer.

Especially as, now, more than ever, Nat was more convinced that Walsh was not a murderer. She just needed more time to come up with solid evidence to support her conviction. And that meant finding a witness to confirm his whereabouts Thursday between 5 P.M. and 7 P.M. It would be lovely if someone came forward of their own volition, but Nat doubted she'd be that lucky.

The ice pack slipped from her head and landed on the floor.

Leo's gaze shifted from her eyes to her latest injury. "She takes a licking but she keeps on ticking," he murmured. Then he leaned closer and Nat assumed he wanted to inspect the damage more thoroughly. She was completely thrown when, instead, he placed a feather-light kiss on her angry bruise. The pain almost vanished and she felt that peck right down to her toes.

"What is this, Leo? Giving me the third degree didn't work so now you're switching from *bad cop* to *good cop*?" Her look might be speculative, but her voice was shaky.

He shut her up with another kiss, this one smack on her lips and not so light.

"I'm not going to talk, Leo." She spoke in a hoarse voice, when he lifted his mouth a few inches away from hers.

"I know." And then he was silencing her again, this kiss as much hers as his.

When he moved away, she was speechless. And bereft.

"Let's go."

Her stomach clenched, the honey-sweet aftereffects of that kiss souring fast. "Are you taking me in?"

"What's this?" she asked.

"What's it look like?" Leo's comeback was clipped.

What it didn't look like was a precinct house. Leo was out of the car, slamming the door shut before she reached for the passenger side door handle. He was parked in the lot of the Sunset Motor Inn, a fifteen-minute drive from Hutch's house.

Her throbbing head was whirling and her movements were tentative as she got out. Leo was standing a few feet away, his arms crossed over his chest, a deep scowl on his face. As soon as she had both feet on the pavement he turned away abruptly and strode off for the front entrance of the motel. She shut the car door and meekly followed him inside the nondescript lobby, hanging back as he signed a registration card at the desk. The clerk handed him a key.

Leo didn't so much as glance back at her as he headed for the elevator of the four-story building. Nat caught up to him as the doors slid open and, silently, they stepped inside the elevator together. He pressed "4" on the brass panel, the doors slid shut and they were alone in this mirror and steel five-foot-square box.

"Leo, what are we doing here?"

"Walsh could come looking for you this time 'round, to finish off what he didn't get a chance to do earlier today. Best to put you someplace where he can't find you. I'll let Hutchins know so he doesn't worry."

"Is that the only reason you've brought me here?"

His eyes narrowed.

Nat took a tentative step closer to him. "Talk to me, Leo."

But now he was the one who'd gone mute. Instead, he pulled her roughly to him, the scowl not softening one iota. He kissed her like he'd just as soon strangle her, but the fierce pressure of his mouth, of his whole body, pushed all thought from her mind. The elevator stopped with a little jolt on the fourth floor. Nat's stomach lurched. Leo let go of her and she fell against the wall, gripping the steel bar for balance.

He held out the key to her room as the doors started to slide open. "You can take it from here and I'll head back down."

Nat realized what drew her the most to Leo was that he was giving her the choice. It was also what scared her the most.

Not trusting herself to speak—not sure what would come out of her mouth—she managed only to shake her head and, jelly-legged, preceded him out of the elevator, leaving him to follow with the key.

Her arousal took a dip as they entered the large, but tacky, motel room. A burn mark and a few stains decorated the worn gray tweed carpet. The room was done up in drab blue and gray decor, the heavy tapestry drapes that framed a picture window looked out onto the parking lot, faded bedspreads covered the two full-sized beds separated by a scarred white melamine night table.

Leo left her standing near the door, crossed the room and pulled the drapes closed, save for a slit wide enough to let a sliver of light bleed into the room. The dimness was a definite improvement. Now if he'd just return to where she was standing and take her in his arms again—

He stayed put. Silent.

Nat found the quiet unnerving. And so in typical fashion she started talking.

"Do you really think Walsh will come looking for me? He had the chance to gun me down in that . . . alley, and he didn't. Doesn't that tell you something?"

"It tells me you're damn lucky."

"It tells me—"

"I know what it tells you," he said flatly.

"Is that homeless woman's alibi for him holding up?"

"Seems to be." He hesitated. "There's something else."

"What?"

"It doesn't necessarily mean anything, so don't go getting your hopes up. In my book, Walsh is still right up there as a prime suspect. Even if that homeless woman's story holds up, a smart prosecutor could decimate her testimony in no time flat. Walsh is going to need more than that to clear him of the mess he's in."

"So what have you found out?" she asked impatiently.

He slowly walked toward her. "A neighbor of Alison Miller's reported seeing a car on the street the night she was murdered. She remembers this particular car because she thought at first it was her son's. The son owns a 1986 Pontiac. Only this one was dark blue instead of black. And it had a busted brake light."

The hairs on her arms stood up. "Keith Franklin. It's got to be—" Her excitement started to mount. "Leo, Walsh told me he saw Franklin hanging outside the English Department building that Thursday night after his class."

"Interesting," Leo said in that noncommittal way he had.

"Maybe he intended to go after Maggie that night and for some reason wasn't able to act on his plan until the next day."

"You're getting ahead of yourself."

"What time did that woman see his car?"

"We haven't established it was Franklin's car, Natalie." He was trying to keep her from jumping to conclusions. But he was too late. As far as she was concerned, the pieces were all falling into place. Franklin's obsession with Maggie, his hatred of Walsh, his weak alibi for his whereabouts the day Maggie was murdered. And now someone was placing him at the scene of the Alison Cole murder.

"Okay, what time did she see this '86 Pontiac with the broken brake light?"

Leo sighed. "Sometime around five o'clock."

"Have you brought Franklin back in for questioning?"

There was a troubled look in his eyes. He took a couple of moments before answering. "We will when we find him."

"He's taken off?" And then it hit her. "You're not necessarily protecting me from Walsh, are you? You obviously think it might be Franklin who'll come looking for me."

Leo put a finger to her lips. "Nothing's obvious except this." He replaced his finger with his mouth.

Desire and relief mingled as they kissed deeply, all the while clumsily grappling with each other's clothing and stumbling their way over to the bed.

She had never cheated on Ethan during their courtship or their marriage. Not that she had never been tempted. Especially that night at Jack's place when she'd rushed over there to see if his drunken wife had, indeed, killed him.

But she took her vows seriously. She'd remained faithful. For close to nine years, Ethan Price had been her only lover. When he left her, Nat never imagined that she would be with another man so soon.

And that that man would end up being Detective Leo Coscarelli—no way. Impossible.

What troubled Nat wasn't that she'd been so wrong about Leo—hadn't she been wrong about Ethan and Maggie, to name two? No, what troubled Nat was the other woman in bed with them. The other woman being Suzanne. The mother of Leo's child.

But for a long stretch, Leo managed to erase this female ghost from Nat's mind.

In terms of technical proficiency, she would have had to say that Ethan won hands down over Leo. Ethan was your typical take-charge man in bed, exuding not only confidence but arrogance. He knew he was desirable. He had no doubts about his sexual prowess. And because of this, at least in part, Nat allowed herself to be drawn in, to follow his lead, to let Ethan set the pace as well as make all the decisions. In a sense, this allowed her to absolve herself of personal responsibility. A time out for a woman who regularly shouldered crushing professional responsibilities.

With Leo, it was totally different. For starters, even as they fell together onto the bed, he said, "It's been a long time for me, Natalie. And you know how they say, it's like riding a bicycle?"

She nodded.

"Well, I never did ride a bike."

"Neither did I," she confided with a breathless smile.

So, from the start, Nat felt like they were in this together. That what they were really both acknowledging were feelings of vulnerability. And the truth was, this shared admission both thrilled her and scared the hell out of her.

Leo's trousers were hanging somewhere between his knees and his ankles, trapped there because of his shoes which he was struggling mightily to kick off. But they were laced too tight. He finally rolled off her and started to untie them only to end up with the laces hopelessly knotted. He was cursing about this under his breath as he finally managed to yank the shoes off, laces still intact.

While he was busy with his shoes Nat started to pull her sweater over her head only to have a loose strand of wool catch and wrap itself around one of her diamond stud earrings. She'd gotten the sweater half over her face, as Leo focused his attention back on her. Thinking he was helping, he started to pull the sweater the rest of the way off.

She screamed in pain, hurriedly tugging the sweater back down far enough to get the stud out of her ear. She caught the look of confusion and panic on Leo's face. Even though her ear was still smarting she couldn't help laughing at this ludicrous comedy of errors. A few seconds later, instead of feeling embarrassed, humiliated or angry—feelings she was certain Ethan would have experienced—Leo joined in. They fell against each other, laughing so hard tears were running down their faces.

The laughter was cleansing and freeing. And for reasons she didn't fully grasp, incredibly erotic. They finished undressing each other without further comic incident. But Leo was still smiling boyishly as they lay there naked, facing each other on top of the scratchy bedspread.

Slowly, his smile faded. He looked very serious. And very desirable.

"I didn't want this to happen." His voice was barely audible.

Nat knew he wasn't referring to their farcical mishaps.

She agreed. "It complicates . . . everything."

His palms glided lightly over her already erect nipples. The sensation made her arch her back. Her breasts pressed into his hands, his erect penis jabbing at her just below her belly button. A low moan involuntarily escaped her lips and she closed her eyes.

"No," Leo murmured. "Look at me, Natalie."

This was not something she did during sex. She always told

herself she liked to make love with her eyes closed in order to fully lose herself. But it was a lie. She closed her eyes because she felt too self-conscious. Too vulnerable. Afraid to connect on such an intimate level.

But Leo was determined to engage her. "Tell me what you like."

She opened her eyes. This was a first for her. Her short list of lovers, including her husband, always presumed to know what she liked. Sometimes they got it right. Often enough, they didn't.

Nat felt both desperately shy and sexually charged by Leo's request. "I'll show you." Her breathing shifted, became shallower. "If you show me."

They both smiled. Then he took her hand and guided it down over his erection, then over his balls. She stroked his soft, tender skin with the tips of her fingers and felt his erection swell against her, heard his own breathing quicken.

"Touch me everywhere." The words came out of her mouth of their own volition. Pretty soon, with their hands, their mouths, their eyes, they were both fully engaged in an intense, uninhibited sexual exploration of each other's bodies.

Nat discovered a jagged scar about two inches long on Leo's right outer thigh. She pressed her lips gently to it.

"How—?" The question slipped out. She felt Leo tense. Not meaning to, she'd broken the mood.

"A bullet. A pimp took a shot at me when I was on Vice. He was pissed because I was depleting his resources."

"Arresting all his girls?"

"Not so much that. Like most successful pimps, he had plenty enough cash flow to get them bailed and back on the streets within hours. But a few of us Vice cops got involved in a rehab program for prostitutes run by an ex-nun and an ex-hooker."

"That's a combo for you."

Leo smiled. "Yeah, and if you met them I'd lay you odds you wouldn't know which was which. Anyway, what we'd do is when we'd pick up a hooker we'd offer her a choice. Get run in and spend a few very unpleasant hours or days in the clink or agree to a mandatory forty-eight hour stay in this rehab house. A lot of the women opted for the latter."

"And forty-eight hours was enough to turn them around?"

"Not all of them, but surprisingly more than any of us cops anticipated. Enough to put the noses of quite a few pimps out of joint. One of them showed up at the house to reclaim his property. I got called onto the scene and a few shots were exchanged. One of them got me in the thigh."

"And the pimp?"

Leo didn't answer right away. That grim expression which aged his otherwise boyish face had returned.

"You killed him."

He winced at her words. Tension seized his body. "First and only time I took someone out. It . . . stays with you. Even though he was scum."

He lifted himself up on an elbow and gave her a long, slow head to toe survey. "What about you, Natalie? Any scars?"

Her eyes met his. "Plenty. Just none that show."

He drew her against him, kissing her deeply but tenderly.

It was the tenderness, missing so much in her life, that heightened her yearning to such a degree that she began to cry softly. Leo held her to him, rocking her gently, understanding that the last thing she wanted now was for him to pull away from her. And this was how he entered her.

Nat couldn't remember ever being this sexually aroused. Or this completely unnerved.

thirty-three

Non-violent men who have been raped on the inside re-enter the community brimming with rage and the potential for violence.

Samuel Dobson, MSW
Corrections Social Worker

THE RING OF her cell phone intruded upon the lovely afterglow. She was tempted to let the caller leave a message. But she could feel Leo's body tense. The lover was gone. The cop was back. Nat reached for her bag and dug out her phone.

"Please . . . you must help me," came a panicky voice as soon as she clicked on. "I . . . killed him. He was going to mutilate Christine. Kill her. Oh my God . . . what should I do? I had to do it. I had to—"

"Mrs. Walsh, please slow down."

Leo sat up, watching Nat intently. She held the phone slightly away from her ear so he could hear the call.

"My baby, my poor baby." She broke off into sobs.

"Are you saying you killed your son?"

"No," she cried. "He wanted my son. He held a knife to Christine's chest and ordered her to call Dean, set up a meeting. She tried to tell him she didn't know where Dean was. But he wouldn't believe her. He threatened to do . . . terrible things to her if she didn't do what he ordered. But she wouldn't give her brother up."

"Who did you kill, Mrs. Walsh?" Keith Franklin was the name that instantly popped into Nat's head.

"I . . . I don't know. Neither does Christine. We never saw him before. Oh God. She's in a bad way."

"Did he hurt her?" Nat asked anxiously.

"No. No, but—"

Leo grabbed the phone away. "Are the police there, Mrs. Walsh? The ones who've been parked outside your house?"

"No. I don't know where they are. They must have heard the shot. I . . . I can still hear it. In my head. It's still in my head. Oh my God . . ."

"Mrs. Walsh, we're coming right over."

"I had to do it. I had to . . ."

The two cops were slumped against each other in the unmarked Ford. One of the men was unconscious but his breathing was steady. The other was starting to come around. He groaned in pain, his hand going to his head, mumbling something about an "ambush" and "never saw it coming." Leo patted him gently on the shoulder. "I'll get an ambulance over here pronto. Take it easy. You're both going to be okay."

Leo called in for a couple of ambulances—not yet knowing the condition of the gunned-down man inside the Walsh house—and got hold of his partner as he and Nat proceeded quickly up the walk. The front door was ajar.

Inside the living room, the body was sprawled facedown on

the pale blue carpet a few feet from the sofa. Even though Nat couldn't see his face, she recognized him. A single bullet hole in his black leather motorcycle jacket was visible just below the left shoulder blade, a clean shot that must have gone straight through to the heart. There was a small patch of blood oozing out from the wound and more blood spreading out from beneath him onto the carpet. A .22 caliber pistol was lying a few inches away from his body.

Christine was sitting stiffly erect on the edge of the sofa, her glazed eyes staring down at her assailant. Her hair was disheveled, her green blouse half unbuttoned and out of her skirt. Her lipstick was smeared. Her eyes were unblinking. No question she was in shock.

Marion Walsh looked frail and red-eyed as she hung back behind a patterned red and white wing chair, positioned in such a way that her view of the body was obscured. Her eyes rested anxiously on her daughter as she kneaded the top of the chair. Fortunately, she had pulled herself together sufficiently to be relatively responsive. Nat asked her if she had any brandy in the house as Leo bent down, his gloved hand checking for a pulse they all knew he wasn't going to find.

"Brandy? Maybe. I think . . . there might be something. . . ."

"Bring the bottle and two glasses." Nat almost said three glasses, thinking she could use a good belt herself. But she decided she needed to be as clear-headed as possible.

Marion Walsh left quickly, a woman eager to escape the scene of mayhem. But she wasn't gone long, returning with an unopened bottle of Southern Comfort and two juice glasses. "It's all I could find. We don't drink. This was a gift from my boss—" Her speech was flat and rapid.

"It's fine." Nat took the items from the older woman's icy hands, guided her to a ladder-backed wooden chair near the doorway and gently eased her into the seat. Then she quickly opened the bottle and poured out double shots into the glasses.

She handed one to Marion, ordered her to drink it, which she did without argument.

Then Nat crossed over to Christine, who had as yet not uttered a single syllable. She knelt down in front of the stricken woman, blocking the view of the body.

"Here." Nat extended the glass, but Christine made no move to take it. She stared straight through Nat like she was invisible. Like she could still see the body behind her. Nat imagined she did. Just like Nat could still see Maggie on her bed. They were both condemned to horrific visions that would be a long time dissolving. If visions like that ever did.

Nat glanced back at Leo. "I'm going to take Christine and her mom upstairs."

"Yeah," he muttered, getting to his feet at the sound of approaching sirens. Relief showed on Leo's face that the ambulances had made it there so quickly. Down the line, he'd no doubt call his men on the carpet for having *fallen asleep on the job*, but Nat felt certain it wouldn't be until Leo was sure they were really okay.

As Nat went to help Christine to her feet, she shirked away. "Who is he?" she asked in a strained whisper.

Nat glanced back at Leo again. He nodded.

"His name is Owen King. He . . . knew your brother in prison."

"He said Dean was out to get him. That Dean had been calling him. Threatening him. Saying how he owes him. He said he wanted to meet Dean face-to-face and . . . clear the air. But I knew he was lying. He wanted to kill Dean. I don't understand. . . ."

"Did he hurt you, Christine?"

She didn't answer. She was staring in Nat's direction but not really seeing her.

"Maybe we should take Christine to the hospital," Nat said to Leo.

"No," Christine said sharply, her eyes finally coming into

focus. "No. I don't need a hospital." She looked over at her mother who was standing nearby, clutching her empty glass. "I didn't know where Dean was. But I wouldn't have told him anyway. I'm sorry, Mom. I'm so sorry."

The glass fell from Marion's hand and she sank to her knees, sobbing. Christine rushed over, dropping down beside her mother, gathering her in her arms. "You saved my life, Mom. Please don't cry. I love you. I love you, Mom."

They got the details of what had happened earlier that night, close to an hour later, upstairs in Christine's bedroom. Meanwhile, Leo's partner and a crime team were busy at work downstairs. Surprisingly, it was Christine who did most of the talking as she sat beside her mother on the bed, the two women clutching each other's hands like the bond was their lifeline.

"I was watching TV. The news. I never used to watch the news. But now . . . I'm always hoping there'll be something about Dean being cleared. . . . But there never is. It's never good news. There hasn't even been anything about that homeless woman coming forward. It isn't right—" She fell silent, her lips compressed in a tight line.

"How did King get into the house?" Leo asked.

"I was so stupid. The front doorbell rang. I thought it was my mother, that she'd forgotten her key."

"What time was this?"

"A little before eight."

"I was visiting a friend." Marion cast her eyes down at her daughter's hand clenched in hers.

"As soon as I started to open the door he barged in," Christine hurried on. "Knocked me against the wall. Demanded to know if anyone else was in the house. Dragged me through every room to make sure. When he was satisfied we were alone he took me into the living room, handed me the phone and told me to call Dean." Now she gave Nat a quick glance. Just as quickly Nat looked away. But Nat was sure Leo caught the little exchange. Leo didn't miss much.

"Was he alone?"

"I didn't see anyone else."

Leo nodded. Probably thinking what Nat was thinking. That there must have been some flunky who King had posted outside the house. A flunky who took off like the wind when he heard that gunshot.

Leo's gaze shifted to Marion. "Can you pick it up from when you arrived home?" His tone was gentle. But they all knew it wasn't really a question.

"I heard a scream as I was unlocking the front door. I suppose that's why . . . he didn't hear me come in." Her chin quivered, but she bit down on her lip to keep herself from losing it. "He had a knife against her . . . chest." The quivering intensified. "Her blouse was . . . off. And her bra . . . he'd cut it down the front. Her . . . breasts . . . were . . . exposed." Marion's last words were faint, her eyes full of horror.

"Go on, Marion. You came into the house and saw this terrible sight of your daughter being held at knifepoint by an intruder," Leo prompted her. "What did you do?"

"I . . . I keep a gun . . . for protection . . . in my bedroom."

Nat spotted the faint arch of Leo's brow. So, too, must have Marion, because she hurried on to explain. "There was a rash of burglaries in the neighborhood about a year ago. Two women alone in the house . . . I was scared. My friend from next door told me she'd got a gun and so had most of my neighbors on the street. She urged me to get one, too. Just . . . in case. I never thought . . ." A sob erupted from deep in her chest and her hands sprang up to her face. "I never fired it before—"

Nat was wishing Leo would let up a bit. The poor woman was on the verge of collapse, in part because she was being coaxed into reliving the abominable event. In part, Nat thought, because her daughter seemed stronger now and less in need of her mother's strength.

But Leo was determined to get the whole story from Marion Walsh. "So you crept upstairs and got the gun."

Slowly, she lowered her hands. "Yes," she said in a barely audible voice, looking like she was forcing down the stream of sobs that were building up inside of her, threatening to erupt. Silent tears ran unchecked down Christine's face as she looked at her mother.

"You didn't call 911." Leo said. "Or rush out to the cops parked outside." Of course, the two officers were in no shape to come to her assistance at that point, but Marion wouldn't have known that.

"No time. I could hear him . . . screaming at Chrissie even from upstairs." She bent over as if hit by fierce stomach cramps.

"Can't you leave her alone?" Christine pleaded.

"What was he screaming, Marion?" Leo asked, his gaze fixed on the woman, his voice still gentle but determined.

Marion lifted her head and stared back at Leo, a flicker of anger in her eyes. "He screamed, 'You bitch. You fucking bitch. Get him on the phone or I'll cut your fucking tits off and shove them down your throat. I'm going to count to ten.'"

Christine began crying in earnest now. Once again, the daughter's deterioration seemed to spark renewed stamina in the mother. "He was on 'eight' when I got to the entryway of the living room. His back was to me. I walked up behind him and fired just as he said 'nine.'"

"How many times?" Leo asked.

"Just the once. I'd never fired a gun before. When he fell, I watched to make sure he wasn't moving. And then I dropped the gun."

"And then?"

"I buttoned my daughter's blouse and called Mrs. Price."

"Why not the police?"

"Because she was scared you'd come bursting into the house and cart her off to prison, that's why. I told her to call the Superintendent," Christine said, then cast Nat an accusatory look. "I didn't think you'd be in such a rush to call the cops."

Heat rose up Nat's neck. She was certainly not about to tell Christine it wasn't a matter of having to phone Leo as he'd been next to her in bed.

"My mother saved my life. She did it for me. It was self-defense. He would have finished me off and then done the same to her. And if Dean had shown up, that monster would have killed him, too."

"Shhh, Chrissie," Marion soothed. "It's going to be all right, baby. As long as you're safe. That's all that matters to me." She disentangled her hands from her daughter's and put her arms around her.

"You're not going to arrest her, are you?" Christine asked Leo plaintively.

Nat joined in with her own plaintive look.

Marion closed her eyes as if waiting for the worst.

"We'll need a formal statement from you, but that can wait until tomorrow. I'll have a talk with my chief and the district attorney. I can't make any promises, but I doubt there'll be any charges pressed against you."

There was a collective sigh—Marion's, Christine's, and Nat's.

"Maybe you can take Christine and go to your friend's house for the night, Mrs. Walsh."

Marion nodded slowly.

"I'll get one of my men to drive you over. I'll need your friend's name and address."

Marion hesitated for a moment. "Donald Barton. 17 Porter Street. It's here in Natick. On the north side of Route 9."

Leo scribbled it down on a pad.

"We're . . . just friends," Marion felt the need to add.

*　*　*

Something was nagging at Nat like a toothache as she and Leo drove off, but she couldn't put her finger on exactly what it was. Pushing it aside for the moment, Nat focused on a troubling point that she could readily identify.

"This business about Walsh calling King. I don't know. It doesn't feel right, Leo. Walsh is on the run again. The last thing he'd be thinking about is making threatening phone calls to King."

Leo didn't bite, so she continued her one-way conversation. "I think it's possible—" Nat was carefully couching her theory so that she wouldn't end up having him accuse her of jumping the gun again—"that Franklin might have been the caller, pretending to be Walsh. Franklin had to have known that Dean was King's *boy* inside. For all we know, so was Franklin. He might have wanted to provoke a showdown between Walsh and King. Get King to finish Walsh off while Franklin still believed he'd successfully framed Walsh for the two murders. That would tie the whole thing up in a neat bow. Total retribution. I'm not suggesting Franklin anticipated that King would attack Christine or her mother to unearth Dean's whereabouts. Franklin probably believed King had the kind of resources available that would make finding Walsh possible."

Still nothing from Leo.

"Why is Franklin on the lam now? Why's he running scared? Because he suspects his plan may be falling apart. Because he's worried I know too much."

"Maybe he's running scared because he's been getting threatening calls from Walsh as well," Leo said finally. Raising a point Nat had to admit had also crossed her mind. "Or maybe Walsh already got to him and finished him off."

Now Leo was a frightening step ahead of her.

As she started to open her motel room door, Leo grabbed her sharply and pushed her aside. Nat saw his other hand make a quick reach for his gun. And then she realized what Leo had already observed. The light was off inside the room. Before they'd left, close to two hours ago, Leo had told her to leave the light on when she'd gone to flick the switch.

Maybe housekeeping had come in and shut it off, she thought, as she heard the click of his safety go off. Then Leo nudged the door open just enough to slip his hand in to spring the light back on.

She heard a gasp of surprise—alarm?—from inside the room.

Leo kicked the door open wide, both hands on his gun, aiming it at the intruder who was standing in a pool of light in front of the unmade bed.

"Hey, hey . . . Don't shoot. I was just waiting for Nat."

Recognizing Jack's voice, she breathed a sigh of relief and appeared in the doorway. Leo still had his gun trained on her deputy.

"What are you doing here? How'd you know where to find Natalie? How'd you get into the room? What the hell were you doing sitting here in the dark?" Leo barked out each question without giving Jack time in between to respond.

"Slow it down," Jack said, grousing. "I needed to talk to Nat. Hutch told me where she was staying. I come over, it's almost midnight, and she doesn't answer my knocks. I get nervous so I show my prison ID to the clerk and he lets me into her room. She's not here. I didn't know what to think." He eyed the unmade bed with its tangled sheets. Like he knew what to think now. And his expression said he didn't like what he was thinking one bit.

"Why were you waiting for her in the dark?" Leo demanded, his gun still on Jack.

"I was bushed—haven't been sleeping much since . . . all this went down—so I decided to get a little shut-eye. Which is why I turned out the light. Last I heard that wasn't a crime."

Jack pointed to the clock radio on the bedside table. "I set the alarm to go off at half past twelve, figuring if she hadn't shown up by then I was going to put my worry into action."

"What'd you need to talk to her about that couldn't wait until morning?" Leo let the gun drop to his side, but there was no missing the edge in his voice. Nat couldn't tell if he was grilling Jack out of a lover's jealousy or a cop's suspicion.

"I found something out that I thought might be important," Jack said, his gaze going past Leo to her. "I was going through Walsh's file again. Trying to see if there might be some clue as to where he was hiding out. And I came upon something that was right in front of our faces the whole time."

"What?" she asked, stepping around Leo.

"It was in Alison Cole's police statement. It was taken in the hospital right after the rape. She described how Walsh picked her up at a bar and she went to that party with him. Well, she also mentioned in that statement that Walsh wasn't alone at the bar. He was with one of his good buddies who tagged along with them to the party. The buddy's name was Rick." Jack waited for the light to dawn on Nat's face, but she gave him a blank look. Leo didn't look particularly enlightened either.

"Rick. Short for—?" Jack arched a brow, waiting for her to complete the sentence.

"Richard," she answered automatically. But then her pulse jumped like she'd been zapped by an electric shock.

Jack gave Leo a sardonic look. "You want to take a guess at the last name, Detective?" Now it was Jack's turn not to give Leo time to respond. "Miller. Richard Miller. Alison Cole married Dean's best buddy, Rick Miller. Seems they'd already begun dating while Walsh was cooling his jets in a county jail cell awaiting trial for Alison's rape."

"Miller never said a word about any of this," she muttered, looking over at Leo.

Jack smiled in Leo's direction, but there was no warmth in that smile. It was tinged with obvious contempt. "You really need to brush up on your detecting, Detective."

Nat knew Jack was itching for payback, both because Leo still had him down as a murder suspect and because he'd put two and two together as to who'd shared her bed earlier that evening. What Nat couldn't decide was whether Jack was jealous or just angry.

Jack's needling had no effect. Leo was not about to lose his composure. He still had the upper hand. The same argument she could make as to why Keith Franklin was their man, Leo could just as easily make regarding Jack. There was even a witness placing Jack on the scene during the time Maggie was murdered. And there was only Jack's word that he never left his car that day.

Nat thought back to last Thursday afternoon, the afternoon Alison Cole Miller was abducted and murdered. What time did Jack leave work that day? Her breath caught in her throat as she remembered him coming into her office. It must have been a little after four. *Hey, Nat. Mind if I cut out early today. I think I'm running a fever. Must be coming down with a damn flu.*

Jack left work before five P.M. on Thursday and Alison Cole was murdered soon after. Jack was out of work the next day. The day his lover—as well as Dean Thomas Walsh's—was murdered.

Now, he'd shown up at the motel to throw suspicion on Alison's husband. A shiver went through Nat. What might have happened if she'd come into this motel room without Leo, if she'd come in here alone? If she'd expressed some of her suspicions?

"You have anything else you want to share with us, Dwyer?" Leo demanded gruffly.

Jack's smile took on a self-satisfied edge. He was starting to enjoy himself. Apparently, he wasn't worried about suspicions not yet laid to rest. Or he wasn't worried because—as Nat dearly hoped—he simply wasn't guilty. Whatever her feelings were for Jack Dwyer—and, God knew, she certainly hadn't begun to sort through them—the notion that she had been both emotionally and physically drawn to someone who might be a vicious and conniving murderer was certainly not a comforting thought.

"While you've been busy scratching itches, Coscarelli, I've been doing some of your legwork." Jack's tone was glib. "You might want to chat up a gal by the name of Sandra Gershon. She's a paralegal who worked with Alison. Told me this afternoon that on more than one occasion Alison showed up at the office wearing dark glasses. Making up some story of a chronic eye infection. She had a chronic problem all right. But I don't think it came from a virus."

Neither did Nat. Far more likely a fist, Nat thought. Rick Miller's fist. Poor Alison certainly hadn't done very well in her choice of men. *But then who was she to talk?*

"Is that it?" Leo snapped.

Jack ignored the question, his eyes resting on Nat. "Is he staying the night, Nat?"

"Screw you, Dwyer," Leo hissed.

"No thanks," Jack said with mock guile.

The question embarrassed Nat as she was sure it was meant to, but it angered her even more. "I think you should go now, Jack."

Leo smiled smugly. "You heard the lady, Dwyer."

She looked over at Leo. "I think you should both go."

Leo didn't make a move. Neither did Jack.

If she weren't so filled with guilt and confusion, Nat might have felt flattered.

thirty-four

One thing I can say. I did my time like a man.

G. V.
Inmate #205764

NAT WOKE UP—alone—in her motel bed at 10:15 A.M. fighting a fierce headache thanks to the lingering after-affects of Walsh's parting whack with that gun. The throbbing was exacerbated by that elusive thought, continuing to nag at the back of her mind. It was like a missing puzzle piece. Fit it in and the picture would be in clear focus. Without it, she simply couldn't quite make out what it was supposed to be.

Telling herself it was bound to come to her when her head cleared, she stumbled into the bathroom and threw some water on her face. It didn't help her pain or her memory. On a plastic tray on the counter next to the bathroom sink was a mini-coffeemaker with all the fixings—a single packet of ground coffee, a packet of non-dairy creamer, and a couple of packets each of sugar and artificial sweetener. Hoping the caffeine would help, she made up a pot and showered while it dripped.

As the hot water beat down on her, Nat tried sorting out the muddle of dilemmas rolling around in her cobwebby mind. In the matter of a few weeks, she'd lost a husband, a best friend, a job. She'd been nearly run down, assaulted twice, almost died in a fire. She'd broken a cardinal rule about not mixing pleasure with business. She had an escaped convict on the loose who might be a victim or a savage rapist and double murderer. And if Dean Thomas Walsh was a victim, then she had a list of suspects longer than her arm.

Stepping out of the shower, she eyed the full coffee pot and realized there wasn't enough caffeine in the world to cure all that ailed her.

The hotel phone rang as she started to dress.

"Hi."

"If you've called to lecture me, Jack—" She grabbed for her sweater.

"I called to see if we could have dinner together. We need to talk, Nat."

"It's . . . too soon, Jack."

"Too soon for what? Nat, what are you doing? Do you really think this is going to help anything, jumping into bed—"

"I thought this wasn't going to be a lecture," she said sharply. "I'm hanging up, Jack."

"No. Please. Wait. I'm sorry. No lecture. I just want you to know that you mean a lot to me, Nat. I hate for you to think I was trying to take advantage of you the other night."

"Maggie's barely cold in her grave," she said tightly.

"You think I don't mourn her loss with every fiber of my being?" Nat could hear the hurt in his voice. "But I can't deny that she betrayed me. Just like she betrayed you. I can't deny that she was sexually confused. That she was never going to really be able to commit to anyone."

He hesitated. "It wouldn't have lasted, Nat. And, in time, I really believe you and I would have still come to where we almost did the other night. And it would have been a start. Not a mistake. Not a regret. Not an ending."

Nat's palm went sweaty as she gripped the receiver. Jack's seduction didn't ring true. Too intent. Forced. She wasn't buying it. "Maggie's dead, Jack. So . . . we'll never really know how it might have been."

"And how is it with that cop?"

She hung up on him and immediately dialed the desk, asking the clerk to call her a cab since her car was still back at Hutch's place. She was outside in front of the motel when the taxi pulled up.

She slipped into the back seat and gave him Hutch's address. Not that she intended to stay put over there. She just needed her car.

On the ride over, Nat phoned her sister to see how she was holding up. The instant Rachel picked up the phone, Nat sensed that something was wrong. She was convinced of it when Rachel hung up on her right after she heard her voice.

She was shocked by Rachel's appearance when she opened the front door. It was close to eleven A.M. and she was still in her bathrobe, her hair wasn't combed and, although she had makeup on, it looked like she'd applied it the day before and simply hadn't washed her face since then.

"What happened?" Nat asked immediately, stepping inside and shutting the door.

"I told Gary about the phone call."

Nat was inwardly relieved, but she understood how much it must have taken out of Rachel to confront her husband with the truth.

"What did he say?" she asked gently.

Rachel laughed hoarsely. "He told me I was incapable of understanding him. He walked out."

Nat took a deep breath. "Rachel, I'm sorry."

"Are you happy now? Now that you're not the only one who's been dumped?"

"Rachel, please—"

Her sister turned away from her, her hands going up to her face as she broke down in sobs. Tentatively, Nat placed her hand on Rachel's shoulder. She felt her sister tense up, but this time, to Nat's relief, Rachel didn't pull away.

After leaving her sister's place, Nat decided to take a quick run by her apartment to pick up a change of clothes. Although she knew everything in her bedroom had gone up in smoke, she kept a few things in the spare bedroom. Hopefully, those garments wouldn't have been damaged.

She heard someone moving around in the apartment as soon as she stepped into her living room. She froze, caught in a fight or flight dilemma. Realizing she'd been on the losing end of recent battles, she very quickly opted for flight. She was almost at the front door when a voice behind her put her back in freeze-frame.

"Holy cow, Nat. You scared the hell out of me."

She whirled around to see her husband standing at the open door to the spare bedroom in a pair of khaki trousers and bare-chested. His hair was damp, slicked back from his face. Like he'd just showered.

"What are you doing here?" she demanded. "Is . . . she in there with you?"

"Jill and I had a fight. I spent the night here. The contractor's supposed to show up sometime this afternoon with his estimate for the work on our bedroom. And I didn't have any classes today so . . . here I am." He tried for a smile but didn't succeed.

"You okay, Nat?" He moved into the living room while she remained in the hallway a few feet from the front door.

Nat had no desire to give Ethan an update on all the reasons she was not okay. One of them being his presence in her apartment.

"You got a few minutes?" he asked. "I could make a fresh pot of coffee."

She bristled at the way he'd nonchalantly moved himself back in and taken over.

"I just came by for a change of clothes," she muttered.

"You've got some things in the spare bedroom. I even found a few things of mine still there." He put his hand to his bare chest. "No fresh shirts, though. I stuck the one I wore last night in the wash. It's probably dry now. I'll go check. What about that coffee?"

It was obvious Ethan wanted to talk. What Nat couldn't decide was if she wanted to listen. But she made no move to leave as Ethan headed into the kitchen where both the washer/dryer combo and the coffeemaker were located.

"You got a bunch of calls. Last night and this morning," Ethan called out.

She walked into the kitchen. Ethan was pulling a blue and white pinstriped shirt out of the dryer and shaking it out.

"You listened to my messages," she said, steaming.

"Take it easy. I thought the contractor might have called and I wanted—" Ethan was examining his shirt. "Think it needs pressing?"

"Who called?"

"Some guy."

"Does he have a name, Ethan?" she asked in a clipped tone.

He raised his eyes to her. "Where'd you stay last night? I called your sister early in the evening but she hadn't heard from you. She didn't even know about the fire. I decided maybe I shouldn't say anything. Didn't want to get her upset."

Nat didn't mention that Rachel had more than enough of her own problems to be upset about.

"Did you stay at Dwyer's place? Or was it that pipsqueak cop—Coscarelli? I get the feeling that detective may be using you to try to get at me—"

Nat wanted to throw something at him. "It's always about you, isn't it, Ethan? Well, it's none of your damn business where I stay, who I stay with. You gave up your right to know anything about my personal life the day you walked out on me."

At least he had the good graces to flush. "You're right, Nat. About it not being my business. But you're wrong if you think I'm only worried about my hide. I'm worried about you. I'm sick with worry, if you want to know. Can you blame me? Some mad killer on the loose. The fire."

"I thought you were convinced it was an accident."

"I'm not convinced of anything anymore." He crumpled the shirt against his chest, suddenly looking older and haggard.

"So, what did the two of you fight about?"

"She's not sure the baby's mine." He gave a hoarse laugh. "I won't blame you for gloating, Nat."

He sank into one of the kitchen chairs, still clutching his shirt. "There's this other guy she was seeing while we were getting . . . involved. Last night she told me the baby could be his. Here's a laugh for you. She met him in one of my classes. A dumb little jerk with a scrawny goatee. Squeaked by with a D. I should've flunked him."

Nat didn't like herself much for admitting that she felt some perverse satisfaction in Ethan's misery. But she wasn't about to gloat openly, if for no other reason than she didn't take any pleasure in hitting a person when he was already down. And, yes, damn it, her feelings weren't cut and dried. She'd be lying to herself to say there wasn't a part of her that still felt drawn to Ethan—albeit a masochistic part. But she'd loved this man for such a long time. Thought, when they married, they'd spend their whole lives together. Happily ever after. So much for coming down on her sister all this time because she clung so fiercely to her denial of reality.

She poured two mugs of coffee and brought them to the table.

She sat across from him. Ethan stared down into the cup, but he made no effort to pick it up.

"She's so young. I forgot what it was like—being young. Funny, because at first that's what drew me to her. Her youth. Her spirit. Her hopefulness. All things bright and beautiful. I wanted to feel that way again. For a while, I did. I felt young, brimming with optimism. I'd tell her all my secret dreams and hopes and she'd say to each and every one of them—*just do it, Ethan. You can do it. You can do anything.*" He let the shirt slip out of his hands and held them out palms up in a gesture of defeat.

"Why did you stop sharing your dreams and aspirations with me, Ethan? When did I ever discourage you—?" Nat's tone was sharp and accusatory. She was angry and glad for it. Anger brought clarity.

Ethan was shaking his head vigorously and made a grab for her hand. She moved it out of his reach. She didn't want him to touch her. She didn't want to be touched by him—physically or emotionally. "It wasn't you, Nat. It was me. I didn't believe in myself. So how could I expect you to believe in me?"

"But I did." And feeling every bit the fool for it now.

"You scared me, Nat."

"What?" She was dumbfounded.

"You have always been so clear about what you wanted. So determined. So strong. I never felt you needed me. Except for one thing. The one thing you wanted from me and that I couldn't give you was . . . a baby."

"My not getting pregnant wasn't your fault," she said quietly, not adding that she knew her failure to conceive came as a relief to him.

"I was afraid to have children. Children meant having to be an adult. I'm forty-two years old but I never really grew up." He pressed a hand to his chest. "Not inside. I was terrified of the responsibility. Even more terrified of being no good. My father was lousy at being a parent. He was selfish, demanding, impatient, critical. I . . . didn't want my kid to hate me . . . like I hated him."

In all their years together, Nat really believed this was the most honest Ethan had ever been with her. It was a little late coming, but she couldn't deny feeling moved by his admission.

"You're not your father, Ethan." Any more, she hoped to God, than she was her mother.

Tears spiked his eyes. "No. That's one thing I learned. Once I was faced with . . . with being a father, I realized I . . . wanted the baby more than I ever imagined. I wanted a shot at being good at parenting. I thought . . . I could."

And if the baby wasn't his? What then? Would he still want it?

"What is Jill going to do?"

"She's . . . not sure. Last night I told her I want her to have a blood test to determine paternity. That was really how the fight started. She got very upset. Told me Sam—that's this kid—wanted the baby no matter whose it was. That he'd asked her to marry him when she told him she was pregnant. I flew into a bit of a rage that she'd told him weeks ago, but didn't have the guts to tell me until last night. Jill came back at me, shouting that this was exactly why she hadn't told me. Because she knew I'd go berserk. Then she tells me she'd turned him down when he proposed, but that now she's not so sure she made the right decision. She's worried I'm carrying around too much baggage. That this whole thing with her is a mid-life crisis for me. And—" he hesitated, "she thinks I haven't really gotten over you."

Unabashedly, he met her skeptical gaze. "I think she may be right, Nat."

She got up from the table, putting some much needed distance between them. "What is it you want from me, Ethan? Jill's tossed you out and now you think you still love me?"

"It isn't like that, Nat. Jill didn't throw me out. I left because—"

"Because she screwed around on you? Because the baby may not be yours? Because your pride—"

Ethan leaped to his feet and started toward her. "No," she said sharply.

He stayed by his chair, tightly clenching his hands together. "I'll tell you something, Nat. The night of the fire, when I carried you in my arms to the hospital, terrified that you might die, I . . . I couldn't bear the thought." His voice cracked and he pressed his hands to his face. "I've made such a colossal mess of our lives, Nat. And I'm so, so sorry."

"How do I know you didn't start the fire?" She wasn't sure if it was her suspicion speaking or her desire to strike out at him.

"What? Nat, what are you saying? How could you think—?" He sank back down into his chair, shoulders sagging, arms hanging limply at his sides. "My God."

Seeing him like that—looking so sad and broken—it was hard to imagine he really could have done anything so heinous. An apology was on the tip of her tongue when he said, "I don't blame you for not being able to think straight right now, Nat. It's been such a nightmare, what with Maggie—"

The instant he mentioned her name, Nat's sojourn into temporary insanity ended and she was catapulted back to her senses. Whatever unknown dark deeds Ethan might or might not be guilty of, there were some sins he'd committed that were all too indisputable. All too painfully vivid. "You betrayed me, Ethan. You lied to me. You cheated on me. Not just with Jill, which was bad enough. But with Maggie. With my best friend. That was even worse. I don't know how I could ever forgive that."

His hands muffled the sound of his crying.

His sobs inspired no pity. Nat was relieved to realize he couldn't push her buttons as easily as he once could. If anything, her suspicions mounted. What if this was all an act on Ethan's part to convince her he was innocent of an attempt on her life and the murders of Maggie Austin and Alison Miller? While it still felt farfetched, Nat couldn't completely dissuade herself of the possibility of his guilt.

The one thing she'd learned since Maggie's death was that no one was turning out to be what they seemed. She remembered Leo telling her to trust no one. She doubted he was putting himself in that grouping, but the truth was, Nat didn't trust him either. They'd had sex and it was great. But he never spoke of his feelings for her. She had no idea what he felt. What it meant to him. Not that she'd come close to figuring out what it meant to her, either.

She turned away from Ethan—her mind a jumble of confusion, rampant suspicion, and exhaustion. "I'm going to get some clothes together. Stay here for a few days if you want. I won't be back until the mess is gone." She was sure he knew when she said *mess* she wasn't only referring to the construction.

She started out of the kitchen when she remembered about those phone calls and, once again, asked Ethan who called. Curtly, this time.

He lowered his hands from his tear-stained face, giving her a wan look. "A guy by the name of Richard—he said he had to speak to you. He left a number. It's on the desk in the spare room."

She was grateful that Ethan remained in the kitchen while she tossed a few items in a duffel bag. Eager to get out of the apartment, she didn't waste time changing there.

As soon as she got into her car, she tried the number Rick Miller had left for her.

He picked up on the first ring. "Mrs. Price?"

"How were you so sure it was me?"

"You're the only one, other than my mother-in-law, who has this number. And I just spoke to her a few minutes ago."

"What's going on, Rick?" she deliberately used the old nickname rather than referring to him as Richard.

If nothing else, he was quick on the uptake. "I haven't gone by

Rick in years." He hesitated. "I guess you found out about Dean and me being buddies back when."

"Back when the two of you went to that party with Alison and her friend. The party where Alison was raped."

There was another pause. "I was the one who drove Alison home that night. She was so messed up. Not just physically. Mentally. It was awful. I never felt so helpless. Poor kid, she was afraid to go home. Afraid her mom would blame her for what had happened because she'd gotten drunk. So I offered to go in with her. Talk to her mom. Jean was terrific. Oh sure, she was upset, but she believed, like I did, that Ali wasn't the guilty one. She was the victim. No guy, I don't care how whacked out he is on booze and pills, has the right to take advantage of a girl in that state. I hated Dean's guts for what he did to Ali. I thought he should have gotten a much stiffer sentence than the judge handed down. You don't know how long it took for Ali to get over the trauma. I don't think she ever really did. But she was an amazing woman. In her eyes, Walsh had served his time and deserved a break. Can you imagine that? It made my blood boil when she'd talk like that."

"Were those the times she showed up at work with a black eye?" Nat asked coolly.

"What? I don't know what—all right. Okay, I admit it. I lost it a couple of times. But I never meant to strike out at Ali. Never. I'd just start boiling over like I said and Ali would be trying to calm me down and . . . okay, yeah, she got in the way once or twice—"

"Of your fist?"

"It isn't like you think. We loved each other. I was getting help for my . . . temper. Seeing a shrink. You can check if you don't believe me."

"Was it Alison who insisted you get psychiatric help?"

"Alison never made me do anything. I wanted to get help. And it had nothing to do with me being fucked up mentally. I just had this problem with my temper and I wanted to get it under control.

I wanted to get back with Ali. I wanted to be the kind of husband she deserved. I was making a lot of progress in therapy. Alison could see the change. See that I was really making headway. That's why we started talking about my coming back home."

Nat was losing patience with Miller's saga, didn't buy most of it. "Let's cut to the chase. Why have you been calling me?" she asked brusquely.

"Could we meet face to face, Mrs. Price?"

"Where are you?"

"The Parkcrest Hotel. It's off Tremont in Boston. I'm registered under the name Dan Jarett. I'll explain why when you get here." There was a brief pause. "Can you come right away?"

Leo got her on her cell phone just as she was maneuvering onto the South-East Expressway.

"I got up on the wrong side of the bed this morning."

She smiled faintly.

"Make that the wrong side of the *wrong* bed," he corrected.

Her smile widened. They definitely had meltdown. "I didn't sleep very well either."

"Where are you?"

"On my way to a meeting with Rick Miller." She quickly filled him in. And felt better for it. Not the least reason being, she was scared of going there alone. In her eyes, Miller was far from being off the suspect list. A man with a violent temper who beat up his wife and hated his one-time best friend—he would have been killing two birds with one stone. With poor Maggie thrown in as one more bird for good measure.

"I'll meet you in the lobby." Leo's curt order stopped her ruminating. "Don't go up there without me."

"Okay."

"I mean it, Natalie." His tone was ice again.

So much for meltdown.

thirty-five

*There is no question that incarceration provides disci-
pline and surveillance, but only while prisoners remain
behind bars—once they leave the institution there's
really no way to keep them in check.*

Ethan D. Price
Professor of Criminal Justice

SHE BOUGHT A paper in the hotel lobby, which was empty save for
the desk clerk—a kid in his early twenties who was wearing head-
phones and reading *SPIN* magazine.

The lead story on the front page of the *Boston Monitor* had a
banner heading that read: MOTHER OF ESCAPED CON KILLS
INTRUDER. The first paragraph laid it out—a break-in at the Natick home of Marion Walsh, mother of escaped convict and suspected double murderer, Dean Thomas Walsh; her gunning down
of knife-wielding intruder, Owen King, an ex-con with a long history of violence.

Nat started skimming the second paragraph, containing more of the details of the incident, when she saw Leo approaching. He definitely *did* look like he'd gotten up on the wrong side of the bed. She saw lines edging his mouth, shadows under his eyes and a tension in his walk.

She folded the paper and set it down on a scratched glass and wrought-iron side table near the lobby entrance.

They exchanged a bland greeting. She was feeling as edgy as he looked. "Miller's in room 601. Under the name Jarett. I was thinking maybe I should go in alone. He might freak if a cop walks in with me. You can stay right outside the door if there's a problem."

"We'll go up together," Leo said decisively.

Nat didn't argue. She really wasn't expecting otherwise.

A white-haired threesome in matching windbreakers, comfy walking shoes and cameras dangling from their necks exited the elevator. Another couple—a fifty-something man in an off-the-rack business suit and a twenty-something blond in a skimpy sweater and an even skimpier skirt started to follow them in. Leo flipped his badge at them, asking them to wait for the next elevator. As the doors started to close, Nat saw them hurrying, instead, for the lobby exit.

"Are you expecting trouble?" she asked Leo.

Leo arched one eyebrow. "Every time I lay eyes on you."

"Miller called me. I didn't go looking for him."

Leo arched both brows.

"Any leads on Franklin's whereabouts?" Nat asked as the antiquated elevator creaked and groaned its way slowly upward. He shook his head.

"You think he might be dead, don't you?"

He gave her a long look. "I don't know what to think, Natalie."

The elevator doors jerked open on six, the hotel's top floor. Room 601 was the last door on the right. Nat knocked a couple of times and identified herself. She saw the light from the peephole darken. She was being checked. As soon as the light returned, Leo edged her out of the way. He had his gun out and aimed as they heard the rasp of the dead bolt being thrown. A moment later the door opened and Leo was face to face with a gun in the shaky hand of Rick Miller.

Miller looked more than a little surprised to see Leo instead of Nat standing in the doorway. Nat was more than a little unnerved to realize Miller meant to be aiming that gun at her.

Miller blanched, quickly dropping his gun hand to his side. "I . . . was afraid . . . you might have been followed," he said to Nat by way of explanation. A rather weak explanation in her book. And, she was guessing, in Leo's.

"Put the gun down on the ground nice and easy and step away from the door," Leo ordered in the firm voice of a no-nonsense cop.

Miller's eyes shifted nervously from Leo to her and back to Leo again. If Leo looked like he hadn't gotten much sleep last night, Miller looked like he hadn't slept in several nights. His eyes were bloodshot, he was sporting a thick stubble, and he smelled of a rank mix of body odor and booze. "I'm afraid for my life."

"We'll come inside and talk about it after you put that gun down," Leo said, his weapon cocked and ready if Miller decided not to cooperate.

"When did you get the first call?" Leo asked.

Miller sat on the edge of the unmade bed, ringing his hands. Miller's loaded .38 had been emptied, gun and bullets tucked away in Leo's jacket pocket.

"The day you came to see me. To tell me about . . . Ali. He called maybe twenty minutes after you left."

"And what exactly did he say?"

Miller scowled. "He said . . . he was sorry."

"Sorry for what?" Leo pressed.

"I guess for . . . what he did. You know . . . to Ali."

"You guess?" The words came out of Leo's mouth like a snort of derision.

Anger flashed on Miller's face, but he reeled it in fast. "Well, that's all he said. 'I'm sorry.' That time, anyway."

Miller dropped his head in his hands and heaved a loud sigh which Nat was sure was meant to denote anguish. But she detected a hint of irritation in that sigh as well. From the first time she'd laid eyes on Miller, she'd both disliked him and distrusted everything he had to say. If anything she felt that way even more so now. Rick Miller reminded her of a lot of chameleon-like inmates she'd seen over the years. Whether or not he'd resorted to murder, Nat had no doubt he was capable of that degree of violence.

"Why didn't you report the call?"

Miller gave Leo a helpless look. "I didn't know where Dean was. I didn't buy his apology, that's for damn sure. And I didn't see how it would help—" As he talked Nat could see him struggling to keep the rage out of his voice and facial expression. He didn't quite succeed.

"When did you get the next call?" Leo cut him off.

Miller didn't respond right away. "Two nights ago."

"Where were you?" Leo demanded.

"At Jean's place. The kids and I have been staying with Ali's mom." Another pause. "I put the house on the market."

"That was fast," Nat commented.

Both men's eyes shifted to her. Up until now she'd been sitting quietly on the sidelines—to be precise, she'd been sitting on a ratty orange and blue plaid upholstered chair with bad springs by the solitary window. Maybe they'd both forgotten she was in the room.

"I got two kids to look after and only one salary now. We need the money," Miller said defensively.

"How'd Walsh know where to reach you?" Leo brought Miller back to the topic at hand.

"That's what freaked me. I don't know how he knew. It's not like he asked if I was there when Jean picked up. She didn't recognize his voice and he didn't identify himself. Just asked for me like he knew I was there. Which made me think he's been following me."

"And what did he say this next time?"

"He wasn't feeling sorry anymore, that's for sure. He was belligerent right from the get-go. I'm pretty sure he was on something. He always did go overboard with the booze and the pills when he was on the street. Uppers, downers, you name it."

"What did he say?" Leo repeated impatiently.

"He started ranting and raving about how he'd been betrayed and screwed over royally. Then he came right out and told me point-blank he was coming after me next." He looked back over at her. "And you, Mrs. Price. He said he owes us both for what we did to him." Again, he paused. "That's the reason I called you. I wanted to warn you. I thought you might want to find yourself a place to hide out as well until, hopefully, the cops smoke Walsh out and send his ass back to jail for life this time."

Miller gave Leo a desultory look. "At the rate you guys are going, I'll be hiding out for the rest of my damn life."

"You could have warned me on the phone," Nat challenged, vividly recalling Miller standing at the open door with that gun in his hand.

Miller met her wary gaze head-on. "Would you have believed me? I know you think maybe I had something to do with my wife's death. I could see it in the way you looked at me that day you came to our home. I thought if I could see you in person . . . I could convince you I was sincere."

He'd have had an easier time convincing her he was the Tooth Fairy.

"Look, I don't want Walsh killing any more people."

"Yourself included," she was quick to point out.

"Damn straight."

Leo cut in on their testy interchange. "What exactly did you do to him, Rick?"

"Huh?"

Leo didn't repeat the question. They both know Miller had understood it perfectly.

Miller rubbed his hands together vigorously. "Okay, back when Dean first got busted, I did go see him this one time. After he did a lot of begging and pleading. And when I finally relented, you know what the bastard wanted? He tried to get me to . . . cover for him. You know, tell the cops he was with me the whole time that night. Be his alibi." Miller stood up and started pacing the small room, running his fingers through his greasy hair as he walked. The gray threadbare carpet showed the wear and tear of many other pacers.

Be his alibi. Miller's words had an inexplicable impact, falling like a shadow over Nat, reverberating in her head.

"I was already dating Ali," Miller was continuing, oblivious of her reaction. "Dean didn't know. Ali didn't want me to tell him. She was scared that if somehow he got off, he might come after us. His head was all messed up back then. Like he'd con-vinced himself what went down with Ali that night wasn't rape. He kept telling me—'She wanted it, man. She loved it.' And I lost my cool. I screamed back at him—'Loved it? She was uncon-scious.' And he's going—'no, no, it's not true. She wanted it.'" Miller stopped pacing. He was standing a few feet from Nat. "I called him a sick pervert and told him that I'd rather die than lie for him. And now . . . he's planning to make me eat those words." He exhaled a loud sigh. "If he finds me."

Leo was giving Miller a thoughtful study. "Maybe that's not such a bad idea."

Miller looked aghast. "What the hell—?"

"Like you said, Rick, so far we haven't exactly been winning any prizes getting our hands on Walsh."

Miller's eyes narrowed as he regarded Leo, his earlier bout of anguish subsiding as rapidly as it had flared. "I get it. And you can forget it. No way, man. I got two kids who already lost their mommy. No chance in hell I'm gonna be a sitting duck for you screw-ups, risk my ass—my life—so that I can lure that fucking murderer out of the shadows."

"We won't let anything happen to you, Miller. We'll cover your ass night and day. The second Walsh steps out of the shadows and makes a move on you, he's ours."

Miller started pacing again. "Oh man, oh man," he muttered. "I don't know—"

"Think it over for a little while," Leo said. "But if I were you I wouldn't wait too long to decide."

"If you'd stop focusing all of your efforts on nabbing Walsh," Nat argued with Leo as the doors of the elevator started to open, "you might realize that that wife-beater back in that room is a prime candidate for having murdered Alison. And then, realizing he'd be the first person the cops would suspect, he cleverly decides to throw suspicion on Walsh by—"

Leo nudged her into the elevator as she was proposing her theory.

They both heard the shot ring out just as the elevator doors rattled closed. Leo frantically tried to pry them back open, but the elevator was already starting its descent. He pounded on the button for the fifth floor, cursing at the slowness with which the elevator moved. As the elevator inched downward, he snatched his cell phone from his pocket, calling for backup.

When the elevator finally got to the fifth floor, Leo was squeezing through the doors when they were no more than inches apart. Nat was right behind him as he headed for the fire stairs at the end of the hallway.

"Stay here," he barked, not even turning his head.

Nat's steps slowed for a couple of moments, but then she disregarded his orders and raced through the fire door right after him. Leo's pounding steps on the metal stairs drowned out the sound of her steps. It wasn't until he burst through the door on level six, his gun gripped tightly in his hand, that he realized she was still nipping at his heels.

They both saw the door to 601—the door on the right nearest the fire door—gaping open. A handful of guests were nervously peering out their open doors. Leo brusquely used his gun to wave them back inside. They didn't need any coaxing. Doors slammed shut fast.

Leo edged over to the door of 601, cautiously peering into the room.

Nat was behind him, holding her breath. Expecting Leo to be viewing the dead or wounded body of Richard Miller. Which wouldn't exactly have been a boost for her latest theory.

Leo kicked the door open until it slammed against the wall, a sure way of making certain no one was lurking behind it. That *no one* most likely being, Nat was afraid, Dean Thomas Walsh.

"Is Miller—?"

Before she could finish her inquiry, Leo stepped into the room, motioning her to stay put. This time, she was more than happy to comply.

After less than a minute, Leo came back into the hall. "He's gone."

She swallowed hard, going clammy all over. "Gone as in . . . dead?"

Despite the look of frustration and irritation on Leo's face, he took a moment to touch her cheek. "Gone as in not here." He crossed over to the hotel room diagonally across from 601, where moments earlier a very nervous looking young man had been peering out.

After a few brisk raps on the door and Leo's announcement that he was a cop, the door inched open. Leo waved the badge in the young man's face. "You see anything after that gunshot?"

The young man, bare-chested and clad in a pair of boxer shorts, hesitated. "My fiancée doesn't know I'm here." He glanced nervously back into the room and then returned his edgy gaze to Leo. "My fiancée isn't the understanding type."

Leo nodded. "Just tell me what you saw and we'll forget we ever saw you."

Beads of sweat punctuated the potential witness's pinched forehead. "I hear the shot and at first I think it's a car backfiring. Only the sound wasn't coming from out in the street. My . . . lady friend starts to freak so I go to check it out . . . you know, to calm her down."

Leo's impatience is showing. "Yeah, yeah."

"When I look out into the hall I see the open door across the way and a guy bursting through that fire door—" He pointed to the very door they'd just exited.

"Only one guy?"

The young man frowned. "I'm not sure."

"What do you mean?"

"See, the fire door was half open when the guy was heading for it. Like, maybe, somebody had already gone through it." He swiped his sweaty forehead with the back of his hand. Even as he was perspiring, there were goose bumps popping out all over his scrawny, hairless chest. The air in the hallway was chilly. "You know, like it could be the guy I saw was chasing someone."

"What did he look like? Did he have a gun?"

"I only saw the back of him. You know, I couldn't really tell if he had a gun. Or what he looked like."

"Hair color? Height? Weight? Come on. Give me something here." Frustrated.

"He was wearing one of those hooded sweatshirts. Dark gray or maybe black. I guess he was . . . kind of average. I only saw him for like, five seconds, if that. Hey really, I can't help you out any more than that—"

Leo was heading for the fire door before the kid finished.

"Thanks. You better go inside and warm up," Nat said, then quickly turned and followed Leo.

He was racing down the stairs, two, three at a time. She did her best to keep pace with him even though she was pretty sure Miller and his pursuer had made it down the six flights while they were creeping their way down the elevator to the fifth floor. By the time she and Leo were scrambling up the stairs to six, they'd probably made it through the lobby and out the building.

On the other hand, if they hadn't got that far, it was possible they could find the dead body of Rick Miller on their way down.

Winded and trying to catch her breath as she hit the lobby, she saw Leo rushing over to question the desk clerk. Except for the clerk, the lobby was empty. Sirens whined as several cruisers squealed up to the curb. Six uniformed officers and one plain-clothes detective, Leo's partner, Mitchell Oates, came bursting into the lobby, heading directly over to Leo.

They all stepped away from the desk and held a brief pow-wow. Nat decided to go outside and see if she could spot either Miller or his pursuer, although she was sure the cops had been on the lookout for them as they raced over to the hotel.

As anticipated, there was no sign of Miller or the guy in the hooded sweatshirt. But what she did see that definitely brought her up short was an old black Pontiac parked on the other side of the road. Dodging the traffic, she raced across the street, and checked the rear of the car. The red glass covering the driver's side brake light was shattered. Now Nat knew what the expression meant *to feel your blood run cold.*

Squinting against the sunlight, she was almost certain she'd caught a glimpse of a hooded figure darting at top speed across Tremont Street toward the grassy, tree-studded Boston Commons across the way. Afraid to lose any more time by rushing back across the street into the hotel to report her sighting to Leo, she took off after the man she was convinced was Keith Franklin. Which meant that Keith Franklin was the man in hot pursuit of Rick Miller.

What Nat couldn't figure out was where in the world Dean Thomas Walsh fit into the equation.

thirty-six

I hear stories day in and day out from cons telling me how they're gonna do this or do that to certain individuals when they get out 'cause it's their fault they're in here. When these badasses finally get released, they walk out with one mean, mother-fucking attitude. . . .

M. B.

Inmate #968473

IF ONLY IT was one of those bone cold autumn days that occasionally hit Boston that time of year. Instead, the sun was out, the sky was clear, and the weather couldn't have been balmier. All of which computed to the Commons being bustling with people who were eager to lap up the last golden rays of sunshine before winter set in with its inimitable Northeast vengeance. Families with young children were picnicking on the grass, couples were strolling the meandering paths, elderly folk were sunning themselves on the benches. All, as yet, oblivious to the potential danger in their midst.

And Nat, unfortunately, had lost sight of Keith Franklin. As for the assuredly panicked Rick Miller, he, too, was nowhere to be seen. Weirdly, she felt as though the nightmare was drawing to a close and unraveling at the same time.

She was about to call Leo on her cell phone to give him her exact location, when she heard the nerve-shattering blast of a gunshot followed by raucous screams. Another shot quickly followed. Then more frantic screams. People started racing in all directions, desperately trying to scramble out of harm's way. Nat froze for an instant, then sprang into action.

Nat seemed to be the only one running toward the mayhem, all the while feeling like she was crossing over minefields instead of a grassy knoll. She heard someone shouting her name and allowed a quick glance over her shoulder. Leo was racing toward her. Coming up behind him, but spreading out, were Oates and the uniforms. No one, including herself, was exactly sure where the shot had come from.

Until the next blast.

Her first sight as she rounded the bend was of a huge elm tree in front of which was the cowering figure of Rick Miller. He was on the ground clasping his bleeding leg. A sweatshirt clad arm was clamped around Miller's neck. His assailant was kneeling behind him, his back protected by the enormous trunk of the tree. The hood had fallen off his head, revealing a shock of thick dark brown hair. Electric blue eyes locked onto Nat, silently warning, *don't mess with me.*

It was the eyes more than the gun Dean Thomas Walsh had pointed at Rick Miller's head that stopped Nat dead in her tracks about twenty yards away from him. Leo and the rest of the cops who were fanned out in a wide semi-circle also came to a halt just behind her.

Silent tears were streaming down Miller's ashen face which

was contorted with pain. It was as if not merely fear, but pure primal terror, had rendered him incapable of sound.

There was no sign of fear in Walsh's features. Instead, he exuded an almost eerie calm, producing an equally eerie hush all around him. It was as if none of them was even breathing.

It took Nat a few moments to come to grips with the reality that it was Dean Thomas Walsh, and not Keith Franklin as she'd thought, who had tracked down—and finally found—Miller. The only puzzle piece out of order was what Franklin's car was doing at the scene.

Miller groaned in pain. Nat wanted to get a closer look at how badly he'd been hit, but she couldn't pull her gaze away from Walsh. She had this crazy notion that as long as they maintained this intense eye contact, Walsh wouldn't squeeze the trigger again. There was no question that the next bullet that hit Rick Miller would kill him.

"I tried to tell you I was innocent," Walsh said quietly. "The day the cops came to arrest me, charging me with rape, I thought it was some bad dream. Or, at the very least, a terrible mistake. I couldn't believe it when Alison identified me as her rapist. I never got much beyond kissing her that night before I passed out cold. My mother came to see me a couple of days after I got arrested." His eyes never moved off of Nat's, but for a few brief moments they glazed over and he seemed not to even be in her time zone.

"She had such a look of revulsion on her face. I'll never forget that look. It wasn't even a guilty-until-proved-innocent look. There wasn't an iota of doubt on her face that I'd done it. When I begged her to get me a decent lawyer, she looked at me like I must be mad. Without a single word, she got up and walked out of the visitor's room."

Pain, not rage, suffused his features. "I want her here. I want to see her face when she learns the real truth. Get my mother here, Nat."

Before Nat could answer, Leo cut in. "We'll get your mother here, Walsh, if you put down that gun."

"Only guns going down are yours," Walsh said with a scarily calm demeanor. "Or else it all ends here."

Miller's eyes squeezed closed as if in prayer.

"You kill him, it's your death warrant as well," Leo responded evenly.

Walsh seemed to be contemplating Leo's challenge.

"Okay, Nat. I changed my mind," he said finally.

Somehow, she didn't think this change of mind was necessarily for the better. Her assumption was quick to be proven correct.

"Nat, come over here and see what you can do about this asshole's leg wound."

"No, Natalie," Leo commanded sharply.

"He's bleeding pretty bad. You know some first-aid, right?" Walsh said, ignoring Leo's orders to her. "Come on, Nat. You don't want to have more blood on your hands."

"Don't move an inch, Natalie." Leo's harsh voice held an edge of desperation. They were both fully aware that if she did as Walsh wanted, all that would happen was that she'd become another of his hostages. One whose life Leo would be more unlikely to risk.

Her breathing was labored. She was sweating so profusely that her sweater was plastered against her back. She was scared to move. Scared not to. She felt helpless.

Walsh's lips curved in a condescending smile. "The longer you procrastinate, the more blood he's going to lose, Nat. I won't even need to use this next bullet." He leaned against the broad tree trunk, the movement forcing Miller's neck to be jerked back. "I have all the time in the world."

The sun slipped behind a voluminous cloud, the area around them darkening.

"We're not even sure where your mother is," Leo called out. "You must have heard about what happened to Owen King at your house."

A full-fledged laugh erupted from Walsh. "Such wonderful irony. My mother, the murderer."

Nat wasn't sure which was more chilling—the laugh or his words.

Leo continued without any visible or audible sign of a reaction. "She took your sister and went to stay with friends. We don't know—"

"Don't bullshit a con. Your lies flash like a neon sign over your dumb head. Chrissie called me last night, you fuck."

So Christine knew where her brother had fled. She'd lied to her mother when she said she didn't know where he'd gone. She'd risked grotesque abuse and quite likely death at Owen King's hands to keep her brother from harm.

Thinking back to that night Nat was once again attacked by the nagging feeling that there was something here she was missing.

"She told me exactly which friend's house they were staying at. The friend my sweet, pure Mom happens to be screwing at the moment. Guess you jerks didn't move fast enough to tap Donnie Barton's phone. Although I was a little miffed at Chrissie for taking the risk of calling me from there. But I never could stay mad at Chrissie for too long. She's been the only one who has believed in me without ever wavering from day one."

"What about Maggie?" Nat asked, a rawness in her throat. "Didn't she believe in you?"

Nat saw a flicker of grief move across Walsh's face. But all he said was, "Come over here, Nat. You tend to my one-time buddy while the detective sends one of his boys for my mom. Once she gets here, everything will be straightened out, and it'll all be over."

Miller's glazed, terrified eyes looked pleadingly at her.

Nat imagined that same look in Leo's eyes.

One of them was pleading for his life. The other, for hers.

"All right, Dean," she said with far more calm than she felt. "I'm coming over." She started toward him.

*   *   *

Within minutes of the shooting, the news of the standoff must have hit the local radio and TV stations because there was a media frenzy going on at the Commons, reporters and cameramen swarming the area like hungry vultures. They were being held back a safe distance by makeshift barriers set in place by the police. Two men who weren't reporters had managed to squeeze their way to the front of the obstructions. Nat recognized them both. Jack Dwyer and Ethan. They were standing there no more than ten yards apart, but she wasn't sure either knew the other was there. Both their faces were etched with fear and helplessness. Nat had been managing a brave front up until she saw them. Now tears welled in her eyes. Still, she clung to the hope that Walsh would release them and give himself up once his mother arrived.

At least she'd managed to stem Miller's bleeding with a makeshift tourniquet she'd fashioned from the shirt sleeve she'd ripped off his arm. But, as she'd already entreated Walsh to no avail, Miller was in serious need of a doctor.

Marion Walsh looked like she'd aged ten years in the last twenty-four hours. Her face was gaunt and pale as parchment. Her colorless lips were pressed tight and her blue eyes so washed out as to be almost gray. Her daughter, whose face was almost as pallid and drawn as her mother's, was holding tightly onto her mother's arm. Marion Walsh appeared very much in need of her daughter's support which Nat was guessing was as much mental as it was physical.

"Been a while, Mom. You miss me?" Dean asked with the nonchalance a son might exhibit upon returning home from a college semester. Only this son was an escaped convict surrounded by police and holding a wounded man and a prison superintendent hostage.

A wrenching sob escaped Marion's lips. "Please, Dean." Her voice quivered.

"I want to know one thing, Mom. In all those years I was rotting in prison, being reamed out by my man Owen or by any of his buddies for the price of a pack of smokes, did it ever—*ever once*—cross your mind that I didn't do it? That I was innocent?"

"Dean," Christine pleaded, "you've got to let it go. She is the way she is. It doesn't matter."

"It matters," Walsh screamed, rage and despair erupting with the force of a volcano. Abruptly, he grabbed a hunk of Rick Miller's hair, yanking hard, forcing him to look up.

"Tell her," Walsh shrieked into his ear. "Tell my mother the truth. Tell her who raped Alison that night."

"Oh man, oh man . . ." Miller moaned.

"Tell her how you let me suffer eight long fucking years for a crime you committed. Tell my mother how it was you who convinced Alison it was me that did her. You think I didn't know you started dating her right after it went down. Chrissie found out. Oh, neither of us knew how sick you were—that it was really you that night—but Chrissie never doubted it was somebody else who was guilty. We stupidly thought it was just that you were hot for Alison and wanted your competition out of the way. Because it was me she was interested in before you set me up, you piece of scum."

Nat looked square into the eyes of Rick Miller. "Did she find out the truth? Did Alison discover it was you who raped her that night?"

Miller shook his head pitifully. "It's not what you think. I loved my wife. It was a terrible thing, I did. I know that. But it was one mistake. The crazy thing was, I went looking for them that night because I was worried that Dean might take advantage of her. See, I liked Alison right off the bat. I walked into that room with the best of intentions. I swear to you. But there she was. On the bed. Dean passed out beside her. And she was . . . pretty much out of it herself. But she was nudging Dean. Rubbing up against him. Mumbling how he should kiss her again. I don't know what came over me. I closed the door, locked it. It was so dark inside the room. I shoved Dean off the bed. He landed with a thud and didn't so much as make a sound. Once it got started I couldn't stop. I think maybe someone put something in my drink 'cause I just went wild. And the whole time I'm telling myself she was enjoying it. Wanting it. Loving it." Exactly the words Miller had sworn Walsh had spoken.

The absolute silence around them was broken by the ragged sobs of Dean's mother as she crumpled to the ground. Christine knelt down to console her. Nat could hear her saying, "I tried to tell you, Mom. I tried to tell you Dean wouldn't do such a terrible thing."

Nat stared with utter revulsion at Miller. Because of this man's act of violence and his subsequent concealment, not only were eight years of Dean Thomas Walsh's life stolen from him, but from his loved ones as well. All of them had suffered and would continue to suffer needlessly. This was a tragedy that should never have happened.

Leo edged slowly toward them, his gun tucked in his holster. "Let us take him in, Walsh. It's over now."

"No, it's not over. It's never going to be over." But there was more hopelessness than wrath in Walsh's voice.

"Please, Dean," Chrissie called out to him. "They won't take you back now. We all know you're innocent. It's just like you told me. Rick killed Alison when she threatened to tell you the truth. And then he went and killed Maggie to make it look like it was you. It's finally going to be Rick's turn to pay the price."

Leo had continued to cautiously approach them. "She's right, Dean. Time to let the police deal with Miller here."

Miller scrunched his face up in panicked consternation. "No. No, wait. You got it all wrong. I didn't do it. I didn't kill Ali. Okay, we fought that day because some woman from work I'd seen maybe once or twice called her up and told her some cock-and-bull story about how I'd gotten rough with her or something.

Next thing I know, Ali's accusing me of being the one who raped her that night of the party. Saying how she'd finally put it all together. How she'd known, deep down, for a long time, but didn't want to admit it to herself."

"And you killed her to keep her quiet," Dean said, his voice drained of emotion. "Then you went after Maggie."

Miller was shaking his head vigorously in denial. If he was still in pain from the gunshot wound, it had taken a back seat to his realization he was about to be arrested for double homicide.

Christine came running over to them, dropping to her knees as she threw her arms around her brother, mindless of the gun still gripped in his hand. He laid his head on her shoulder. She stroked his hair and crooned softly to him. After a few moments, Walsh let the gun drop to his side. Nat quickly reached for it before he had a change of heart and grabbed it back up and shot Miller in cold blood. A part of her wouldn't have blamed him.

Leo motioned for the EMT boys. They scooted over carrying a stretcher. As they lifted Rick Miller onto it, he was sobbing and screaming. "No, no, no. You got it all wrong. It's a set-up. I never killed anyone. I'm innocent. I swear, damn it. It's Dean. It's Dean."

As Nat watched Miller being carted off, still loudly protesting his innocence, she found herself thinking of that old childhood story about the little boy who cried wolf.

thirty-seven

I still proclaim my innocence and that's all I have to say.
J. A.
(executed 5/17/90)

WALSH AND HIS sister remained entwined in each other's arms, but as Christine saw their mother nervously approach, she helped her brother to his feet and stepped aside. The media was still being held at bay, allowing the family the barest modicum of privacy. Nat, too, left them this moment, wondering how they would ever repair the damage that'd been wrought.

She walked shakily over to Leo, handing him the gun she'd taken from Walsh. What she wanted—what she yearned for—was for him to take her in his arms and tell her, like Christine told Dean, that everything would be all right now. But Leo made no move to embrace her. Instead, his gaze shifted over to where Jack and Ethan were now standing together, both arguing with a policeman to let them through. Leo called out to the uniform and gave him the okay.

Nat gave Leo a wounded look, but all he said was, "You've got a lot of unfinished business, and so do I, Natalie."

Nat wasn't sure if he meant Walsh—who was now facing a possible charge of assault with a deadly weapon—or Jakey's mom.

Ethan beat Jack to her and pulled her into his arms. She didn't fight the embrace. She simply didn't respond to it. She couldn't. Ethan was quick to sense her lack of involvement and let his arms drop to his sides. He regarded her with a sad, winsome look. "I made one mistake, Nat."

She smiled ruefully, hearing Ethan echo Rick Miller's words. She really thought neither man had any true understanding of the momentousness and enormity of his *mistake.*

"I spoke to your sister," he said. "She called as soon as she heard what was going on here. She wanted to come, but I persuaded her not to. I didn't think you'd want her to be here."

Nat nodded her gratitude.

"She said to tell you she loves you."

Tears spiked Nat's eyes. Ethan looked puzzled. She made no attempt to explain her emotional response.

"Well, I'll call you in a few days, Nat." Ethan's voice cracked and he turned away looking lost and confused. Nat knew the feeling. God, how she knew the feeling.

Jack waited on the sidelines until Ethan trudged off, shoulders hunched against a wind that wasn't there.

"You okay?" Jack asked as soon as he approached.

"I will be."

"You're the girl of the hour, Nat. The Commissioner will probably pin a medal on you for risking your life to prove a condemned man innocent. And I'm sure he'll be begging you to shorten your *vacation* and get back to work on the double."

"It doesn't feel like it's really over," she said wearily, glancing back at the Walsh family. Marion was standing close to her son, her hand ever so tentatively resting on his shoulder as she spoke to him. Christine was smiling luminously. For the first time, Nat saw that she was really as striking-looking as her brother.

"Can I give you a ride back, Nat?"

She shook her head, her gaze drifting over to Leo who was conferring with his partner, Mitchell Oates.

"You know about his kid's mother?"

Nat looked back at Jack. "How do you know about her?"

"I read her Exit Assessment yesterday. In four weeks, she's being transferred to Horizon House. She'll be finishing out her last year of incarceration with us."

Nat tried to conceal her dismay, but she wasn't successful.

Jack touched her arm. "You really care about him, huh."

"I don't know how I feel about anything or anyone right now," she said, meaning it, at least partly. "You better get back to the House, Jack. I need to see what the police are going to do about Walsh."

She started to walk back to Leo when Christine broke away from her family and came running toward her.

"I don't know how I can ever thank you, Superintendent. For a while there you and I were the only ones who believed in Dean's innocence. Even after that homeless woman came forward, the police still didn't—"

A gasp escaped Nat's lips, a chill whipping through her like an icy breath. *Oh my God. That's it. That's what's been nagging me.* With dawning awareness, Nat stared intently at Christine.

"What . . . what is it? What's wrong?" she asked anxiously.

"You couldn't have known, Christine. I never told you. Leo never told you. And the police deliberately kept it from the media."

Christine was starting to look alarmed. "I don't know what you mean. Known about what?"

"After King was shot you said almost the same thing."

"What? I don't know—"

"There was no way you could have known the witness who came forward to support your brother's alibi for the time of Maggie's murder was a *homeless* woman." Nat took in a ragged breath. "Not unless you or your brother was the one who got her to come in."

Color suffused Christine's face. Ironic how all this time she had lied so well and now she gave herself away so easily. Nat imagined it was because she'd thought it was finally over and had let herself drop her guard.

"It wasn't Dean's idea. And it wasn't as though she wasn't there that day. She's always hanging out there."

"How much did you pay her to provide your brother with an alibi, Christine?" Nat wanted to be angry at her, but the only one she felt angry at was herself. Because, for all her suspicions and skepticism about everyone else, she never saw through Christine.

The radiance and joy evaporated from Christine's face, leaving her almost plain-looking again. "It was the truth. But no one would believe us. I had to do something." She stepped back, stumbling on a rock.

Walsh darted over and caught his sister as she was losing her balance. She clung to him. "It is the truth, right, Dean? It was Rick who killed your teacher. Who killed Alison. That's why I paid that homeless woman to back you up."

Instead of assuring her, he shook her angrily. "Shut up, Chrissie. Shut up. Do you hear?"

The second the media spotted the activity, they smelled something hot again. Cameramen jockeyed for a good position to get the siblings on video and stills, and the reporters were clamoring for an update. More uniforms lined the barriers to keep them from breaking through.

Christine was oblivious of the renewed commotion in the background. "Dean, please tell me it's the truth."

"Of course it is." Walsh told her dismissively. Then he glared at Nat. "Haven't I suffered enough?"

Leo and Mitchell Oates stepped over to them.

"What's going on?" Leo asked.

"That witness—the homeless woman—was arranged," Nat said shakily. Out of the corner of her eye she saw Marion Walsh standing a few feet away, her arms tightly crossed over her chest. As if to keep her heart from exploding.

"What difference does it make?" Christine cried. "You heard it with your own ears. Rick confessed. He confessed."

"He confessed to raping Alison nine years ago," Leo said. "He vehemently denied murdering either his wife or Maggie Austin."

"Rick's lying," Christine insisted. "Just like he lied nine years ago. You can't do this to my brother again. It isn't fair. It isn't."

Leo reflected for a few moments before responding. "That may be, Miss Walsh. But as things stand now your brother has no supportable alibi for the times of either murder. And you are in some serious trouble of your own."

"But don't you see," Christine entreated, "he had no reason to kill them. He forgave Alison long before he left prison. And he loved Maggie. He loved her and she loved him."

Something corrosive flickered in Walsh's electric blue eyes. It lasted only an instant, but it was so profound a glimpse into his dark soul that it stole Nat's breath away.

The truth was, Maggie hadn't loved Walsh. Any more than she'd loved Jack. Or Ethan. Nat believed the closest Maggie ever came to loving someone physically as well as emotionally probably had been Karen Powell. Karen was right. She had understood Maggie better than anyone. Certainly far better than Nat had.

But Nat was beginning to understand Dean Thomas Walsh. A wrongly convicted youth vainly proclaiming his innocence for eight long years to deaf ears—save for his sister. Alienated, isolated, humiliated, victimized, brutalized. Subjected to endless days spent see-sawing between terror and tedium. All for a crime he never committed. A terrible injustice befell him. He entered prison an innocent boy. And came out a hardened man with enormous and justifiable rage. Nat was sure his relationship with Maggie held that rage in check for a time. But then something went horribly, terribly wrong.

Leo started reading Walsh his rights. He and Oates were joined by two armed uniforms for back-up. Christine was telling her brother that it would all get straightened out, not to worry, as always, more concerned about his plight than her own. Well, Nat guessed, everyone wanted to believe in someone. Sadly, Christine Walsh had placed her belief and trust in the wrong someone. As had Nat. They'd both been duped by Dean Thomas Walsh, each for their own reasons.

Walsh was oddly subdued as he took it all in, his eyes fixed on the ground. Then, just as they were all thinking Walsh was not intending to cause a rumpus, he suddenly lunged for Nat with the swiftness of a cougar. Even as she heard the almost instantaneous clicks of the uniforms' weapons, she felt Walsh's arm clamp viciously around her ribcage, perversely close to her breasts. Her back was slammed hard into his chest. Once again, Nat was Walsh's hostage. His shield.

"If you want me, you'll have to go through her," Walsh spit out. "I told you before, Nat. I'm not going back. You owe me."

Walsh's other arm locked around her throat. "One of the nifty skills I picked up in the joint is how to snap someone's neck. Kills them instantly. Amazing, the things you learn behind those walls."

"No, Dean," Christine pleaded. "Don't do this. You're upset and panicked. But this time Mom and I will get you the very best lawyer. And he'll prove you didn't kill anyone."

Terrified as Nat was, she felt a flicker of pity for Christine. Even now, she wouldn't let go of her belief in her brother's innocence.

Walsh was deaf to Christine's pleading. He was in his own zone as he backed the two of them cautiously up against the huge trunk of the elm tree so that he was protected from the rear. The media had quieted to a hush. But the cameras continued to snap and roll. In the back of her mind, Nat wondered if Ethan and Jack were still out there. But as she found herself having to gasp for air, all thought but survival quickly evaporated.

She tried to tug Walsh's arm from her neck but it wouldn't budge. "You couldn't let it alone, Nat. You've got only yourself to blame."

"Okay, Dean," Leo said with remarkable calm. "Let's figure a way out of this with no one else getting hurt."

"No problem, man. Just clear the area and let my sister drive me and Nat here away. I'll leave the Super off without so much as a bruise on her in, say, twenty-four hours. That is, if I don't have any unwanted interference."

"I can't do that, Dean," Christine said quietly but firmly, for the first time refusing to be maneuvered by him into complicity. "If you're innocent—"

"So, now even you are doubting me." Walsh sounded more disgusted than disappointed.

Tears streamed down Christine's face and she turned away from her brother.

"Dean." The sharp sound of Marion Walsh's voice startled him, as though he'd all but forgotten she was still here.

She started toward him.

"No, Mom. Keep away," he warned.

She continued approaching, her step not faltering. "You can't let what happened to you turn you into a monster, Dean."

"It's too late." His voice was a strained whimper. "See, Alison called me at work that day, Mom. Told me she had something terrible on her conscience that she had to confess. She asked if I would come over. I knew seeing her could get me shipped out of pre-release and behind the wall again. But . . . she sounded so upset. Really pressed me to come. She was nervous when I got there. Worried Rick would show up again. She told me they'd just had another of their blow-ups. She wanted to walk. So we walked. Must have walked close to a mile. Not saying a word.

"I didn't press her. I waited till she was ready. And then she told me. She told me she'd lied about me being the one who raped her that night. That she knew who really did it. I demanded to know who it was, but she wouldn't tell me. I asked her straight out if it was Rick, but she wouldn't say it was him. All she kept saying was it would only get me into trouble to know and that she didn't want to see me end up back in prison again."

He laughed harshly. It might have been the same laugh he gave Alison that portentous afternoon. "Can you believe it, Mom? Here was this bitch telling me she was trying to protect me when she was the one who destroyed my whole life in the first place."

Christine began crying in earnest, but Marion Walsh's face was as stony as alabaster. "You killed that poor girl. And then you went and killed your teacher." There was no doubt in her voice. Nor was there any emotion. It was as if all feeling had been drained out of her. She turned her back on him and walked over to her daughter.

Nat couldn't see Walsh's face, but she could hear his sharp intake of breath. She envied him his ability to breathe so easily as she fought for each shallow breath, terrified that each one might be her last. What did Walsh have to lose? He was already facing double homicide. One more would be mere icing on the cake.

Nat's only hope was that as long as he believed she could provide him with an escape route, he'd keep her alive.

Once that hope was gone, they were both dead.

"I thought Maggie loved me." Walsh continued his oratory. "I poured my heart and soul out to her. No matter what god-awful things I told her about my life in prison, she accepted me. Comforted me. Told me how much I was growing as a poet by facing the horrors that had been done to me. And because she knew, like no one else, what I'd suffered, I was sure she'd understand when I told her about Alison. I was sure she'd be horrified by what Alison had done to me. I thought she would forgive me. Help me."

Nat shivered as she pictured first Maggie's dawning realization of who this man really was. Then the horror. The revulsion. The fear. And, yes, the awful disappointment that she had been such a poor judge of his character. All of which Walsh would read on Maggie's open face.

"It was the ultimate betrayal, wasn't it, Dean?" Nat said raspily.

"You can't know," he half-sobbed.

"I *can* know. I *do* know."

Walsh's grip on her neck loosened a fraction. Nat wasn't sure if it was her words or the conviction behind them that had gotten through to her captor. All she knew was that she had to tread carefully. Walsh's hint of capitulation was exceedingly touch and go.

"You never wanted to hurt anyone, Dean. Least of all Maggie."

"She was going to turn me in. I . . . couldn't go back. It . . . wasn't fair."

"You'd already done the time."

"I tried to tell them I was innocent. No one believed me."

Nat was acutely aware of the silence all around her. Everyone literally standing there with bated breath. Nat was the only one breathing a little easier now that Walsh's grip on her neck had loosened some more. But still, he did not release her.

"It should never have happened, Dean. I'm truly sorry for everything you were put through. But it isn't true that no one believed you. Christine believed you. She put her absolute faith and trust in you."

Christine, who'd stopped crying briefly, began again in earnest. This time, Walsh paid attention.

"Chrissie, don't," he pleaded.

Okay, Nat thought, *he's out of the zone. If I'm ever going to reach him, this is it.* "Then don't betray your sister's trust, her love, Dean. Don't make her an eye-witness to more carnage."

Nat could feel Walsh's whole body trembling with what she knew must be a mixture of anguish, panic, fear and an unresolvable rage.

"I don't know what to do," he said wretchedly, sagging back against the tree.

At first he drew Nat back with him. But then he exhaled heavily and let his arms drop to his side.

It took Nat a few seconds for it to get through to her that she was free. This was followed by a few seconds of abject relief. But the relief was quickly overwhelmed by fear. Not for her own life now, but for Walsh's. If she stepped aside, no longer providing cover for him, and he made even the slightest move to run, Nat knew, without doubt, that Walsh would be gunned down by one or more cops.

What if it were Leo whose weapon brought Walsh down? Killed him? How would Leo live with more blood on his hands? How would she?

Slowly, Nat pivoted in place, remaining Walsh's shield as she now faced him. "Take my hand, Dean. We'll do this together."

Walsh's features were pinched, his arms clutched around his own middle. He gave a haggard sigh, his eyes meeting hers. She held out her hand. Wordlessly, he took it. Just as he did, a shot rang out, the bullet slamming into the trunk of the elm tree inches from where she and Walsh stood. Stunned, Walsh released his hold on Nat's hand.

Nat's legs buckled, fury warring with fear. It couldn't have been a cop who'd fired. No police officer would ever have risked a shot with her standing so close to Walsh. Someone had managed to sneak through the barrier during the stand-off. Easy enough to do with the cops all focused on her and Walsh.

Screams, shouts, cries, erupted all around them like a storm, drowning out the sound of the next shot. Nat might not have heard it, but she literally felt it whiz past her head.

A piercing shriek escaped Walsh's lips as he grabbed for Nat and started slipping to the ground, pulling her with him. Nat felt something hot and sticky against the side of her head and, dazed, wondered if she was the one who'd been hit.

Oates was holding back a sobbing, struggling Christine. Leo and a couple of uniforms came rushing toward Nat and Walsh. Marion was on her knees, her hands clasped tightly together as if in prayer. Nat was only vaguely aware of the gurgling noises coming from Walsh, who even now maintained his hold on her as they half-sat, half-lay on the ground against the tree.

It was only after Leo pried her free that Nat realized it was Walsh and not her who'd been hit by that second bullet. There was a gaping hole in the side of his neck and blood was gushing both from the wound and from his mouth.

His lips were moving, but Nat couldn't hear him. She leaned a little closer. "I . . . told . . . you . . . I . . . would never . . . go back." Dean Thomas Walsh's lips curved into a twisted smile as he took his final breath.

Leo shut the dead man's eyes and then gently lifted Nat to her feet. She wanted to ask him to hold her, but before she could get the words out, he was already gathering her in his arms.

It would all be on the six o'clock news.

Including the unconditional surrender, without further incident, of Dean Thomas Walsh's shooter.

HEART OF JUSTICE

I do not see the walls, the bars, the barbed wire trails.
I do not hear the slurs, the orders, the threats.
I do not smell the piss, disinfectant, pungent reefer smoke.
I do not feel the invasions or pervasions.
I do not taste the rancid chow, the jail-brewed hooch.
I do not weep for all that I have lost.
I have no regrets.
I have given it all away knowing full well what I would pay.
My heart is light.
For you are with me day and night.
With my eyes closed or open
I see your beautiful face.
I hear your soft, sweet Southern drawl.
I smell your intoxicating lilac scent.
I feel your tender touch.
I taste your warmth, your goodness, your purity.
I am not serving life.
I am serving your loving memory.
And I am free, Maggie.
I am free.

Keith Franklin
Inmate #304585

epilogue

AFTER WEEKS OF investigation and then a *real* four-week vacation, Nat was back at Horizon House. Following Franklin's arrest at the Boston Commons, some serious powwows were held at the Commissioner's offices downtown. The end result was that the Commissioner—deciding that there'd been so many screw-ups across the board, starting with Dean Thomas Walsh's wrongful arrest over eight years ago right up to his being gunned down—decided to return all that could be returned to the status quo.

"Do you have any qualms about being back?"

Nat looked across her desk at Leo. Did she have any qualms about returning? Yes. Dozens. There were days—more often nights—that she still wondered if she'd made the right choice. But she was there. This was her life. This was where she'd meant to be before it all went haywire. And, in the final analysis, self-recriminations, doubts, and fears aside, this was still where she wanted to be. One terrible misjudgment did not alter her belief in the program or her commitment to it.

"No," she said.

Leo nodded, but somehow Nat knew he was not responding

to her terse answer but to her thoughts. That was the thing about Leo. He had this unnerving ability to read her mind.

"If Franklin had gotten to Maggie's apartment ten minutes earlier than he did, she'd still be alive," Nat said, still feeling the pangs of loss. As it turned out, Franklin probably arrived at Maggie's place no more than five minutes after Walsh had murdered her and fled her apartment. Like Jack, Franklin, too, just missed saving Maggie's life.

Life seemed to be a collection of so many *if onlys*.

"I gotta hand it to Franklin. He laid it all out for us," Leo said. "Staging Maggie's dead body to appear like the handiwork of Walsh—he told us down at the jail how he'd researched Walsh, read old newspaper clippings about Alison Cole's rape so he knew just what to do. There was never any question in Franklin's mind that Walsh was Maggie's murderer. He was determined to see Maggie's murder pinned on him."

"And," Nat added, "just in case the police didn't get him, there was always Owen King. Until Walsh's mother killed him."

"Yeah, Franklin told me he made those calls to King, pretending to be Walsh. He wanted King to join the hunt. He confessed to intoxicating visions of Owen King torturing, raping, and ultimately killing Walsh. Not that he wouldn't have settled for seeing Walsh thrown back in prison for life, knowing as Franklin surely did, the life Walsh would lead inside."

Nat knew that Franklin had also admitted to having tried to run her down, and when that failed, assaulting her and starting the fire in her bedroom. He worried that she was beginning to suspect him and meant her death to bring the focus of attention back on Walsh. There was no sign of any remorse about having tried to cold-bloodedly take her life.

Solving a last piece of the puzzle, Franklin openly and even proudly admitted having taken the lewd photo of Maggie and Karen, as well as dozens of others, all of them snapped from the fire escape outside Maggie's bedroom window. He kept the other photos hidden away in a safe deposit box. He never thought of himself as a voyeur. Rather, he viewed himself as Maggie's true lover. He was able to pretend that it was him rather than Jack or Dean who was making love to her. In each of the photos, he deliberately avoided a clear shot of the lover. He confided that the only time he had trouble with the pretense was when he discovered Maggie and Karen in their sado-masochistic sexual encounters. These sexual liaisons troubled him greatly. It was the reason he sent Maggie that photo. He was hoping that once she realized there was tangible evidence of her *misbehavior* she would be alarmed enough to stop carrying on with Karen.

"I should be appalled by what Franklin did," Nat said quietly, "but just between the two of us, Leo, I—"

Leo held up his hand to stop her. "I know."

"I'm glad there was no trial," she said. "I'm glad it's . . . over."

Keith Franklin had pleaded guilty, thus waiving a jury trial. Given a court-appointed lawyer, he'd refused to have the young attorney try to plea bargain for a lighter conviction—there being some small chance he could have argued second-degree murder. Franklin had been especially vehement in his opposition to an insanity plea. It was as if Franklin prided himself on being charged with the first-degree murder of Dean Thomas Walsh. Although he was also charged with arson and Nat's attempted murder, this appeared to be a matter of complete indifference to Franklin. At his sentencing hearing, because he was still on parole from his first offense, the judge dealt him an especially stiff sentence—thirty-five years to life. He would not become eligible for a parole hearing for 18.5 years.

"By the way," Nat said. "I heard from Terri Franklin a couple of weeks ago. She's filing for divorce. Planning to marry her boyfriend this summer. I wished her the best."

"Hear anything from Christine Walsh?" Leo asked.

Nat shook her head. "Don't expect I ever will. I read in the paper that she and her fiancé were married last month."

"She's one damn lucky gal that she isn't spending her honeymoon in jail." While Christine had been arrested for aiding and abetting her brother, a high-priced lawyer hired by Christine's mother had managed to strike a deal with the D.A. Christine pled No Contest and was given two years probation.

"I really do wish her the best," Nat said. In her opinion, Christine was one of the people who'd suffered the most from the whole ordeal, her only true crime having been that she loved her brother so deeply that she couldn't see him for who he truly was. Or rather, who he had become. Because the first victim here had been Dean Thomas Walsh.

"What do you think, Leo? How much of what happened to Walsh in prison—the countless emotional, physical and sexual assaults on his mind and body—played a role in shaping him into a killer?"

"I don't know," Leo said. "But I imagine it was considerable."

"There's something terribly wrong with the system."

"That's why you're back."

She smiled. "Yeah, that's why I'm back."

She saw Leo studying her. "What?" she asked.

"I . . . uh . . . hear your ex is no longer living with his girlfriend."

"Who told you?"

Leo shrugged. "Just heard it through the grapevine."

"She had a miscarriage. Ethan never did find out if the child was his." She looked away. "I was surprised at how hard he took the loss."

"So the two of you have been . . . in touch."

Now it was Nat's turn to shrug. She decided not to mention that she and Jack had bumped into Ethan that past Saturday night when they'd gone out to dinner at Pomodoro. Ethan was with a very pretty brunette who looked to be in her early twenties. He introduced Nat to her as his new T.A. Nat honestly couldn't remember the girl's name.

The reason Nat didn't bring up the encounter had nothing to do with her ex. She didn't mention it because she knew Leo didn't much like her dating Jack.

But then Nat didn't much like Leo's *dates* with Suzanne Holden. The inmate had been transferred from CCI Grafton to Horizon House almost a month ago. Leo's mother and Jakey continued their weekly visits to Suzanne at Horizon House just as they'd done at Grafton. The only difference now was that more often than not Leo joined them.

Suzanne was clearly happy to see Leo when he visited. Sometimes Nat saw him linger with Suzanne after Jakey and Anna Coscarelli headed out of the visiting room. Nat never saw them kiss, but she did see Leo squeeze Suzanne's hand or briefly put his arm around her. Suzanne always appeared to welcome the contact. In Nat's estimation, so did Leo.

"Is Suzanne still against letting Jakey know that she's his mother?" Nat asked, trying to keep her tone casual.

"How'd we jump from your ex to my . . . to Suzanne?"

Nat smiled sardonically.

"Yeah," Leo said, "no change there."

Where was the change?

"So, we on for a movie tomorrow night?" Leo asked after too long a silence.

Nat hesitated. It had been a couple of weeks since they'd gone out. Not for want of Leo asking. Nat simply was being cautious. While she went out with Leo every now and then, she was careful not to let these encounters occur too frequently or get out of hand. She was leery of getting overly attached to him, until he'd sorted out just how attached he was to Suzanne.

"Okay, a movie sounds good." There was such a thing as being too cautious.

Leo smiled. "Great. That's great. I'll pick you up at your place—say seven o'clock."

She nodded.

He got up and started to leave.

"By the way," she said. "I'm not living alone anymore."

He looked back at her, concern etched in his features.

"Who are you—?"

"Her name's Hannah. Don't worry. Her bark is worse than her bite. Of course, if I'd gotten that pit bull I was considering instead of a golden retriever—"

Leo grinned. "You're not the pit bull type."

"Don't be so sure, Leo. Don't be so sure."